A Traitor's Confession

Palmer Carroll

Contents

List of Main Characters:

- Tenenbrani - the "dark creatures"
- Clairdani – the "light creatures"
- Elves – forest fairies
- Luz, aka the Advocate - young girl who lives with the dragon in the caves
- Simão - leader of the Enlightened/Traitors
- Rowan - magistrate of the town of Tomar
- Anehta - the owl that is Luz's constant companion
- Hawthorne – the gaoler
- Noyette - the gaoler's wife/widow
- Cenellot - the gaoler's son
- Florenço - the elf that helps Noyette and Cenellot survive
- King Abrimel - king of the elves
- Ma'elrich - the inquisitor, Rowan's childhood friend

Towns/ regions:

- Lusitania - the name of the regional country that was affected by the curse.
- Tomar - The central town of the story. There are many other towns in the same predicament, but they haven't progressed as far in figuring out what was going on or finding an answer/solution.
- Batalha - the name of the cave region. So named for the echoes and noise the wind makes as it whips through the caves and the echoes of the dragons' roars, since this is where the dragons lived (and the only remaining dragon still does).
- Cidade dos Corações, the city of hearts - the graveyard for dragons

- Osses Degrotto, the "cave of bones" - the sacred burial ground of the dragons where they hide their hearts
- Sintra- the lands of the elves. Within the lands are
  - Monserrate- the palace of the elfin king
  - Palmela- the living area for most of the elves
  - Sintrentejo- the periphery of Sintra
  - Torre de Verdade, the Well of Truth - the great hall of the Elfin King

Chapter 1: A Substitution

At the hour before dawn, the torches that lit the entrance to the newly white-washed town hall and the rough timber prisoners' gaol were the only lights visible in Tomar. A lone, strongly built man clad in a coarse woolen tunic, leather vest, greaves, and simple leather shoes stood within the lintels of a well-concealed entrance on a dark wall of the gaol, determining whether there was another movement beyond the known threat nearby before proceeding. Feeling the large open oval bow and three teeth of the required key, he unlocked the wooden pieced door, stepped inside, and closed the door quietly behind him in one smooth motion. Inside, the gaol was darker than staring at ebony wood a hand's breadth away from the face, but it mattered not. His memory of the corridors after his virtual occupation for the past half-generation guided him until his eyes made their quick adjustment to the eternal murky dank of the dungeons, the lower level of the gaol itself.

Save for the sounds of rustling rats, all was quiet –the forlorn prisoners were still fitfully sleeping, as best they could in their manacles without any bedding. His destination was at the end of the last corridor on the right, the Traitor's Corridor, where gratefully, contact with anyone would have been impossible, but better yet, no one should register his presence in the area before his escape. Swiftly, he unlocked the cell door. He raced into the cell, the smaller bowed key with only two teeth in his hand to unlock her manacles, trying to wake her while doing so. There wasn't any more time – she had to wake quickly. "Luz! Wake up! They are coming!" he whispered in her ear.

She stirred, mumbling, "They are alwayth coming..." she slurred her words through her many broken and missing teeth, but then she absorbed the urgency in his tone.

"Wha' happe'ed?" She tried to stand, but her broken legs wouldn't support her.

He bent down and gently picked up her frail skeleton – it was miraculous that she still possessed life within her, with her many broken bones and internal injuries. He could feel her wince when he touched her, but there was no time to find a more comfortable position to carry her if they were to escape in time. He began retracing his steps through the corridor maze of the gaol, created so that any prisoners escaping would never find their way out before they were caught. Left, straight, straight, right, right – he navigated the corridors automatically while trying to update the situation to Luz, her arms around his neck as best she could.

"The Inquisitor is on his way. He's already inside the town walls. The magistrate called for him last night, and he came straight away. His interrogation techniques are... unparalleled in their cruelty. I've never known anyone that can resist the Inquisitor's techniques, especially if it follows the magistrate's."

The steps up to the market level were wearing on him now, his words coming more in bursts than the quick torrent they were at first. "Your animal friends are here to help take you to safety – they told me about the Inquisitor and have been keeping a lookout."

"They are within the walls? But they will be slaughtered if anyone sees them!" Her body now seemed fully alert, although she didn't yet make a move to leave. "But what can we do? There is no escape from this place, and I will probably die soon anyway…"

She began to struggle, trying to stand, not afraid to meet the Inquisitor and the fate meted out to her. She had nothing to hide – she had told the truth from the beginning, but the magistrate refused to believe her. If she could convince the Inquisitor to believe her, although she knew she was too ill to continue for long in the dungeons, perhaps the others like herself would be safe…

Her futile struggles against his grip only invigorated his determination. She had survived somehow so far, but he had seen the inquisitor's methods and could not bear to have her innocence destroyed under the inquisitor's hand. With a moment of clairvoyance, he knew what he had to do, and he only hoped that his wife and family would be spared or allowed to leave Tomar once they knew of his capture. His family knew nothing of what he suffered or knew of this "traitor." For the sake of their own lives, he had kept them away from the truth until he could sequester safety for them.

They reached the gaol's main corridor just as the magistrate and inquisitor stepped into the area from the opposite direction, blocking the door leading to their freedom. Their short statures, hunched backs, and swarthy appearances sharply contrasted with their finer silk tunics, gold-and-silver encrusted velvet doublets, and buckled shoes, as if trolls had eaten the rightful owners of the clothing and tried to wear them as disguises. Behind them stood a dozen guards clad in rough woolen tunics, leather breastplates, greaves, and closed leather boots. A few seconds' glance at the gaoler carrying a prisoner towards freedom told them all they needed to know, and with a shout of "Traitor!" the magistrate and inquisitor demanded the immediate capture of both Traitors.

As the guards ran towards the gaoler, he put Luz somewhat roughly on her feet. "Go! I'll hold the guards until you can get through the door. They are waiting for you!" She hesitated, not knowing which way to go, but he had already turned to face the oncoming teeth of death the guards carried - a bear guarding its child regardless of the inevitable death that would follow. Unable to stand, she crawled towards a door down the corridor to the right, negating her pain and brokenness in her efforts. Guarding her escape, he faced the guards, daring his prior comrades to arrest him. They still came forward, mechanically, swords and daggers drawn, as he mirrored their actions with his own arsenal. Resigned to the hateful task, he took on the guards two at a time, using his sword and dagger efficiently in the tight space the corridor provided and moving slowly towards the escape door as the bodies took the space in the corridor. With only two guards left, he felt, rather than saw, a blinding white light grow behind him before it shrank into nothingness, taking Luz with it.

Stunned at the suddenness and novelty of a bright light in a faintly lit dark corridor, they all stared briefly where the prisoner had stood a moment beforehand, as if the light had just as suddenly turned them to stone. The magistrate's scream of "Do not let him escape!!" returned everyone to themselves, recovering as if they had to think through thicker air.

He followed his awakening bellow with more commands to the other guards. "You two – go to the tower and sound the alarm! A prisoner is escaping, and she will not get far in

4

her condition!" The last two guards immediately returned in the direction they'd come and disappeared up the stairs.

The gaoler, his task complete, threw down his sword and dagger with a serene determination on his face as the two remaining guards recovered and roughly threw him to the floor at the feet of the magistrate. "You'll never find her now. She's with the Clairdani, who will have her out of this town and area before they get the alarm out."

Walking deliberately to the gaoler, the inquisitor grabbed a fistful of hair to pull the gaoler's face upwards. Staring into his eyes, he growled, "Perhaps. Regardless, we have a placeholder. You are now mine!" Stepping back, he addressed the guards on either side. "Take him to the interrogation chamber at the end of the inquisition hall and strap him in. I will come anon."

Smiling to himself, the inquisitor said to no one in particular, "This will be... an enjoyable first day." Knowing anything he said would only be returned with physical pain, the gaoler said nothing while the guards bound his arms and goaded him down the hallway. It didn't matter that they had known each other their entire lives and worked together for a decade. He had lost any peer status by assisting a traitor to escape and was doomed to die at the hands of the inquisitor and his ruthless interrogation methods. Now, he was someone they had *carte blanche* to torment, and having just killed ten of their fellow guards, they had enough anger, bitterness, and knowledge of his weaknesses to torture him during the long march to the interrogation chambers.

The inquisitor rubbed his hands together gleefully while the magistrate looked both irate and confused about the gaoler's treachery. "I wonder if perhaps she was also an enchantress who cast a spell on him – he was my most loyal and trustworthy gaoler! I had him trailed for many months to ensure his loyalty, and not once did he go outside the walls or meet with those suspected of being Traitors. Maybe I should question him first..." the magistrate began.

"No, I'll handle it. I'm already here, and my methods are more efficient... I will have something from him by the end of the day for you, and you won't have to worry about finding a cell for this one! He is resilient since he hasn't been interrogated yet but that will allow me to truly test some of the newer methods I've been contemplating."

The inquisitor's disdain for traitors was palpable, but his true satisfaction came from dismantling a person, regardless of their identity, on every conceivable level—emotionally, physically, and spiritually—until nothing was remaining. His obsession and purest source of joy in life revolved around extracting every last ounce of a person's soul. This pursuit not only brought him pleasure but also served the purpose of unraveling the mystery behind why someone became a traitor. Ultimately, it aimed to put an end to the mutilations and deaths these traitors facilitated.

The magistrate had long harbored reservations about the inquisitor's ruthless methods, considering them excessively severe. As a result, the inquisitor was always a measure of last resort, summoned only when all other avenues had been exhausted. With a heavy heart, the magistrate accepted the grim reality of losing his most accomplished gaoler.

With a sense of dread gnawing at him, the magistrate led the inquisitor through the hushed corridors that honeycombed underneath Tomar, where shadows seemed to cling to the walls. The inquisitor's reputation as a relentless interrogator cast an unsettling mood over the magistrate's thoughts.

Finally, they arrived at a small, dank space that served as the magistrate's office while he was working interrogations in the gaol. After exchanging terse nods, the magistrate left the inquisitor to make the space his own. "I'll return shortly, this space is now yours to use as you see fit."

He then continued down the stone-hewn passageway, stopping at the interrogation room. The gaoler's eyes betrayed a mix of trepidation and curiosity as he glimpsed the magistrate's arrival. Waving aside the two guards, he stepped into the room and stooped to stare into the gaoler's eyes for a long moment. Without any preamble, the magistrate spat in his face, then departed, leaving a trail of hostility in his wake.

He returned to the gaol office, each step echoing with the weight of a decision that had cost him his best gaoler. Thoughts raced through his mind, pondering which among the many gaolers could possibly fill the void left by the most recent betrayal. The somber, morbid atmosphere of the gaol mirrored the magistrate's unease as he contemplated the uncertainty of the future.

Chapter 2: The Gaoler's End

Despite awakening the town before their normal time, the alarm had produced nothing. None of the guards that were summoned by the alarm had been able to find a trace of the escaped prisoner. They had all returned to the irate magistrate with nothing, who stood glaring at the collected horde. Unable to decide about a replacement gaoler, the magistrate assigned his oldest gaoler to the traitor's corridor, threatening to cut his tongue out if there were a word spoken to any prisoner over the next three days in the gaol. He gave the remaining guards similar threats if they spoke to anyone in town about the "false alarm" before allowing them to return to their posts.

In his red fog, the magistrate left his rough-hewn desk at the musty gaol with a strong feeling of betrayal. The traitorous gaoler! Had he always been a traitor, helping other Traitors in the dungeons? No, he decided. He himself was a close friend of the gaoler's wife… indeed, a very close relationship. He knew there were no deceits with her or their son. His heart desired her assurance that they knew nothing of the treachery the gaoler had committed. However, he knew that he might be associated with the Traitors himself if he were to show any form of compassion for their family after one was convicted of treachery. They would be burned, all of them, to ensure there was no trace of the traitor's blood left in the town.

He decided a change of scenery might help him clear his feelings of betrayal and his memories of the friend he had lost to the other side. Leaving the gaol, the magistrate turned left at the edge of the market square and headed towards the center of town and his much grander office at Town Hall. The clear autumnal air helped cool his anger and frustrations.

8

As his townspeople began their work in the streets and farmer's market, he forced an air of unperturbed calm to not solicit questions he was unprepared to answer. He paused at the renewed pile of wood and broad stake pole in front of Town Hall - It was their eternal monument to their efforts to rid themselves of the Traitors who held connections to creatures that wantonly crept into their town, spreading death, destruction, and mutilations amongst the people. This would be where he would last see the beautiful woman, the gaoler's wife, and her only son.

She had always been his object of desire. In their youth, they had been very close and always acted as if they would be together forever. He was never sure what had happened to change that. One day, she asked if he knew anything about Hawthorne, a new youth to Tomar, supposedly orphaned by his parents and needing a new life. Without a child of his own, he had hoped to adopt the child as his own someday if anything ever happened to Hawthorne – the child had a brilliant mind and would be valuable in bringing about prosperity to the town when he himself could no longer control the people. Shaking his head as if to rid himself of pesky thoughts, he entered through his private entrance and instructed the Town Hall guards that he was not to be disturbed.

Gathering the scrolls and codices he had neglected over the past few days as he had concentrated on his interrogations of the traitor, he sat heavily into his goose-feathered wooden chair, placing the documents on his wood-inlay, ebony desk. The gold leaf embellishments reminded him of the bright light that had removed his quarry after so many years of hunting. "The Advocate," those Traitors called her, although he did not understand for whom she advocated – the Traitors received nothing from her in return for their apparent devotion. He had noticed she was different from any other traitorous prisoners he had met– her story never wavered, despite the fantastic aspects that permeated her story more than any other he had heard. Her tales of the murderous creatures forming sides, speaking to humans, guarding over the town – these were impossible. Only occasionally did she say something that was somewhat connected to what he already knew. He was aware that the Traitors had a rendezvous with the creatures. While the Traitors claimed it was for the greater good, he believed it was solely to provoke the creatures into launching more attacks on the town. His previous attempts at finding her grimly reminded him of the futility of a search party. In her ability to be unseen, she was definitely unique! Only he knew that the only reason she had been captured after many years of relentless pursuit, was her nobility of character, as she turned herself in to him for questioning.

There was a magical quality about her, of that there was no doubt. He would have to scourge the remaining gaolers to see how far her treacherous charm had carried within the gaol itself. With hope, this was the only gaoler affected, and they could continue their interrogations with the other Traitors currently held in the gaol until they routed out all of the conspirators. Hopefully, this would end the brutal attacks, maulings, and mutilations that had marred this town for as long as the town remembered. Slowly, these memories drifted away as he immersed himself in the multiple edicts, tax collection notices, and sundry items that reminded him of his joys – complete control of all aspects of the town, including the new edict proclaiming the official size and thickness of horseshoes for the blacksmiths in the town.

Inside the only office in the oldest gaol of the region, the excited inquisitor made himself ready for an enjoyable day of questioning in the magistrate's gaol office. Rather than feeling betrayed or remorseful, the inquisitor was ecstatic about his new prospects for the day – interrogation of a powerfully built gaoler, one of their own, would give him a better understanding of the strength of his methods. He had never had the opportunity to interrogate someone from the beginning – many of them were, at most, one day away from death before he could see them, so he had to use other methods to retrieve the necessary information since most chose death first. He surveyed the tools of the trade he had brought with him, assuming it would have been the girl – thin chains, small snakes, leeches, blindfolds, knives of various bluntness – and decided that he might still be able to use those in addition to larger knives and other elements the guards would be able to find around the town for him while he was at work.

The inquisitor was on good terms with the magistrate, but his taste in decorating left much to be desired. While the inquisitor enjoyed his work around the region, he regretted the austerity that traveling required. He missed his creature comforts – a ready flask of wine, trays of food to help calm the nerves and feed his weariness after his work, fresh bowls of clean water to bathe the blood off his body after a particularly intense interrogation - and the magistrate had none of these available to him.

Chuckling to himself, he reminded himself how lucky he was that he left Tomar at an early age, enabling his rise above the baseness of this town. He was born here and felt a connection to the people, and he had been sorrowfully sent away after the sudden death of his father. With only ten sun cycles to his life, he had been sent away to live with his wealthy uncle in another nearby town. Like here, the town of Clod Pollux also suffered from random creature attacks, but not even half as many as Tomar seemed to. Even though the magistrate and he had been like brothers until that fateful day when his father was killed by the nightmarish creatures, he now felt that his uncle had helped him become a wealthier man, better suited to enact necessary change regardless of the cost to life, love, or liberty.

Leaving these thoughts in the magistrate's gaol office, the inquisitor took his bags of tools – one of live tools, one stained with blood from the other instruments hastily stored before he cleaned them each day – and a flaming torch from the wall and called for the guards. He waited until there were four guards available for his use, then followed them to the inquisition rooms in the deepest part of the gaol where sunlight never entered. Awaiting orders, the guards called a halt at the beginning of the inquisition corridor, unwilling to enter unless required. There was an air of death beyond the mildew and the nauseating stench of rodent droppings in the corridors did not prove to be very inviting. After the echo of their footfalls, the inquisitor listened carefully to any noises beyond the scurrying rats and beetles that outnumbered the occupants by five score, but there was nothing. It was deadly quiet. Secretly, the inquisitor hoped that the gaoler hadn't denied him the pleasure of working with him, and the silence only meant the gaoler had fallen unconscious or was trying to be brave. The gaoler would soon find out there was no such thing as bravery. Bravery was only an assumed power over an internal weakness, but he would show the gaoler what true power was.

Pointing to two of the guards, he indicated the entrance to the corridor, giving instructions as he unlocked the rusty metal door. "You two stand guard at the entrance there. Ensure I am NOT disturbed on any account, not even by the magistrate himself!" To the other two guards, he pointed to the sides of the room he would be using. "You two – stand guard on either side of this entrance, and on penalty of death, you will not disturb me!"

The two guards looked quizzically at each other and glanced at the guards at the end of the corridor, then nodded their heads in assent. One made to take the torch from the inquisitor, but he only chuckled. "No, this is for my own use. You should have thought to bring your own." With that, he entered the room and clanged the inch-thick iron door behind him, leaving the two guards in pitch darkness. He had ordered that the gaoler be stripped and put first on the rack for the hour while he prepared himself for the rigor he would be exuding shortly. Grateful that the guards here did as they were bid, the inquisitor gave a growling chuckle, slapped the gaoler out of his unconsciousness, and began his work.

At first, the inquisitor only tested the gaoler's ability to withstand pain, which proved very informative and hopeful. This being was strong and resisted all but the most intense manipulation of his phobias. Once the initial assessment was over, the real work began. As the inquisitor prepared himself mentally for the new tasks, he withdrew into the corridor to address the guards in the corridor on either side of the room.

"You two, I will not need you for the next two hours. Find his house. Torch it and everything inside to the ground. Leave nothing behind. Bring me anything you find."

"Should we give notice before lighting…" began one guard, but the inquisitor interrupted with

"Everything in it burns!! NOW!"

The two guards clicked their heels together in a manner of salute and acknowledgment of the direct order. Turning, the two guards shuffled out of the interrogation corridor, gathered the other two guards, and marched in step, up to the market level. Fetching the lit torches from the entrances, they continued their quick march towards the designated hut, through the market square towards the edge of town in the awakening dawn.

Aware that there had been an alarm earlier, the townspeople knew to stay out of the way of guards in pursuit of their new quarry. The torches created haunting shadows, adding to those preceding the rising sun. At the market square, a young child dared to whisper to his mother, "Where are they going…?" He was snatched back by his mother and shushed before he could finish his statement, but not before a guard had noticed.

The closest guard only waved his flaming torch in the child's face as the mother defended her son. "Please, spare him! He doesn't know what he's asking!" Glaring at her for her impertinence, the guard recalled himself to the task at hand, realizing it was of more consequence. He continued on in step with his fellow guards, leaving the mother to comfort the frightened lad and lead him back to the safety of a side alley. Many others quietly followed the guards, hoping their home wasn't the one to be burned.

The gaolers' huts were all at the edge of town in an effort to put stronger townspeople nearer where the creatures entered as further protection. Even though this one was separated slightly from the other townhouses by enough space to allow a husky man to walk between them, it was still made of wood, thatch, and mud and would burn quickly, perhaps catching the nearby houses on fire as well. As the parade began to center on the gaoler's house, many shouts of "Get a bucket!", "here!" and "Go ahead and see if anyone has left for the market yet," to which the guards replied, "No warnings allowed!" and prevented any townspeople from getting ahead of them in the parade.

Silently, the two guards moved towards the gaoler's house, and immediately a gasp of horror and wonder escaped many from the gathered crowd. A murmuring chorus of "Are they at the market or in the field?" "Did anyone see them this morning?" "No, I haven't seen them yet this morning – I hope they aren't still inside!" started amongst the steadily growing crowd of onlookers.

Any continued attempts to give warning were thwarted as the guards touched their torches to the eaves of the thatched roof and watched as the tiny tongues of flame licked the sides of the roof before growing and consuming the rest of the roof. With a nod of understanding, the four guards patrolled the hut, each blocking exits or entrances through the door or windows with their spears. Although they waited for some resistance from within, none came from within the hut. With the flames consuming the roof, the smoke was thickening quickly, and soon, the timbers would begin to fall into the hut, potentially crushing anyone still inside. Two of the guards pushed the townspeople back, deeper into the street, preventing anyone from going towards the flames. In a macabre mood, the townspeople asked each other unanswered questions about what this gaoler's family had done to incite the magistrate and wailed for the lives lost in the flames. They could only watch in horror and use the water they had gathered to quench the flames that tried to spread to neighboring huts.

After the flames died out and the smoke drifted and cleared, one of the guards spoke to the crowd. "Let it be known that this hut was destroyed by order of the Inquisitor himself. Anyone seen rummaging around the hut will be convicted as a traitor and brought directly to the magistrate. Clear out!" The four guards stood posted around the burned remains until all the crowd had cleared, then rummaged through the ashes themselves. Using their swords to turn over anything still solid, they searched for bones or other evidence of what might have been still in the hut but found none. Charred fabric, ceramic pieces, and charred shards of wooden furniture constituted most of the remains. As they cleared away the debris, one of the guards heard a hollow sound resound as he stepped near the hearth.

"Oi! There's another room underneath. Did you know they had a meat locker?" As the guard cleared the area, an embedded metal ring emerged, attached to a small, hinged door on the floor.

All of the guards shook their heads and moved towards the ring- a potential answer to how the inhabitants had escaped their dictated fate. There hadn't been enough time to leave the town since no one knew about the gaoler until now. With only those few moments to escape, perhaps the condemned were still within reach? Using his sword to handle the metal ring, the first guard lifted the door, which creaked open, revealing an opening that was not deep enough for anyone to climb into. Baffled, the guard felt around inside the space, finding it narrow and only roughly scraped out to create a small storage area. After a few moments of searching, he touched something, and a quizzical look froze on his face. Slowly, he pulled out a smoking leather-bound codex and rose to his feet.

"It doesn't seem to be burned at all, even though everything around it was scorched to ashes," the scroungers revealed.

"Can anyone else sense the magic that surrounds this codex?" The guards next to him moved away as he made the observation. Demonstrating any knowledge of magic could mark someone as a traitor, and they feared death too much to allow themselves to become suspects of such knowledge.

"Not only does it have the ancient runes on it, but there's no obvious means of opening it. It seems to be held together by a magic I've never felt before," the scrounger continued. Passing the codex around to the other guards, they each looked over the codex warily, trying to determine a means to open the codex to no avail. Finding nothing else in the remains, they marched determinedly through the now deserted streets back to the gaol house. Moving deep into its interior to the inquisition corridor, they were led by the sound of intense screams and cries of agony. Waiting for a pause, the oldest guard bravely knocked on the door. After a few moments, the inquisitor came to the door, and careful not to allow the guards to see inside, he stormed into the corridor.

Looking at the guard who found and carried the codex, the remaining guards nodded encouragement at him as he held the codex so the inquisitor could see it. One of the guards mustered up the courage to report to the intimidating presence in front of him, "We torched the house and everything in it. Nothing escaped. We thoroughly rummaged through the burnt remains of the hut and discovered this book, concealed within an underground storage." Stepping forward, the guard placed the codex in the inquisitor's hands and stepped back into the safety of his fellow guards.

Speechless, the inquisitor stared at the four guards and the codex until he found his voice, his veins pulsing dangerously in his temples and his eyes flashing gold with occasional red sparks. He moved to a position among the four guards, staring each one down in turn as he pursued a line of questioning. "And? What of the rest of his family? Were there any other traces of creatures having been at the house? You have nothing else to report but that you found one codex?" The guards felt trepidation rising and stared straight ahead, saying nothing.

"Sir," one of the guards began, and the inquisitor stopped his rant to stare at the interrupting guard. "The codex is a mystery. It is impossible to open, but it looks well used…" he broke off as the inquisitor bore down on him in fury, brown eyes staring back into the eyes flashing gold with red. The inquisitor seemed frozen in thought and anger. "You deemed yourselves worthy to try and open something that could be evidence??" The sudden slap on the guard's face echoed in the halls, but the guard made no sound. He had realized as soon as he spoke that he would be lucky to keep his life, especially with the implication that he might also have other forbidden knowledge. The inquisitor stared as if deliberating for a moment, then decided to let the breach slide. Breaking the stare, he looked more intently at the codex in his hands. Fingering the sheaves, he controlled himself and spoke a bit more calmly to the guards.

"Return to your stations in this corridor. Do not interrupt me for ANY reason, and do not look in on the procedures, regardless of what you hear. If I come out and ask you to get anything, you must get whatever I ask, regardless of what it might be, without question. Is that understood?" The inquisitor stated the order with a thinly veiled promise of swift and painful punishment if the command was not met with an affirmative. The four guards nodded their heads in assent as one, then mechanically took their former positions in the hall.

As the inquisitor closed the door, the guards heard him ask the gaoler, "So you have a codex?" before the sound was muffled closed through the door. In between sounds of flesh hitting flesh, a tearing sound. "Who taught you to read?" A thud followed by the sound of a fluid splattering on the walls. "Where did you get this codex? What is the secret to opening the codex? ANSWER ME!!" The voice transformed into growls that were then intelligible. The guards never heard anything other than screaming after that moment.

Knowing death was imminent, the gaoler drew courage and hope from what the Advocate had told him – stories of serenity and opportunities to help others after death. The pain was insurmountable and unbearable to the point where the gaoler kept hoping that death would soon take him and give an end to his agony, yet he still refused to break. But that mattered not, as he provided the inquisitor with everything else he desired – the pleasure of watching pain spread throughout his body, every moment, hoping it would be the last he had to endure before he died.

After five hours of intense screaming, muffled thuds, bequests for various insects found in the woods, rats from the gaol, or hot tallow from the candlemaker, amongst other things, there was a cry of anger, then sudden silence. After the first moments of intense noise, the guards had plugged their ears to avoid their own imaginations terrorizing them with what they knew the gaoler was suffering, though they were intensely aware of the proceedings. The sudden silence, then, was deafening. A few moments later, the inquisitor emerged, splattered with blood and other unidentifiable organic material. "He is dead," he stated, leaving the door open to the sight of a dismembered gaoler with a gaping mouth. After controlling himself, he was able to speak. "You are dismissed. I can find the office once I've finished disposing of this, on my own."

Although highly irregular, the guards preferred the dismissal to the usual detestable order of bringing bags into the room to collect the full complement of a body. Without retort, the guards turned, marched through the corridor, and returned to their normal guard duties around the gaol. Each pondered the events of the gaoler's betrayal, the disappearance of his wife and family, and the mystery of the codex. What might the codex contain? Would they be allowed attempts to open it? Without a traitor to question, would the Inquisitor leave, or how long might he stay? His purpose was complete with the flight of the traitor, and now that he had taken on the destruction of the gaoler, who was now dead and would join the other bodies outside the town at dusk, there was no reason to stay.

Each of them admitted to themselves that there was a sudden chill in the air whenever the inquisitor was nearby. There was also that odd odor in any room the inquisitor occupied, which returned and lingered when they lit the fires in the rooms he'd occupied. Fearing what it might mean and thinking others would laugh, none were willing to admit anything out of place openly. Pretending everything was as it should be, they had enough thoughts to occupy them through the remaining hours of their shifts and enough to gossip about the odd behaviors and mannerisms of the strange man.

Chapter 3: The Meeting at the Pit

Every evening, guards patrolled the wall surrounding the town, covering the perimeter almost six times during a standard evening. They searched the surrounding area for creatures looming from the forests or anything amiss that might indicate a potential attack on the town. Unlike other towns, which feared other people's armies storming and pillaging their people, Tomar had never been attacked by other people. Tomar was infamous as a cursed town that seemed to draw in all sorts of destructive forces through creature attacks. Not wanting to share in this curse, the other regions shunned Tomar, and over the years, a dense forest had grown up around it and helped drive the town into obscurity. Patrolling guards watched the woods for signs of movement or proximity of the known creatures that lived in the denser regions of the forest – werewolves, unicorns, minotaurs, goblins, brownies, vampires, griffons, and others. At the slightest indication that a creature was in the area, the alarm sounded, and a patrol would exit the town to destroy the creature or at least ward off its attack without too much cost to the town in life and limb.

At dusk, just after the first patrol declared the southeastern area clear of any threat, a few people gathered. They remained hidden behind the bushes surrounding the Pit, waiting, out of sight of the patrols. Located just outside the town's southwestern walls, the Pit was the receptacle for any of the town's dead at the end of each day. Tonight, a few townspeople dared to leave the protective walls two or three at a time to acknowledge and mourn any dead they knew from the town. Most Tomar townspeople, raised on the tales of horrendous creatures that occasionally roamed in the woods that surrounded the town, feared to venture outside the town between dusk and dawn. Not all of them. There were others - "Traitors" – who had no substantial fear of what lay outside the town, and they continued the superstitions in town to protect the truth they knew. It was this superstition that kept the streets and alleys clear at night and superstition that allowed them to move freely while others quaked in their homes, afraid of what might lie outside. On this particular moonless night, the patrol had just passed by, and it was sufficiently dark. The town's streets, hidden from view by the closed gates and high walls, seemed devoid of noise and activity. At that moment, these Traitors emerged from their hiding places behind the bushes around the Pit.

"Is it safe?" whispered a wavering, childish voice amidst the sound of rustling branches of the bush he was emerging from, apparently to no one in particular. A pale, tear-stained round face under a rough crop of dark hair emerged. This face had not yet seen a decade of solar cycles, and his youth cautioned his movements from the bushes as he huddled behind a woman who shared his likeness. She too, had shining eyes that reflected the moon's light and a worried air that made her check her surroundings every few minutes.

A more resounding, huskier voice answered just as quietly. "Yes, Cenellot, you are safe now. The patrol has passed. No one else from the town will come by here tonight, I promise you. If any were looking for you, they would have come before now, with more strength in numbers." The tall, thin owner of this deeper voice made his way towards the very edge of the Pit, surveying the contents for any new additions. His beard did nothing to hide the creases of worry between his eyes. "I don't see any new additions here..." His words were broken off by his need to attend to the struggling woman he held next to him. Her arm held in his hand, a

22

woman who had definitely seen thirty solar cycles but yet retained her youthfulness in her dark eyes and face was not entirely submissive in the scene. Her long, woolen tunic showed through her rough overcoat of brown wool, both of which had bits of twig and leaves on them from her forced hiding place of the last few hours behind the bushes.

"Perhaps he did not die today, then, and you have kidnapped us as a sacrifice to the creatures that roam around the forests?" her clear, determined, flute-like voice asked as she freed herself from Simão's grasp. "You say you rescued us, but we have nothing to hide from the magistrate or anyone else in the town. I know you are Traitors… your secrecy gives you away. My husband was extremely loyal to the magistrate as well! You know he's guarding the most powerful traitor in the region, and you are just using us to get what you want. Admit it!" She spat on the dirt to punctuate her wrath.

Looking to the ground, Simão gazed at her with a gentle and patient expression. He knew that the truth, despite its beauty and harmony, was a delicate thing that must be administered slowly for true understanding. She had not had any opportunity to adjust to the reality that her husband, unbeknownst to anyone, had quietly sided with the Traitors over the past months. It was a surprise even to Simão and his co-conspirators to hear that this gaoler had assisted the Advocate to escape certain death, and for this, they owed his family what protection they could. Luckily, they had been alerted by the Clairdani of the gaoler's plan, with only enough time to get to the gaoler's house to give a warning and smuggle them out of the town. Taking his wife and child by unfortunate surprise, they forced them to safety far from the town with only the warning that the magistrate was probably coming to burn the house and they must leave immediately. Without time to collect anything more than their shoes, they were rushed through quiet alleys so as to avoid detection by anyone. She had come willingly enough at the time, perhaps from shock, but now that she had had time to dwell on the events of the day, she was becoming more suspicious and reluctant to believe what they had told her. Evidently, her husband had tried to keep her safe by keeping his conversion secret, even from his own family. Well-intentioned though his efforts may have been, the reality was that the magistrate's fears clouded any rational thought, and asking forgiveness rather than permission was the general rule.

Looking into his kind, understanding eyes, she found no argument from him, only compassion. Since she and her son had not yet been hurt, she decided to go along with these Traitors for the time and perhaps collect information she could use later. She thought about her childhood friend, now turned magistrate. Surely, the magistrate would remember their friendship and excuse her later when she brought him important evidence? She drew a deep breath, and tears filled her eyes. Tears filled her eyes. "We are so very grateful for your alarm that saved us from the fire and for your hiding us while everyone was looking for us in town, but we have nothing to hide! Hawthorne never gave us anything – information or otherwise – that would leave us in harm's way…"

Simão shook his head wearily. He knew the politics of the town too well. "I only wish that were true." He paused, wondering how best to word what he knew as compassionately as he could. "We know he died today, horribly, for allowing the release of a high-level traitor. I think he knew he might die today, as well, and as much as he tried to protect you, you are still associated with him and thus not safe in this town, ever." He paused again to let them absorb the reality. Rather than the tears he expected to renew in her eyes, Noyette seemed to draw herself up into a stone-like pillar.

"So it's all HER fault, then, that he's now dead!" She took a moment to compose and focus her rage. "Is she here?" She paused to look around at each face she saw. "Why did he need to let her go free – so he could die himself!?" Hostility radiated through her as she glared at those around the Pit.

Simão took a defensive stance between the hostile woman and his friends, with Cenellot standing out of reach, confused. He watched her momentarily, ready to contain her again if needed. After a minute of no physical hostility, he replied as calmly as possible to help diffuse the fear and hurt driving her aggressiveness. "She is not here – the Clairdani took her to safety as he asked them to do. Yes, HE asked them to take her from the gaol. We had nothing to do with her escape, actually," he remarked in answer to her dubious scorn that she flashed his direction. "We heard from the Clairdani what his intentions were and were as surprised as you that a gaoler would risk his own life to help one of our own, especially after the number of us that he's helped torture." A shadow of sorrow passed over his face, then vanished as he focused on the matter at hand. "The few of us who were told about the plan agreed to do what we could to honor Hawthorne and his wishes, which meant rescuing you from the same fate. That's all we know about your husband's plans and involvement in her escape."

The matron sighed in resignation, and defiant tears streamed down her face. "Hawthorne was always kind-hearted, and I know..." Faltering, she wiped the fresh tears from her face. "And I know he struggled daily with the cruelties he was required to condone. He thinks he kept it to himself, but his sobs and terrors in his dreams woke me and let me know the true state of his heart..." She could not continue. "Why does kindness have to be repaid with cruelty?! Why does one man's kindness have to destroy so many other lives?" Her anger only made her checks flush and her tears hotter.

Kindly, Simão offered her a scrap piece of linen for her tears. Allowing her to wipe her eyes, he looked to the Pit and surveyed the town walls to give her time to collect herself. "We've heard more about what happened since her escape, though. The guards shared the story in the taverns, divulging all they knew about his demise as soon as they left the gaol earlier today. They told everyone of the new Inquisitor and boasted of the strange things he asked for to help torture him, although they were definitely disturbed by the fact that it was one of their own this time. Given that it was one of their own, I would have thought they would have made a bigger spectacle of his funeral procession out of town. It is bizarre that no one has seen any bodies leave the gaol to come here today..." Turning towards the two new refugees, the tall, father-like figure continued quietly, "We are glad you both are safe, at least, and we are sorry for your loss and what it will mean for you now. Know that we are here to help you and that you will not be harmed by any one of us."

After exchanging subtle smiles, the mother and son's lips almost curled up to their cheeks. The more maternal, concerned voice continued, "We thank you, sincerely, for our rescue, and you are right. Now that they think we are Traitors, regardless of the truth, we cannot return to the town." Now that the storm may have passed, she searched the faces of the people who stood nearer her. These were faces she had never known well, and knowing her life was only safe beyond the town walls, she would never know them now…

"What are we to do now? How and where are we to live? By now, the magistrate will have signed our death warrants in case we are ever found!" Breaking into renewed sobs, she could not continue.

"Noyette, we will take you and Cenellot to a place where you both will be safe this very night. The other Tomarans will expect you to be dead after the magistrate's declaration and treatment of your husband, so your disappearance will not cause a search from them. However, since the guards know you escaped from the house, the magistrate's guards may look for you for a little while, even though they spread stories of your deaths. Thus, time is of the essence. We will have to introduce you to the Clairdani – the elves and the Creatures of the Light, who will help provide for you while you make a new life for yourselves. I am still hoping that your husband, Hawthorne, will be brought to the Pit in time… I'm still hopeful that you will have this opportunity to say good-bye. Perhaps we missed the procession?" He paused to give her time to absorb his words and recover from her renewed tears. "He was very brave, sacrificing himself for all of us. You can be very proud of what he did, although I know it is too difficult to do so now."

As if on cue, a creature with a striking resemblance to an unusually large dark brown cat with golden eyes materialized suddenly. Only four feet tall when walking on its hind legs, it came near the circle, heading straight towards Simão. As with all creatures, the Brownie made no noise on the tufted, large paws that were the size of lunch plates. A gentle, calming, purring sound emitted from his throat, affecting everyone in the circle somewhat differently. Noyette and Cenellot, as conditioned, gasped in fear and scrambled back towards their hiding places. When the others made no moves other than welcoming the Brownie into the circle, the fearful duo paused and watched. The overgrown cat-like creature did not seem to say anything or do anything to anyone, but the Traitors seemed to nod their heads as if they had heard something. Perhaps it was a whisper? Just as quickly as it had appeared, it suddenly vanished out of their circle around the Pit, and Simão looked around for the cowardly duo. "There is nothing to fear, my friends. That was a Brownie, one of the Clairdani. He came to tell us that he had not seen any Tenenbrani – the Creatures of the Dark – nearing the town. You can come back now, and I'll explain a bit more. He will not return soon."

The pair slowly made their way back to the spot between the bushes and the clearing, then sat down on the ground. Although their faces were turned towards Simão, Noyette's eyes searched the night around them, not wanting to be surprised by another sudden appearance. Once they were settled, Simão explained further. "The Brownies are part of the Clairdani, who are the magical creatures who are trying to help people and protect them from animal attacks. They speak mostly through their eyes, and once you establish a connection with them, you will be able to hear their voices in your head as clearly as I am speaking to you now. The ones who attack people in the town are called the Tenenbrani, and a wicked lot they are. We do not get too many opportunities to speak to them, for they are mostly more animalistic in their minds. They only think about food, which the people mostly provide, but we have made some progress. Those of us who can speak to these creatures work with the Clairdani to try and prevent those attacks. It gets more complicated than what I've just told you, but the rest can wait."

The boy, listening intently, had crept even closer as Simão spoke and gently tugged at Simão's tunic. "Could I speak to them too, then?" asked Cenellot imploringly. Then, he had another thought. "I've always loved the unicorns, and I never could believe they were evil. Do you think, once they get to know me, that the unicorns might let me ride them?"

Chuckling at his impatience and excitement, Simão answered, "Normally, we try to hold off teaching people how to communicate with them until they are older. Remember, it does have a permanent effect on you: your eyes will turn green, forever marking you as one of us in the town. But yes, maybe the unicorns or even the centaurs..."

"But your eyes are brown! How do you communicate with them, then, if your eyes aren't green?" The youngster interrupted.

"Ahh! You're quick. I like that. You're right - I do have brown eyes, but don't let looks deceive you. We have learned that we must use eye covers to make our eyes seem brown while in town because having green eyes would make us seem suspicious since everyone has brown eyes." As proof, he quickly turned, putting his finger in his eye, and showing the deep brown cover to the boy, who gasped appreciatively. "See? They aren't impossible to wear, but they do take some getting used to, and they only come in one size, so it works better once you're fully grown." In the ensuing pause, Cenellot stood perhaps a little taller to show that his eight solar cycles had indeed made him taller than others his age. "However, if you and your mother are to live amongst them and with us, you will need to be able to speak with them because they may have important messages for you that may be a warning to flee. We have also recently learned of other towns in the area and are hoping that in these towns, the green eyes will not mean anything to make them suspect you of any wrongdoing."

He paused, his face falling as he grew more serious. "But know this -from the moment you become a Traitor, or as we call ourselves, an Enlightened, you live in fear of discovery, in fear of your very life, every day…" He grew quiet as the memories of the many friends he had lost over the years because of the blindness of the magistrate and his people flooded his mind. In equal frustration, he sat hard on the ground and stared over the Pit, bringing the discussion to an end for the time being.

They all stood or sat around the Pit, in constant vigilance for any signs that the guards might be bringing Hawthorne's body to the Pit. At the faintest sound of rustling or any movement, they hurriedly retreated to their respective bushes for concealment until the fear had subsided. In between times, they whiled the time until the midnight moon by whittling sticks and telling occasional tales of victory. Occasionally, they were interrupted by the appearance of a brownie or unicorn that came towards the circle, reporting what they had seen on their own patrols. The reports were very similar – no Tenenbrani had emerged or approached the town tonight, although occasionally, one that the Clairdani were on speaking terms with was spotted alone in the forest. Simão translated for the newcomers each time so that they would begin to understand the new world around them, letting Cenellot stand next to him while he spoke with them. There would be time to absorb the newness of their situation over the next few weeks while they lived away from everything they knew and depended mostly upon the Clairdani.

As midnight drew nigh, they gathered in a circle around the Pit, and Clairdani who had hidden beyond their view, came nearer, making impatient sounds as they moved forward. The bright moonlight shone fully on the Pit now, illuminating each rough woolen, blood-stained cloth of the town's dead laid to rest in neat rows in the Pit below. Moments passed. The moon began to create shadows on the western part of the Pit, and nothing changed in the Pit. Bewildered, the Clairdani came closer and made inquiring noises that echoed the thoughts of the Traitors. The largest unicorn was twelve-hands high with a silver mane and tail, its hide so brilliantly white that it reflected every beam of the moon. As midnight came and went, this walking luminescence approached Simão and looked into his eyes.

"I know. You did say that no one came to bring anyone to the Pit, so it was foolish to risk exposure for something that wouldn't happen. But maybe we just missed the body transfer, and his body was here? I wanted to be sure." Simão gestured to those around, indicating they should move back away from the Pit and behind the bushes. In a quieter voice, he resumed his discussion with the Clairdani. "OK – keep a watch tonight to see if they are waiting until tomorrow to bring him out, and in the meantime, we will take his family to safety." After another pause, most of the Clairdani left the area, disappearing into the darkness. A few hid in the shadows just out of sight of the patrol to keep watch while two of the unicorns stayed with Simão and followed him back to the townsfolk.

"All of you, return to your families and remember to act as surprised as everyone about the gaoler's death. Ask questions but be careful not to be too curious. Carefully find out what you can about the details. Remember, we know the truth about why the gaoler died, so do not let on about what you know, or it will mean exposure of who we are. If you uncover any information about what happened to the body, come to my house tomorrow night after dusk once the streets are clear."

The area cleared out in silence, the people leaving in twos and threes so as not to make too much noise that might attract attention from the patrol. Once the others left the area, Simão and the two unicorns met with Noyette and Cenellot alone. Simão gave them a small bag of provisions and patted the backs of the two unicorns. Looking down at the exhilarated Cenellot, Simão explained, "the unicorns are only allowing you to ride because of the dire nature of your distress. Do not insult a unicorn by assuming you would ever be allowed such travel again in the future. These are our friends and guardians, not beasts of burden, and as such, you will be completely safe while in their care." He lifted Cenellot onto one unicorn, then offered his clasped hands to Noyette so she could sit astride the unicorn nearest her.

"These are trusted friends, so you are very safe with them. Cenellot – this is Markus, and Noyette, yours is Celina. They will take you to a safe location, a hide-away, until the town stops looking for you. Then, we can try to find a town that will accept you as a widow and her son and help you find a product to sell in the markets. It must be a product that people from other places won't come looking for and draw attention to who you are. For now, stay hidden until we come to find you. We will not abandon you, I promise! We will come visit and help you understand everything, although it won't be regular visits, mind you."

With a nod to the unicorns, Simão let them depart into the darkness, watching to ensure they passed safely out of sight of the town. Turning towards the town, he looked over at the Pit again, puzzling over the delay in the deposit of the gaoler's body. The townspeople were very superstitious by nature and believed that death drew the maniacal dark creatures to them. In a way, they were right – both the Clairdani and the Tenenbrani could smell death regardless of how far away they were, but only the Tenenbrani dared to destroy a town over a corpse. If there were still a corpse inside the walls of the town, there would be Tenenbrani collecting outside… but no one had seen any. This mystery meant the balance had changed, and he wasn't sure whether that bodes good or ill.

He approached the gate, side stepped to the right, and appeared to gaze at an indistinguishable triangular mark on the wall. Mirroring the triangular figure with his right hand, he seemed to pass through the wall. Once on the other side of the wall, he scanned the streets. Seeing none of the others in the streets, he hoped they had safely reached their homes. Reaching his own house a few minutes later, he continuously scanned the town for any unusual movement. The only sources of light were at the Town Hall and the Gaol, same as always, no torches, then leading guards with new prisoners. Something was different, but he would have to wait until the morrow to gather more details to help him determine what the change implied. Until then, he had to trust that the Clairdani were on patrol outside the town and that they were safe inside these same walls.

Chapter 4: The Alliance

After dismissing the guards and returning to his temporary office, the inquisitor stared at the codex in front of him as he slowly lowered himself into the wooden seat of judgment that would be his for the next few weeks. The codex, a dark-brown, well-worked leather cover reinforced by intricate iron work at the edges and iron clasps, seemed well used. Many of the iron finials along the spine and the front were loose and spun easily when touched. There didn't seem to be anything remarkable about the codex itself. In appearance, it looked like any other codices he had seen, other than the lack of an apparent means to open it. The very few codices in existence were hoarded by those with wealth. Even the ability to read a codex was a highly sought after yet guarded skill, seen as unnecessary for the everyday town inhabitants. On a gaoler's salary, how had the simple gaoler afforded a codex? More intriguing, however, was why a gaoler needed a codex, having come from a town of illiterates? There was more to this simple gaoler than it had appeared. It was apparent that he must have gained some secretive training in his early years, if he had the ability to decipher a codex.

If only he could unlock it to discover what the gaoler had concealed, even from his own family!

For the next two hours, the inquisitor tried every method he knew of opening a codex – saying "open" in every language he knew, dropping it from the ceiling, even using the weight of the desk to try to bend the clasps. The codex even seemed impervious to the elements - fire seemed to leave the codex unmarred, and water made no impression or mark on the leather or pages inside. Were these enchantments something the gaoler had known to do, or had he bought the codex already enchanted for a specific purpose? If so, then what was this gaoler concealing from the rest of humanity? Surely, if he had something to conceal, he must have told someone about it, in case something happened to him... If not a person, perhaps he had hidden a clue in his hut? With a stab of resentment, he wished he hadn't been so hasty in demanding the hut be burned to the ground. He would have to try tomorrow, once there were fewer prying eyes around the hut, and see if there was anything left that might indicate a method of gaining access to the codex.

The inquisitor felt exhausted by the day's proceedings that had not gone well. He had not intended the gaoler to die so quickly, and he was disgusted that he had nothing to offer to the magistrate. Despite his failures, the inquisitor knew his presence in the magistrate's office at the Town Hall could not be put off any longer. It was already dusk, and he had discovered nothing other than this codex, which he was reluctant to reveal to the magistrate. Somehow, it seemed to him a personal challenge on a mental scale, one between himself and the gaoler. While he may have triumphed in the physical test, the gaoler had clearly outmatched him in this mental challenge. He would wait until he had at least seen what the codex contained before entrusting any knowledge to the magistrate.

He debated what he should say about the codex as he left the gaol, walking through streets that recalled memories of his past life in this town on his way to Town Hall. He nodded his head in acknowledgement of the townspeople's greetings to him but otherwise, seemed unaware of the present. With any luck, the magistrate would be hungry and anxious to get to his evening repast and not need a full report at the moment.

The Town Hall was lit by torches along the walls, both at the entrance and throughout the low, one-story, whitewashed timber and mud building. To signify its importance, it was guarded by a handful of guards in leather-metal armor with spikes in hand and daggers in their belts. They each stood to their full height in salute of the inquisitor as he passed by on his way to the Magistrate's chamber immediately opposite the entrance on the other side of the central atrium. Upon reaching the open iron wrought doors, the door guards announced the inquisitor's presence to the magistrate, who acknowledged with a vague, distracted phrase, "Enter."

For the tenth time that hour, the magistrate looked out his oiled sheepskin window to see the lateness of the day before he looked at his visitor. "You're later than I expected, Ma'elrich."

"Pardon me, Rowen, I was … rather occupied."

"So I see." The magistrate took a moment to re-evaluate the man in front of him. "In the future, do not carry out interrogation, executions, burnings, or… any other form of justice you decide on without consulting me first."

"Of course, Rowen. I got … carried away. It will not happen again."

"Good. Now that we have established our understanding, how was your… interrogation?"

Ma'elrich began to pace in front of the desk, trying to formulate a reasonable answer to the seemingly simple question. "It was informative on one scale – I discovered that regardless of a person's physical strength, a person can have an inner strength of character that has no direct correlation with their physical strength." Reflecting that he may be speaking in riddles, he reformulated his answer. "In simple terms, just because someone is strong physically doesn't imply that they can tolerate mental torture any better than someone who's already been weakened…"

Impatient with the unimportant details of whatever experiment Ma'elrich was running on his own time, Rowan decided to ask more boldly. "And the gaoler? What did you discover? What information can you give me about the Traitors??"

"He was unresponsive to any form of interrogation I gave him. He seemed to know his end was coming regardless and chose not to give me anything other than the joy of hearing him scream through my various techniques. Ultimately, he was destroyed…"

After staring at Ma'elrich, with what he hoped was a disdainful and abhorrent stare, the magistrate adjusted his tone to be more stern and hoped for a better answer to his second question. "And the burning of his residence? Was that part of the torture you were administering?"

"No… that was more, uh, insurance that the gaoler would… cooperate," the inquisitor answered, somewhat mumbling his inadequate response.

"So, you spent from sun-up to after midday destroying the gaoler. Meanwhile, you had the guards destroy what was left of his existence, to no avail??" The magistrate's voice rose with each word, ending with a shrill tone that resounded throughout the building.

Desperate not to allow the magistrate to take the upper hand and dictate all terms, Ma'elrich fought back. "He was a traitor! We are no worse now than we were before, and now there is one less traitor in the town than before today. Don't forget that!"

For a few moments, the two men held a silent struggle for power as they each looked at the other defiantly, neither willing to look away first. Ma'elrich spoke first, having taken a deep breath to calm himself and think more clearly.

"You said yourself that the gaoler had no connections to the Traitors and had never visited any of their people or wandered outside the town. What you have not yet heard is that there were no bodies at the residence – somehow, they were forewarned. Maybe the gaoler told them to leave when he left for the gaol, and he would find them if he could." He bided his time, waiting until he sensed the magistrate's interest was piqued before revealing the crucial piece of information he held. "The only thing left in the hut was a codex."

"A codex?? Wha..." he broke off as the inquisitor continued as if he hadn't been interrupted.

"It contained nothing, though. I've already read through it." He fabricated a tale on the spot. "It was an old manuscript of old legends, nothing more..."

"Why would they have a codex? I had no knowledge of commoners who were proficient in our language's writing." The magistrate seemed more unnerved than even Ma'elrich himself had been, so he pressed his advantage while the magistrate was still befuddled.

"With your permission, of course, I would like to stay here until I have read through the old legends to see if there is anything there that might tell us of the origins of the Traitors. I'd like to extend my assistance in uncovering the meaning behind this, as we haven't achieved anything else today."

The magistrate considered for a moment, carefully weighing each aspect of his proposal as he slowly replied, "You may stay for one week. If you find you need more time, we can consider what has been accomplished that week to determine whether staying another week would be feasible. While you are here, you may use the office in the gaol for your sole use – I will stay here in the Town Hall. We shall meet every day to discuss any new discoveries, even if it is only the briefest of meetings. As for accommodations, I shall consider our shared history and the respect I have for our friendship and have your old room ready for you at my residence. I assure you; my servants would give you the best at table, and we need not discuss anything more than days long gone. It would be better if we did not discuss these things outside these walls, in any case. What say you?"

"I thank you for your offer and hospitality, Rowan and will enjoy dining with you at your house. I accept your proposal, then, in its entirety." Stepping forward, he proffered his hand, and the two shook hands briefly but firmly.

"To my humble house, then!" The magistrate offered a smile, but it lacked any warmth. The two men then gathered their belongings to walk to the magistrate's house, a short distance from the Town Hall on the main street of Tomar. Just outside a two-story, newly whitewashed stone-and-timber building with pieced glass windows, the magistrate held up his hand to have the inquisitor wait. "Wait here while I have your room readied and our evening meal put to order." The magistrate called to the house, and when his manservant, Oliveiro, came forward, they discussed details of the inquisitor's stay. Oliveiro bowed his head in acknowledgement of his orders, and went inside, immediately dispensing orders to the cook and other servants of the house.

Orders given, the Magistrate turned to the Inquisitor. "Welcome to my humble abode, my dear Ma'elrich! May this be your home away from home for your duration here!" He gestured for Ma'elrich to enter the house, and followed, both in the high spirit of a new alliance.

Chapter 5: A Fluttering Light Gains Strength

With the alarm echoing faintly in her mind, Luz lay limp in the cradling talons of a mountainous red dragon. A small indistinct cloud seemed to fly nearby in perfect symmetric undulation with the dragon wings. Upon closer inspection, the whitish cloud is actually a very fluffy owl with large wings and even larger eyes, constantly watching over Luz carefully. From the moment Luz had been rescued, the owl had hovered around her, giving constant reports about her condition. Luz's eyes briefly fluttered open, just enough to catch a glimpse of the owl, before her remaining strength faded away.

Metulas, we're too late! She's dead! You need to stop now so we can revive her!

I can feel her heartbeat under my talons. Faint though it may be, she's still alive. Don't worry, little one! Metulas flew a bit higher. *Her body needs proper rest to recover, and my fire magic will speed her healing once we get back to our lair. You know she is strong. She will survive.*

Soon, they were out of sight of Tomar, and at that exact moment, her breath eased. It was as if she had finally cleared her lungs of the foul, dank air of the dungeons. Yet after two more hours of flying steadily, she had yet to show any other signs of awareness, and her friends grew worried.

I was hoping that by now she might open her eyes, since she is breathing more easily now. The town is far behind us, and we've seen no other change in her condition!

After a minute of contemplation, Metulas decided to help Anehta see the obvious. *Anehta, hang back and look again*

41

from a different perspective. Then, come back and tell me what you see.

Fluttering in place, Anehta did as she was asked, then sped back to her vigil beside Luz. *There's a slight pinkish glow around the two of you. Is that what you mean? I didn't notice anything else. But you know I've never been as observant as either of you are, and it's still rather dark!*

The dragon rumbled his acceptance of her answer. *Remember that magic happens in many forms and appears strongest where it is needed the most. For instance, right when we thought all was lost, we were finally able to succeed where we had always failed before. Magic finds a way when it senses urgency. After all these years, I'm still unable to predict what will happen.*

Oh! Anehta exclaimed with sudden clarity. *Is that how you were finally able to rescue her? I know we've tried so many times before.*

Yes, exactly. I was finally able to create a scrying portal inside the gaol for Luz to escape. While she was in captivity, I was not able to sense her at all. There must have been a magic dampening spell near her cell. It was solely the strength she possessed that had kept her going all this while, so I am happy to see that she's still alive. I worried that the drop in the spell meant that she was lost.

Anehta sighed deeply and gave a slight shudder to rid herself of that horrible thought. *I've watched you train her for many years now, and combined with her own inner strength, she's probably the only human that could have withstood what was in that gaol.*

The dawn's light finally overcame the darkness, and Luz began to twitch and flutter her eyelids. The slow emergence of light fluttered her eyelids open, granting her the final additional strength required for her to awaken. The feebleness of the light provided her eyes with more than enough light to see the world around her after being in the continual dark for the past few months. As she took in the world around her and where she was, she was comforted by the sight of her two friends with her.

"Metulath...?" she slurred.

Metulas nodded his giant head in rhythm with his next wing flap as he lifted her higher above the land and out of sight of any bowman or patrolman seeking an escaping prisoner. Luz smiled and as she was overcome by weariness and security, she slipped back into unconsciousness. She felt the blanket of security lull her back into a restorative slumber.

The owl began squawking in earnest, flying as close to Luz as she dared, trying to wake her.

Stop your mothering, Anehta. She will be restored by all that's in heaven! She's with us now, and I will not let anything harm her while she heals. Her breathing shows she is now gaining strength and is no longer in danger.

Anehta still fluttered about, unconvinced. A constant companion to Luz for many solar cycles, the mothering owl ensured she stayed on alert nearby Luz during the long flight. Despite her friendship with Metulas and his assurances, Anehta wasn't sure the dragon really understood death. As an immortal being with immortal friends, Metulas never saw death as the final element as Anehta did. More than once, Anehta had seen Metulas being more careless than necessary when it came to actions that might cause a loss of life, and she secretly pledged to be the guardian of all those that existed around Metulas.

By the time the sun had come above the horizon fully, the trio had landed at a shallow cave located mid-level in a mountain side overlooking a vast, barren canyon. Its seemingly narrow ledge at the entrance defied its constant use by a large two-hundred-foot-long dragon, and had been overlooked through the centuries by those seeking to slay any remaining dragons in these parts. Metulas sighed at the entrance, partly in relief and partly in frustration. While the narrow, hidden entrance had helped preserve his life for many centuries, it was no longer necessary since most assumed he was already dead, as had been the fate of all the dragons in the land. To the task at hand, it was a more awkward entrance with someone's life hanging in the balance in his talons.

There was also a much smaller cave, slightly above this main cave and hidden by the brush from onlookers from below, with just enough shelter from the elements to be called a cave. Despite its smaller size, this cave had the comforts attributed to human comforts - a hay mattress and rough woolen blankets for warmth, a floor covered with animal hides, walls decorated with drawings ranging from simple to elaborate, and a small fireplace. It had been Luz's home for the many years since Metulas had found her as a young girl wandering in the desert without much life left in her.

In this smaller cave, Metulas laid Luz on a bed of healing grasses within the dragon's reach from the entrance, ensuring they were out of sight of any inquiring eyes that might be searching for her. Despite the lack of hands, Metulas and Anehta's talons, wings, and head prods were able to complete most human-like maneuvers. Nods and gestures communicated their needs to help the two caregivers keep a reverential healing silence.

After giving Luz a small amount of warm liquid and food, Anehta steadily administered herbs to Luz's wounds while Metulas´ fire-breath kept both the cave and the poultices warm. Slowly, they saw Luz's breath normalize as she sank into that deep healing sleep enabled by the purification of her wounds. By unspoken agreement, both stayed within the small, cramped cave- Anehta standing guard at the bedpost and administering healing herbal waters, and Metulas lying across the entrance, a large boulder protruding from the mountain that emanated heat to those inside. There was much to think about now that things had changed in the town, and the two spent time in a shared quiet, occupied by their thoughts and loving hope for Luz.

All they could do now, was wait.

Chapter 6: Flight

The first couple of hours of riding on the backs of the unicorns were fascinating for Cenellot. He enjoyed every nuance of riding other than his constant slipping off to the side. From being free of doing the walking himself to seeing beyond the walls of the town for the first time, everything caught his attention. Although he could not understand his unicorn's speech, he felt they understood each other. Cenellot felt more secure in his companionship with his unicorn than he ever had with anyone inside the town, a thought which made him rethink his friendships and acquaintances. As he thought back on them, he was forced to acknowledge that the friendships had mostly been children laughing at him and his good-natured laughing at himself for all his blustering, missteps, and overall detraction from all the misdeeds others caused. With this fresh start, this seemed to be a natural connection, and a friendship developed that the boy had never had. At each new sound they heard, Cenellot would whisper his questions, and Markus would nicker, nod, or shake his mane to show his agreement or negation of the statement, which was enough conversation for him.

Noyette was less assured by Markus' head answers and spoke not at all, flinching at each sound around them. Celina would respond by sharing a kind and reassuring look. Having lived longer in fear of anything beyond the town's walls, Noyette was horrified by every sound she heard around her. Having listened to and understood the implications of their situation, she wished ruefully that her ignorance and innocence could be restored. In her mind, each shrill bark was a werewolf calling to his pack to attack them. Each ghostly hoot seemed like a Fury giving its warning cry to frighten its prey before its inevitable death. Any sudden rustle was a minotaur or griffin watching them before its attack. Markus and Celina neither flinched nor reacted to the strange sounds, which did give her some confidence that they were still safe. It would be a long time before she would be able to sleep well now that she was outside the only life and protection she had ever known.

Within that first hour, the four had crossed the plain and entered the forest, from which most of the town's animal horrors had come. As they entered the forest, the familiar brownie that had visited them at the Pit met them and exchanged words of sorts with the unicorns. All Noyette saw was head bobbing, whinnying, snorts, gurgling or whimpers, which seemed to constitute speech for them. Markus seemed assured after the exchange, and after helping Cenellot balance again on Markus's back, they continued their forced ride. They then plunged headlong into the forest, diminishing the moonlight and making visibility difficult for humans. As the forest grew thicker, Cenellot could only see his mother as a dark blur astride Celina's shining coat. In contrast to Noyette's rising anxiety with the loss of visibility, Cenellot seemed to grow more wondrous and confident with the dark. His slips off Markus' back had slowed to only once an hour, and he seemed able to sit straighter, allowing his legs and lower back to keep rhythm with the motion.

After those first two hours, however, the chill of the night air began to make them shiver, even with the heat from the unicorns' bodies warming their legs. Neither was used to riding animals, and their backs and legs were aching and raw from the unaccustomed use. Mental discomforts added to her physical discomforts as well. The forest created its own terrors in her mind as she recalled the many town stories about maulings and lost limbs of townspeople who had gone into the forest on patrol. Despite her constant terror, Noyette forced herself to resist her urge to scream out or give away their location. She kept looking to the distance, willing them forward toward the other side of the forest and the promise of a sunrise.

Suddenly, a deep growl seemed to thrum through the forest in a wave. Noyette froze with terror, and a short cry escaped her lips before Celina looked back at her to calm her. They all froze as Markus and Celina's ears swiveled to track where the sound had come from. Cenellot looked over Markus's ears to see if he could see anything as well and thought he could see two pinpricks of red floating in the forest a little distance to their left. Markus gave a slight lurch, indicating that Cenellot should dismount, which he did quickly. Markus lowered his horn and plummeted into the dense forest brush. Cenellot huddled next to Celina, his mother's hand on his head to steady them both. Within seconds, another snarl of challenge erupted to the left, and more growls reverberated around them. Celina prepared for an attack by allowing Noyette to dismount, then took a guarding pose near her charges.

The continuous growling and snarling, punctuated by yips of surprise and pain, lasted an eternity for the two hapless refugees awaiting their delayed demise. One set of red pinpricks grew in size until the group could discern the large, gray wolf they belonged to; its teeth gleaming brighter as he entered the slanting moonlight.

Noyette screamed, pulling Cenellot close to her on the ground, closing her eyes and mind to the threat of death by teeth. Celina charged the wolf with horn and hoof, barely able to dispatch the first before a second and third came to the fray. Fantastically, Celina's horn worked as quickly as any swordsman's blade and her hooves as quick as any fighter's mace, ending the three of them in only a few heartbeats. As suddenly as it had begun, it was over, and Markus returned to the bloody quiet of the group. Markus and Celina looked at their human riders and, agreeing on something, turned their horns to their riders and moved towards them.

"What are you doing? You can't kill us. We are under Simão's protection!" Noyette's maternal instinct for her son's survival gave her strength that she didn't feel in her aching and bloody legs.

Markus stopped where he was. Raising his horn, he tried to communicate to Cenellot with his eyes as best he could. The eyes were kind and concerned, not hostile or angered.

"They aren't going to hurt us, mother. This is about something else. We have to trust them, or we won't survive here."

Noyette stared long and hard at the two Clairdani and finally nodded her head. Markus turned his horn toward Cenellot's legs while Celina mirrored the action for Noyette. Gently, their horns touched their pants, and within a few moments, the aching and pain in their legs began to disappear! Cenellot touched his pants, and the blood that had soaked him from the ride was also disappearing.

"Thank you!" Cenellot stammered.

Just then, a Brownie arrived, jumping from carcass to carcass and turning flips in the air as he landed amongst them. His head swiveled, and his ears cocked this way and that in a way that made Cenellot clap a hand over his mouth so as not to grin too broadly. Finally, the Brownie looked at their pants, and he clapped his hands as if in approval of their past actions. Markus and Celina nodded their heads in thanks.

It was easier to read the Brownie's thoughts with the mime, and Cenellot was happy for the lighter company. In further reassurance, the Brownie stood upon one of the wolf carcasses and, pointing at himself, mimed that he would be staying closer by to protect them from any other stalking Tenenbrani.

"Thank you, Brownie, all assistance is welcome!" trilled Noyette in a voice that still descried her anxiety. While speaking, she failed to notice the reluctant nods exchanged between Markus and Celina, signifying their grudging acceptance.

With the brownie prowling in the forest nearby (although not entirely quietly), Markus and Celina continued at a slightly brisker pace nonetheless. Cenellot didn't seem as worried about new noises from the forest, taking it all as part of the forest, and his enthusiasm kept Noyette from letting her extreme terror show through – one terrified refugee was enough at the moment.

As the trees began to thin and the moon highlighted more ground, a griffon, as large as the hut they had lived in, dropped in front of them, shaking the ground as it landed. Folding its large eagle wings into its sides, it turned its head from side to side to see each of them better with its large eyes. This last surprise was too much for Noyette, who suddenly fainted and almost fell off her mount.

"Mother!" Cenellot cried as he clumsily slid off Markus' back and saw that the griffon was a friend, not a foe. Running to her side, he supported her slumped form as best he could from Celina's side. Celina was moving slightly so as to support the weight as it shifted.

"Mother, wake up! Mother, mother!" While the griffon and the unicorns conversed about which of the Tenenbrani were about the area and the status of anything beyond the forest, Cenellot shook his mother gently until she could rouse herself from her temporary stress-induced paralysis.

"Mother! It's OK, he's a friend!"

As if she had already forgotten what happened, she started to say, "Who?" while she looked around her and again saw the griffon. Seeing the two Clairdani speaking together was less of a surprise than the sudden appearance. She gave a wane smile and replied, "It would appear so."

The fact that they were all still alive when she opened her eyes gave her a little comfort. Slowly, she gained confidence that the griffon was a protective Clairdani as she took in the conversation from what she could understand of it by watching their interaction.

The apparent additional protection gave her the courage to voice her requests when it seemed that there might be a break in their exchange. "Celina, Markus – would you mind if we stopped soon so we could rest? We are not used to riding or staying awake all night... Could the griffon stand guard for a while until the sun is almost overhead?"

In response, the griffon seemed to take on an additional air of dignity and bowed his head as if to say, "As you wish." Celina knelt so she could dismount more easily and join Cenellot, and the griffon turned his back to begin his watch over them. Exhausted, Noyette and Cenellot unpacked the blankets, and Noyette found a hard soda biscuit for each of them along with a singular animal-hide skin of watered-down wine.

"Eat, then sleep, my dear boy." Cenellot was too tired to mind the mothering. They had barely finished eating and taking sips of the wine before they were stretched out on the blankets, lying next to the kneeling unicorns. For the next few hours through dawn break, the unicorns blocked the two refugees from any wind and provided more warmth against the cooling night air, snoozing on and off as the griffon stayed on watchful alert.

Chapter 7: Breaking the Codex

The inquisitor found himself running in underground corridors lined with rough-hewn dark stone. Light from somewhere in the distance reflected from the ridges formed by the stone, hopefully guiding him towards an exit. He was winded from running, but whenever he stopped to take a breath, another creature came behind him, spitting fire, sporting talons or teeth that threatened immediate death. He ran on, the stitch in his side growing as the time between breaths grew shorter. If he didn't stop soon, he would collapse from exhaustion. He began stumbling, hearing the beats of the hoofs of whichever creature was closest to him now, knowing that he would die one way or the other very soon. Suddenly, he tripped and fell. Gathering his remaining strength, he tried to stand, but the animal was upon him. He smelled the sulfur and felt the flame's heat from the creature's mouth. A blood-curdling scream came from his own throat, and he awoke.

Gasping for breath, he tried both to forget the dream and remember it. In many ways, it was the same dream he had had every night since he obtained the codex. It was always the same rough-hewn corridor, but the danger changed each night. The creatures of tonight's nightmare alternated with sudden fires, cave-ins, or immense winds that prevented him from moving forward. The worst horror was the floods that dragged him under and swept him breathless until he felt he was drowning. Each time he died, he awoke screaming. Breathing a bit easier now, he tried to remember his dream, trying to connect the repetitive elements with the changes. Were the dreams trying to give him clues to help him decipher the codex or warnings about an impending attack that would cost him his life? He had enough experience with the various creatures that in life, he wouldn't be afraid of them. Why the fear in the dream, then?

After a few days of attempting to open the codex by ordinary means to no avail, Ma'elrich was no closer to opening the codex than he had been when he first tried. His fatigue grew as he put off sleep each night until it overtook him. The nightmares that always followed left him feeling drained and more exhausted when he awoke. On the seventh day, after spending the entire time before breakfast staring at the codex's design, he decided that perhaps it was the iron scroll clasps that held the sealed book together. He spent the rest of that day finding tools within the gaol and endeavored to remove all the iron-worked scrolls from the codex. With a breath of relief, he pulled at the book's cover.

"Aaughh! Of all that sets the stars in the heavens!! It still won't open!" A stream of profanities oozed from Ma'elrich's mouth, which he reiterated at each reminder of his failure that afternoon until he had composed himself. He was very silent that night, only somewhat answering questions from Rowen that evening at their evening repast. Each day, he had another inspiration, but each inspiration was as fruitless as the previous one. Even his visits to the hut led to very little. Although no one had cleared the ashes from the site yet, the only identifiable piece he could find at the site was a small, scorched wall placard reciting the town's motto of "Love's Truth Will Set You Free" in the old runes. The stonework on the floor also contained the ancient runes in combinations that did not create any words he recognized at the time. He knew them well now since they reappeared thereafter in the stonework walls and flooring he retraced in his dreams every night. If he couldn't break into the codex soon, he would have to pursue this other path. Other towns existed, and perhaps there might be someone able to translate these other runes for him. More questions to answer!

Bleary from his self-imposed insomnia, Ma'elrich's dreams and realities began to run together. Each sunlit path from the magistrate's house to the gaol became fires rained down from the heavens. The young high-pitched voices of the town's children recalled the squawks of the attacking rooks on his flesh. The darkness and twisted nature of the gaol's corridors intertwined with the corridors of his nightmares. Worst of all, the pile of iron work on the desk at the gaol became a nest of snakes, writhing into various runes on the desk. Imaging them suddenly bursting into flame, the image would startle him with a cry of agony as if he had been burned. The townspeople hid their faces as they laughed behind his back, pretending they did not notice him. But they did, indeed, notice his fear at every sound coming from the streets, and how he staggered, seemingly intoxicated, reacting to unseen elements around him. After the thirteenth day of Ma'elrich's delusions, he reeled into the magistrate's house, screeching as if he were being attacked."Ma'elrich? MA'ELRICH!!" Rowen ran towards his old friend who continued to screech to the heavens. He was fending off any offers of help violently as if the proffers were attacking vultures. Fearing Ma'elrich was under a curse, he stopped short of actually touching him. "This cannot go on!" Standing away from him, Rowen called to his personal physician, running through his residence to find him more quickly. "Hale! Hale! Where are you!!"

Abruptly, a tall, thin man in a long white silk tunic with a red velvet cloak appeared from a room upstairs, walking quickly towards the staircase. "Here, milord!"

Rowen met his physician halfway. Out of breath, he kept his voice down in case there were others listening to his concerns. Glancing around first, Rowen stage whispered, "A tonic... a sedative, ...anything! Ma'elrich is entranced and thinks he's under attack. The people of this town have already started laughing at him, and if he becomes aggressive, he could be dangerous." The two men descended the stairs to the entrance, where Ma'elrich was still quivering. Looking out to ensure no one was in view, Rowan quickly closed the door to keep any townspeople from hearing more than they already had. Ma'elrich then suddenly collapsed, lying motionless on the floor, twitching.

The physician-healer evaluated the new patient's health from afar and weighed the safety of everyone else in the vicinity. Walking over to Ma'elrich and looking into his eyes, he attempted to determine how much of Ma'elrich's mind was in the present and substantial world. Ma'elrich's eyes could not focus and did not seem to see him at all. Hale stepped back towards Rowen to return the stage whisper. "How permanent do you need this solution, milord?"

"Let's just do something to get him to sleep for a couple days, something that will help him to settle down. After that, we will see if the enchantment has lifted. If not, we will have to determine a more permanent solution."

After a long pause in which the physician recalled what combination of tonics he had with him, he thought of a solution that might work. He cautiously stated, "I have something in my laboratory that could work. With your leave, I'll return in ten minutes time."

With Rowen's nod of permission, the physician left for his own residence, and Rowan reclosed the door behind him. Trepidatiously, Rowan approached Ma'elrich again. He was now comatose on the floor in the same place and position as earlier. Studying him, Rowen saw that Ma'elrich's back rose and fell automatically. He breathed a sigh of relief over his sleeping friend as he stood guard, waiting for the physician.

The sudden, distinctive tattoo drummed on the wooden door announced the physician's return. Rowan swiftly opened the door and then closed it behind the physician. "Here it is – is he yet conscious?"

"Well, he's breathing, he's just not moving." They hovered over Ma'elrich, and Rowen moved to a position to support Ma'elrich's head while the physician unstoppered the tonic mixture. After pouring the mixture into a small enamel jug, the physician put the jug to Ma'elrich's lips.

"Come, now. Open up, Ma'elrich…". Being unresponsive, the physician took the initiative. "Milord, close his nostrils. It'll make him open his mouth… Right - just like that. "As if on command, Ma'elrich's mouth opened, and Rowen poured the tonic into the open mouth. Rowen removed his hand from his friend's nose, allowing him to breathe again. He hoped this procedure worked and would be done soon. The inquisitor was very heavy.

"There, now, that's it, now swallow." The physician stroked the inquisitor's throat, encouraging the swallowing reflex. "One more…" They repeated the procedure, and with the second swallow, Ma'elrich's body relaxed, and Rowen lowered the body to the floor.

"Let's take him to his room and let him be for a while. Leave some water and food in case he awakes hungry or thirsty. When he is fully conscious, we will see if rest has helped release his enchantment." The two men carried the inquisitor to his room and placed him carefully on his bed.

Before releasing the physician to his own affairs, Rowan held his arm. "Not a word or sign of this to anyone, Hale. The results would be disastrous to this town! I worry enough that the creatures will be drawn to his new condition..."

Hale held up his hand to quell the flood of fear. "I completely understand, milord. Not a word to anyone. I'll also burn some incense in this room to help dispel any smells or enchantments he may have and hopefully ward off any potential attacks."

Nodding in silence, Rowan exited the room, leaving the physician to follow through with what he had promised.

Chapter 8: Simão, Lead Traitor

As Simão lay on his bed in the morning twilight, he was trying to keep the dream of his wife and son fresh in his mind. Their fleeting and unreal presence in his dreams was as close as he was able to get to them now. His eyes burned as he remembered them. They had been entirely innocent of any wrong-doing. They had simply been in the wrong place at the wrong time and had become another set of victims of the Tenenbrani. He could still remember their cries for help and alarm as they had been attacked while taking a short walk outside the town walls sixteen solar cycles ago or so before the current magistrate was assigned to Tomar. There was no provocation on their part, so someone must have been transforming right when the two of them strolled into the area, and in that initial loss of self, the Hydra decapitated and destroyed his family in one instant. It had been so long ago, before he had become Enlightened, and even now, he wondered if he would have been able to prevent it or at least witness their resurrection so he would have been able to connect with them.

The resurrection of the innocents usually occurred on the night of their death. Knowing it was a possibility, they had begun a vigil at the Pit, where they witnessed a reincarnation after innocents died. It was truly awe-inspiring, as they seemed to be reborn from the ashes into new creatures. The more current ones were now many of his friends amongst the Clairdani, and their connection helped establish a working relationship between the Clairdani and the Enlightened. Together, they were beginning to show some promise in stopping the Tenenbrani attacks. Perhaps his wife and son were Clairdani now somewhere? They had never recovered their bodies or connected with them if they transformed, so there was no way of knowing. Creatures on both sides, the Clairdani and the Tenenbrani, were free to roam the lands, and not all of them stayed close to the town they had come from. He had learned that over time, once he had become Enlightened and connected with the Clairdani himself. Just as not all those in the area were from Tomar, many of those he knew must be Clairdani were not among those who stayed nearby. Names were something that meant nothing to the animal minds and seemed to be mostly for humans to differentiate between them.

He had seen the mirror of his own grief in Cenellot and Noyette as they mourned for Hawthorne, and their faces had haunted him every night for the past few days. Even now, he remembered that ancient grief, although now it was more a dull ache and not an acute pain he could not escape. And, like himself, there was a loss with no sense of closure or understanding. *If Hawthorne had been brought to the Pit...* He understood her fear, her pain. He had felt the same pain and fear himself, although he hadn't been hunted by the Magistrate as a criminal after his own losses. *Seeing Hawthorne reincarnate as one of our creatures might have helped Noyette understand that not all creatures are evil, just as not all people are good. Why hadn't his body been brought out? I feel sure that over time, Cenellot will forgive his father for sacrificing himself. Noyette... not so sure. She had such mistrust in her eyes... By not trusting her with his transformation, I'm sure she felt betrayed both by her husband and then by his former friends, now his enemies, and now her enemies. Time, like fate, can see wrongs righted, although not always in the ways we hope or expect...*

He continued musing about the many other reincarnations they had witnessed in his history with the

60

Enlightened and finally decided he needed to catch up on any news. Reports from Markus about the fugitives, what anyone had heard about the Inquisitor and what he might be doing with the codex, and if anyone had any clue about what was in that codex would do for starters. As for that codex, *what would the Advocate have told him that both converted him to their cause and inspired him to write it down?* There was a reason nothing was ever written amongst them beyond the fact that few people knew how to write or read, for that matter. Even though what they knew about the connection between the people and the Tenenbrani and Clairdani was helpful, the distrust about all creatures was too strong to breathe out loud. *I'm sure she wouldn't have told him everything, wanting the final pieces to come from us once he joined us. The Advocate worked in mysterious ways, it was true, although she had never mentioned writings before and may have thought he didn't know how to read or write. She had this power that made you feel like she was reading your very soul and could hide nothing from her. If she told him about us, she must have seen his genuine goodness with no trickery and hoped he would connect to us to rescue her. His sacrifice certainly manifested that goodness and should have been rewarded with a resurrection...* Again, the question. *So why wasn't he brought out to the Pit?!*

At last, fully dressed and breakfasted, Simão opened the door to his forge in front of his house. Putting on his tool belt and protective apron, he used the flint and billows to rekindle the forge fires. He opened the door to the alleyway in front of his shop, signaling to all that he was open for business. As one of the many blacksmiths in the town, there was a healthy competition for business. This made it easy to miss a day or need to leave for a bit since there was always someone else happy to pick up any slack business that day. Between the

61

late nights, green eye covers, and constant searching for information around the town, the headaches and arthritis provided enough excuse for the suspicious townsfolk. A quick glance up and down the alley told him no customers were waiting for him, so he had time to make his contact rounds. *Times like this remind me I need an apprentice. The shop could keep regular hours then, and I would be less missed and draw suspicion away from us.*

With the Inquisitor in town, Simão needed to know his history, what anyone knew about the Codex, and whether Noyette and Cenellot were still safe. He might need some time to get the information on the Inquisitor, although hopefully, his novelty made many tongues wag without drawing suspicion. Today would be a fact-finding day – either from customers who are willing to talk about the gossip in town or from the gaolers or folk at the inn this evening after their tongues were loosened a bit.

A gently aging man strode into the forge with the shuffling gait and stooped posture that suggested the barrel he carried was heavy. Simão turned his eyes towards the sound, offering help automatically.

"Can I get that for you, Noé? It seems pretty heavy!"

"Mush oblige, Simão! I dunna have the strength I ust ta." Without the weighty barrel, Noé seemed ten years younger. His brown eyes twinkled as he smiled his somewhat toothless grin at the blacksmith.

Years of pounding metal in the heat had melted the fat from Simão's body, sculpting his muscles as if they were carved from stone, a transformation that persisted well into his later years... Simão took the heavy barrel from Noé's arthritic and wrinkled hands and easily carried it gently towards his workbench. Inside were wine and beer taps that needed cleaning and perhaps some refurbishing… so this was a social call more than a need for serious smithy work.

"I can finish this for you while you wait if you prefer?"

A simple nod as Noé came nearer. A few pleasantries about business and the weather, and in a flash, the cleaning rags were already at work. "Simão, have ya hirt the stories dey tellen roun 'ere? Tale o' dis strange Inquizider… now I ask ya, whudt wuz wron' wid de ways we was doin' de interrogatin' by uself? Why'd dey need ta goo an' git someun new? I tell ya, dere's summa not quite righ' wid 'im…"

"Oh?" was all that Simão could muster in response.

Noé was the local tavern owner, and after hearing everything from everyone else, he needed no prodding to pass along anything he knew. Simão pretended to be wholly absorbed by his work while taking mental notes of anything he said. You could always count on the innkeeper to know the local news, and this would give him as much information as there was in Tomar.

Noé prattled on about what he'd heard – rumors, of course, so nothing certain. He hadn't known that the Inquisitor had been like the Magistrate's brother – still was, although they certainly weren't close. The Magistrate had returned to them from another town many years ago after spending a few years away at school. Perhaps the move to Tomar had something to do with their estrangement? He wondered which one had initiated the distance. His hunch was the inquisitor since the Magistrate seemed more personable, although that was comparing unyielding ice to an uncompromising rock. *What was their childhood like, if this is what they've become?*

"Did ya 'ear wha' 'appen't to da jail'r, Simão??"

"Hm…"

Without waiting for any response, Noé verified everything Simão had heard or guessed already about Hawthorne's last day. In his telling, the Gaoler had tried to free a prisoner and was caught right as the Inquisitor arrived. Not only was he tortured in place of the prisoner, but they'd also destroyed everything that had anything to do with his life: they had burned down the house with his family inside and nothing was left except this mysterious object they carried out of the ruins. No one knew of its existence or what it might be except that the Inquisitor had it.

"I guess we will know soon enough what was in it since the Inquisitor has it. Maybe it'll lead right to the Traitors so we can be free of the creature terrors around us?" Simão had perfected the role of cool indifference to the happenings in town, his face a perfect mask of focus on the task at hand and nothing more.

"Not frum wha' I 'ear…". Chuckling, Noé continued. "Ya see, he no can opin it! 'e bin lokt up in 'is office, swearin and 'itten it wuf everytin' 'e got, and it don't opin! Sum myst'ry t' us all!"

Simão gave a sigh of relief, which was interpreted as a sigh of incredulity.

"Innit it? So we haf ta wait a bit logger for to rid usself of dose blastit 'orrors, but de ent should be nigh!"

"Maybe…" Simão placed all the taps back in the barrel and carried it to the door. "All finished. Shall I add it to your tab or come by tonight to settle in kind?"

"Whae'er way works fur ya. I'll see ya, den?"

A nod as Simão held the door open for Noé to sidle through. He watched him lumber down the alley to the wider alley and close the door as the alley emptied itself again.

Noé had been… very helpful. Markus should be at the Pit this evening to make his report about the refugees unless something was amiss and he gave a message to someone else to relay it to him. There were quite a few owls in the area, which were convenient for messages if one happened to be around. If he saw one, he would give it a message to send along to the Advocate. He doubted that Anehta would come about any time soon. With the Advocate as near death as she was, Anehta would be a mothering hen for a while.

As the tenth star's light appeared, Simão scanned the Eastern wall near where he hid in the alley's shadows. He watched as the guards made their pass and changed direction. There was a small timeframe where the furthest was too far to see anyone passing near the wall, and with the focus on large creatures outside the town, it was easy enough to get out of Tomar. Hiding in the various shadows, he turned his right hand in a triangular salute to the wall, where three stones glowed a dull green before the ground became a set of stairs that led under the wall out of Tomar. Once on the other side, the ground seemed to heal itself as he stealthily crept towards the Pit. He saw Markus just past it, his white coat shimmering in the dark shadow he hid within. A quick glance behind at the wall to verify the passing of the guards, then a short, slow crouch to Markus' location.

"All is well, my friend?" Simão whispered the echo in his mind as he patted Markus' slender white nose.

Markus nodded his head, sending images of Cenellot and Noyette as he had left them at the entrance to their new stone home.

"Any indication of them being followed by the Magistrate?"

The pause before Markus shook his head gave Simão pause. "What else might be following them? Anyone we need to watch ourselves?"

In his head, he heard the response. *Elves or some forest spirits maybe… although they are supposed to be neutral and hate your kind. They might watch only to ensure no harm will come to their own kind.*

"I thought they were the talk of legends and myths?" He shook his head. More mysteries! "They exist, here, now?"

Markus whinnied, making nothing definitive., . Simão couldn't determine whether the presence of elves made him feel safer or put them in more danger. The legends were of the massive war between the people and the dragons, which had sided with the elves. Afterward, the elves had disappeared, as if by magic, and were never seen again. Over the centuries, their existence seemed to vaporize, and people either thought they were legends or had left for other lands. Apparently, neither was true. "Interesting…" more to himself than to Markus.

"At each definite phase of the moon, let us know what they are doing, and if they need immediate help, send word through the usual channels. With this new Inquisitor, things are amiss, and we might not be able to get out as regularly as we used to." He scanned the wall to check on the guard's rotation. One of their own was watching their section tonight, making him feel a bit more at ease. Still, to avoid questions, he made sure no one else might see them. "They might be on their own for a bit, I think."

Markus nodded his acknowledgement, and Simão put a companionable hand on his side in thanks before sauntering back to the stairs under the wall and his home above the forge.

Chapter 9: A Light Returns

With only his head in Luz's cave, Metulas sighed contentedly in his sleep. The night had been a little fretful as Luz's fever had spiked again. Anehta had been beside herself, flying to the nearby river to cool rags in the water and apply them to her head. Alternately, the fever spikes would cause chills that Metulas would try to dispel with his own heat. Anehta had changed all the bandages, trying to determine the source of the infection with no success. This was something Luz had to battle alone again. Thankfully, the fever broke, leaving everyone exhausted and now resting comfortably. Or at least Luz and Metulas were resting. Anehta was already out getting breakfast and herbs for a restorative draught for Luz.

Anehta was awake and attempting to be productive. Her attempts would have been wonderful if it weren't for the clumsiness and noise. Metulas never understood how such a small creature with wings could be so clumsy and noisy when there were no footsteps to make! Nonetheless, Metulas awoke shortly after Anehta returned to the cave and needed to reach in with his foreleg and claw to help steady the pots from falling.

We're trying to let her sleep, remember? Metulas growled softly. A little smoke accompanied his thoughts, and Anehta fanned the air with her wings to clear the air.

It's been three days, and she was physically healed until the fever hit. Anehta fussed. She flew closer to Metulas so she wouldn't have to hoot too loudly. *Do we have time to wait before we learn what happened?*

Maybe. We do need to hear what she knows, and with the new Inquisitor, we need to know sooner than later. We may not have a choice but to talk to her today. We've wasted enough time already...

Anehta flew right next to Metulas' ear. *What do you know, Metulas? I saw the gaoler's family leaving the town with Markus and Celina. Is there something else happening? Aren't we safe once Luz is healed again? Won't that be the end of the danger for now, unless we decide to return to the town?*

Metulas seemed to deliberate something. Cautiously, he gave more information. *I sense a lot of change in the land, and not all good. Yes, the family got away, but where was the gaoler? There seems to be unrest in the air - plants shift differently, and the animals are a little quieter than usual. Something worries them, and that worries me because I don't know why there's a change. There must be something else happening that we haven't seen coming.*

Under his fiery gaze, Anehta felt small and insignificant. *While Luz is resting, maybe I can go look around and see what might be going on? I can hide more easily than you can, and then I'll report back what I hear from the Clairdani I meet. A hootaloo, keep her safe!* In anticipation of an agreement, Anehta left the cave with a hoot of goodbye, almost flying into Metulas' lower half that was still bunched up outside the cave.

At that moment, Luz stirred again. Metulas sensed that her fever was gone and her energy was returning. Looking back out the cave entrance, he saw that Anehta was already too far away, and perhaps this part of the story would be better just between them. Anehta fretted too easily when she heard about anything unpleasant or troubling, much like an elderly woman, when she heard about the troubling events. Less chatter, more focus, fewer accidental, well, anythings.

As he waited, Luz slowly remembered where she was and looked around. He let her decide when she wanted to let him know she was lucid.

"Metulas…"

Here, Luz.

"What day is it?"

Quinta. It's been four days since we left the gaol.

"What happened to my gaoler? What about his family?" Luz started to rise, but Metulas' quick claw kept her from rising too quickly.

Careful, you still need time to recover fully.

"I'm fine."

Metulas' growled his disagreement.

"I'm recovering well, thanks to you, I'm sure. I'm more worried about all those we were trying to protect in Clod Tomar. What about them? Who is with them now?" She attempted to rise again, finally getting to her feet to stand. She managed for a minute, then had to sit back down on her makeshift bed.

Let's agree that I will give you information as long as you allow yourself to recover. Metulas ' red eyes glowed warmly at Luz, which gave her some assurance and relief.

"Agreed." She glanced around. "Is Anehta with them? Are they still in danger, then?"

They are not in any more danger than we are at the moment. However… the gaoler has died, of that we are sure.

Luz sighed deeply. "We both knew his fate when he freed me. He was sincerely a good man and made my life as bearable as it could be in a dark pit of despair." She paused, wiping her eyes and giving herself time to think about what they could still do. "So which unicorn is he now, then? Have they been able to talk to him? Was his family pleased that they hadn't lost him forever as they thought?" Luz grinned a bit at the thought of how she might react to finding out that her father had suddenly become a unicorn!

Silence.

"Metulas?" With no answer, Luz hobbled closer, grabbing onto his forearm for strength. "Metulas??"

He never appeared.

"What? He transformed into a Tenenbrani? After all the good deeds and sacrifices he made? That wouldn't make any sense…"

No, he was never brought to the Pit, and nothing else emerged that night either. He just… disappeared or… something.

"Disappeared? How…"

I don't know, Metulas said a bit harsher than he intended. *It's a mystery for all of us.*

"So, if he disappeared, what happened to his wife and son? Were they able to get away with the Clairdani? Where are they? I thought maybe they would be here with you?"

Luz, you know people cannot know that I exist! You are the only one. The Clairdani are protection enough against any Tenenbrani, and the guards never venture too far away from Clod Tomar. They are safer away from Clod Tomar than in it, I think.

"What happened at the gaol, exactly?" After a breath, Luz seemed to understand something and grew angry. "Did we exchange my life for everyone else's safety??"

Luz stumbled, and her anger brought her to the mouth of the cave. Here Metulas' massive build was able to support her and prevent her from leaving. *No, that is NOT what happened, and if you want to know what did happen, you will at least sit down to rest!* Red eyes met green as the battle of wills ensued.

Once Luz seemed a bit calmer and sat down on Metulas' foreleg, Metulas told her of the events in the town beginning with her escape. He told her of the family's flight from the house, what he had heard about the gaoler's interrogation, and about the Inquisitor.

"I'm sure that Hawthorne never gave away any information about us. He was both the hardest and kindest person I could ever know in Clod Tomar. At first, I only saw his cruelty. He was just following orders though, I know. He also didn't understand who we are and what we do, so at first, he treated us like Traitors. Duty, and no more. We don't fight our imprisonment like others do, though, and he began to notice that we were different. Eventually, no matter how much we were tortured, he would offer kind words to us and try to heal us as much as he could. Many died, so when he saw that I was a survivor, he began to ask me questions. He told me of his beautiful wife and intelligent, although ungainly, son, and they were all the family he had left. Over time, he learned all about us and never gave away anything he learned from me, so there shouldn't be any way to find us."

Metulas pondered her words. *Did he ever say what his wife's opinions were of Traitors?*

Luz thought for a while. "I got the sense that she was a very proud woman. Proud of her husband's position and the opportunities for her son in the future. I do not know if he told her anything of the Traitors' truths. If he did, then she is in danger. If he did not, then she will be very unpleasant when she discovers her husband's dealings with us!"

My thoughts exactly, agreed Metulas. *Given her surprise at seeing the Clairdani, I will wager that Hawthorne never told her anything, though. She's in danger even without any knowledge of us, unfortunately.*

"So, if Hawthorne didn't make it to the Pit, I wonder what happened to him? You said the Interrogator was invited by the Magistrate from another town, and they have an old connection. Hawthorne seemed terrified by him and refused to tell me anything that might weaken my courage. What else have you heard? What aren't you telling me?"

Metulas stared into Luz's eyes, assessing her strength and fortitude to hear the last of what he knew. *Hushed whispers at the tavern speak of strange voices and sounds coming from the interrogation room as if there were a multitude of Tenenbrani in the room with him. The screams weren't always human, either. That is all I know.*

Luz stared, dumbfounded. This was beyond anything she had imagined! What connection was there between the Interrogator and the Tenenbrani? Was there a network with the Tenenbrani to parallel the one the Enlightened had with the Clairdani?

"Metulas..."

I have no knowledge of what happens with the Tenenbrani, so I can only guess as much as you. It is unlikely that the Tenenbrani have won over humans that would help them, and they are too selfish to be able to work together. However, since the Interrogator never left the room while those voices were heard, there may be a link there we need to investigate. Carefully.

They fell into a dark, thoughtful silence as they both pondered various possibilities and their implications.

Remembering the tangible darkness of the gaol, Luz's mind imagined various Tenenbrani and where they might hide in that warren of death. She had stumbled through most of them during her months of captivity and had never sensed the evil of the Tenenbrani near her and said as much.

Your ability to sense things may have been affected by the same magic-dampening elements that kept you from succeeding against the magistrate in the first place. Something about that edifice feels wrong.

"But..." Luz began.

Let me finish, then we can speculate further.

Luz nodded, and the dragon continued. *I don't have the same knowledge of the gaol as you do, although it is not very large, even considering its upper floor where the magistrate offices are. I doubt that it could hold that variety of creatures within it, and others know nothing of it. There are laws against having creatures within the walls of the towns, and the magistrate wouldn't break the same rules set to keep him safe. Lastly, remember that there were gaolers outside the door at all times, and nothing but the Inquisitor left or entered. Perhaps there is a tunnel that connects the room to outside the gates, but that would be another consideration after we exhaust many others first.*

"You've had some time to think on this. Have you told Anehta any of this?"

No, she would just grow more worried and fretful than she already is. Until we have more solid confirmation of facts, let's not discuss this with her. We need her strong and confident, and as long as she is not going to Clod Tomar, she will stay safe.

"Do you have any ideas where he might come from? Where did he and Magistrate Rowan learn of one another? I was too young when I left to know anything about the people not part of our enlightened circle."

The answers to those questions are only from what I've heard. He has only recently become the Inquisitor, the previous one having had an accident, leaving the post open. His given name is Ma'elrich. Since his promotion to the post, there have been more arrests and less crime overall. Apparently, he is most recently from Clod Pollux, which has a history of secret dungeons, prison towers, and disappearances. Some townspeople remember him from his youth, when he lived in Clod Tomar. He was extremely brilliant, and after his father died, he went to Clod Pollux to study the legal trade with his uncle. Magistrate Rowan was one of his closest companions when they were children, and they kept in touch. Having heard about your arrest and muteness, he offered to come and help get answers.

Luz's eyes kept closing while she tried to listen to the history, and she finally lost the battle. Metulas nuzzled her with his soft, velvety nose and was able to get her back into bed.

Sleep, miudinha. I'll keep watch.

Chapter 10: An Enlightenment

In his enchanted sleep, drinking the tonic seemed to lighten the dark corridors. He no longer stumbled with his arms outstretched and could see the ground at his feet. The animals that generally seemed to attack him in the darkness he could now see were only shadows of the iron scroll works he had removed from the codex. During the two days of his enchanted sleep, the inquisitor's mind manipulated those iron scrolls into many objects – alive and otherwise, in a constant kaleidoscope. They seemed to transform themselves into everything he had seen in the town – children, buildings, the burned hut, the placard… the codex itself. These finials moved, snake-like, transforming smoothly from one shape to another. In his mind, he saw the codex, and the loose finials created runes as they rotated until they formed words from the ancient texts…

With the sudden insight, the inquisitor awoke, understanding what he must do to open the codex. His coverings stymied and deterred him for a moment, resembling the many finials he had just been fighting in his dream. With a violent tug, he untucked the vermillion cotton bedding from its associated mattress and threw it to the ground triumphantly. Satisfied, he hoped this would be the first of many final undoings in the future.

"Guilherme!" He waited a couple heartbeats for the sound of any response. Hearing movement, he dressed hurriedly while he waited for him to appear. Hesitantly, Guilherme lurked in the doorway, verifying whether the inquisitor had regained his sanity or would come to attack him once he entered the room.

Seeing the manservant, Ma'elrich regained his former air of superiority. "Ah, there you are. Bring me some nourishment and refreshment. Let your master know I'm alive and well so I can tell him what I plan to do."

"Very good, milord," and bowing, Guilherme turned and traversed the hall towards the stairs.

A few minutes later, the magistrate appeared with a wooden plate containing a wedge of hard cheese, two bread rolls, and a flask of brown ale. "Seeing how I was going to see you anyway, there was no point in bringing others too." Rowan took a moment to look over his friend, nodding to himself in affirmation. "I see that it is true – you are doing well!"

An involuntary smile touched Ma'elrich's lips, and he reached Rowan in two strides allowing the smile to suffuse his face. Gently, he took the wooden plate from Rowen's hands with a hurried thanks. With his free hand, he took a loaf of bread, gesturing to the singular chair in the room so Rowan would sit down. Exchanging the roll for the ale, he drained half the wooden goblet before taking a seat for himself on the swan-down stuffed mattress. There were a few moments of silence while Ma'elrich doggedly ate his bread and cheese, spilling the ale down his chin in his haste to wash down his first meal in three days. With only a couple of crumbs left on the plate, Ma'elrich finally put down the plate and looked contentedly at the magistrate. Not wanting to tell Rowan that there was more to the codex than he had already told him, he fabricated a story about the ancient legends.

"I have a lead about how the ancient legends connect to the codex and this town, so it won't be long now before I have the codex secrets in hand and can leave. I apologize for my odd behavior these past few days, but I have, thankfully, recovered. I will need only a couple more days before I'll have enough to give you a report about the Traitors and their beginnings!"

"But you were sleeping for the last three days. You can't possibly have any information. You haven't left this room, and you need time to recover. Let me…"

"No, no – I'm fine! I insist! I am not asking for your permission to get back to work – I'm telling you that I am well and will have a report for you in two days." Ma'elrich stood up at a measured pace and strode to the doorway. "I just need to know that I can still count this as a place where I may rest until I leave…"

Rowan's eyes and face betrayed the emotional conflict within him between anger at being so dismissed by his guest and his relief at hearing an end to his stay. Changing from red to puce, then back to normal, Rowen stood from his chair and walked to where Ma'elrich still sat on the mattress. Looking at the window, then at Ma'elrich, he stated simply, "Yes, of course, I will extend my hospitality for a few more days. After all, we are like family! Please report to me what you know about the Traitors once you've completed your investigation here." Clapping Ma'elrich on the shoulder, he continued, "Then we will celebrate!"

"Thank you. And now, with your leave, I need to get to the gaol to continue my work with this codex." Without waiting for any response, the inquisitor pushed past the dumbstruck magistrate in the doorway, descended the stairs, and left the residence.

Chapter 11: Homestead

With the warmer sun's rays breaking through the trees toward mid-day, the two refugees began to stir, slowly awakening to a much less frightening atmosphere than they had when they drifted into unconsciousness. Instantly aware of his surroundings, Cenellot searched the area visually for the griffon. He found the winged creature in silent conversation with the two unicorns, whose heads were nodding throughout the conversation.

However, as he tried to move, the pain in his legs and back from the day before was excruciating. He looked at his mother, whose face reflected the pain he felt. It would be a more difficult and painful day of travel today; one he didn't look forward to. At least the wounds would not be a problem. Since the smell of blood attracted the Tenenbrani, the touch from the unicorn horns had healed the skin on their legs and they didn't bleed anymore. Sore muscles weren't part of that requirement though, unfortunately. Who knew riding used muscles? For his mother's sake, he tried to be brave and gave her a determined look. He was the man of the house now, with his father gone, and he would do what he could to protect his mother. Holding her gaze, Cenellot nodded his head toward the unicorns to signal that he would go talk to them, and his mother nodded in grateful consent. To help his legs remember how to move, he spent the first few steps exaggerating his walk to loosen the muscles. As he moved carefully towards the Clairdani, he felt his mother's eyes watching him protectively. She tried not to laugh at his exaggerated walk, yet it was good to have something to smile at in all this! She hadn't tried to move yet and didn't revel in the thought of what pain the day might bring.

Hoping for news, Cenellot approached the Clairdani respectfully to avoid interrupting them. They heard him and allowed him to join their small circle as he eyed the griffon curiously. Not able to understand them, Cenellot allowed them to continue until the unicorns had finished nodding their heads and they had turned towards him inquisitively. Questions filled his head, but most would have to wait until he could speak to them directly, which he hoped would come sooner than later. He fumbled with their attention on him and only managed to squeak out the one word, "soldiers?"

The griffon shook his feathery head. Cenellot felt relieved, although he knew they had a head start and might still be found today. "Then will we be led to our hiding spot today?" The unicorns nodded their heads. "I hope it won't be too long or far. Not for me, mind, I think I can manage the riding even better today. I'm not sure my mother can handle the weariness or the fear of being outside Tomar for much longer." He continued his rambling. "I mean, I think we can travel another day, but it would be nice to be settled somewhere. Is it far?"

The unicorns were split on this answer. One shook its mane, the other nodded its head. They seemed to understand the quandary they presented and reversed their motions, which still left the question unanswered. Cenellot understood this to mean that their destination wasn't too far, but also wasn't nearby.

Satisfied, Cenellot ambled back to his mother to convey the news. Sotto-voce, he half whispered, "We should be at our new place today! I asked the unicorns, and they seemed to say that it wasn't too far." In his enthusiasm, he embraced her around her neck tightly, being the easiest part to reach while she still sat on the ground.

Lovingly, Noyette took his hands from her neck and squeezed them in confirmation of her understanding. Cenellot had no idea how much effort would be required to set up a new home or live in the middle of an unknown land. And that was possible only if they survived this second day of travel with who knows what other creatures waiting for them or the soldiers in pursuit! With just the two of them, there would be no one to help with the chores required to survive. Noyette looked at his uplifted, smiling face and returned what smile she could with an encouraging nod of agreement. His youthful optimism would help them face the loneliness and frustrations they would face in the weeks and months ahead. As long as his clumsiness and impulsiveness didn't alert them to the world around them, they might survive. She rallied what enthusiasm she had. "So, let's start this new adventure with some food to break our fast, shall we?"

Despite the unicorn's impatience to move on, the two sat where they had slept. Resigned, the unicorns stood near the edge of the forest where some fresh grass grew with dew-kissed flower buds. After some cold biscuits, salted meat, and watered-down ale, the two were ready to continue their journey to the undisclosed destination. Noyette took a turn at trying to make her legs move again, although a bit less clumsily than Cenellot's attempt, and she was resigned to another day of riding.

Smiling, they finished collecting the rest of their belongings with as little leg movement as possible.

As one, the four of them looked to the griffon. Cenellot, seeing the unicorn's bow, offered an awkward bow himself and saw the griffon nod his head in response. After standing guard for them, it was time for the griffon to return to his own needs and requirements. He gave a meaningful glance of benediction to Cenellot and Noyette and flew away.

Markus and Celina crouched to allow Noyette and Cenellot to sit astride their backs. Rising, the riders held onto the manes to keep their balance. Slowly, at first, the unicorns started at a walk, eventually gaining speed until the world around them became a blurred streak. Forests, streams, distant mountains, and meadows they had never seen and would most likely never see again blurred past them. Even if they had wanted to, the dizzying speed and shuffle of the scenery would make return on their own impossible. They noted that this was definitely a different speed than they had used last night, although perhaps Noyette had been so terrified that life seemed to slow down? She would have to ask about it later if she remembered. At these speeds, she wondered how they were able to stay warm with such winds buffeting them, and remembering the magical powers of the unicorns, she wondered no more.

She allowed her mind to drift from where she was and think about what she had always known about her town and her people. Had everything she known been part of a lie? She refused to believe anyone in the town had deliberately kept her from the truth. The town leaders were also victims in this deception created by the Traitors - the townsfolk were playthings for the Traitors' own ends. With the powers she saw that they possessed, she would have to learn who the real leaders were of the charade. Whoever was orchestrating the creature attacks among the Traitors had to be stopped. Once she and the magistrate knew who was truly orchestrating the deception that controlled their vila, they would be free of the terror that had kept them all prisoners for as long as anyone could remember.

Cenellot had his own musings, although not as conspiratorial in nature. Despite the speed, he accepted the scenery as it flew past. He caught glimpses of what he had never seen before, trying to commit it all to memory as he wondered at the lack of villages they encountered. Perhaps there were only a very few other vila in existence? Perhaps the effect of the unicorns on everything around them kept them from seeing others as well as keeping others from seeing them? With unicorns and other Clairdani around, what were the magical possibilities? How had his people lived for so long without knowing the wonders of this beautiful magic and only the terrors? The number of questions he had left him speechless, and although he did tumble off Markus a couple times during the day, there wasn't any conversation between the two otherwise. His thoughts kept him in good company, and the amicable silence was welcome from the chaos that had ruled their lives for the past two days.

Towards evening, the unicorns slowed as they emerged out of the forest into a valley with some low wooded foothills on the lee side of the heavily forested mountain. The change of pace roused the travelers from their respective thoughtful stupors, and Cenellot bent forward to speak to Markus. "Are we getting close to our new home?" As if in response, Markus and Celina slowed to a walking pace as they approached a less dense forest with the many boulders defining the foothills of newer mountains.

Markus simply nodded a couple of times, then whinnied to Celina as they changed direction, hunting for the path through some very rounded boulders that lay as guardians against any unwanted visitors. A short nicker and nod towards the northwest direction, and the two gained more speed as they found their trail. After many twists and turns on this unmarked path, they slowed, then stopped. Since there wasn't enough room for the unicorns to kneel down to let them dismount, Cenellot and his mother used the nearby waist-high boulders as stepping stones to dismount from the unicorns' backs. Markus pointed with his muzzle towards a larger boulder that had two smaller boulders immediately in front of it. "What's there?" Cenellot tried to ask Markus, forgetting that the only answers were "yes" or "no." In response, Markus simply nodded again to the boulders, and since they didn't seem to be afraid, Cenellot moved forward and braved a look behind the two smaller boulders.

"There's a cave here, mum!" cried Cenellot. His voice echoed a little against the boulders, giving his voice a strange distortion. Noyette followed him, and they disappeared behind the two boulders into the cave. There was an opening, just big enough for Cenellot to walk through unimpaired, which Noyette could use if she bent down almost double. The unicorns weren't able to get in, but they stood guard outside while the two of them examined the cave. Without any light, they couldn't explore the darker depths, which made Cenellot trepidacious of staying. They could hear the dripping of water somewhere, so there was more than just this small entrance to the cave. If the cave continued far into the mountain, what else might be living further in? Noyette tossed a stone into the darkness, which seemed to roll for a while before coming to rest. If the end of the cave wasn't immediate, how safe would they be?

Cenellot and Noyette emerged from the entrance, a little cautious.

Fueled by her maternal instinct, Noyette found her strength and asked, "What else lives in the cave? There doesn't seem to be an end to it, and anything could be living there. We wouldn't be safe."

Markus whinnied and pointed at one of the packs. Cenellot opened the pack and found a flint firestone and torch, which he gave to his mother.

"Let's see where this cave ends, shall we?"

Returning to the cave, the two struck the flint and were able to get the torch lit. As they entered the cave, they walked straight back, and right as they found the thrown stone, there was a small pool of water and the end wall of the cave. There seemed to be a small opening at the bottom of the pool since it didn't overflow, and there were no other hidden refuges they could find.

They emerged from the cave, seeming to breathe easier. Quietly, Noyette exclaimed, "This is wonderful! There's no one around the area to see or hear us, and no one should be able to find us or guess we are here if we see anyone coming. The water will be helpful as well, especially if we have to stay hidden without venturing out for a couple days." Looking around the area while deep in thought, Noyette added, "Do you think there's enough wood around to make another torch so we could explore the area?"

Celina nodded her head, and Cenellot snaked his way back to the unicorns through the boulders while Noyette sat on a boulder, enjoying the warmth of the sun. Together, Celina and Cenellot walked back through the maze of boulders to find and gather what firewood they could. Wind in the area had blown drier branches and twigs from the trees in the area, and many had become wedged amongst the boulders. Looking around, Cenellot saw that there were some taller pines scattered around the foothills for more wood if needed. Even though there weren't any trees closer by, the walk to the nearest of the pine trees was no more than the walk to the market square had been to gather tinder wood and firewood to start a fire. With his arms full of branches as thick as his own arms, Cenellot turned to return to the cave, only to realize he had gone too far! He froze in terror, dropping the wood. Sensing his distress, Celina magically appeared and nudged him with her head, gesturing in the correct direction. With a deep breath of relief, Cenellot recollected his kindling and followed Celina back to the cave.

The remainder of the day, they spent exploring their small cave, collecting wood with the help of the unicorns, and creating a usable supply for various purposes all under the unicorns' watchful guard. To host a regular fire, they would need to make a safe fireplace so they would be able to sleep at night. For lighting, they would need to make torches to light the remaining parts of the cave. This would require a bit of imagination between the constant darkness and lack of ready-made places to place them along the walls. When the shadows grew longer outside, Noyette refocused her attention. "We need to survey what is edible around here so we do not starve once our food runs out." She had been thinking about how barren the land was around them. While it was suitable for protection, it did not present much for sustenance. Her fear of starvation encouraged her to speak to the Claridani.

"Markus or Celina, could you show us where we might find berries, seeds, nuts, or anything else around here that we might be able to find to eat? I know Simão said you all would provide for us, which is very kind of you. I worry though about a day that something happens, and we need to fend for ourselves…"

Markus nodded his white, gleaming head. Knickering, he waited for Noyette and Cenellot to follow him. At every turn, he would look back at their new abode and nod at it, and Noyette eventually realized that Markus was trying to help her remember her way back along the trail. She was grateful since it was quite a while before they arrived at anything that resembled a bush or tree. First, he led them to a few bush hedges of berries, allowing them time to make mental notes about their harvest and location before moving on. Since it was still early spring, most of the berry bushes only had blossoms, but there did seem to be enough different types of berries already ripe that they wouldn't starve. He also showed them the trees that produced nuts or fruit, many of which Noyette and Cenellot had never seen before in Tomar. It was all very new, and her heart sank a little as she tried to remember what the bushes and trees looked like. When the fruit came, it would be obvious which trees had anything edible - it was remembering which ones were edible and not poisonous that worried her. Tears came to her eyes as memories of Hawthorne in the forest around the town sprang to her mind. At Tomar, he had always been the one to brave venturing out of the town to gather anything they might need and had protected her at all costs. She only knew the basic edibles available inside the marketplace and was unsure of the plants they came from. She wiped her tears quickly and wished she had some way to mark a path or the areas for them to find later.

The unicorns were helpful, although they had a habit of pausing to munch on plants that were toxic to other creatures, and Noyette hoped she would remember which plants were edible and which weren't when they were gone. Before too long, between the berries, mushrooms, and other fragrant leaves, they were able to create a nourishing soup.

It was only somewhat satisfying since it put something in their stomachs if they ignored their taste buds.

The unicorns stood watch over the area for a time, then nodded their heads in dismissal before departing. Noyette and Cenellot spent time outside collecting what they needed for their first night alone. Despite the number of small rabbits and rats in the area, no other forms of creature life existed. *At least there might be meat available if we had a way of capturing the rabbits or rats,* thought Noyette. The relative quiet gave them both a sense of comfort and foreboding – comfort that nothing was around that might eat them, but the quiet seemed like the indrawing of breath before a dragon spewed fire, destroying all in its path.

For three days, the fugitives spent their time making their cave into something more comfortable. They gathered grasses for mattresses and found ways to capture the rabbits for food. The bones gave Cenellot materials to make small tools, and Noyette used the tallow to make candles. After the third day in their new abode, they had hoped for that promised company. Shortly before the sun reached its zenith, they heard hoofbeats that stopped exactly in front of their cave. Not hearing anything, Noyette sent Cenellot to take a quick look to see if it was friend or foe.

"Markus!" Noyette heard Cenellot cry out happily. She exited the cave, seeing Markus and Celina alone with Cenellot. They were carrying riding packs as if they had had riders. The unicorns didn't seem upset by the lack of riders, however.

"Is anything wrong?" Noyette asked, worried that their appearance indicated a precipitous event back home.

Markus and Celina shook their heads, and Markus pointed with his nose at the satchels on their backs. The main satchel on Markus's back had a note inside for her. With much difficulty, Noyette managed to decipher the words somewhat coherently:

The town is being watched, and we are unable to come at the moment. We are giving you some basics to help you get started in your new life, and we hope to be able to come visit before the moon's next cycle. In the meantime, if you have need of anything, the Clairdani are on the watch and can report anything you need to tell us. Stay together, do not roam far, but find something you can create well enough to sell at the market. Stay safe!

They emptied the satchels, and, to their delight, found wooden mugs, plates, a full tinderbox, some night clothes, a couple of blankets, yeast, flour, salt, cheese, and biscuits. Amazed, they awed and gasped as they pulled out each item – each one, ensuring their survival for at least the next week. They would need to find some eggs, but at least they now had something more solid on which to build new items for their lives.

Looking intently into their eyes, Noyette offered her heartfelt thanks. "Thank you so very much, you two! And send our thanks to your friends in Tomar. We never could have survived without your assistance. Please help them stay safe from the Magistrate, as best you can. I've begun to agree with Simão after this time to reflect on his words. We do not know what Hawthorne's intentions or allegiances were, but we should honor what he has done for us and keep anyone else from suffering as best we can."

The two unicorns nodded their heads in agreement and nuzzled her face with the sides of their muzzles in assurance. Their business was complete, the two unicorns departed swiftly, and the two refugees brought their prizes into the cave to put them to use.

Chapter 12: The Jigsaw

Returning to the gaol, the inquisitor immediately set to putting the ironwork back in place around the leather codex. Although much of the ironwork was bent beyond his ability to reuse it without reforging it, he was able to find those pieces that he had initially thought were just loose and work those into the small holes that had held the iron to the leather. By spinning the iron in their places, he was able to form words using the text of the ancient runes. All he needed now was the word that would open the codex, and he would be able to find the secrets this traitor knew to hide… In his excitement, the ancient runic words would not come to him. He would need to immerse himself in the runes to help him focus on this last delicate task.

"Guards!" he called, and within moments, the two door-guards appeared in front of him, wondering what demands he might have this time.

"Diogo, Tiago- I need you to correct these scrolls. They've been bent and need to take these shapes." He hurriedly drew three different shapes, placing the 5 misshapen pieces atop the designs each one needed. "As soon as possible, now go!"

Ma'elrich thrust the metal pieces into Diogo's hands while Tiago collected the paper designs, and they turned to leave. They waited until they left the office and were out of earshot before examining the pieces in more detail to see if they could determine a plan. There was a forge down the way, and a couple attempts told them they wouldn't be able to complete the task themselves.

"He didn't say it was a secret, so I think we can go to the gaoler's forge with this one?" Diogo asked, hopefully.

Tiago agreed, and they departed for the forge, hoping there wouldn't be too many other forge requests in the queue already. They dared not leave their charge for too long, or the Magistrate would make examples of them for desertion. Yet, they wouldn't return without the task completed either for fear of what the Inquisitor would do.

"So, if we can't be gone for too long and can't return before the scrolls are completed..." Diogo began.

"We simply threaten the blacksmith." Tiago finished. "We won't have to physically hurt him unless it comes to that, and anything we do to him would pale compared to what would be done to us if we fail either of our lords."

Diogo squared his shoulders and sighed. After Hawthorne's screams and sudden disappearance, the concept of torture had derived a new meaning for all of them. It was different when you tortured the Traitors – they coordinated with the blood-thirsty creatures and tortured others. However, when torture was used as a punishment on themselves, that began to turn his stomach, and he didn't know if he could manage another gaoler being tortured. Hawthorne was kind, not a Traitor! Perhaps kindness was weakness, but he had seen how many prisoners had given Hawthorne information - much more than any given through torture!

"As long as you do the threatening, I'll stand by you. I just pray that there isn't any need to fulfill the threat."

Tiago looked at his compatriot asking, "Turning soft, are you?"

"No!" Diogo answered vehemently. Almost in a whisper, he added, "After Hawthorne..."

"I understand," Tiago answered quietly, then looked around to see if anyone had heard them. Retribution would be quick and severe if anyone thought they had any weakness for an alleged Traitor. "Let's go. We have only an hour before someone is punished for our tardiness.

Animal sounds met Ma'elrich as he entered the tight residential alley streets. "Raugh!!" called children from a safe distance. Jeers from children met his scowls and flashing red and black eyes as he searched the town for ancient runes. Some grew bolder, wanting to see his reaction up close, while most melted away. Finally, he reached the gaoler's house and stood among the ruins and ashes. Moving slowly through the remains, he looked again for the placard of runes and tried to remember what it had said. *Something about "truth" and "freedom,"* he thought.

Not wanting to dirty his clothes, he used his feet to shuffle the dirt away slowly and find the area where the placard had been. *Ahh.. there it is!* He re-read the ancient runes to himself: *"The truth will set you free."* Pulling the codex from under his cloak, he fingered the loose ironwork to experiment with creating words with the iron. He knew this had to be the key, however many combinations there might be between the words and the ways to move the ironworks. *What words were there that the gaoler might be able to use for these movable pieces?* He thought. *There are too many pieces to this! ...OK, if each runic letter requires at least two iron pieces, then perhaps it's a long word?*

Searching through the letters and the placard, he looked for any word to determine which of the iron pieces fit together to form the runes. Turning each piece on the codex showed that some of the iron fit together neatly, while other neighboring pieces wouldn't touch no matter how he turned them. His excitement grew – he knew he would have the codex opened before the night's end. There were eight letters in total, and there was only one eight-letter word in the ruins – *SANLEKUR,* Truth. He replicated the word into the codex iron work, ensuring each piece was placed precisely at the correct angles to form the runic letters, and attempted to open the codex. Nothing. It still would not open! He knew he must have the right word, but maybe one piece had moved? In frustration, he struck the codex with all his might, and the pieces he touched sank into the codex itself… then stopped. A wail of frustration poured from him, and his eyes flashed red as he pounded on anything nearby. Of course, every scroll would be required, and he would have to wait for those imbecile guards to return. Again, he could only wait…

At the other end of the gaol in the forge, the guards and the blacksmith heard the unholy sounds of a mixture of animalistic growls of pain and human anguish. "Wha… what was that?" the blacksmith stammered.

The blacksmith paused in his work. Studying both guards one after the other, he continued in a hushed whisper, "you know, don't you!" It was a statement, not a question.

The two guards simultaneously slapped and punched him in the stomach for his delay and quesiton, causing him to double over in pain.

We thank yTiago wasn't about to give Ferrer the whole truth, just enough to get him moving again and at his fastest speed. "Yes, and that will be what awaits the person who doesn't get the correct scrollworks to the Inquisitor within the hour, Ferrer."

Ferrer's questioning glance was only answered by uncompromising stares of command from Tiago and Diogo. Ferrer worked more quickly, and soon, the scrollworks were completed.

Hastily, Diogo took the still-warm scrollworks and fled back down the warren passages, Tiago giving Ferrer instructions to charge the work to the Magistrate. The two arrived at the Inquisitor's office and quickly knocked on the door, eager to terminate their task.

Having heard the commotion in the halls, Ma'elrich was able to recompose himself, feigning indifference to the task at hand. He forced himself to speak calmly and bid them enter.

After the appropriate salutes, Diogo placed the scrolls on the desk and then stepped back.

"Thank you, men. You may go."

Ma'elrich waited until he heard the click in the door, which meant the guards were out of sight, before he collected the missing pieces. Quickly, he pushed them into the codex cover. A slight, popping sound issued from the codex, as if a small, rusty metal lock had released its hold, and he was able to turn the cover of the codex. Eagerly, he looked at the first page, then the second and third pages, then the remaining sheaves.

They were all… blank!

Chapter 13: The Trapper is Tracked

After a fortnight at their new abode, the quiet that always surrounded the cave-dwelling began to give the two refugees hope. They still checked their surroundings every morning and anytime they ventured out of the cave, but each day it was with decreasing awareness and caution. Cenellot spent almost all the sunlit hours outdoors, exploring their new surroundings. Once a game, the traps Cenellot had created at home for the cats in the town became a means to their survival. After a few days of growing hunger and unsuccessful attempts closer to the cave, Cenellot finally found a rabbit warren not too far away and was able to catch a rabbit for their dinner.

"Mother, we can eat something other than roots tonight!" Cenellot displayed his catch- a large brownish-grey rabbit hanging over his shoulder and tied up with string.

Noyette came to the entrance and beamed with pride at her son, who was quickly learning how to be a man at a young age. Her mind flashed to Hawthorne, and she lamented that he wasn't here to show their son this important process of hunting. Catching the food was only the beginning, and she would need to teach him the rest. Sitting together with the rabbit outside the cave, she taught him the words to their Song of Thankfulness and of sorrow, asking that the spirit of the rabbit give them strength and nourishment.

We thank you, our kind Creator,
For this life provided to us
For our own sustenance.
In thanks, we use its life
To continue your good
In the world around us.

At the song's hopeful conclusion, she placed the knife in his hand and held his hand in her own so that together, they stabbed the rabbit through the eye so as not to destroy any meat.

"Any time you take a life for yourself, you must sing this song, or else the flesh you eat will only decay in your stomach and not grant you strength. Promise me, you will always do this, even if you do not get to eat the flesh you catch."

"I promise, mother." After a minute, he continued. "So, now what do we do? Do we just put the rabbit over the fire?"

Laughing, Noyette replied, "No, we actually do not eat all of it. We need the meat and perhaps some of the viscera for eating. The fur will be a soft covering for a small place to sit or place your head, but we first have to tan it, or it will grow hard and unusable." Guiding his hand again with the knife, she showed him how to cut the skin off of the rabbit to minimize fur loss and prepare it for the spit.

"I will let you tan the hide so you can use it later while I get the meat cooking." In response to his quizzical look, she answered with, "You will need to place it on the ground and pee on it, then while it's wet, stretch it without tearing it and hang it so it can dry."

Cenellot gave a disgusted face but took the skin from her and walked around the back of the cave. After a couple attempts, the rabbit fur was stretched between two wooden branches outside, where the stench wouldn't waft into the cave. The aroma of the cooking meat, as he entered the cave, erased all the sour memories he had associated with the preparation. After a solid meal of rabbit and wild carrots, Cenellot and Noyette found sleep easily without the usual nagging pangs of hunger.

After their first great catch, each day was very similar to the next. About once a week, Cenellot would trap a rabbit, and that was the highlight of the week. For the rest of their time, Noyette stayed inside the cave and was able to watch over Cenellot by sound. Between his exclamations of surprise, delight, and painful stumbles, she was able to track his location. At first, she had gone out with him each day to ensure there were no signs of wild beasts or soldiers. Luckily, even though Cenellot tripped often and made enough noise for five people, nothing disturbed them. They grew bolder as time waxed on, leaving unnoticed signs of their existence beyond the cave entrance. The broken twigs and picked berry bushes were hopefully not too noticeable to the casual eye, and only a trained scout would know these signs meant people were nearby.

Even though they weren't disturbed, that did not mean that they weren't observed by others. If they had looked closely, they would have realized that some of the green leaves in the bushes weren't leaves but actually eyes of the forest watching them. For now, these visitors seemed harmless, having no weapons of any kind, and were more in need of protection than offering protection or danger to anyone else. Being in close connection with the animals of the forest, they had heard about the visitors and decided they warranted watching, especially if they were taking lives for sustenance.

Humans of any kind were never to be trusted, regardless of how harmless they initially seemed. History had reminded them of this fact time and again, although it had been a couple centuries since any of them had seen an actual human. In this, the observations were an outlet for their curiosity. Only tales of dangerous treachery and grotesque mutilation remained of this human race, and many were anxious to verify the reality of their lore. A handful of elves shared the reconnaissance of these humans, each shift requiring a short debrief to the next elf, as well as their king upon return.

The cave-dwelling was well situated, with multiple groves of berry bushes and nut trees nearby, ensuring survival if they were careful about their usage and storage for later. The more adventurous elves had wandered upon these very berry bushes many eons before, and even now, they were a fun excursion for a young elf or a secretive rendezvous. Cenellot and Noyette had discovered the grove for themselves after a couple of days. In their excitement, they had walked all around the grove hunting berries and leaving crisscrossed paths of shoeprints throughout the grove.

As Cenellot grew more comfortable with his daily trip to the grove, he began to notice more of the small animals around him, the types of trees, and the prints he left behind. The forest was no longer a generic place of mystery - elements were taking shape with recognizable landmarks just like the town he had left behind. He was fascinated by the other prints he saw – deer and rodent, mostly, and he fantasized about what it might be like to be able to track a deer. It was easy enough to see their prints on clear dirt, and he vaguely wondered if anyone would be able to track them. *We should be more careful when we are out, just in case, and walk more on tufts of grass and not the dirt when we can,* he thought once or twice, but then the thought eluded him as soon as he got back to his mother and showed her what he had found that day.

At the end of that first fortnight, Cenellot made a discovery at the grove. As he arrived, something just seemed different, although he couldn't decide what it was. He collected berries quietly from the first bush, and as he turned to the next one, he realized what it was. He remembered all the prints he and his mother had left around the grove; somehow, they had all vanished except the prints he had just made! Afraid, he froze while he tried to think of any explanations. Racing back to Noyette, he panted as he approached the cave entrance.

"Mo-ther!" Cenellot called between breaths. "Come… quick!" After his second repetition, Noyette heard him and rushed out of the cave to protect her son.

"Here!" She called and raced to him, checking him for any physical harm. Finding none, she searched his face and eyes to focus the concern.

"In… the … grove, … come… see!" He panted while holding his sides from bursting after his run.

Gesturing for him to go, Noyette fell in line behind Cenellot, running as best she could between the many bushes that crowded all around. Expecting a fire or other emergency, she looked toward the grove eagerly as she ran, catching herself as she tripped over the many roots. After a while, they finally arrived at the grove. She saw nothing.

"What is it, Cenellot? There's nothing here!" Relief and exhaustion warred in her mind as the emergency seemed unwarranted.

"Exactly," Cenellot replied. "There's nothing here. Remember how many times we've walked around this grove? Look behind you - do you see all the prints we have left behind us? What do you see in the grove now?"

Looking again, Noyette understood what he meant. The ground looked as if they had never been in the grove! Questions erupted in her head, competing with the questions that Cenellot asked. "What do you think did this, mother?"

"It could be many things that we know nothing about or that we forget about, such as wind, rain, or …magic."

"Magic? Do you really think it could have been magic?" Cenellot seemed in awe with this new thought.

"After all that we've seen recently, would magic surprise you?"

"I guess not. I just don't always think about magic being possible."

"Nor do I," Noyette answered truthfully. "Whatever it is, it knows about us and hasn't come for us. If it were the soldiers or some other evil, they would have come after us before now."

Cenellot had to agree with this logic, although it made him even more curious about what else was in this forest. If whatever it was wasn't evil, then perhaps they had allies, if not friends, here?

"Until we know better, though, I think I shall go with you to the grove from now on. If something happens, it would be better for us to be together. Markus and Celina said nothing to us about creatures or people to be wary of, so I'm sure it is safe enough. All the same…"

Silently agreeing with her, Cenellot held his mother's hand and gently led her into the grove. They spent the next hour or so silently collecting berries, each absorbed in their own thoughts about who else might be here and staying close to the other for company since neither would be good security against any threat that came nearby.

"Let's go back, Cenellot," Noyette finally said after they had filled a large sac with the berries. "Simão said they would return when they could and not to worry. All the same, I would feel better if we stayed closer to our cave for the next while. When they come, we will ask them for an answer what we saw."

A small sigh that released his tension told her Cenellot agreed with her, and they walked carefully and quietly back to their abode with no disturbances. They had enough berries for a few days, and hopefully there would be answers before those were finished. Those days couldn't go quickly enough!

"Markus!!" Cenellot raced out of the cave, stumbling on a small outcropping at the base of the opening.

Markus was alone, but he was there, sending waves of reassurance with his presence. Noyette smiled despite herself, and for the first time in her life was happy about seeing a creature approach her. "We are truly thankful you are here! Are you here alone?"

Markus could only nod his head to this and gesture to his back, where he had more stores of food and supplies for them. As they unpacked, Cenellot rambled on about all of his adventures and discoveries, how he learned to trap rabbits for food, and the berries they had collected at the grove. At the mention of the grove, he remembered the footprints and froze.

"Markus, we think someone is watching us," he whispered.

Markus's ears swiveled forward, his complete attention on Cenellot, who took this as encouragement to continue.

While Cenellot retold Markus about his discoveries at the grove, Noyette decided to watch Markus during the retelling. What she saw gave her confidence. She saw Markus look interested yet not worried, which relieved her a bit.

Moving to be in front of Markus with Cenellot, she voiced her relief. "You know who it was, I can tell."

Markus shifted his gaze to Noyette and nodded his head slowly.

"So, is it someone that can help us, or is this another part of this mysterious world we can't understand?"

Rather than answering, Markus only stared intently into her eyes as if trying to speak to her, and his lack of a movement for yes or no was enough to tell her that it was part of the mystery they couldn't understand yet.

"Fine, it's obviously part of the mysterious elements that we don't understand yet. As long as whatever it is is safe to us…?"

Markus slowly nodded his head with a small whinny of assurance. Instantly, they felt more assured and calmer about whatever was in the grove.

"Thank you, Markus, for bringing more supplies and your information about the mysterious strangers. Do you know if you'll return in another three weeks, or will it be someone else?"

The responding whinny and shake of the head seemed like an answer of uncertainty, and that would be the best he could do. After trotting around the area and peering in the cave entrance, Markus looked deeply into their eyes once more, blinked slowly, and then departed as quickly and silently as he came.

Chapter 14: Moonlighting

The Inquisitor sat, dumbfounded, in the gaol's office, staring at the blank pages of the codex. *Why would there be so many protections on a codex if there were nothing in it?* He wondered incredulously. *Maybe he had just recently obtained the codex and had only hidden it so no one knew of its existence?* He answered his own thoughts. *But there wouldn't be a necessity for these extreme protections until after he had written something to hide in it!* Around and around went his logic as he puzzled and fell asleep, his body slumped over the desk.

These thoughts circled through his mind continuously in his sleep. The smoking tallow candles slowly burned down to the nubs and then sputtered out of existence. Asleep, he hardly noticed the growing darkness in the room while the waxing moonlight streaming into the office lit his desk and everything on it. The roars and hissing of the scrolls encircled him in his dreams, forcing him into a bottomless pit from which there was no return. He couldn't fight these inanimate things, yet they were exacting his life from him! Retreating from this certain death before him, he felt the earth give way under his left foot, and he jerked forward, jerking back into consciousness. Slowly, Ma'elrich awoke, lifting his head slowly off his desk. Looking around the room, he assured himself of the solidity and inanimation of the objects around him and reminded himself that the scrolls were now deep into the codex, unable to do him any harm. *They weren't doing him any good either,* he thought. Absently, he flipped through the sheaves of the codex, hoping for inspiration or a clue as to how to move forward. Everything he had done had pointed to this codex, and now it seemed to have been a hoax, a diversion from the actual truth that was hidden somewhere else.

As he berated himself for being taken in so easily by a lesser being, he saw a flash of silver in the sheaves. He stopped abruptly, slowly turning back to the sheave on which he saw the flash and stared at the page. There, in glistening bluish silver, was a manuscript in the common tongue of the area! *At last! Writing! But why only on this one page, as if it's a partial recording of something, here in the middle of a page?* He picked up the codex and carried it with him to find a candle and read the page with help from a better light, but as soon as the codex left the moonlight, the writing disappeared. He moved back to his desk, and the writing returned. He turned around so his shadow was cast over the codex, and the writing vanished. Turning back around to face the window, the writing reappeared!

Suddenly, he understood. *Brilliant! Moonlight writing!* He had heard of this in the legends of Tomar. He would have to research those legends to see if other elements might solve this place's riddles. For now, the inquisitor was beside himself with this new discovery. Quickly, he moved back to the window to ensure full moonlight on the codex. Then, he flipped through the codex to see which pages had been used. *Was this where the traitor started his secrets, knowing most would start at the beginning of the codex? Or was there a pattern to where he wrote his secrets?* Ma'elrich searched, flipping back and forth, then began counting pages. *The writing is definitely patterned - tonight, I can only see portions and every 30 pages or so.* He paced the floor as he pondered the meaning of the pattern.

He froze, mid-thought. Bluish silver ink, he remembered, was another essential element of the moonlight writing and was also part of the legendary elves from the area. But no one had ever seen elves, and they were assumed to be bedtime stories for the children, not bits of truth. So, what he had heard recently about elves in the forests WAS true. Interesting…

Elfin ink?! Somehow, the gaoler must have gotten a store of elfin ink! Those blasted elves and their moon-worship. Of course, it would be writing that can only be read in the same moonlight it was written in! A stream of profanities ushered forth that helped express his frustration but did nothing to solve the problem. Moonlight writing meant that the author wrote in a special ink that could only be read by the light of the same moon. Since the moon rose at a different time each day, he would have to find the best time to read the given page and hope there was enough moonlight that evening to read the script.

Although wanting to read the one page he had, he wanted to know what began the gaoler's traitorous transition, so he needed to read the codex from the beginning, whichever moonlight that first page might have used. Counting pages, there were about fifteen blank pages before the first writing was visible. He would have to check every night until he saw writing on that first page of the codex and only hope that it would not be a full moon cycle before that day occurred.

For the next fortnight, Ma'elrich secluded himself in his bedroom, locking the door and extinguishing any light in the room. He set a chair by the window, ink pen in hand, to copy what he might see in the codex. On the tenth evening, the moonlight stole into the room, highlighting the codex. The first page began to shimmer, and writing appeared! Sighing a deep breath of anticipation, he began reading what seemed to be an introduction.

I have been haunted by nightmares about this new traitor I've been guarding. Unable to sleep, I feel I will only find rest once I have these images written down. Please forgive me if, despite my efforts to keep this hidden safely from the magistrate, anyone I know is hurt by my indiscretion.

The inquisitor gave a cruel chuckle as he thought about how he had now become the ultimate victor in this game and the irony of how well the gaoler would be served his share of retribution, not forgiven, now that the codex was in his own hands! After a few moments of musing about the end of the gaoler, he turned the first page and continued to the gaoler's real intentions. If these were the images that gave a gaoler nightmares, it would do well to take notes so that he could use them in his future interrogations, as well.

Chapter 15: Not All Berries are Friendly

They stared at the place Markus had been only seconds before, then at each other. The initial relief they felt gave way to their feeling trapped by the walls of their new home, and they set out to gather more berries at the grove. Their light-heartedness gave them a sense of security for the first time in a long time, and they smiled despite themselves. In his happiness, Cenellot raced ahead to the grove, Noyette trailing behind unconcerned. She wondered how many berries Cenellot would collect before she got there. She had to admit he had gotten better at collecting them, so if he could just learn how not to spill them all before she could cook them, that would be a true success. In front of her, the dirt told a story of someone having tripped on a root, lost his footing, and fallen. There was quite a scuffle in the dirt! *Well, thankfully, it was before he had the berries this time!*

At the grove, she expected Cenellot to come running to show her how many berries he already had. The grove was silent, as if it were peacefully dozing in the sunlight. No sign of him anywhere. "Cenellot?"

No answer.

Trying to focus, Noyette searched the ground to see if she could tell if there were fresh prints on the ground. Since they had only been there once since the dirt was cleared of its prints, she hoped she could see something. After a few moments of trying, she realized it all looked the same and stopped trying. "Cenellot, if you're hiding from me, I'm not going to let you come here by yourself again! Answer me, where are you!!"

Still no answer.

Back near the cave, Florenço checked his surroundings, then climbed effortlessly into the fir tree a short way from the cave's opening. Silently, he reached a branch twice as high as a standard man, where almost no one would think to look for him. Out of sight, he sat comfortably on the branch with his back to the trunk and began his watch over the interlopers. As an elf, Florenço's forest leaf clothing, dark green eyes, and shoulder-length ebony hair camouflaged him perfectly among the dark green needles and bark of the fir tree. It was his favorite reconnaissance spot, and so far, the humans still seemed oblivious to his company.

The king had heard from the forest friends and Clairdani that there were humans residing in the forest, and he had ordered them to observe until he made a decision for or against their presence. After a few days, the three volunteers had developed a rotation so as not to take over the entirety of their other duties. Having never seen the human form before, they were first amazed by how similar and different they were to humans: similar in stature and sociability, their rounded ears and heavier features certainly set them apart from the elfish finer, slighter figures. Moreover, humans seemed so loud and clumsy. It was amazing that they were able to survive in the forest at all. Not for the first time, he wondered, *This was the race they feared?*

After some time reminiscing, he realized something was wrong at the glade. True, he might be too hasty in his suspicions, as his friends were quick to point out. A couple of weeks ago, there had been hoofprints and the dead-meat scent of Tenenbrani around the grove. Fearing the worst, they had searched the area and region and found no other traces of the cursed creatures. His friends had dismissed the episode with a laugh, but he sensed there may be something still amiss. Independently, he decided to erase the footprints so as not to alarm the humans. His fellow elves were furious. It was not their place to save humans from their own folly or from the Tenenbrani, and they should never interfere. They had reported him to their King, Abrimel. Thankfully, he had forgiven their interference but still refused to allow them to contact them directly. Under the Threat of Banishment or Grounding, Florenço kept strictly to his reconnaissance role, knowing that he was watched more closely by his friends as well. In the aftermath of that particular incident, the child had noticed the erasure of the footprints, and they had stayed in safety in their cave thereafter. He had further proof that these humans required protection from the Tenenbrani when he saw Markus with them. Humans hadn't even known about the existence of the Tenenbrani or Clairdani until fairly recently, and those that did, seemed to have short, cursed lives themselves.

Scanning the area now, Florenço finally realized what was wrong this time. Usually, the child ventured out shortly after the sun emerged, and the older female began preparing their nourishment for the day. Today, there was nothing, not even the beginnings of a fire. His predecessor had said nothing was amiss, so perhaps they had already gone out somewhere already? He reached out with his mind to the animals in the area, trying to sense their emotions or thoughts for clues. Amid their preparations for the day, a small team of ants was carrying a fellow ant in physical distress. Her thoughts rambled about a sudden large weight that pressed her into the ground and then lifted, and she was unable to move until her colony arrived to lift her. Seeing the distance, the ant caravan had carried their comrade. It had been a while since the child had stepped on her.

"Cenellot!"

A cry of anguish broke over the choruses of songbirds, silencing them. Alighting to the ground, bow in hand. He feared a Tenenbrani had found them. Although they were forbidden to interfere with the Tenenbrani regardless of their destruction, Florenço's curiosity sped him through the forest to their aid.

As he ran, his nostrils and ears fed him the needed information. There were no strange scents or smells beyond those of the two humans, so whatever fate befell the child was of their own making. He slowed his pace a little, wanting to ensure a silent approach. The berry patch. It was mid-summer, quite late for any edible berries and too early for the deadly nightshade to have their telltale black coloring. Unripe, the nightshade could easily kill younger children without the proper precautions. Even though there were not many children amongst the elves, learning the different berries and their markings was one of the first elvish lessons for precisely this reason. The elves used nightshade to tip their arrows, although its use had to be sanctioned by the king himself and only during times of war. Instinctively, he touched his small pouch, in which he carried a small vial of antidote for poisons. He hoped it would be enough and that he wasn't already too late. These humans were frail and not the enemies he had been trained to hate ruthlessly. Regardless, allowing any child to die was wrong. He decided he would live with the consequences.

That same child now lay in the cave, still near death. He hadn't eaten more than one or two berries, so while the mother was panicking in the grove, he had quickly picked up the child and taken him to the cave. After laying him down on the leaf mattress, he had gone looking for the herbs that would absorb the poisons and keep him alive. Hopefully, humans were stronger than they appeared.

Walking around the grove, Noyette hoped for something to guide her. Just behind the right-most bush, there was a gap in the smaller bushes behind the grove itself, and lying underneath the bush just out of reach was the basket Cenellot was using, although it was empty. There was more dirt shuffling here as well and… a footprint that was too thin and long to be hers or Cenellot's! Now that she looked, there was only one set of prints in this area. Beyond the grove, the strange footprints led away, and she couldn't find Cenellot's prints anywhere. He had disappeared!

Terror flooded her heart as she called again and again, "Cenellot!" listening with all her strength and hope for an answer. She grabbed the basket and followed the prints, hoping she was following something that would lead her to her son. Moving as swiftly as she could through the rugged undergrowth, she scoured the area as she went, searching for any signs of Cenellot. Perhaps he was in a bush somewhere, hiding from this creature? If something else had happened to him, perhaps the creature would have dropped him? She could only hope that the creature needed him alive as much as she did.

Tears began to blur her vision as she remembered his life and how much he meant to her, especially now that Hawthorne was gone. She wouldn't be able to live out here by herself. It would be too much! In her agony, she could only focus on the footprints and not on where she was going. The prints came to an end, and she finally realized that she was back at their cave. She stormed into the cave, calling to her son. "Cenellot!!"

There was no response, but something lifeless lay on his bed.

Chapter 16: The Witch Hunt Continues

The writing of the first pages ended, and desperate for information he didn't already know, the inquisitor turned the remaining sheaves. Not finding any more written than the first two sheaves of the codex, he slammed the codex shut. "This is going to be a very slow moon cycle," he mumbled to himself as he thought about the words he had read. The magistrate had done well to ensure the gaoler understood the depth of his position and his duties with regard to the new traitor, and he had warned the gaoler that she was powerful. Indeed… she was powerful, but not in the ways most people expect. The Advocate never mentioned what powers she possessed or admitted to Hawthorne that she had any. The fact that she outlasted all other prisoners in all methods of torture meant that she had something supernatural about her. *What power is this that allows her to feel pain and show injury and still survive? Surely, it isn't just a matter of her will. Was Hawthorne giving her something that sustained her, maybe?*

Reading the first part of the codex, Ma'elrich witnessed Hawthorne's slow corruption. At first, his reports were very stoic, as if he were making an official evening gaol report. Very subtly, however, the tone changed to one of awe and then subservience… *Her methods must be cunning and mental, not physical, since there was nothing in the codex indicating her demonstration of anything supernatural.* She exuded an effortless blend of kindness and simplicity, managing to not only be empathetic herself but also inspire empathy in those in her presence... *That must be it! She must be able to control their minds with her voice and make others want to help her. She uses their emotions to manipulate them! Showing injury and pain would definitely be part of what won others over quickly rather than using any physical means to overpower others.*

Rowen did order the gaoler not to speak to her, but maybe it would have been better to use a deaf gaoler so that her voice wouldn't be able to persuade him? He would have to suggest that to Rowen for the future – ensure that only the mute and deaf are employed as gaolers. It might help them tolerate the screaming better as well, making them more useful in the interrogations themselves. Yes, he would include this suggestion in his next report to the other towns in the area as well. Since there were so many attacks, not many of the townsfolk remembered that they weren't the only ones that existed. They were entirely controlled by their fears of the forest around them, and many moons would go by before they ventured out beyond where the patrols patrolled. With that one positive thought from his entry into the codex, the inquisitor considered the first day a success and went to bed for the rest of the night.

From that day on, the inquisitor followed the same daily agenda. He would wake up late, read what he had written over the night before, and write any insights as suggestions to the locations of treacherous lairs. Deep in his own world of thought, he would also take his meals alone and speak to no one. When the moon rose and it was dark enough to see by the moonlight, he settled in the same room at his residence with a few candles and read the next entry, writing over the letters in regular ink so he would be able to read the entries whenever he wanted to. Way into the wee hours of the morning, Ma'elrich wrote over as much of the text as he could. Often, the writing became mesmerizing, and the words blurred together, not making any sense. However, when he fell asleep on his work for the third time, he would force himself to sleep in the actual bed. There, again his mind would replay what he had subconsciously consumed in the writings, making the transformation of their best gaoler into a nightmare he couldn't control.

He reveled in the despair he felt in the earlier writings. Despair was giving in to a higher power, usually his own power, and he was accustomed to causing said despair for his own manipulation tools. However, as the writings continued, they lost that sense of total loss and control and gave way to a hope he couldn't understand. It was as if the intervals between the writings gave a brief summary of feelings rather than the actual details and facts of a storyline. He needed the details and facts, not some sappy emotional dribble. He hoped that once everything had been written down, re-reading it in its entirety would give better clues to actual locations, people, and events that might help him catch those not explicitly called out in the text.

Despite himself, Ma'elrich had to admit that the gaoler was undoubtedly clever! He didn't seem to be concerned with these details, giving details about events long ago, nothing very recent. In fact, it was a bit like reading about someone's life. Some little girl who got into trouble and got lost outside Tomar. *More than likely, she ended up as a snack for some of the Tenenbrani. Who likes obnoxious children anyway? Horrid, wretched things that they are. So weak and needy.* He shrugged off the chill he got whenever he thought about children wanting something from him. Thankfully, most of them avoided him when they weren't taunting him. He had done well in his pretense of being a crotchety miser. *If they only knew that I was the source of all their nightmares, they wouldn't dare come near me. Patience...* Hopefully, as the gaoler gained confidence in his secrecy, he would get careless and begin putting actual places and people's names in the codex. Then, he would have people he could torture for information and finally get the Advocate herself!

Thinking that the parents of a missing child might be easily goaded into giving him information, he revisited this thought. ...especially if he led them on with false hopes of finding her. *The only information I have so far is the father and mother of a young child who ran away... It might be a dead end, but it could lead to somewhere. Perhaps the girl knew something, and they sent her outside of Tomar to protect the information?* A plan quickly formed in his mind. *I'll wager they would give me anything to protect her or bring her back?*

"Guards!"

Diogo and Tiago reported immediately, snapping to sharp salutes.

"I need you to bring me a listing of all children born about eight to twelve solar cycles ago and whether they are still alive. If they have died, I need to know how. Do you know how you might obtain that information here in Tomar?"

Diogo glanced quickly at Tiago and answered for both of them. "We can find that. There is a guild of midwives amongst the women. I'm sure one of them or collectively they could tell us and perhaps write names for us. We should be able to return by midday on the morrow with your request."

"Agreed, as soon as you can. Go."

The two snapped a quick salute to acknowledge their dismissal, then turned in unison to depart.

Rather than sit at his desk while waiting, he decided to do a little digging of his own. He enjoyed watching others wilt under his stares, avoid his approach, and try to hide what they thought he might be looking for. All of it made him feel more powerful and would be a good antidote for his current frame of mind.

He carefully donned his most official-looking cloak and decided he would go bareheaded to ensure everyone would recognize him. After some consideration, he decided to take the Codex with him as well and pretend to be looking at names. That way, when he looked at anyone in particular, they would more likely avoid his gaze or slink away if they had something to hide. It would also give him paper to write down descriptions of people looking suspicious, as well as where they were going. For some reason, when people felt guilty or hunted, they always seemed to go to the others being hunted, which made it that much easier to find others. *Then, the real fun begins!*

Trying to hide his smirk, he carried the open codex with him down the hallway and into the narrow street. He wasn't expecting anyone to be there, but he was disappointed all the same. Turning toward the main market square, he hoped it was a market day with many vendors. Selling or buying wares made it more difficult to suddenly leave the area and would make it easier to see the people's connections. As he approached the square, though, he realized the calm and quiet meant it must not be a market day, and all he could hope for were sudden changes in direction when they noticed him watching him.

In the center of the market square was a stone dais, upon which a large stake and firewood were piled. This was where most traitors met their public and fiery end, as a warning to all that cavorting with murderous creatures was not to be tolerated. These Traitors invited these vicious creatures into the town, where they then maimed, trampled, or otherwise destroyed the innocent townsfolk. The ashes from these public displays of punishment were then collected and dumped outside the town walls so as not to attract any flying monsters into the town. Standing at that location would be a tremendous boost to his fear-mongering and a perfect place to people watch. He settled into a nearby comfortable spot on the firewood, opened the codex, took out his quill, and began taking notes on everyone around him. With luck, tomorrow would be a great day to let the interrogations begin.

Chapter 17: Mateus

Mateus' late patrol shift had just ended, and he was still shaking from what he had overheard and seen of the Inquisitor. His legs automatically carried him where his thoughts led him – to the forge, where his mentor, Simão, might have some words of comfort and guidance. As one of the oldest gaolers, Hawthorne had been one of his best friends even though they were on opposite sides of the "traitor" question. Until the Advocate had disappeared, he had thought that Hawthorne was the most likely to turn him in and torture him himself before lighting the pyre under him. How wrong had he been? Hawthorne would have hated himself for turning in a friend, but his allegiance and loyalty had never been questioned, especially when the Tenenbrani were such murderous creatures. On that, they could agree. With this new inquisitor holding the town in an Iron Fist of Fear, Mateus wondered if humankind was potentially worse than the Tenenbrani? The Tenenbrani at least seemed to kill indiscriminately, whereas the Inquisitor was a lethal hunter who killed with impunity.

He remembered the day he had lost everyone in his family when he was about to begin his gaoler training. His father had never been kind, and part of becoming a gaoler was to help prevent the pain he had endured in others with the law on his side. Over the years, his father had become more spiteful, not just to his family but to neighbors and anyone who might owe him money. Ultimately, his father had been devoid of companionship, and his mother and siblings lived in constant terror. The week before their end, he had noticed his father's eyes blinking black every once in a while, and sometimes, he thought he saw fire in those eyes.

He didn't dare question him or anyone else about it for fear of any repercussions.

That last night, he had been awake late, practicing his latest swordsmanship techniques in the main room so as not to awaken anyone, when he heard a loud, hair-raising growl that froze him in fear. His mind searched for a location or reason for a Tenenbrani to be anywhere near them in the town and determined that the continuing growls were from the loft – where his parents slept. Stepping backwards to the far wall, he was able to see their makeshift bed, where he saw a shadow growing in the night and heard cloth ripping as a prelude to his mother's screams. The screams were short. The creature assaulted them, and within moments, all that remained on the bed were tattered shreds of their existence.

Before the creature could jump from the loft, he had run through the door and began the town warning of a Tenenbrani in the town. The Patrolmen, who slept with their weapons nearby in their turn, instantly created a path to the nearest opened gate, clearing the path of any potential victims. The creature had stumbled out of the town without further incident, although it was too late for what was left of his family. His sister and brother, both younger than himself, had perhaps awoken at the noise and had tried to flee. Their remains were scattered by the front door. His father's body was never found, although remnants of both his father's and mother's clothing had been strewn around the room. It still haunted him that he hadn't tried to rescue his brother and sister before he left his house that last time.

Alone, he had resolved to join the patrols in addition to being a gaoler to further protect the town from wonton violence and death. Those sharing in the grueling hours of training and practice became his best friends, people he would trust with his life, and they trusted him in return. People like Hawthorne. Hawthorne hadn't joined him in the Patrols, though, having already found a wife and a life outside of the gaol. The Patrols was a different group of people- some were patrols because of personal experience, like himself, and all wanted to protect the town from any outsiders.

That first night on patrol after a few months of training, he glimpsed movement near the southern wall and walked slowly towards it to check on it. There, glowing almost as brightly as the moon, was the most beautiful creature he had ever seen, a pure-white unicorn! Its purity seemed to shine from its gleaming coat, and its round, golden eyes were only a little higher than his own. More than that, despite the legendary lethality of the twisted bone-colored horn protruding from its forehead, the unicorn did not hold its head in any threatening way and rather made him feel at peace. After a few seconds of assessing each other, he felt it was trying to say something to him. As he walked closer, the unicorn made no move to step away but dropped its head to see eye-to-eye with him. Something about the look and the eyes reminded him of his mother, and he reached out to touch her. Amazingly, the unicorn leaned into his touch, and he felt something in his mind shift and connect.

"Mamãe?" he started to say.

"Mateus! Careful! Don't make any sudden moves!"

As Mateus turned to see who it was that was disturbing his moment, he saw Afonso running at him with his spear ready to throw. At the same instant, the unicorn bolted and disappeared into the forest, never to be seen again.

"Mateus... you weren't... speaking to it, were you?" Afonso asked accusatorily. "You know that they can control you if you make eye contact."

"What? Of course not. You can't talk to animals. Everyone knows that. Besides, I remember everything, so I wasn't being controlled..."

After a hard stare, Afonso looked appeased, and Mateus wanted to encourage the positive momentum.

"I've never seen unicorns that calm before. I've always imagined them as fierce, invulnerable fighters, although maybe not as bloodthirsty as some others."

"Don't get comfortable with them. Any of those creatures will kill any of us for any reason. You were just lucky I came when I did. As close as that one lured you in, you would have been dead as soon as her horn pierced your chest!" In emphasis, Afonso thumped Mateus' chest with his fist. Mateus caught himself before he fell backwards, making Afonso grin.

"Yeah, well..." Mateus took a quick look around to see if perhaps the unicorn had stayed nearby, then sprinted into Afonso, knocking him over.

"Hey!"

"Come on, back to work. With any luck, since the unicorn was that calm, there aren't any other creatures out tonight. At least, none with plans for us!" The two pranked each other back through the gate and up the stairs to their wall positions.

His meeting with the unicorn had earned him a badge of bravery amongst his fellow patrols, and Simão had wanted to hear all the details when they met at the tavern. After the fifth retelling of the story, Simão started asking more probing questions, and Mateus began to suspect he knew more than others about unicorns.

"Have you seen other unicorns before, Mateus?"

"Maybe... or I've only heard so much about them I feel like I've seen them before. They're known for their healing and speed, right? Afonso says they're killers, with that magic horn of theirs..."

"They're not killers."

His solid assurance gave Mateus pause. "So... you've really seen unicorns then?" He looked around to see if anyone had heard them, and in his haste, he almost fell off his stool. In the local tavern, the noise level was enough to cover most conversations, although keywords seemed to still draw attention.

Simão removed his steadying hand once he knew his friend wouldn't fall. He conspicuously avoided looking around as he mumbled with his ale mug covering his mouth, "You could say that." His penetrating stare at Mateus made it all too clear that further questions would not be answered in the tavern. "So... how are you doing, by yourself, and doing both patrol duty and gaol training?"

Understanding flashed in his mind, and Mateus answered, "I could definitely use some help." The two sat in companionable silence, watching those around them, laughing occasionally at a pretend remark to avoid drawing attention to their observations. When they had finished their drinks, Simão gave the barmaid a few coins and met Mateus at the door, two friends ensuring the other made it home safely.

From then on, Mateus had become one of Simão's mentees, trusting him over anything ever said by the magistrate and learning how to play both the ignorant and the knowledgeable roles as the current company required. Simão became the kind, caring father he had never had, and Mateus became the son Simão had lost many years ago.

Mateus figured that Simão would need to know what the Inquisitor was doing, if he didn't already know, and would have a plan for how they would all survive this flushing out of Traitors in Tomar. With renewed determination, Mateus ensured he took a circuitous route and slowed his pace so that he would be the only one that arrived at Simão's forge that afternoon.

Chapter 18: Strangers Become Friends

Cenellot lay on his bed with a small candle by him, unconscious. His skin looked pale, and he was unresponsive, although he was at least breathing. Noyette scanned the interior of their home and saw nothing out of place. How had he come to be here? What had happened to him? She shook him, hoping he could tell her something about what happened. No response. Something fell on her foot. Glancing down, she saw berries – nightshade. Hadn't she told Cenellot that these were poisonous?? Had they seen any before now so she could tell him? She couldn't remember. She rechecked him, looking for signs of what he might be suffering and hoping he hadn't eaten too many. She had some medicines in the pack Markus just brought, although much of the healing would have to be Cenellot's doing. He was strong, and hopefully, his system would be able to process the poison without taking too much of a toll on his body and her mind.

She looked through the medicinal herbs and eventually was able to concoct an infusion she could administer to him when he woke up that might help dissolve the poison in the system. Organizing the herbs by their uses gave her something useful to do while she waited for progressions of the poison through his system. At the first sign of life from Cenellot, she attempted to wake him fully so she could understand what had happened. His eyes fluttered, and she saw that nothing registered in his unfocused eyes. "Cenellot, I need you to drink this. It might be disgusting, but it will help you heal. Drink!"

She tilted the cup to his lips, pouring small quantities into his mouth and then waiting for a swallow. After a few sips, he drifted off again into unconsciousness. *At least he got some medicine before he fell back unconscious. Now, all we can do is wait.*

By the time it was fully dark outside, she had all the herbs organized and a few overnight infusions ready in case he awoke during the night. She set up her bedding next to Cenellot and fell fast asleep.

The convulsions and fever began at the darkest hour of the night on the second day. Noyette heard Cenellot thrashing and rose to reassure him and do what she could to clear the area of anything he might hit with his tremors. He was extremely hot and still unconscious no matter how much she tried to wake him. She lit a few candles far away from his reach and soaked as many rags in cool water as she could to try and reduce the fever. The first night was full of his violent, projectile vomiting as his body tried to rid itself of the poison, and she hoped that the herbal teas she had been able to get him to drink would help eliminate the remaining poison. The fever and convulsions proved it had not worked completely.

Forcing herself to remain calm, she thought about what she needed to do. She could treat the fever, and there *were* some bark teas she could use to calm the convulsions. *But would that be enough? If only Markus or someone would come with a more specific herb for this poison!* She could only hope that forcing the herbal teas and cooling the skin would help sweat out the poison. After she was able to get some bark tea into her unconscious boy, the tremors ceased, and he fell into a deep sleep. Between changes in the cooling rags on his body, she cried tears of fear and worry for herself and Cenellot. Had the Traitors left them here in the forest alone and without aid hoping they would fall victim to the dangers therein? So, it was true! They were just as dangerous as the other creatures! They were just more devious in their scheming!

Sensing that Cenellot would sleep for a while, she ventured to the front of their cave and breathed in the cool night air. The stars shone with all their might, adding to her sense of insignificance in the world and universe. *Is there anyone that can help my only son? Anyone at all? Are we to die here, or is there a place for us here?* The light of the half-moon reflected on her silent tears, highlighting her high cheekbones and beautifully fair skin. The tranquil night offered her solace, and after wiping away her tears, she found the strength to return to Cenellot and sleep.

After the third night of Cenellot's worsening, a tearful Noyette began to prepare herself mentally for possibly losing her son. Without the proper herbs, he would die as surely as she existed. It would be too long before Markus returned to be of any help. Her grief had driven her hunger from her, although she and he both needed water, and he might need food if, by chance, he had any moments of strength. Without Cenellot to help, she would have to go herself and hope he survived a little while until she could return. Thankfully, there were berries on the first bush in the grove, and the water was clear enough with her first draw. There was even a small rabbit in the trap they set a few days ago. Hurrying back as quickly as she could with the heavy load of water and sustenance, she thought she heard voices as she approached the cave. *Hallucinations? Or is Cenellot talking in his sleep?* The voice sounded calm and reassuring, although it wasn't in a language she understood. The words crashed over her and calmed her just as she saw the same strange set of prints leading to their abode. She rushed in, worried more about Cenellot than her own safety, to encounter a being of extraordinary beauty, strikingly human-like, yet distinctly non-human, helping wipe Cenellot's brow.

"Who are you, and why are you in our house!" Noyette grabbed the cloth from the being's hands, shoved him aside, and began looking over Cenellot for any sign of mistreatment. She found none. Rounding on the stranger, she found him a few steps away, standing perfectly still. She looked him up and down and noticed pointed ears sticking out from long, dark gossamer hair and large, slanted eyes that seemed to follow the slant of their very pronounced high cheekbones. His limbs were thin, with overlong hands and feet that were covered with a beautiful tunic of leaves, finely woven together in a manner that highlighted the various shades of the forest. With his greyish-brown skin, if he had been standing in the forest, she would have thought him a part of a tree or bush. She looked again at his feet, matching these long, thin feet with the footprints she remembered. So maybe this is the being that brought her Cenellot home when he had been poisoned? She hid her thoughts by returning the Cenellot and continuing to wipe his brow. Nothing seemed amiss. Perhaps this creature was here to help?

Looking back at the human forest creature, she asked, "Who are you? What are you doing here?"

The being gestured that he didn't understand her language and tried to speak to her in his. "*My name is Florenço. I've been watching you and saw that you needed help.*" Seeing that she didn't understand him either, he pointed to himself and spoke only his name, "Florenço."

Understanding, Noyette repeated the gesture with herself. "Noyette."

He then signaled that he would like the rag and helped Noyette resubmerge it in cooler water to refresh it. Sensing that Cenellot was safe and this forest creature wasn't endangering anyone, she lapsed into a quiet companionship with Florenço. After a while, she sensed her eyes growing heavy, and despite her efforts, she involuntarily drifted into sleep. Startling awake some time later, Florenço was nowhere to be found, and Cenellot's fever was thankfully broken at last.

Chapter 19: A Treacherous Ploy

Ma'elrich was frustrated. His observations of the Tomarans yielded no apparent clues that any of them were working with anyone outside Tomar itself. They seemed to be naturally suspicious of strangers but not of anyone from Tomar, regardless of their authority or position. *They really feel that Rowan is doing everything he can to protect them? They have been secluded for too long and don't realize how unusual these attacks are nowadays. I wonder if they even suspect that their ringleader might be from Tomar?*

The first list the guards gave him had a couple of promising suspects. Not wanting to cause any alarm, he had decided to visit the couples at their own houses to put them at ease. It would also allow him time to see how recently they had lost their child by how much the child's presence was still in the house. Over time, surely anything that belonged to the child would be reused for other things, and any decorations or marks would be covered by dirt or wear. Both of the houses he had visited had other children, and neither family seemed to be deferential to any particular seats or locale. People were never his favorite creatures to deal with, especially the smaller, whiny ones. For information, he would try to be pleasant.

After knocking assuredly on the first door he was visiting, he waited for the door to open. A somewhat tall, balding man with dull drown eyes answered. Doing his best to sound pleasant, Ma'elrich opened the conversation. "I had heard that you lost a child in the recent past. I'm very sorry for your loss." He was sure he sounded sincere in his statement... and their reaction wasn't hostile, which boded well.

Trying not to show his fear of this man who was widely known for his success in torturing not conversation, the father spoke for the family. He hoped this conversation would be short and satisfactory, and not become awkward so that he would have to invite him in. The longer the Inquisitor was with anyone, the shorter that person's lifespan became. "It was a while ago, and life is fragile. Any one of us could die tomorrow. We can only make the most of the life we have."

Looking past the man's shoulder, Ma'elrich observed what he could. The eldest child, almost as tall as her mother, and as thin as her courage seemed to be, grew quiet as her father spoke. The others seemed oblivious to adult conversation and continued their play amongst themselves. Seeing that the Inquisitor was not going to be easily appeased, the man stood aside and allowed the Inquisitor to enter. As he entered, the entire family stood and came toward the door.

Looking over at the parents, Ma'elrich nodded in the child's direction for silent approval. "Child, may I speak with you for a moment?" To the others, he continued, "The rest of you may continue with what you were doing. This will only take a moment or two and no harm shall come to her, I promise."

Looking to her mother for approval, the girl followed the crook of his finger to stand near him. Ma'elrich waited until the rest of the family resumed other activities before beginning his questioning. "Who was older, you or your missing sister?"

Shyly, the child pointed to herself. "I was, sir."

"I'll wager that the two of you were the prettiest and fastest children in this town…?"

The girl shook her head. She gave a short curtsy, and walked back to her other siblings, too shy to continue.

If the missing girl is younger than this one, these are not the traitor's parents. The Advocate was much older than these girls now that I see their age personally. Yet another dead end!

Aloud, Ma'elrich excused himself. "Thank you for your time, and if you think of anything that might help us find your missing daughter, let us know and we will continue the search."

They bowed him out the door, and he thoughtfully returned to his temporary office. *Perhaps the parents of the Advocate never had other children, or maybe they've both fallen victim to the creatures they pretend to befriend? Or maybe…* He would have to consider these options as he watched the townspeople this week.

After a week of detailed descriptions of anyone looking suspicious, Ma'elrich had created quite a list of names. Reviewing which names repeated themselves over the week gave him a solid base to start his interrogations. Gleefully, he played finger games with his pen and then called the guards. "Tiago! Diogo!"

Tiago opened the door to the bare room, and the two stood at attention, hoping they would finally be doing something more than paper chasing.

"I need you to gather the garrison. Have them help you collect the first 10 names on this list as well as one parent of any children that have gone missing or have died in the last few years. Arrest them in the name of the Inquisitor, and that will tell them all they need to know about why they are being arrested. Take them to the dungeon, and we will begin the interrogations this evening."

"Dead … children's … parents, sir?"

"To help keep people from looking for her, the parents may have declared her dead and buried an empty coffin. It's what I would have done if it were my child anyway."

Stunned into silence, the guards took a careful glance through the list. Neither of them moved as they read through the list, preparing a mental plan for how best to collect the ten with the least amount of warning. None of them were parents of a missing or dead child, meaning a select group would need to scout those out separately.

"Well? What are you waiting for? Get moving, now!"

"If I may, Sr Inquisitor…" Diogo bravely defied the order to move lest he make a graver mistake that would undoubtedly cost him his life. "There are only first names on this list with vague descriptions. There could be many that fit any of these descriptions. How do we know which one to arrest?"

The Inquisitor growled, annoyed by their naivety in terror tactics. "Simply arrest the one you are most suspicious of that fits the description, or if you see someone that matches the description before that person, arrest that one instead. It matters not whether these are actual traitors."

Tiago looked incredulous at this order; They had always taken pride in upholding the principles of law and order, but they had never received directives that went against basic moral standards.

"Do as I say, or you will be included in the next list of names! You are soldiers and follow my orders, you have been given to me by the mayor to eliminate the threat, and this is how we must do it."

After a moment's pause, Ma'elrich added, "Since you will not think of this for yourselves, have a few guards patrol the walls outside to catch anyone trying to run – those will be the true traitors. They will panic when they see that we are arresting potential Traitors and will want to save their own necks. We will exchange these true traitors for the first group, especially those least likely to be traitors."

"As you command." Tiago and Diogo bowed, saluted, and left the gaol. Both of them hoped they did not run into too many friends that might match the descriptions on their vague lists of suspects and wondered how much their magistrate knew of the Inquisitor's methods.

Chapter 20: A New Hope

As he returned home to Sintra, Florenço felt something inside had shifted. He had been taught his entire life not to trust humans, and he had knowingly broken the elfin vow never to get involved in any of their lives! For days, Florenço felt that someone would report him or challenge what he had done. He did his best to return to the regular routine – he kept himself busy and never strayed outside the elfish land borders. He hoped that the distance would help him forget them and that his fellow watchers wouldn't discover his interference or grow suspicious about the boy's unlikely recovery. As part of resuming normalcy, he couldn't totally ignore the humans' existence. As oddities in their forest, their news was whispered throughout their kingdom, and as part of their spider network, he was expected to be well-informed and participate in the information gathering. Thus, on Florenço's turn to watch the humans, which he managed to contain to every few days, he stayed with the orders to see without being seen.

Despite his efforts to disconnect, Florenço found opportunities to speak to the Clairdani, asking quietly about how the boy was doing beyond what he could see physically. Instead, they conveyed Noyette's moods as she moved from distrustful anger at the Traitors to effusive gratitude to the stranger who saved her son's life, filling his heart with hope. Even harder to resist were the reports that as the boy gained strength, he started asking questions about his savior. Thankfully, the Clairdani gave them no direct answers, in accordance with the elfish ban on humans knowing of their existence. What he found most interesting was their reports about Cenellot's other transformations. As Cenellot's transformation quickened, he increasingly understood the Clairdani and his eyes were slowly turning green!

Cenellot's transformation was happening quickly! Once he was fully healed, Cenellot asked the Clairdani through their mental link about his savior when they came to check on him. This time, he sensed the picture of the elf that his mother had told him about! He finally knew how to communicate and felt more like a part of their world. Markus even shared Cenellot's hope that they might survive this, especially if they could link up with this forest creature!

After a couple weeks of limited information, Florenço was astounded to hear about this final revelation and felt he would need to verify for himself. He vaguely knew that some humans were able to connect with the Clairdani, although none had been this young that he knew of. On his next solo vigil rotation, Florenço checked the environs for any animals and then edged nearer to their living area. Surprisingly, he smelled a Clairdani as well as the woman and her boy! Slowly, Florenço appeared from behind one of the larger bushes.

The two startled human faces turned to him, while Markus gave him a nod of welcome. Cenellot rose to his feet as he recognized this forest creature as the one who had saved his life. Humbly, he bowed to Florenço. "We owe you my life. For that, we thank you." He bowed, not knowing how else to show his gratitude to this stranger.

Florenço, although not understanding the speech, nodded in return in acknowledgement of the obvious sentiment of thanksgiving.

Without the panic of before, they were better able to study each other. The mother and son pair still did not seem frightening, although Florenço was still dismayed by their smell. Elves bathed at least daily and ensured they smelled of the forest – pine, mostly, although in the spring, when many flowers were in bloom, it was easy to use the honeysuckle that was everywhere in bloom. For their part, the thin, chiseled features set Florenço apart and were in stark contrast to his natural fighting stance. The large bow on his back suggested a strength that defied any frailty suggested otherwise in his thin frame. "My mother tells me you are called 'Florenço' and that you live in this forest." After a pause, he added, "What exactly are you? We have never heard of any humanoid creatures living in the forest before now."

Florenço shook his head, not understanding the complicated human speech.

They speak it now, too? Florenço asked Markus as he approached the small group.

Markus nodded his head in affirmation, adding *He does, she does not,* while Cenellot and Noyette stared at the elf.

Cenellot was surprised to hear the foreign thoughts in his own head as if he were a Clairdani. *I am glad to see you well,* Florenço continued, this time to Cenellot. *I am relieved to know you can speak with the Clairdani. Now that you are one of the Enlightened, we can acknowledge you and perhaps even give you aide.*

Sensing that she was missing something in the looks the three were giving each other, she asked, "Cenellot, what are they saying? Can you understand him like you understand Markus?"

"Yes," came Cenellot's curt but kind reply as he looked to his mother. He then turned back to the stranger.

Cenellot's mind suddenly caught on one word he had heard. *We? Are there more of you? What are you? I've never seen a creature such as you before.*

I am an elf, a fairie type of being with similar features to humans and yet very different lives and strengths. We have been in this area since the beginning of this forest In fact, it was our song that brought it into existence. Unlike humans, who tend to live as far away from nature as possible, we are part of nature, each helping the other in our mutual survival.

Cenellot took the opportunity to study Florenço more closely. There was something green about him beyond his simple brownish-green tunic that seemed woven from leaves. His hair was long, straight and held back by a simple band possibly made of vine, and he wore a simple type of pointy-toed moccasin. Otherwise, his thin, wiry arms and legs were bare, and he didn't seem very old. His mother had told him about Florenço but seeing it for himself solidified his image of who this was.

Can I ask you how old you are? You know so much, although you don't seem any older than my mother.

A gentle smirk crossed Florenço's face. *I'm much older than I look. We elves do not age as humans do and do not die naturally. We are still mortal, although, without war, we each live many eons.*

That thought was hard to really comprehend and would take time to sink in. Cenellot gave a head nod to accept the answer and asked a more general question.

What do you mean about the Enlightened? Is that what this connection is?

Markus answered this time. *We refer to the humans that speak with us as the Enlightened since their eyes have grown lighter in color, and they seem to have a light within them. Being able to communicate with both Clairdani and Tenenbrani, the Enlightened are also our link with other humans, and we work together towards a victory over the Tenenbrani.*

There was a wealth of unspoken meaning in that statement, and many more questions left to be asked.

What are the Tenenbrani? Was the biggest question. *Are they a different group of people I haven't seen yet?*

The Tenenbrani, or 'dark creatures' are the creatures that destroy others. These are the creatures that maim and kill and are the source of all the terror in the area. Those of us who are helpful are called the Clairdani, or 'light creatures' since we are doing all we can to rid our land of the Tenenbrani.

Markus didn't seem like he was going to explain anymore the moment, so Cenellot moved on to the next question, this time to Florenço.

We've been working with Markus for a long while now. Why wasn't that enough before? What do you mean by 'acknowledging our existence'? Haven't you helped us and thus acknowledged us in that way?

Florenço ducked his head as if in shame. *Normally, we are forbidden to contact humans by the ancient laws. When you were moved into our forest, we needed to watch you to ensure that you did no damage to the forest. The various Clairdani worked with us to verify that you were not dangerous and that there would be no interference from us. When you were poisoned through your ignorance, I was moved to help you. I was not allowed to interfere with your progress, though, so I could only give you the correct herbs.*

We speak regularly with the Clairdani, and anyone who also is in close communication with them. Since you have now joined in that number, you are also welcome. He looked suspiciously at Noyette, who returned the look with a suspicious stare of her own.

Annoyed by the silent communication of looks transpiring between the three of them, she spoke up.

"Cenellot, what's going on! You three seem to be playing a shifty eyes game. You make me nervous!"

Thus reminded of his mother, Cenellot startled out of his reverie. After looking at both Florenço and Markus and nodding, he told his mother everything he remembered Florenço saying. Satisfied for the moment, Noyette relapsed into silence, standing even closer to Cenellot for assurance.

Florenço continued, pausing after each sentence to allow Cenellot to translate for his mother. *I will report to our king and let him know of this development. You would be safer closer to the elves, and I will request his permission for such a move.*

Cenellot, do not tell your mother this: if she doesn't learn how to speak with the Clairdani, there may be little I can do for her. It's not something you can force. It comes from a true desire and love for all others, not just a desire to speak and make yourself heard. Do you understand?

Cenellot nodded his head imperceptibly and translated to his mother, "he says the king can be difficult, so we must expect some delay and be on our best behavior."

"We can live here just fine on our own, as we've shown. We now know which berries and dangers to avoid, and there haven't been any creatures around other than you, Markus…"

141

Markus shook his head. *There is more danger than you know. It is because the elves protect this forest that you are safe here. If your presence brings the Tenenbrani or other threats to the forest, the elfin king will kill you rather than protect you. His hatred of humans runs very deep, and he will never sacrifice his people to protect you. Why does a fairie group we have never even known hate us so much? Surely no one we know has done anything to harm them or this forest to earn this wrath?*

Cenellot saw Markus and Florenço share a look, but the only thing Cenellot saw in his mind was war, blood, and death. Having never heard of any wars, this must have been many generations ago!

Markus had a few parting words to share. *I'm glad to see you are healed, and now that Florenço can help you, I know you will be safe. I will only come now if there is trouble. I am needed around Tomar to keep the Tenenbrani away from the town. They have grown bolder lately, and all of us are working to halt their rampage. Some have converted to our side through the Enlightened's work, but their numbers seem to be growing unnaturally, and each day brings a new conflict somewhere. In Tomar, the Enlightened are in danger from the Inquisitor and dare not meet outside lest another person be captured and tortured in gaol. It is not going well. We have to find an end to the Tenenbrani terror and find peace!*

Did my father start a war between Clairdani and Tenenbrani" Cenellot's eyes gleamed with pride in his father's significance and concern for what lay ahead.

No. He was just one piece of this craziness. This has existed as long as we remember and has increased with the arrival of the Inquisitor. We are trying to discover his past and why his presence might be drawing evil to Tomar, but no one has any information. After a pause, he restarted his exit. *Do as Florenço tells you, be strong, learn as much as you can. If you get into trouble and Florenço isn't nearby, call any bird to you and tell it about your troubles, and it will find one of us to help you. Stay well!* And with that final salute, Markus turned and quickly disappeared under the trees.

A more friendly routine that included Florenço commenced for the next few weeks. The three shared much laughter and more smiles as Florenço attempted to teach Cenellot how to use a wooden sword and walk with them every day through the forest to point out edible fungi, berries, and roots that became their new staple for life. Each shared their own lives – Noyette told Florenço about her husband and all the things she admired about him, and Florenço told her of his people, using Cenellot to translate. To make this less awkward, Florenço attempted to teach Noyette some of his language, and she began to use the elfin words more and more, to his delight.

One day, Florenço attempted to explain how far away the elfin lands were in the forest, and Noyette grew curious. In elfish, she haltingly asked and used hand gestures to help explain her thought, *"Why do we not move closer to the elves? It would be easier for you, yes?"*

"I don't mind the travel every day."

"But you alone watch over us now and are not with your fellow elves. They need you, yes?"

"Yes, but the elves are very distrustful of your race, and if you were too close, they may see it as an attack and kill you."

Noyette took a while to process this last bit. *"How would they know? If we could smell more like you, speak the language, and stay hidden and far enough away that no one would see us?"* That was a lot of *"ifs"*. Why did this have to be complicated?

Florenço stood silent for a long time, gazing into the distance. Finally, he spoke. *"It might be possible, but we would have a lot of work to do. You and Cenellot would need to be elves in all but physical appearance: mannerisms, language, bearing, what you eat, and swordsmanship, for Cenellot. Amongst my people, even the females are able to wield swords, so you will need to at least be able to hold one as if you knew how to use it."*

"But..." Noyette started to interrupt. Florenço silenced her with a look, then continued.

"When we accomplish all of this, I will talk to the King. Not before."

Cenellot finished with his morning chores of hauling water and collecting berries, tubers, and fungi from the forest. He still had to show everything to Florenço before he was allowed to eat any of it, and his knowledge of which berries were poisonous had significantly improved these past couple of weeks. The review no longer required an hour of discussion and caution, and only one or two berries had been tossed out this past week. Sensing the small tension that follows a momentous decision, his eyes darted between his mother and Florenço. *"What happened?"*

"Nothing, dear. We were only discussing the possibility of being closer to the elves, where we might be safer, and be around a community...."

Cenellot whooped in glee and knocked over his forest collection of edibles.

Florenço smiled and shook his head. *The boy will need a LOT of training. He is so uncoordinated!*

Stooping to help Cenellot recollect their food for the day, she cautioned, "It won't happen anytime soon. We need to be able to blend in with them, which will take a lot of work."

"Indeed. Starting today. We must only use my tongue, and I will teach you how to bathe before breakfast."

And so the work began.

Chapter 21: A Frightful Escape

The dungeons were full of frightened parents, worried both about their own children still at home and their own. There wasn't an obvious connection between any of them or order or rationale as to who was being tortured. As womanly screams filled the dungeons, the remaining prisoners either tried to stay calm or were crazed about the fates of their loved ones. Xofre and Mercurio sat with the other prisoners, doing their best to give each other courage and hope. Their own daughter, Luz, had suddenly disappeared a few years ago, and they had told the authorities that a Tenenbrani had carried her away. There were so many such disappearances that they hoped it would be believable. They knew she was not dead and did not believe that the Tenenbrani were all evil.

Towards evening, a guard unlocked their cell and grabbed them roughly into the corridor. After a few minutes of stumbling in the dark on the rough-hewn flooring, they were shoved into a dimly lit room and seated across a desk from the Inquisitor. They tried to hide their surprise – they had expected a torture table and instruments, not a civil discussion with The Inquisitor! Wary, they sat down while the guard stood behind them.

Much after dark, Xofre and Mercurio were allowed to leave and walk home. They had remembered the story they gave the authorities those many years ago. Although seemingly sympathetic, the Inquisitor kept pushing about their knowledge of the creatures around – both the Tenenbrani and the Clairdani. He seemed to have expertise beyond the usual citizen of the area, and his questions were very perceptive. They feigned ignorance and fear of all creature activity in their town and were allowed to return home … unharmed. However, the questions asked definitely pointed to a renewed, intense search for the Advocate. Murcurio only dared to say one phrase to his wife that evening: "Tomorrow, we see Simão."

After interrogating multiple couples, some more intensely than others, Ma'elrich had released all of them with strict instructions to a few of the guards to tail them quietly over the next few days with reports every day. Overall, the interactions had been fruitless, and perhaps another feint was in order. If he left, pretending to follow a lead, that may lure the Traitors into meeting, and he could get many of them at once. A plan formulated in his mind.

However, he could do the remaining transcriptions of the codex and searching the surrounding area from his own residence, where he would be surrounded by people he already controlled and not this cursed town. If only he had learned the whereabouts of the traitor's wife and child, he might have been able to have more fun before he left. That would have to wait another day, he supposed.

A week later, after more harried random searches and watching for traitors in the city square, the sun rose to find the inquisitor outside the Magistrate's house, finishing his packing for his return journey. Seeing the sudden move to leave, Rowan, the Magistrate, was equally relieved and concerned. "You are leaving, then? So suddenly? At least allow me to give you a coach for your comfort." And without waiting for approval, Rowan motioned to his manservant, who quickly alerted the livery that a coach would be needed immediately.

"It's really not necessary, Rowan…"

"I insist. We all know too many creatures attack outside the town's walls, and I would be remiss to let such an important visitor leave without additional protection!"

Ma'alrich grunted as he cinched his large brocade sack, taking it off the larger of his two horses. The magistrate wasn't sure if that was an affirmation or not, so he continued. "I had hoped that once you'd found any evidence, you would share it with me. Remember our agreement?"

The inquisitor stopped unpacking and stared dispassionately at his co-conspirator. Again, unsure of his meaning, the magistrate tried to achieve a less enigmatic response. "When might you be returning so we can have your rooms prepared?"

At that moment, his coachman arrived out of breath, interrupting their conversation briefly, and Ma'elrich gave no indication of a response. Rowan signaled to the bags and instructed him on their handling and destination.

The arrival of the coach and activity drew quite a few spectators from the town. While the Coachman readied the horses and coach, Ma'elrich pulled Rowan aside conspiratorially. "My work here is finished, actually." He allowed the concept to penetrate as he watched Rowan's face change from worry to delight. He continued, "I was able to really get into the codex yesterday and read some of the entries last night. There wasn't much there – we caught up with him too early, honestly."

He took a deep breath as if to relieve his frustrations in the case. "It seems the traitor was angry about the misfortunes of the town, which he felt we deserved. He had joined forces with these Traitors to help punish us for our own wickedness." A flash of red-gold flashed in Ma'elrich's

148

eyes, and disappeared just as quickly. Ma'elrich blinked, seemingly unaware of it.

Seeing this, Rowan couldn't look away from Ma'elrich's face, and the seed of mistrust planted itself deeper in Rowan's soul. Briefly, Rowan scanned the townspeople in the area to see if anyone else had seen the flash. None seemed to be willing to look anyone of authority in the eyes. Quite the opposite – they did everything possible to seem busy and look everywhere else.

Sensing the distrust in his counterpart, Ma'elrich continued. "Come now, brother! Trust me! In the end, the traitor earned the death he received, and Tomar is better off without him. As for the other traitors, the attacks these past few moon cycles seem to have rid your town of most of them, so you are clear." Striding to the coach, which had been hastily packed and readied for the two-day journey, Ma'elrich glanced back at Rowan. "I will return if you decide that anything else is needed of me."

He climbed into the coach, then looked down at Rowan and proffered his hand. "I want to thank you sincerely for your… 'hospitality' and will gladly return the favor if you are ever in my care. If you need me again, you know how to reach me. I will hope that the example made here will keep any remaining Traitors from acting in the open again."

The two men grasped forearms and held tightly for a few moments, and Ma'elrich released his hand to sit down and allowed the coachman to close the coach. A small gathering of townspeople waved their goodbyes at him, happier to be rid of him than out of any sense of loss. The coach set off slowly, carefully maneuvering around the tight corners and small alleys between the grand center and the outskirts of the town. Once on the main thoroughfare between the market and the gate, they were able to move more quickly, knowing that they might only be safe as long as it was daylight.

Rowan stood, staring at the departing figure, wondering if bringing Ma'elrich here had been a waste of time. What had he actually accomplished other than killing his best gaoler and family? He had tortured some of the townspeople and made an enemy of many... could he use that somehow to his advantage? In his many solar cycles in the town, he had yet to make any headway with the creatures or the traitors.

He had hoped that having the Advocate in his gaol might weaken their resolve. They might have tried to rescue her so he would be able to destroy them all at once and be finished with it, but neither had happened. Since the Advocate had appeared, it was true that there had been slightly fewer attacks. Supposedly, she had powers, although he hadn't noticed any in his office when she came to confront him, and she was easily overpowered and imprisoned. *People will follow anyone if it means hope...* Still, he himself hadn't engendered that type of loyalty amongst the people, and he remembered a time before the Advocate arrived.

On the road at last, Ma'elrich was slowly feeling more himself in the fresh air outside the town. As they rumbled down the rough cobblestone road, Ma'elrich pulled out the Codex, excited about his new plan. There were too many curious people in the town, and he needed his secrecy if he was going to truly find the Advocate and wipe out the Traitors. They had been the cause of his dwindling population, he was sure, although he didn't know how. His false farewell would hopefully lead them to a sense of complacency, and he would get to see how they truly were once he set up his observation points.

Around noon, he pulled down the oiled skin window and asked that they stop so he could relieve himself in peace rather than along the bumps and ruts in the road.

"It's not safe, milord. Anywhere beyond the walls, Tomar and the Fortified Cities are haunted by creatures that will kill you day and night. We need to press on for safety."

"I could have you whipped for your subordination, Coachman. You will stop because I ask you to stop. If you don't feel safe, you may stay here at the coach while I go out. I will take care of myself, I promise you. Nothing will harm me."

Reluctantly, the coachman stopped the coach and dropped to the ground. Haltingly, he scanned the area and then opened the door to the coach. "As you wish, milord."

He opened the door, then stood aside, with his arm outstretched to help the Inquisitor down from the coach. The Inquisitor refused any help, jumping slightly to the ground, a bag of food in his hand. "I would stay within sight of the coach while you eat. I will stay here with my quarterstaff in case anything comes at us... Where are you going? Didn't you hear me? The woods aren't safe!"

The Inquisitor didn't seem to care about the warnings and wandered beyond the wood's edge, following a deer path deeper into the woods. Resigned, the coachman muttered choice expletives but stayed at the coach, ready to fight or leave as soon as possible. Given the choice, he would return the coach to Tomar as soon as possible. The Inquisitor would be getting what he deserved, after all. *He certainly won't be missed in Tomar, with all his threats and interrogations of innocent people.*

The horses were getting restless. *Of course, as soon as he disappears, something would happen! Where IS he!?* Refocusing on the Inquisitor, he tried to see if he could still hear him or if he had gone too far into the wood. There was *something*, although it didn't sound like casual human steps. He held his quarterstaff in a crouched-ready position, listening more carefully. The stones on the road shook slightly, then shook a bit more. Various images came to mind of the various creatures he'd encountered and glimpsed over the years, although only a few were large enough to cause the ground to shake. Fumbling with his quarterstaff, he tore the door of the coach open, looked to see if the Inquisitor was coming, and then shut the door. He was able to fit inside the hidden compartment in the seat of the coach, which hopefully would be too hard for whatever it was to open. Silently, he prayed to any deities he could remember from his stories.

As soon as he had disappeared into the coach, a large shadow loomed in the forest. It took on form as it neared the coach, and its rasping and growling would have frozen the coachman in terror if he had heard it. As if waiting for a storm, the coachman held a hand over his mouth to keep himself from crying out and listened to the pounding of its legs as it drew closer. Even with the weight of the coach and the luggage, the coach shook at each step. He tried not to think of the horses as a sacrificial offering, although hopefully, the creature would be sated after eating them and leave him alone...

The coach was suddenly covered in shadow, and a coldness crept into the coach. He could hear its breath as it sniffed around the area. The horses were making enough noise now that there was no way this creature could miss them. *A good distraction, at least...*

THUD. Suddenly the coach dropped a bit and seemed to sag. *Did it jump onto the coach?* Then, long claws scratched at the windows, doors, and canopy, scattering the luggage all around the area. A huge tearing noise announced the canopy ripping apart, and claws were tearing at the inside of the coach, just over his hiding spot. He would be found any minute now... *Well, luckily, I won't have to worry about a bathroom break now. And hopefully, the horses smell enough to cover up this stench!*

Just as suddenly, the creature seemed to stop and sense something else because it leapt off the coach and continued running away from the wood. *Was there something ELSE out here? What could be worse than that??*

He had a sense of another presence nearby, despite the absence of growls, claws, or heavy footfalls. It just seemed to be watching and waiting... After it seemed that the sun's heat was coming from the other side of the coach, he decided it might be safe enough to peak and see if the coast was clear. He couldn't see any dangers within the coach, so he climbed out of the bench and peaked over the gouged windowsills. *Nothing outside the coach... even the horses had settled down, and one was still alive somehow*! He glanced toward where the creature had gone and thought he saw a glint of wings in the sky and nothing more.

Breathing in deep relief, he climbed out of the coach to check on the horses. One was beyond help. The other was badly torn into and could possibly survive. He looked around to see if he could find something to stitch the gauged wounds. He tried to calm the horse in preparation for the additional pain, and settling himself on the ground, he looked at the wounds again to determine where to begin stitching. The wounds were already healing! They had new skin around them, looked at least a week old, and had no signs of putrification! Checking the horse again, he decided he would be well enough to bring back the coach slowly. Slowly was better than walking by foot, which would help get him home to Tomar. He climbed back into the driver's bench and, with a sharp snap of the reins, turned the horse team around and headed back to Tomar without another thought about the Inquisitor's fate.

Chapter 22: Meeting in the Forge

After many moon cycles of worrying about the Inquisitor's Terror, as the period was referred to later in history, the villagers tried not to be too exuberant about the sudden departure of The Inquisitor. The speed was a bit unsettling. He hadn't left while he was ranting about snakes during multiple attacks in the town, but he would quit after torturing and releasing townsfolk. While the regular townsfolk may have fancied that their magistrate finally had rid the town of him, there were a few who were more suspicious. Mercurio watched the departure with great interest, staying out of direct sight of the Inquisitor. His naturally suspicious nature heightened after their questioning and release, and he considered the sudden departure a trap. "Vengeful people never leave before they have their revenge. He must have left a mission behind. Stay on your guard!" He would warn anyone who asked and tried to enlist others to be watchful of the guards. If some had been tasked with continuing the Reign of Terror, there would hopefully be some indications upon his departure.

Elders and children alike watched the events in silence as the coach gathered speed toward the open gate, expecting it to turn around at any moment with last-moment threats. The gates shut behind the coach, and the townspeople collectively seemed to hold their breath until the sound of hooves no longer echoed along the town walls. The townsfolk dispersed slowly, wary lest the coach suddenly return. Mercurio watched the guards during the dispersal. None of the guards seemed to be lingering or watching the people as they had been for these past weeks. Although most of them were grim-faced, a few of the guards struggled to hide their gleefulness at the departure, and these guards weren't all part of the enlightened.

Mercurio took the circuitous route home, first joining the town in the tavern to celebrate their renewed freedom. As he entered, he waved at Noé, the tavern owner, busily tapping ale for his customers. About half the townsfolk in the tavern were lightly restrained in their drinking, the other half raucous in their bawdy humor. How easily they seemed to have forgotten the terrors of the past moon cycles! The additional guards, patrols, check-ins, and searches to participate or attend the daily markets... and despite *or perhaps because of* all the focus on finding "The Traitors," the number of new Tenenbrani outbreaks and attacks had increased! There were so many Tenenbrani outside the walls that it seemed that they had their own patrols mirroring their own! *When will they realize the Traitors are not the ones creating the terror?* He wondered. As he looked around, he nodded to his compatriots and neighbors. The sudden apparent return to their old lives required some adjustment, some needing more liquid lubrication than others to restart.

As the beer ran dry, the tavern cleared out. Most were able to exit on their own power. Some were collective efforts to get in the general direction of home. Deep in his own thoughts and beer, Mercurio said goodbye to most of his fellow patrons before he rose himself. Suddenly, the door slammed open, and the coachman roared at the barman. "whatever you've got hidden, I need it! Now!"

Not a drunkard normally, the coachman ambled towards the bar and sat at the closest stool. Noé, gesturing for the barman to go clean up the tables, brought over a large mug of beer, an unlabeled bottle of fire whiskey, and a smaller glass, which he put on the table. He still held the unlabeled bottle in his hand as he sat down opposite the coachman.

"Tell me the 'cashun, and I'll see how much of dis ya git," declared Noé.

The coachman took a long drag of beer, setting it down with emphasis. "The Inquisitor's gone."

"Yep, we knowed dat. You droved 'im out dis mornin;," droned Noé, unimpressed.

"No. I mean, the Inquisitor is GONE. He wanted to stop to relieve himself after a while, and he walked off despite my warnings. He wandered off deep into the thicket, and instead of returning, some wild monster charged out of the forest right where he had been! This thing had fangs, long limbs, large claws, matted, black hair... and I just had enough time to climb into the coach itself before it was upon me! It clawed at the coach and roared at me, then suddenly left. Not before it attacked the horses, though, and it killed one! I was able to resuscitate the other horse, who was less wounded. Thankfully, though, I was able to get the reins back in my hands and get us both back here as best we could. Maybe The Inquisitor managed to hide, but I'm betting that the monster ate him first, then came for us or whatever else smelled like him. I can't imagine how else I got away with my life!" explained the coachman animatedly.

Noé held the whiskey bottle, weighing how much to give him for the tale. After some deliberation, he poured the small cup to the brim and put the glass in front of the coachman.

"So he's rilly goan t'en?"

"As far as we are concerned, yep!" The coachman downed the small glass contents for effect, and when he returned it to the table, the tavern owner refilled it.

"With that news, I'll be leaving," Mercurio announced and walked towards the door. As he passed the last table before the door, he noticed a symbol hastily drawn in chalk. It was their call mark, calling them to a meeting.

Taking a moment to read the details and erase the mark, he covered his delay by addressing the two men left in the bar. "Good night, all, and may your dreams be as sweet as the news!"

The coachman and tavern owner saluted his departure with their mugs, not noticing his movements.

With the streets now mostly deserted, with only drunk townsfolk for observers, Mercurio wasn't overly cautious about his route or surroundings on his way to Simão's forge. It only took a fraction of the usual time he normally took, even with checking a couple of times for anyone following him. When he arrived, the forge's main room was dark, and only a small lighter area flickered where the steps to the basement were. After listening closely, he decided the meeting must be in full swing, so after checking up and down the street, he quickly opened the door and slid inside. The basement was mostly full by the time he arrived, so he stopped near the bottom step as quietly as he could.

"... these past moon cycles. Any volunteers?" Simão concluded.

No one offered, and after a couple of minutes, a brave hand rose.

"I have a question first." In response to a deep nod, the volunteer continued. "So, after all this time since The Advocate's escape, why haven't we heard from her? Is she dead, or did she give up? Why hasn't she come help fight the surge of Tenenbrani that followed his evil to our town?"

A murmur of agreement followed, and Simão gestured to get them to settle down and listen.

"As I was saying, we haven't heard anything yet. However, that doesn't mean that she is dead or giving up. Even with the increase in Tenenbrani, at least one Clairdani would have been able to get us a message if something significant had happened to her."

Simão waited for a moment for the crowd to accept his logic. "She was badly hurt while in prison and has probably been recovering. She is in good hands and will send us a message when she is ready, hopefully with a new plan to help stop the increasing number of townsfolk transforming."

"That didn't go so well last time now, did it? Wasn't that how she ended up in prison in the first place?" shouted a dissenter, followed by nervous laughter and loud agreement.

"We don't know what happened exactly. For some reason, her abilities were not able to work on the Magistrate. Maybe he's something we haven't encountered before." More murmurs. "Regardless, we will need a different plan to get the city council to stop demonizing us. Until we hear from her, and unless she has information about the Magistrate, we need to work with the Clairdani to clear the forest surrounding us and determine who the prime suspects are that are drawing them in."

"So first, do we have patrol volunteers to connect with the Clairdani about the status of the Tenenbrani in the Forest? Find out if they are withdrawing from the area or waiting for something first?"

While Simão spoke, Mercurio raised his hand slowly. Thinking he was a volunteer, Simão had to call him out.

"Mercurio, I appreciate your enthusiasm, although I need a patrol here."

"I'm not volunteering. I have important news."

Amidst the murmurs and sudden turning of all eyes on Mercurio, Simão gestured for him to tell all.

"Before I left the tavern, the coachman returned from his trip. He says The Inquisitor is gone, never to return again. Not gone to another village, but perhaps eaten by a Tenenbrani – his words, not mine. According to the coachman, shortly after The Inquisitor entered the forest to do his business, a huge monster galloped into the clearing and attacked the coach. Slashed at both horses, then clawed at the coach until it grew tired and left. He had just returned with the one horse he was able to revive when he came to the tavern."

"Hmm… perhaps the Tenenbrani have a new member, then?" Simão shouted over the loud murmurs that erupted at the story's end.

"It would make sense – there were reports of his eyes flashing black, and there was an increase in the number of attacks, just like there are when one of our townsfolk becomes a Tenenbrani," Matteo said out loud. As one of the guards, he had seen The Inquisitor more than others had and knew more of his personal details.

The room was filled with nodding heads as if all their necks had been replaced with springs recently set in motion.

"I think it makes having a patrol contact that much more important. There shouldn't have been the surge of Tenenbrani that we saw recently, even with the couple of morphs that came from here. After this long pause, we can let them know what we know about The Inquisitor, as a starting point. Ask that they look out for him and have them find out about his creature if that is indeed what happened." Simão began searching the crowd, hoping for a volunteer. Matteo caught his eye.

"I'll be going with you," began Matteo. "Discreet as we have to be, it would be good to have two Enlightened out there with our message, double the chances we get the message through. I also think we need to see if they know anything about the additional Tenenbrani. Are they connected somehow to the ones we've been fighting for years, or did they come from somewhere else? Has our Ring of Protectors been destroyed or compromised?"

With Matteo's words, the Enlightened grew bolder. A few hands went up, and Simão was pleased.

"Thank you. Stay behind, please, and the rest of you know the departure routine."

As they slowly left up the stairs to depart the forge in pairs or alone along deserted streets, Simão and Matteo huddled with the four volunteers.

"Just start slow. It's been a while since we've been allowed beyond the walls. One of you leave the mark, and the rest of you can follow up at your next patrol time. We aren't in a rush, so stay vigilant above all else! Without The Advocate's help, we are only catching up on what we know from their perspective."

All agreed. These last ones also joined the last people at the top of the stairs. Matteo hung back.

Matteo whispered, "have you heard any more about Rowen's Codex...?"

"No, nothing. We can hope that with the morph, The Inquisitor won't be able to decipher any more of it. Do you know if he left it at the goal, by chance?"

"I'll look. If he had it with him when he left Clod Tomar, it could also still be in his luggage. I'll have my guards relocate his bags to the goal as well so I can search them myself."

Matteo looked closely at his friend, seeing an unwarranted tenseness in his eyes. "What aren't you telling me, Simão?"

"Beyond the Codex being written in code, it may have been everything The Advocate told Rowan while in goal. If so, the Inquisitor may know more than many of us do about her whereabouts and was harassing all of us, trying to find the connections here to bring her back into town. That may have been where he was going when he transformed."

Matteo cursed. "Then we will need more help. If she's still recovering, and the Inquisitor knows where she is, she might not live for much longer."

"Exactly, Matteo, exactly. Let's hope we can find the Codex and figure out how much he could decipher. And Matteo, pray the Advocate has recovered enough to save herself for now."

Chapter 23: A New Beginning in an Old Place

After a few days of travel, the Inquisitor finally returned to his homestead. With the coach, horses, and everything gone, he had walked along the high road for most of the day, eventually finding an inn with some bed space for a weary traveler. A simple meal of slightly moldy cheese, crusty bread already being enjoyed by a couple of weevils, and warm, flat beer was provided, and he accepted it with a quiet sneer. By paying attention to the patrons around him, he was able to determine which ones were headed towards Clod Pollux and secured a spot in a goat cart going that direction.

Right away, Ma'elrich wondered if walking might be the better option, even with the wear on the feet. The small wooden cart was pulled by two goats and had one seat for its owner. He didn't think he'd drunk that much the night before, but he must have done so, or he wouldn't have missed that the owner didn't smell any different than the goats and had just as much hair! There was a small space in the cart that he could fit into only by wrapping his arms around his legs or by letting his legs hang off the edge, which had its own clearance issue with larger objects on the road.

All along the road, rather than talk to the driver or other commoners who sometimes walked alongside the cart, Ma'elrich kept reliving his last moments in Tomar and his departure. There was something that irked him about it, although he couldn't quite determine what it was. Thankfully, the townspeople seemed satisfied with his story, which suggested he was giving up on his work. No problems there. *There was something else, something I've overlooked... I'll have to think on it again later.* It was difficult to think clearly between the stench, the large rocks that blocked the road or threatened to overturn the cart, and the commoners who insisted on having conversations with him regardless of his rude silence.

After a day of dealing with goats and commoners, Ma'elrich staggered out of the cart, waved a general thanks in the direction of the driver, and hobbled the remaining stretch home. In his filth and stench, he was thankfully unrecognizable and left alone until he could wash off the travel grime. As he entered his palace under his manservant's watering brown eyes, he ambled straight to his washroom and asked the help to burn the clothes as he was peeling them off of himself.

Tall and slender with a tendency to disappear when viewed sideways, the manservant, Rabicho, gladly took the clothes to the kitchen fire, where he had started preparing dishes as soon as he saw Ma'elrich coming through the gate. The grime, sweat, and other unknowns that had become part of the garments changed the flames occasionally to blue or green, announced by small explosions. As the last of the threads turned to ash, Rabicho placed the finishing touches on the various dishes he had prepared for his master, Ma'elrich. Fruits from the orchard and freshly made cheeses purchased that week at the market would help soothe his travel woes and restore his better humor... hopefully.

Sealed back in his own workspace, Ma'elrich accepted the proffered meal with orders not to be disturbed for any reason. He was eager to continue decoding the codex and ready to begin the real work he needed to do to finally destroy the nest of Traitors – a gang that had killed his father and left him orphaned so many years ago. Maybe if his father hadn't been destroyed and his family obliterated that night, he might not have become what he was…

He checked the moon cycle once more. While traveling, he was careful not to open the codex, and the forest had shielded them from a clear view of the moon. He hadn't noticed a lot of moonlight while they slept, giving him hope that the moon would be on the right day of the cycle to illuminate the next page of the codex. Curse the creatures that only used moonlight at night and made him wait for more answers!

In his new routine, Ma'elrich slept much of each day, awaking at dusk to set to work for a night of transcribing, much as he had done in Tomar. It didn't seem that the gaoler wrote every night, meaning that each page wasn't always the next day of the moon cycle. He had already waited seven days to find the right moonlight to illuminate the writing for this one particular day, and his hopes ran high that tonight's moon was right. The inquisitor's eagerness counterpointed the melancholy of a room dimly lit by the light of the waxing quarter moon. The middle pages of the codex in front of him, he relished his goblet of wine while he set to reading and transcribing the next piece of this traitor's manuscript. So far, it had only spoken of her childhood in Tomar and distant past events. He hoped this next part would help give a reason for the gaoler's treason and more clues about where the Advocate went when she left Tomar and perhaps her current whereabouts.

While he waited, he thought about Rowan and Tomar. Had he thanked the magistrate well enough that he would be welcome back once he finished uncovering all the secrets of the traitorous society that lay in secret in Tomar? He had dreamed of his revenge on these people for so many years! *Revenge could be so sweet!*

At last, the moonlight stole into the room, highlighting the codex. The open page began to shimmer, and writing appeared! Sighing a deep breath of anticipation, he began reading what seemed to be a new phase of the gaoler's mindset, writing as quickly as he could:

I've decided that these Traitors are not the cause of the attacks in Tomar. Rather, they are trying to prevent them. They are kind and well-meaning, not cruel and vindictive as the Magistrate believes. I will have to discover a means of communicating with them to let them know I want to help them end these attacks...

Chapter 24: A Star Sapphire

With Anehta back next to Luz, her strength returned quickly, and she was able to return to her training. Determined to help Tomar defend itself against the Tenenbrani, she needed to find her fighting strength again and determine how to counteract the Magistrate's power-dampening abilities. As she regained her strength, Metulas repeatedly asked her to recount her meeting with the Magistrate to uncover any clues as to why her powers had failed her. Where had she been in the room? Was there anyone else there? Was there anything not from Tomar in the room? Did she feel any difference in one part of the room than another, or just in the whole room itself? Together, they guessed that the Magistrate had power-dampening abilities himself. It had to be something near him, although there was no lore about such objects that Metulas knew about. Also, if he truly had powers, then creatures near him would have been destroyed or weakened, wouldn't they? Furthermore, if he knew they were weakened, wouldn't he have boasted about his accomplishments and been able to provide more protection to the townspeople? After figuring out at least this much, when she wasn't training with Metulas, these thoughts continued to cycle through her mind. Awakening one day to find that Metulas wasn't anywhere to be seen, Luz had to ask. "Anehta, where's Metulas?"

"He said he needed to see Dawn from a new angle and left," Anehta replied. "It didn't make any sense to me either, but that's dragons for you. It's not like he hasn't seen a million Dawns in his lifetime now, right?"

"So, are you training with me today then? Or would you rather wait til he returns?" Luz challenged while she rummaged around for her quarterstaff to practice with her friend. "He IS coming back today, right?"

Anehta shrugged, then flew into the cave, alighting on the bed.

"Do you remember where my quarterstaff is? I thought it was behind the bedding here somewhere, but it's not there."

"No, I haven't seen it, although I can try to help look."

After a while of turning everything over and moving things away from the walls, Luz felt she was hearing whispers coming from the back of the cave. It was very quiet, and even as she approached, the whispers didn't get any louder. There wasn't room for anyone in the space, so perhaps there was a shaft to a neighboring cave they didn't know was occupied.

"Anehta, did anyone else come live here while I was gone? I hear voices from somewhere."

"No one ever comes here… what voices?"

"Come closer. Maybe you have to be here to hear them."

Anehta flew the short distance, landing on Luz's shoulder. Listening as best she could, she still heard nothing except their breathing.

"Nope, I don't hear anything. You sure it's voices, and not just the wind? You know how it makes those whispering sounds sometimes."

"I know what I'm hearing, and it's not windy out today." Moving closer to the back of their cave, she added, "It's coming from here, somewhere…"

As she closed in on the sound, she lifted a few blankets to search behind them. Not only was the quarterstaff there, there was a perfectly faceted blue heart-shaped sapphire about the size of her palm. As she looked at the stone, the color swirled inside it, and she could hear indistinct whispers emanating from the stone. It was strangely warm in her palm, not cool like a stone normally would be.

"Hello, what is this?" Turning around to show her friend, she hoped for answers. "Anehta, have you ever seen this before?"

"Hmm.. no," she answered vaguely as she flew closer. "It doesn't look familiar to me." Peeking over Luz's shoulder mid-flight, she saw the staff lying on the floor. "You found your staff, let's go train. Ready?"

The sudden change of topic was very odd for Anehta, who was always curious about everything. Luz suspected she knew more than she was saying, although there were more ways to get Anehta talking than a direct challenge. Living with Anehta for years taught her that she would only conceal something when it was absolutely necessary. "Sure, let's go outside where there's more room and see if you can beat me."

Training with Anehta was not about physical strength. Her minuscule size made for better practice with the mind-body connection. As per their routine, Luz tied the cloth strip over her eyes, staff poised to strike, and stood motionless as if listening to the world. Anehta flew to a location nearby, tapping Luz on the head with her wing as she passed to let her know the game had started.

"Ok, catch me if you can!" Anehta taunted.

Anywhere Anehta flew, Luz sensed where she was and pointed to that location with her staff, tagging Anehta if they were close enough. With her intuitive ability to sense the Clairdani, Metulas had wondered if it were part of an intuitive sense that connected her to all other living beings. To test this theory, they had devised a game where Anehta would hover somewhere near Luz, and Luz would have to sense in which direction she was hovering. Initially, this had seemed an impossible task, with tears and too much self-doubt to begin to succeed. With much encouragement, she began to trust herself, and success followed. Now, after weeks of recuperation, Anehta flew only within a few yards of where Luz stood to ensure her strength had returned. Almost as soon as she stopped, Luz found her and tagged her. With a short hoot of joy, Anehta flew further away, back to the game they always played. The two almost seemed in a strange dance sequence, with the twirling, lunging, hopping, and short races across the land in Luz's pursuit of Anehta. It was almost as if Luz was able to watch Anehta's every move.

"OK, stop, please! I'm exhausted!" Anehta finally gasped, spiraling out of the air back towards the ground.

Staking the pole to the ground, Luz pulled the cloth from her eyes. Anehta landed on her shoulder and nestled against her neck.

"So, is the sapphire a present for me, then?" Luz smiled as she turned to look at her friend. She knew that unprepared, Anehta was more likely to say things she shouldn't.

"No, it's not a present..."

"So you DO know what it is, hm?" Luz retorted.

"What? Um, no, I mean, since I haven't ever seen it before, how could it be a present from me?" Anehta sighed.

Luz rolled her eyes. Of course, Anehta would hide the truth behind this statement. "So if it's not a present from you, is it one from Metulas?"

Anehta left her shoulder and alighted on a nearby bush. "No, it's not a present from him either. You know I'm terrible at this! You tricked me! I can't say another word about it. I gave my word. When the time is right, you will know what it is, and not from me."

"So this has to do with Metulas, not you?" Luz took a moment to scan the land for any signs of her largest friend returning. It was past time for his return, and the new mystery made her more anxious about his absence.

Almost to herself, she mumbled, "Why would Metulas need to hide this sapphire? Even if it were a present, we've never hidden presents before, or hidden information about the present to others. Besides, doesn't he have room in the gem vault behind his cave?"

"Anehta, can you answer questions that aren't exactly about the sapphire, maybe?"

"Maybe...?"

"So... when exactly did this sapphire appear?"

"I suppose that won't tell you much, so I can tell you that it appeared while you were imprisoned in Tomar. Honestly, Metulas suddenly appeared with it after another one of his mysterious flights, and other than knowing roughly where he hid it. I know nothing else about it."

"So is that why you all weren't able to come for me earlier? You were unavailable somewhere?"

Anehta shook her head. "It wasn't like that." They had been through this a few times before, and Metulas was much better at explaining why they hadn't come to rescue her when they should have. No one knew about Metulas, which was one of the biggest obstacles. As the last remaining dragon, Metulas did all he could to keep his existence a secret from everyone. Luz and Anehta had stumbled upon him, and as his only family, they kept the secret as their own.

"Weren't you with him, though? You aren't usually here by yourself..."

"You know that we both worried about you and wanted to rescue you immediately, of course!" Anehta raised a wing to give her friend as much of an embrace as she could. "When we heard you'd been captured, we all knew that if anyone could turn events in their favor, it would be you. You are so extremely special, Luz, and have abilities others could never even dream of! Your capture and inability to escape made us realize there was a whole other dimension to this problem, and we needed to make some discoveries for ourselves."

Luz's eyes stared into the horizon as she blinked away the memories of feeling abandoned during those weeks in the gaol.

Sensing her discomfort, Anehta flew back onto her shoulder. "I know it was truly horrific in gaol, ... we both knew!" Anehta gave her a half-embrace with one wing around the neck. "We also knew that since no one knew about the two of us, as long as you were there, the Tenenbrani and Magistrate wouldn't be looking for anyone else to make discoveries about how to stop or end the Tenenbrani. The very moment Metulas returned with that sapphire was when he told me the Inquisitor was coming, and we had to go rescue you."

A small tear ran down Luz's cheek, and Anehta brushed it away with her wing tip. After a deep sigh, Luz reached up to pat her friend. "So I hope you all were able to make some progress?? I know you have been watching over me while I've been healing, but we've been training for a long time now, and things only grow worse. Punishing the Enlightened didn't stop when I was imprisoned, and now with the Inquisitor... "Luz trailed off as she saw a large shadow flying towards them. *I wonder... if Metulas is getting his information from that direction, and the stone comes from that same direction... Maybe the stone is part of that knowledge?* "Anehta, is that where Metulas flies back from each time he's gone for his morning flights?"

Anehta looked at where Luz was pointing. "I think so? I wasn't always outside when he returned, so I didn't always see the exact place. It was always from that direction, though."

They had never gone east, towards where the sun rose each morning. The town was south of them, the denser forests to the Northeast, and it was only desert both west or east, like a river bed run dry that used to separate the town from the Batalha caves. "Anehta, what lies over there? Had you ever gone in that direction before you met me?"

"Me? No, I found Tomar much safer than being alone with the Tenenbrani out there. I'm just a little snack for most of them!"

Luz had to smile at that. It was so true that Anehta, as delightful as she was, was very much attracted to trouble. "Well then, how often does he go? This is the first time I've known him to go anywhere. Usually, he just sulks here near his cave, burning anything that gets too close..."

They both wondered if the desert between Tomar and Batalha had anything to do with an angry dragon trying to force distance between himself and the townspeople. Images of a large forest burning flashed in her mind, and she wondered briefly how many Clairdani and Tenenbrani had been there before. *Had they known about the dragon then? Did they still pass along that knowledge as if it were legend now?*

"You're right, Luz. I think he may have gone a couple of times since you've been recovering. He's usually back before anyone notices, though."

"What changed, Anehta?"

"What do you mean?"

"What made Metulas suddenly decide to leave his cave rather than just guess at answers like he usually does? He spent so much time training me to go to Tomar and rescue the town because he wouldn't be trusted as a dragon. Is this place that he visits where he is trusted? And if so, when did he find out about this other place?" *And what isn't he telling us?*

Anehta gave a shrug. She had no idea herself. Metulas rarely confided in her.

The shadowy figure of Metulas grew ever larger as he approached, and they watched in awe of his size and the luminousness of his scales in the morning sunlight. He landed heavily near them and folded in his gigantic silvery-grey wings. His fiery eyes connected with Luz's, exuding both love and peace. Luz rushed forward to embrace him around the neck, as far up as she could reach.

174

"Morning, Luz, Anehta. Fine morning for flying!"

"That it might be. Without us, though? You could have awoken us so we could enjoy it with you." Luz scolded.

Enigmatically, Metulas answered, "I needed to go alone."

"Why? What's over there that you don't want to share with us?"

Metulas only looked between the two of them, a question glinting in his eyes. They rested on the pole in Luz's hand.

Following his gaze, Luz looked at the pole and was reminded where she found it. With fierce determination in her eyes, she looked him in the eyes. "We found your sapphire, Metulas. You owe us a story, it seems."

Metulas glared at Anehta, who only shrugged back.

"I suppose you are right. I should tell you, both of you, since eventually, it will concern you and everyone else. I'd like to have the sapphire help me tell the story though, so…" Gesturing towards their mountainous abode, he offered a wing to help them onto his back. Luz climbed up easily, Anehta flying to her spot between his shoulder blades, and they flew the short distance back home.

Chapter 25: A Progression of Clues

Ma'elrich awoke towards midday. He had uncovered enough of the Codex to start a list of places the Advocate may be referring to, as well as some of the methods they used to communicate. Both were extremely helpful, and he was elated.

As Rabicho helped him dress for the day, Ma'elrich's mood intrigued him. He practically hummed to himself in his unusually happy state.

"We seem to be happy today, milord."

"Rabicho, indeed! Today, I begin my ultimate destruction of this Advocate of theirs by taking away everything that helps her in any way."

"Yes, milord."

Ma'elrich smiled. "I have it all planned out. First, I will visit these regions firsthand to determine which are the true lands of her creature supporters. Second, I will have to scout out these secret meeting locales closest to Tomar. Last, I will have to return to Tomar and root out the Traitors' lairs."

"That sounds very through, milord."

He finished his wardrobe with a traveling cloak.

"I'll be traveling for the next fortnight. For now, bring me as many ropes as you can find, and while I'm gone, work on creating a large cage that can hold about ten creatures. I'll begin here packing for my voyage and bring my standard traveling fare with the ropes."

"Very well, milord."

Before the sun had ascended far into the sky, Ma'elrich was already mounted, with everything securely packed. He sniffed the air, turning his head to help him determine which way to travel first.

"Be ready when I return, Rabicho. What I bring back with me will not be friendly."

"Safe travels, milord! Everything here will be ready. You have my word."

During the two-day ride between Clod Pollux and Tomar, he plotted to meander towards the desert lands mentioned in the Codex and capture any creatures he finds. He had learned that the Traitors could communicate with some of the creatures, although the methods here hadn't been explained in the Codex, and he needed to find out. *I've made a life of interrogating humans, but how do you get information out of other creatures?* Creatures weren't nearly as fun to interrogate as humans. They had a higher threshold for pain and didn't say very much he could understand anyway. He would have to start with capturing them and see if that breaks down their network enough to bring out other Traitors into the open.

As he traveled, he stayed as far away from human settlements and routes as possible. From the Codex, he learned that the Traitors called the creatures that they worked with "Clairdani" and the creatures that attacked the people of Tomar "Tenenbrani." *If the Clairdani have never attacked anyone in Tomar, what creatures might those be then?* Having only seen or heard of what seemed to be monstrous bears, oversized bats or vultures, basilisks, or enchanted wolves in Tomar, he wasn't sure what other creatures lurked in the forest or deserts.

A flash of orange caught his eye as a large, fiery-colored bird exploded into the sky away from its perch. *A phoenix!*

He started to ride after it but then thought better of it. *I'll be calm and pretend to be a friend of the forest. Then, when it returns, I can capture it when it least expects it.* He eased the pace of his horse and became more observant of the surrounding environment. He could feel himself being watched and forced himself to look straight ahead so as not to give anything the impression he was a predator in their midst.

At dusk, he set up camp, intentionally making noise as he prepared a small fire and cooked his dinner. He left his bags open, thinking a*ll eyes are curious. Perhaps I will get a volunteer!* After his simple fare, he laid down on a blanket near his fire and pretended to go to sleep. Before long, he was no longer pretending, and he did get some volunteers.

As the sun rose, Ma'elrich awoke to find his bags already packed and the fire carefully put out. Some breakfast tack with cheese was laid out on a broad leaf as if it were a plate. Looking up, he saw a brown-striped cat-like creature looking quizzically at him from across the fire. "Did you do all this?" he asked.

The cat nodded in response and gestured for him to eat his breakfast.

"Thank you, you are very kind. Can you understand me?"

The cat nodded again, although he didn't offer any verbal explanation. Ma'elrich got the impression he was reading his mind or expected him to do so. This wasn't a form of communication that would be easily learned if that were to be the case!

Thinking quickly, Ma'elrich made an offer. "I'd be happy to have a friend like you with me on my travels if you're open to that?"

The cat jumped up onto the horse and settled on his rump behind the saddle.

"Well then, I guess we are traveling companions!" Ma'elrich stashed his blanket and climbed into the saddle. *One Clairdani down, at least two more to go. This might be a very simple process...*

With the catlike creature in tow, Ma'elrich was introduced to even more forest creatures. Again, Ma'elrich sensed them understanding each other while nothing was uttered. Evenings were definitely more entertaining with these fun-loving forest creatures around, hustling to find edible roots, berries, grubs, and onions and then cooking them on a small fire. It was at the end of one of these meals when there was a sudden hush around them. All were on high alert, and Ma'elrich felt the hairs on his neck rise. There was a sense of something stalking them. Quietly, he grabbed a large half-burned branch from the fire for his weapon, and his fellow creatures, including his own horse, scattered, sounding a warning alarm to all as they left.

Suddenly abandoned, he backed up to the fire, cursing his horse for leaving him with no exit opportunity. Sense on high alert, he heard low growls from multiple places around him, then a large circle of growing fire-lights floating head-high.

"I'm not afraid of you," he blustered, trying to convince himself maybe more than whatever was out there.

Four stabs of sharp pain as something dug claws into him, and he was knocked backwards into the fire. Roaring in pain, he rolled off the scattered flaming logs and pushed with all his might to throw his attacker off him. Staggering to rise, he quickly doffed his flaming cloak and smacked at the scorch marks on his clothes as best he could while trying to see what monster it was that hit him. A wall of dark, matted hair and a stench of rotting flesh accosted him on all sides. Turning his head, he registered several large creatures dripping bloody saliva from long fangs right before he was slammed to the ground. Pain flared all over his body as the wall of dark hair knocked into him on multiple sides. Then, it went dark, and he knew no more.

Chapter 26: Dragon Lore

Once they had returned to Metulas' cave, Metulas asked Luz to retrieve the sapphire while he settled in for the history. When she returned, her friends were waiting quietly, highlighting the whispers emanating from the sapphire.

Luz wanted to ask the first question, but Metulas silenced her with a glance. *Let me start where I know I can start, and when I finish, you may ask whatever questions you need to. I think all your questions will be answered in due time, if you all agree?*

Luz and Anehta nodded their heads in approval, and Metulas began his tale.

I may be the last dragon in existence, but I remember my family, friends, and clans as long-living and life-loving flights of dragons. There were many of us, and we lived in peaceful harmony with all humans, all animals, and... elves.

"There are elves here?" Luz began and was again silenced by a look from Metulas.

After a moment to make sure he wouldn't be interrupted again, Metulas continued. *We all lived together peacefully. There were no Tenenbrani or Clairdani. All creatures were mere forest creatures with no designs on humans or elves. It was very peaceful, in its own way.*

I was still a young dragon when the wars began, so I am only learning now why the wars ensued and how they ended. From what I understand, it started with one group of dragons and humans fighting with other dragons and humans, the humans divided along clan lines. Then, the humans put aside their grievances and joined together against the dragons, and we felt very betrayed. When it became humans against dragons, the elves joined our side, and we all almost fought ourselves out of existence.

I was too young to be part of the battles, and my parents, sensing and ending of sorts, flew with me here and hid me so that I would not be swept into the fracas of those last days. I do not know exactly how things ended. I only know that it grew quiet in the land, and when I went out to seek out my parents, there was a perceptible but intangible change to everything.

After a time, it became evident that anyone who had fought in the war was doomed to a treacherous death as, one after another, they all fell ill and died. I believe I am the only dragon remaining from those wars, and only because I was hidden here and not near the battlefield. In my youth, I didn't know what to ask, and I mistakenly thought they were dying because they were wounded or old. It was then that I learned about the dragon necropolis, where we bury our dragon hearts. When we die, our hearts can live on if they are offered before our flesh dies. When we commune with these hearts, we can learn from our ancestors and gain strength from our past. Many of us died before we were able to give up our hearts. Their deaths were so quick. When there were only two of us left, and it was evident that he would die soon as well, I asked him to give me his heart so that I wouldn't be completely alone.

He did reluctantly, feeling I was unworthy of it since I hadn't fought with my kind. All I heard from his heart was anger and damnation at me for not being there in the battle with my kind. So, I took his heart to the necropolis, a place of honor we call "Cidade dos Corações", the city of hearts. I was hoping to find others that were kinder and more helpful. When I arrived, I found that the necropolis had been

182

desecrated – not a single dragon heart remained! I wept for the loss of my kind. I would never again hear the sounds of my kind or the histories I had yet to learn. There was only this one heart that remained, and it only had words to torture me. I found a new hiding place in that same area and buried the heart to alleviate my suffering.

After a long silence, Metulas continued. *Many years passed, and the Tenenbrani and Clairdani began to walk the earth. They were strange creatures, able to communicate with elves and some humans, and had a peculiar gravity to humans. Whereas the Tenenbrani would try to destroy humans, the Clairdani were trying to help. This, you know, since you've known it all your life, but to me, it was strange. I knew not to trust humans, and not knowing whether the elves were friends or betrayers, I stayed to myself here. After you and Anehta showed up, you know the rest of my story.*

On to what I've learned more recently. Yes, we had a great plan – use your gifts on the Magistrate to have him stop hunting out Traitors and see the truth. From all that we had learned from the Clairdani and the Enlightened, we were sure that the Magistrate was the key to ending the war against us. Along with your other gifts, your ability to connect with others emotionally and convince them you are a friend, not foe, has enabled you to communicate with the Clairdani and win over Tenenbrani at a much earlier age than ever seen in history. Your connection to me has allowed you to grow faster than other humans so that you seem ages older than your tender years of only 10 solar cycles. You should have succeeded with the Magistrate if he were a ... normal human. His pause gave the intended effect, and Luz could hold her questions no longer.

"Meaning he's NOT human? Is that what you mean?" Luz blurted out. Maybe she hadn't lost her powers as much as she had thought!

When you were captured, we asked ourselves the same question. Between love and claw, we might have been able to rescue you, although where you had failed, we would only have failed completely. While you were captured, I decided it might be time to go back and face the buried past. Perhaps the heart would be willing to share rather than scold after so much time has passed. Despite the years, I found where I had buried the heart, which was still there, and thankfully, without the malice emanating from it. I wanted to hear more about the war: the humans, its causes, and find anything that might help us fight them again but win. Although he was willing to give me the main points, he wasn't willing to give me the whole story. The whole truth would only go to 'a heart of humility that has paid the earth's toll; only such a heart can render of the two, one whole'.

Luz wondered aloud, "What is the 'earth's toll'? I've never heard that before. Have you?"

It could be many things... anything that we pay to the earth for what it gives to us. I'm not sure how a heart would pay, though. So, as it is with all riddles, we can only hope it will become clear at the moment we find this heart paying a toll. For that exact reason, I decided to keep the heart here rather than there so that when we find this new heart, we can find answers without any more delay.

Luz's head held so many questions! Circling back, she remembered the elves. "A bit ago, you said there were elves... maybe they can help us? Perhaps they've already solved the riddle and would be willing to tell us the whole story?"

Metulas pondered for a while. *They may, although elves are elusive. They pretend to stay to themselves, helping no one but themselves, even though they are also everywhere and know everything that happens. I've heard the Clairdani mention them. From what they've told me, they seem to be naturally Enlightened somehow. Regardless, I don't even know where to look for them or how to speak to them...*

A long silence fell while they contemplated all they had just heard.

Anehta piped up. *So... was there anything in the history of the war and humans that was helpful to us now?*

The only addition to what I already knew was that the elves were involved somehow. The humans and the dragons used to help each other, so the details of what changed are unclear. It was after the war, though, that everything changed: elves seemed to disappear; any dragon who fought died very suddenly from even the smallest scratch during the war, and the Clairdani and Tenenbrani began from that moment. These bits are new to you, not new to me. I just forgot as part of my desire to bury the painful past. After the war, I blamed humans for the end of my race and would destroy any humans I found around Batalha, hence the dry desert surrounding this place. It wasn't until you arrived and tricked me into connecting with you that I had anything to do with a human. I still do not trust them, nor they, me. You are our link, Luz, and your goodness is the only reason I have any hope for all of us. Luz blushed, and Anehta gave her a wink and a nod of affirmation.

The only other piece I was able to learn is that whether it was a dragon or human who began the war since both were affected in the aftermath, we must reunite the two to undo that outcome."

"Does our unity count, or does it have to be a lot of humans uniting with you? It's hard enough to get the humans themselves to unite, let alone unite with their least trusted enemy, the dragons!" Luz began to feel it might be hopeless.

"Remember, though, you and I are united in a common purpose now, so if we need evidence that it can be done, we can be that hope." Anehta and Metulas both gazed at Luz with hopeful expressions, as she had been the driving force behind their improbable partnership. Luz returned their gaze with a friendly smile. "So, we must unite the humans first. Let me think." After a few moments, she added, "Now that I think about it, the gaolers did seem to be crueler after they had met with the Magistrate in his office. Their clubs hit more viciously, the words cut more deeply, and they cared less for humanity, even their own families. It seemed to wear off after a time. Hawthorne was never called into the Magistrate's office, which might be why I was able to keep a connection with him. The others seemed closed off when I would reach out to their minds."

Anehta chimed in again. *So maybe the Magistrate has an ability that's the opposite of yours? Whereas you connect with others and bring out their goodness, perhaps he brings out their evilness? Although I didn't feel his darkness the way I feel Luz's light. It may be that I wasn't ever near enough to him to feel that perhaps?*

Perhaps? Was all that Metulas could contribute before falling silently into deeper reflection. After a few moments, he added, *I have told you everything I know, so from now on, we make discoveries together.*

Luz and Anehta nodded their heads in agreement and thanks. Luz still had a few burning questions. "I have a couple of questions about the sapphire we found."

186

Once all eyes were on her, she continued. "First, is that the dragon heart you mentioned?"

With Metulas' nod, she continued. "I can hear whispers when I'm near the heart, although Anehta cannot. Why can't she hear them? Next, although I can hear the whispers, I don't understand what is being said. If it's a dragon's thoughts or speech, shouldn't I be able to understand it like I understand you?"

As to why Anehta cannot understand the heart, I have no idea. Perhaps as we learn more about how the heart works, that question will answer itself. For the second, you assume you could understand another dragon because you understand me. However, you and I speak the human language, whereas dragons speak in pictures and our own language, which is more akin to elfish than any other language.

"Elfish? Why elfish?"

Perhaps because our two races are older than any other race, even if we haven't always been friends or enemies. We had common beginnings and frequent encounters, so our languages developed together. Once humans came to this region, we reached out to befriend them, and found camaraderie with them in their hopeful and playful ways. The elves tend to be too serious and long living, making them a very pessimistic and arrogant race. Perhaps the decision to choose humans over the elves was our downfall. We will have to keep asking questions to make those discoveries, though.

Luz had one last burning question. "One last thing, Metulas. You said that you brought the heart here and that all the other hearts were destroyed. Why, then, have you continued to travel east?"

I know that where I laid this heart, all others had been destroyed during the war. The Cidade is finally restoring itself from the burned shell that it was when I first visited. I have hope that there might be one heart that still exists. One that was buried under the rubble, deeper than the others, and well protected from the destruction that the others endured. Or there might be another older place where dragon hearts existed, or a secret one created once we were at war in case our main location was destroyed. I have not found anything yet, although I do smell the elves in the east. They think themselves invisible to our noses because they blend into the forest. However, because they smell like the forest, if they exist in any groups, there is a much stronger smell of forest than is proper for the number of trees that dwell in that location. The elves have been there in our sacred Cidade dos Corações, although it may have been long ago. They may have kept a heart for safe keeping and that knowledge lost before it was passed along to me.

After a few minutes of silence lapsed, Metulas continued. *I travel east to find the elves since that's the only place left they could be and reconnect with them. Between us, the elves, the Clairdani, and the Enlightened, I hope we can rid ourselves of the Tenenbrani once and for all. We have to be united for their existence to cease, in whatever form that might be. The elves may have our missing links and possibly a dragon heart if they are willing to help us. I just need to find the elves first.*

Chapter 27: The Elfish King Makes a Decision

Back in Palmela, the main elfin city in their lands of Sintra, Florenço gathered wood and vines as he had each day since he had connected with Cenellot and began teaching the humans their customs. He was impressed with their progress and was hopeful that their innocence and abilities would enable them to live within the lands of Sintra someday. He greeted each fellow elf with a nod as he hurried on his way towards their cave dwelling. As he neared the border lands of Sintra and the unclaimed forest beyond, a land called Sintrentejo, he started checking for other elves in the area. Once he was sure the area was clear, he detoured north a little and dropped his bundle of branches and vines beneath a huge yew tree standing solitary within a ring of other trees. A vine hung down from a middle branch, and Florenço easily swung himself up into the canopy, invisible to all. He stood on a simple wooden platform structure that served as the main floor of what would be an elfin hollow. A few other wooden platform structures built into other broad branch clusters showed the extent of his vision for their new tree dwelling. He reviewed his upcoming meeting with King Alfonso as he continued work on the treehouse that would eventually be home to Cenellot and Noyette. Regardless of what the customs and traditions were, the elfin King had to approve any non-elfish people living in Sintra, no matter the duration, location, or cause. With their progress, Florenço hoped that they would be able to blend in even if they would never resemble the elves physically.

Having made some progress on their future abode, Florenço returned to the ground and back towards Palmela.

In the center of Palmela stood Monserrate, where the high court council sat and the king himself resided. The council hall itself, known as the Toree de Verdad, stood centered at the bottom of a spiral staircase with nine levels. This Torre de Verdade was one of the first hollows built in Sintra, sung into the trees of the area by the first council of elves. Through their music, the trees knit their branches together to form walls, stairs, and seats while still maintaining their leaves and seasonal cycles. In fact, the only non-living element within their hall was the hewn stone table that sat at the very center of the chamber.

Trellises covered in floral vines created a long, tunnel-like entrance to the Torre. As he emerged into the elaborately sculpted entrance hall, Florenço noted a shorter, dark green-haired council elf seemingly carved out of ivory, seated on an oaken chair twice his own height at the entrance to the main council chambers. Requests to see King Alfonso were infrequent, thankfully, although that meant that he paid special attention to all requests. He approached the council elf on duty and twisted his hand in a sign of respect and greeting.

Returning the gesture, the council elf intoned his response, "Please make your mark in the roll, noting the purpose of your visit."

Florenço took the quill, noting his name and "request for refuge" as his purpose.

The council elf raised an eyebrow, revealing a set of pale-yellow cat-like eyes, but otherwise made no indication of surprise or judgement. "Very well, follow me."

They entered the large council room, and Florenço felt he had stumbled upon a large, hidden glade in the forest. As his eyes swept around the room, they were drawn to the very height of the room and the tree canopy that all but covered them in shade. At the top of the nine levels of spiral staircases, the sun only shone down directly on the council at the very zenith of its course. This tree canopy provided great protection from the elements above, and their intertwining branches served as living walls, giving them a sense of privacy free from distraction. Vines of various shades of green and brown along with bountiful flowers of every color, herbs, and fruits of the earth hung on these walls and on the council elves' stone-hewn table, which stood centered in the room. At the far end of the room sat King Abrimel between two other council elves, as marked by their light green rings that adorned their right ring fingers, serving as his advisors. The elf he had followed into the hall announced him as "Florenço, with a request for refuge," then departed, leaving Florenço to walk the length of the room unaccompanied amongst a vast array of whispers around the Torre.

Kneeling and gesturing in respect, he tried to be as eloquent as possible in response to the king's silent request for him to speak. The hall fell eerily silent as he began.

"Your Highness. As you well know, I have been one of the pairs of eyes watching over the humans that were deposited east of Sintrentejo to check on their progress and intentions. I have come with a report of considerable progress that may need attention."

The King nodded. "Proceed."

"Some of the Clairdani have been assisting the two humans with supplies and information, which they also share with us. The boy is exceedingly kind and shows intelligence. Indeed, at his tender young age, he is already able to communicate with the Clairdani! It is my understanding that we are allowed to break silence with them if they can speak to the Clairdani?"

The king hesitated, then agreed, adding, "It is one of the conditions we set forth for interacting with humans."

Florenço continued. "Since they are alone and this Inquisitor is hunting for them, I have been instructing the boy in basic swordsmanship, and he shows promise. The woman is also keen to learn about the forest herbs and pharmacy to help when needed."

"So, is the refuge request for you to live with them?"

"Not exactly, Your Highness. The request is that they be granted the protection of our lands and people, and they join us. They are unable to return to their own lands and will not survive for long with the Inquisitor hunting them."

Murmurs again filled the halls as the thought of humans in their midst became a possible reality. The king held up a finger to stem the tide of noise and turned to his fellow council members. After a few moments of fierce conversation, he announced, "we have decided not to extend our hospitality to them. You may continue to work with them and protect them where they are, but they are not to come here. They are human." This last sentence was spat out as if it were a disgusting slug he had to dislodge from his mouth.

Florenço acknowledged the command politely, "yes, Your Highness. Might I add that the boy's eyes have already turned green, like ours? It is nearly impossible to hide such eyes in the human world, and it would be easier for him to blend in with our people."

King Abrimel immediately interjected, his voice rising a little in his growing annoyance. "Their ways are not ours;

eventually, they will succumb to the evil that permeates their entire beings. We do not welcome that here. Besides, ultimately, they may decide they want to return to their own people, which would be too dangerous for our entire existence. We cannot allow it."

"What if they lived at the very edge of our lands and had no interaction with us?"

"The matter is already decided. You may go." King Abrimel stared at Florenço, as if he could move him out of the hall with his mind.

Acknowledging the dismissal, Florenço bowed, saying, "I thank you for your wise counsel, Your Highness, and will heed what you have said."

Unconvinced, Florenço left the council room, thinking carefully about what was said, unsaid, and what he could tell Cenellot and Noyette.

Chapter 28: Normalcy in Tomar

Rowan watched the marketplace from the vantage point of his office window. His townsfolk seemed to have shrugged off the Inquisitor's terrors and returned to their normal routines. The restrictions on trade with other towns had been lifted, easing the shortages in the market and raising everyone's morale. There were smiles and banter among them and purchased goods carried in the streets. It was as if the Inquisitor had been a nightmare, and now all was forgotten. There had been no attacks since his departure, but Rowan was sure the Traitors were still in town, somewhere there in the market like everyone else. He had hoped that returning Tomar to normalcy would see the Traitors return to their secret routines and let down their guard. But they were as allusive as ever, and he couldn't tell one townsfolk from another from here or from down in the markets.

Weeks after the news of the Inquisitor's demise, Rowan was doing his best to continue his search for the traitorous leaders based on what he remembered from the Inquisitor's work. He sighed. *It was fantastic being able to run the town without worrying about the constant search for Traitors and have someone else take the curses from the townspeople!* He thought. *Leaders are never appreciated for what they had to do!*

Even if the Inquisitor is dead, he did stir up the traitors in his short time here. Weren't there more attacks with him here? With the town locked down and exit forbidden, they could still bring in the monsters and increase the number of attacks. Why was that? HOW could they accomplish all of that under the very nose of Ma'elrich himself? Rowan paused for a moment. *Creature attacks had always been part of the history of Tomar, although they had always been rather infrequent and in clusters. There would be an attack or two on a patrol team, then soon thereafter, an attack in town that would destroy either a family or a couple of members of it anyway, then nothing for many months.*

Hmmm. Rowan wondered. *The Inquisitor seemed obsessed with the Advocate and was either locked away or ranting mad while he was here. He instilled the right amount of terror required that made traitors make mistakes, so that might need to continue if we can do so without increasing the number of attacks.*

He had also arrested many suspected traitors and then released them after questioning, and there was no accounting for what he learned in those interrogations. Maybe they need to reinstall the patrols as a warning signal that another attack is eminent in the town? And if there's an attack, gather all the townsfolk into the city hall with extra protection? That's it!

Rowan felt elated. Anyone who didn't go to the protected City Hall would be working with the attacking creatures, and if they wrote down everyone who came, they could easily determine who the traitors were! Or at least, they could find out a couple of traitors that they could then interrogate for more information on the others. *One thing the Inquisitor did do for me. I'm no longer the most hated person in Tomar, even if I was responsible for bringing him in. His shadow will bring down the Traitors and the attacks, I'm sure of it!*

With that, he felt he had a plan. Looking up from his desk, he called his aide de camp, the only person he truly trusted with everything.

"Oliveiro!"

"Yes, milord?"

"I need you to reinstate the patrols in full force. I know we've used the patrols much as before, and the attacks have ceased for now. However, while there are still Traitors, there will still be attacks when we least expect them. So, we are going to use the patrols as bait. We just need to have constant patrols around the city to draw the creatures closer."

"How might that help, sir?"

"These monsters seem to skirmish with the patrols, and then an attack occurs within the town very soon thereafter. So, after a patrol group is engaged, we will gather the townsfolk together in City Hall and plant all of the guards around us. With the strength in numbers, we should be able to fend off any attack. Also, anyone who is not at City Hall will obviously be one of the Traitors who is orchestrating the attack. If we document all of those who are at City Hall and then figure out who is not at City Hall, we will have at least a couple of our Traitors by name. Eventually, we will be able to rid ourselves of all the Traitors in our midst, and these attacks will cease!"

"If you please, milord. What if we start losing patrols to these creatures? How can we replace those lost? It may be harder to find replacements for such a dangerous task."

The Magistrate only thought for a moment. "How are our dungeons, Oliveiro?"

"They are full, milord. If we put those who rebel…"

"No, no, that's not my intent. For any slots unfilled, use any prisoner not suspected of being a Traitor. Putting known traitors beyond the walls will be setting ourselves up for attacks. We don't want attacks, so if no attacks occur, then we have all the Traitors already imprisoned, yes?"

"As you say, milord. I will go do as you've required."

Chapter 29: The Triad Makes a Plan

Euphoric from their decision to involve the elves, Luz, Anehta, and Metulas then moved to the difficulty of deciding exactly how to get the elves involved. Getting the elves involved would require much grace, caution, and diplomacy and none of these were things any of them particularly excelled at. A couple weeks later, they were still finalizing how best to accomplish that task. During those two weeks, Anehta had acted as messenger between Batalha and Tomar to keep herself busy and she was completely exhausted now having just returned the night before from her long journey. The three were enjoying their first breakfast together in many days, the calm, clear, crisp morning providing some serenity before their momentous discussion. Their simple fare of fresh eggs and warmed nuts was accompanied by a warm, dandelion-flavored water they considered to be as fine a tea as could be served anywhere. The routine allowed them to remain deep in their own thoughts about how best to proceed with the elves.

Setting down the bowls and wooden cups, Luz took a deep breath for what she knew would follow. After each return flight, there had been short exchanges of ideas, and although they sought a unanimous decision, Anehta was clearly entrenched in her ideas.

I still don't understand why we can't just go all together, whined Anehta.

"We've been over this, Anehta. First of all, you are smaller and can hide more easily, and until we know what the elves are thinking, we don't want to force their hand," Luz reminded her.

Your powers could be very helpful in influencing them to our cause, though, Luz! And Metulas, you are responsible for helping restore the friendship between your races, which would also help our cause.

You are not wrong, my little one, rumbled Metulas' voice in the cave. *However, we require your speed and stature for now, once you've recovered from your recent excursion.*

Anehta had returned late in the night from delivering her message to Simão. Too tired to do anything but fall asleep, she had tucked in her beak next to Luz and settled in for the night. Now that the initial sleep deprivation had been alleviated, Luz released her enthusiasm full force on her best friend.

"How was everyone, Anehta? Details, please!" Suddenly, it seemed to be a girls' event, and Metula was the awkward father trying both to hear and not listen in.

Well, the biggest news is that... the Inquisitor has gone! They aren't sure what happened because he left town, went into the forest, and never came out. The Magistrate has been pretending everything is back to normal and has required even more patrols than before. That's working for us because it lets us have more meetings with the Tenenbrani and Clairdani alike, and there's lots of other news!

"Tell all!" Luz gushed, happy to finally hear from beyond her prison cell and her two friends.

So Anehta gave Luz all the news she could remember from Tomar, including their suspicions of the Inquisitor reading the Codex and its loss. She cried over the names of friends who had died while imprisoned, gasped at the details surrounding the flight of Hawthorne's family, and sighed with relief that her family was still unscathed and watchful.

198

I gave them the message that we had a plan that required us to be elsewhere and that they needed to be on their own for now, and I didn't give away any information beyond that. Simão understood the need for secrecy and wished us luck and speed on our quest to get more help for our cause.

You didn't make any promises, correct? Ensured Metulas.

Correct. No promises, no mentions of elves or magic or anything.

Good. Metulas felt satisfied with Tomar's acceptance of their plan. *As soon as you are ready, fly to the elfin lands for us. I've never been there myself. Unfortunately, I've only heard stories, so I cannot give you much guidance. The council seat should be at the center of their lands and is probably their largest structure. They are forest creatures and will sense your presence if you aren't careful. Stay hidden, stay high where other birds are, and your presence won't be as noticed. Once you're inside the council seat structure, you should be able to find a high spot near their decision table to hear clearly while being out of sight. Get a sense of their attitude toward the Clairdani, humans, and Tenenbrani, and whether you think they might join our cause to end the curse causing these transformations. I do not think we are in immediate danger, but they need to know that if they don't join us, nothing will protect them from the same fate they set in motion. If they seem amenable, wait till after their council to approach the king with our plan. If not, wait until the room is empty before returning to us.*

Once Anehta had flown off for the third time, having forgotten to peck Luz goodbye the first time and the correct direction the second time, Metulas and Luz grew more serious.

I just have one more thing to teach you, Luz. Now that you're back to health, we must test your strengths again.

Luz turned away from the distant speck that was Anehta and sat near where Metulas squatted in the cave.

"Why don't we go now? I can look for clues around Tomar, and you can keep working on deciphering clues from that heart."

I think I have as much as I can handle from that heart at the moment, and it did give me one thing I can tell you.

"What I'm looking for, exactly?"

Well, yes, and no. I believe there could be two separate objects. When elves make declarations, they write them down, and I wonder if they were able to write the Tenenbrani and Clairdani into existence the same way they can sing a forest into existence. If so, finding and destroying that object may break that chain.

Luz exuberantly clapped her hands, stopping when she realized Metulas wasn't finished.

Metulas huffed out a bit of smoke to release the tension in his stomach. *However, I have no idea what type of object it might be that the elves created or if it's related to the end of the war. The second object is this element in the Magistrate's office. That object is of unknown origin. It may be a human creation, a found elfin object, or a relic of some past creature. I do think that if it's of elfin origin, be on the lookout for natural items that seem out of place. Secondly, elves tend to use moonlight ink, meaning that if there's anything written, you'll need to use moonlight to read it. Lastly, if it is something written and you don't know how to read elfish, you will have to just copy it exactly and return with the writing so I can attempt to translate it. If it's of human or creature origin, they don't usually use writing and prefer to imbue individual objects with magical properties. Simply destroying those objects would be enough to break their powers, although they may be magically protected... which means we would need the elves for those.*

"So regardless of what we find, we will probably need the elves to help us end the human transformations to Tenenbrani and the power The Magistrate has from this object?"

Exactly. While those ideas bounced around in their heads, Metulas continued. *Let's train for a couple more days. Then, you can begin your search for objects here in Batalha and between here and Tomar. Ready?*

When Luz nodded her head, Metulas began.

Close your eyes. Rise off the floor, just enough so we would be able to tell if you drop a little. Now, imagine yourself inside a walled fortress where you can get out, but nothing can get in. I'm going to try to control your abilities with my mind. Don't let me. Try to sense my mental presence and use that mental fortress to push everything foreign out.

Luz dropped as soon as Metulas pressed her. "Is that what a mental presence feels like?"

When Metulas nodded his head, Luz took a moment to take a deep breath. "Okay, try again. I'll do better this time."

For the next two days, Metulas and Luz practiced this new mental fortress exercise. They focused on both planned and surprise attacks until Luz could effectively shield herself. This allowed her to keep working with her abilities despite attempts to mentally dampen them. *Excellent, indeed!* Metulas boomed on the fourth day. *I think you are ready.*

Luz settled down on Metulas' right foreleg, where she could look him more directly in the eyes. "Metulas, if this object can influence my abilities, now that I know what to expect and how it feels, should I be able to feel it if I'm near enough to it?"

That is a possibility and could make it easier to find. It can't hurt to use every sense you have to find it. Until we know, I wouldn't rely on it alone. If you go out during the moonlight, you'll be able to see if something has moon writing on it. It might only look like a reflection of moonlight, so it would be easily missed unless you are looking for it. Otherwise, anything that seems unnatural in that place – anything non-native or in an unearthly formation, for instance – could be a marker for the object itself.

"Good thinking! I'll start near here and sweep towards Tomar, and if I find anything, I'll send word. If Anehta returns from the elves, I mean, WHEN she returns from the elves, have her come to find me and bring me the message as well. Any hope of additional help would be welcome in Tomar."

The Inquisitor may be gone, or may not be… without his human form, he could be a new, dangerous Tenenbrani. Keep your mental shields up at all times, and probe with your own to help protect yourself from being seen by anyone. Of course, the Clairdani can help you, as if you could deter them from doing so.

"I'll be careful, Metulas, as always."

She gave Metula a broad hug, reaching as high as she could, took up her food sac, and left the cave.

Once out of sight, Metulas flew east to continue his search for other clues in the Cidade de Corações. This time, he had the company of the sapphire heart. He hoped the old dragon would recall communicating with any other heart or creature while lying in the Cidade and guide them in that direction, making his search much easier.

Chapter 30: The Return of the Inquisitor

Hours later, Ma'elrich awoke and again found everything around him in order, his horse nearby as if he hadn't betrayed his own master by leaving him to those monsters. Evidently, the creatures that had abandoned him last night had returned, somehow rescued him, and worked on his wounds! There was no evidence whatsoever that there had been an attack in the night other than his own pain. Although he wasn't bandaged, his wounds were healing, and given what he thought his condition had been last night, he was miraculously feeling alive! A plan came to mind. He needed these creatures, for surely there was a connection here to their "Clairdani," as they called themselves, and they could be useful.

The brown-striped cat-like creature noticed him awake and came over to check on him. He checked Ma'elrich over thoroughly and tilted his head as if to ask *how are you feeling?*

"I am amazed I am alive, honestly! Thank you all for your help!" Ma'elrich answered in response.

After a pause, he added, "After last night, I think I need to return home and wait to heal. Could you all, or at least some of you, help me home? I would be able to give you a dinner in your honor if you would…"

The brown-striped creature nodded and made haste, organizing the other creatures into packing and restoring the area to its prior state. Within minutes, all was ready. Some of their retinue dispersed back into the forest, and only four creatures remained with him – the fiery plumed phoenix, a couple of rather large squirrels, and the brown-striped cat-like leader. It seemed the Phoenix was their scout, flying ahead and leading them to his house once he gave them the general description of where it was. The others took turns between keeping him company and scouting along the way for edible food for their meals, saving time along the way.

This way, they managed to get back to the Inquisitor's palace within a couple of days. He was relieved to see that the cage had been positioned next to the house but was hidden from the front. Although a little apprehensive about coming inside, he convinced them they could go through the house to the back, where a feast was being prepared for everyone. The phoenix flew rather than walk and settled on the pinnacle of the palace as a lookout.

"Rabicho! Come meet my new friends who have rescued me from certain death!"

As bidden, the lean manservant came quickly, halting when he noticed that they weren't already bound for imprisonment. He chose wisely not to question the Inquisitors' reasons until they were alone and set to thanking them and unpacking the horse. He heard Ma'elrich's one-sided, easy banter with them as he led the horse back behind the palace to their stables. Once he returned, he began collecting the packs in his arms and heard Ma'elrich's booming voice.

"Rabicho, now that you've unpacked the goods, can you set up for a banquet in the back? I'm sure my friends would help you, and we have brought plenty for all to eat already from our return."

While Rabicho prepared drinks and some vegetables and cheeses, the squirrel-like Bobkin and the cat-like Brownie helped prepare their food contributions. Rabicho wondered what foods exactly they would be bringing that all would enjoy and hoped he had made the cage both big enough and with small enough spaces so the smallest creatures couldn't escape. When all was prepared and the table was set, he called all of them to dinner.

"Fantastic, Rabicho!" With a gesture to the creatures, he escorted all of them into the enclosed outer space. Focused on the table, they all happily carried their burdens to the table. Placing their various foods on the table, they then stood back, waiting for the cue to begin eating. "Just wait until you've sampled this forest fare, Rabicho. Truly, we could learn a few things from our friends here," Boasted Ma'elrich.

To his guests, who were already focused on the food on the table, he added, "Please, have a seat." He sat at the well-laden table while the others stood at or sat on a place setting at the table. After a few moments of silence, he stood as if to give a salutatory speech. Instead, he called his servant.

"On second thought, Rabicho, let's not eat just yet. Please remove all of these dishes from the table, and we will eat later." Without question, Rabicho cleared the table under the apprehensive and wary gazes of the Clairdani. Within minutes, the table was devoid of any sustenance, and the servant was walking back to the kitchen.

To the guests, Ma'elrich clarified what would happen instead of sharing a meal. "You will not be returning to your forest but staying here with me. There is much I can learn from you, and I hope you will help me learn your ways. As long as you cooperate with me, I will provide what you need. If at any time you do not cooperate, I cannot guarantee much of a future for you. "

He then closed and locked the door behind him. The phoenix's squawks rang out through the forest and surrounding area as they realized they had been tricked! He departed, screeching a warning to all in the area and disappearing quickly out of view.

In a few minutes, the Inquisitor returned with a bag that smelled of death and dressed in a bloodied leather tunic, looking like the butcher he was. At the sight of him, the Clairdani all scattered from the table, taking to the edges of the cage as far from where the Inquisitor stood as they could manage. Relocking the door behind him, he strode to the table and whisked off the table cover to reveal four prisoner cabinets that he slowly separated out around the encaged space. From the structure of these prisoner cabinets, they slowly realized that while their heads might be allowed to see what transpired around them, the rest of their bodies would be crammed inside the cabinet, with no ability to rest or sit. They had scarcely registered this fact when they saw the Inquisitor's flashing black eyes seek theirs. In a flash, the Inquisitor somehow moved faster than any human should be able to move, and within a few moments, he had all four creatures imprisoned in their boxes.

Returning to the door to the cage where he had left his tools, he physically disappeared somehow into his small bag of tools and emerged as a large raptor. His body was covered in feathers, his feet now huge blood-red talons, his face dominated by a large, yellow bony beak that didn't hide his black beady eyes. With a large flap of his arms now transformed into feathery wings, he zipped around the cage, puncturing each of the four cages multiple times with his talons. Cries of startled pain emitted from all four as blood trickled out of each of the cages where they had been pricked.

In their minds, they heard his voice. *Now that you know who I am, tell me exactly who you are and where this Advocate leader of yours lives!*

Screeches of outrage at his unjust treatment of them accosted him from the cages, claiming ignorance of the Advocate and her residence.

I'm sure there is something that you know that could be useful to me. Let's start with the smallest, shall we?

And flying to the smallest cage, the Inquisitor took the cage in his talons, and flew around the cage. Occasionally, he would toss it towards the bars of the cage or drop it only to catch it again before it hit the ground. At each jarring movement, the Inquisitor repeated his question in their minds, *who is this Advocate? Where does she live?* In sheer terror, the Bobkin fainted until re-awoken when thrown against the bars. Each time the Inquisitor caught the cage again, his talons pierced the cage anew, mangling it and suffocating the Bobkin further. Whether through fear or bravery, the Bobkin never gave any information and Ma'elrich reached the end of his patience. In annoyance, the Inquisitor tore open the cage and swallowed the bloodied, mangled Bobkin in one snap of its beak.

Calming himself, the Inquisitor flew back to his bag, and transformed back into his human self, looking a little disgruntled at his lack of progress. Hoping that giving them time to think about their own consequences would work for him, he left his bag and departed, slamming the door behind him. For the next few days, Ma'elrich spent time transcribing the Codex and trying every day to begin to understand his prisoners' speech, communication channels, and knowledge about the Advocate, he understood that they knew nothing of her origins and only vaguely of her whereabouts. She seemed to live across the northern desert near Tomar in some caves he had never heard of before, most of the activity still remained in and around Tomar itself. The patrols seemed to be a key piece to the Traitor's link to the Tenenbrani, so he would start there, back in Tomar. Perhaps he could grab a couple of patrols before officially announcing himself in Tomar and get some clarifications before they were on full alert?

"Rabicho, I will need to return to Tomar for a while. I'm not making any progress with these creatures, and no one seems to notice their disappearance. "

"Would you like me to try working with the creatures while you are gone, milord?"

"That won't be necessary for now, perhaps later. For now, pack my bags for a fortnight, and I will hope to make quicker progress in Tomar than I did last time. I don't have names, but I do have more information on ways to recognize the Traitors, so I should be able to make quick work of ridding ourselves of these Traitors."

"Very well, milord. As you command."

Chapter 31: The World Encroaches Upon Solitude

King Abrimel, King of the Forest Elves, listened raptly to the brown-striped sparrow that had alighted on his finger. Its energetic, shrill voice twittered around the council room. Trying to calm the agitated sparrow, Abrimel stroked his feathers calmly with his long bony fingers as he continued his questioning. Once satisfied, the elfish king stood and boosted the sparrow into the air, which flew up and out of the council room. The remaining twelve council members remained seated around the large, round oaken table, waiting for their king to relay the recent, unexpected news. Unseen by all, a small grey owl alighted onto one of the tallest tree canopies surrounding the table and began hopping from branch to branch in hopes of being able to hear the council's deliberations.

"Our friends report that the Inquisitor is alive and well! He has captured some of the Clairdani, tricking them into going to his palace, and they are imprisoned there now. A phoenix who didn't follow them into the palace has escaped and is now alerting those in the countryside about his duplicity."

A loud murmur broke their stoic silence while their king spoke. In the surrounding nine telescoping wooden circles of the Torre, sorted by status and age, onlookers were allowed to hear what was said without being heard themselves. King Abrimel glanced around to see a few visitors in the Torre and raised his hands in a request to reclaim decorum.

Looking around the council table at the outwardly calm faces, he saw a deeper resolve and questions in their eyes that he would have to address.

"Alameas, Lord of the Forest patrols. What have you to add to this fresh news?"

At the far side of the round table, Alameas was both Lord of the Forest patrol and King Spymaster in as much as their primary source of intelligence was from the forest itself. It was difficult to tell whether his black, shadowed eyes, darker bark-like complexion and emaciated frame were what drew him to the position or if the position transformed his physique, but his physical resemblance to a cunning spider put everyone in his vicinity on guard. "We knew he had left Tomar and returned to his own dwelling in Clod Pollux. In years past, he has never had any contact with the Clairdani and has mostly only kept to his business of torturing other humans for information. This is a new development if he is now not only in contact with Clairdani but attacking them as well. It would appear the Tenenbrani have an unprecedented human ally."

At the suggestion that humans were working with the Tenenbrani, even louder murmurs erupted. Any creatures working with these foul Tenenbrani would be considered lower than anything in existence, with a free license for any elf to destroy the human on sight without need of trial or justification. If this list had only one human on it, King Abrimel might put together a hunting party to rid the world of a substantial threat to their forest magic. Every elf knew that if evil penetrated their forest magic, there would be more dire consequences in the shape of disease, hunger, and death for everything that dwelled therein. If other humans were allies with the Tenenbrani, it could be the resurgence of a war like no other. All this, King Abrimel processed while scanning the nine levels of onlookers and his fellow elves on the council. The news only entrenched his determination to continue their estrangement from the human race.

To his right sat a silver-haired female elf in multi-colored vestments and wings who was a bit shorter than the others. Her electric-blue eyes looked around the table in a silent request to speak next. As it quieted, Abrimel gestured for her to speak her thoughts.

"Are humans now manifesting a desire to destroy the Clairdani before they even transform? Have any other humans shown malice towards Clairdani, or is this a singularity?" While she spoke, her blue eyes sought the king's green eyes for any clues he might share beyond his words.

"Evil will always attempt to destroy that which is good, whether that be before or after the humans transform," philosophized an older, mauve-haired elf in vestments that matched her eyes sitting halfway between them and the king. "What is interesting is how he learned of the Clairdani at all. Most humans are not alerted to their presence or origins and avoid them at all costs."

"Clearly, something has shifted. Whether that was while this Inquisitor was in Tomar or something he learned in his own palace, Almourael, matters little," added a slight and very tall ebony-colored elf sitting opposite the silver-haired butterfly elf. "For him to demonstrate this type of destructive intent before transforming is alarming. The point of the transformations was for them to destroy themselves, not other forest creatures."

"But these are Clairdani, not our forest creatures," reminded the mauve-haired elf. "Does that not include them in their own self-destruction? Whether they be human or creature, they will all eventually destroy each other into extinction."

"I realize the Clairdani are also transformed creatures. My concern is whether or not he understands their language. If he can torture information from them, he may be able to learn of our existence and lead other humans into battle against us again." Explained Alameas

"I will agree that there is a certain evil about this Inquisitor that is far beyond what we have ever seen in the human kingdoms," summarized King Abrimel. "For myself, I do not want this evil seeping into our lands or our people."

Trying to redirect the conversation away from philosophy and towards action, Alameas asked, "are we going to help the Clairdani and these Enlightened humans to help protect our lands? For our sake, not theirs, clarified Alameas hastily.

"I would rather leave Sintra forever than help the humans, regardless of their relationship with the Clairdani. They are not to be trusted, and their destruction brought on by Tenenbrani and themselves is their own doing. We owe them nothing and will supply them nothing."

Even though he knew that many of them shared his views, he was aware that a few of the younger elves had different ideas. Searching the faces that watched him carefully, he added for assurance of their agreement, "we will revisit this again if there is other news that concerns us."

Standing, Abrimel dismissed them all without another word. As the last elf left the table, Abrimel seemed to wander around the tree line at the edge of the room, pausing at one particularly leafy linden tree. Grasping one branch, he murmured something quietly, and suddenly Anehta found herself shaken from the tree and in King Abrimel's cold grip.

Anehta felt ice in her veins as she heard his voice inside her head.

You aren't an owl, I know, and you don't smell of the forest. What might you be doing here?

I am Anehta, a Clairdani from Tomar and a friend of Luz, known as the Advocate, and Metulas, the only dragon left in existence, She answered. Apparently, there was also a truth oath spoken in his spell, for she couldn't help but answer him with full disclosure.

You have interesting friends. They aren't here, though. Why are you here and not with them then? continued King Abrimel in his interrogation.

You know how evil the Inquisitor is. I was sent to find the elves to see if they have forgiven the human and dragon races enough to join forces against him and the Tenenbrani. Seeing the obvious 'no' on his face, she continued, *"Or for any direction or help you can offer us that might help us defeat them. One advantage of the truth oath,* she thought, *is at least we won't talk in riddles forever!*

As I have said many times, humans are a destructive race and are coming to their natural end. We will not interfere with the course of these natural events in any way.

But what about the curse you put on them...? Anehta began, forgetting that the curse wasn't something she was supposed to bring up. The increased tension in the King's grip on her legs was a quick reminder and punishment for that betrayal.

How do you know anything about the curse? That was hidden years ago! King Abrimel cut across her thought.

Metulas relayed the story to us from the Cidade dos Corações. *We know your people visit there on occasion.*

The elf did not deny this fact, his eyes fixing on hers in challenge.

Pressing her advantage, Anehta continued, *You must admit that the curse is a large non-natural part of their current destruction. Since your race bound them, can you not at least give us some aide before the evil you caused reaches beyond the human race into the forests and beyond?*

King Abrimel gave no reply until they had walked around the council table twice, the king with Anehta still clutched in his left hand. *Well-reasoned, my little friend. Very well. I will tell you this much: the curse was written in our language with our methods and placed in plain sight of the humans on the battlefield. If it has been moved, we know not when or how. That is all I can tell you.*

Releasing Anehta from his grasp, he added, *Your honesty and directness are refreshing and portray your earnestness. You may return to your friends. We will not expect to see you again.*

Getting far away from his grasp, she turned and faced the king, flapping her wings to keep her stationary in the air. *Thank you. I will let Metulas and Luz know about the clue and relay that they should expect no help from the elves at this time.* With this, Anehta had had enough of his arrogance, and she flew up over the canopy into the sky beyond.

Before she reached the top of the canopy, she heard his reply in her head: *Or ever!*

Chapter 32: A Change in Patrols

Simão was happy about how well the new patrols were working out after the mandated shift from little patrol work to full time patrols. Even though they had to increase the number of people on patrol, there haven't been any attacks on the patrols so far. Rowan's efforts to boost the patrols didn't seem to be yielding results, fortunately. *If the purpose was to reduce the number of attacks, however, the plan was working beautifully,* he admitted. The increase in patrols had also allowed them more opportunities to connect with the Tenenbrani, which had led to a much-needed information transfer about the Inquisitor, where the newer Tenenbrani were coming from, and other news from the Clairdani as well. Still, many questions remained. *I wonder where the Inquisitor is... He was certainly bloodthirsty enough to transform, but if he transformed and had his primal attack, then disappeared? Where did he go? Something must have seen him; they don't hide themselves well. Or maybe it was one of these newer Tenenbrani not from Tomar that we heard about in the reports and went back to its own lair?*

From the Clairdani reports of their skirmishes while the Inquisitor was in Tomar, these other groups did seem to be more consumed by their own animal lust and less capable of remorse or empathy. Without those two emotional capabilities, there was no path back for them. They would have to let the Advocate try to work with them if they returned to the area. Sometimes, she had just enough ability to resurface those deeper feelings in others when all other attempts had failed. *At least now we have our patrols.* As it stood now, there were just enough Enlightened to have one on each patrol, even as often as they were being utilized. Even the forced prisoner labor was serendipitous and allowed them more flexibility in their enlightened patrol assignments.

Despite all the lingering doubts and unknowns, this information exchange was bearing fruit. After months of not being able to meet with them, Simão found that the Tenenbrani they worked with had been able to identify other Tenenbrani who were ready for a remorse-centered conversion. Additionally, with the suspicious actions and departure of the Inquisitor, the Enlightened on the patrols were able to convince a few more of the Tenenbrani that there was a larger evil afoot, and they should band together to help quicken more conversions from Tenenbrani to enlightened Tenenbrani. Many of the newly created Tenenbrani could remember their own transformation from human to monster, the process having been both painful and frightening. While some enjoyed their new forms with their new abilities for destruction, others had remorse for how their avarice or bloodthirstiness had led to the destruction of their families by their own fangs or claws, as well as their separation and vilification from family and friends. These Tenenbrani could be willing to help them and the Clairdani with information and nonproliferation of attacks.

Within a moon cycle, their new spy ring was bearing fruit. Mateus gave short, quick updates to Simão at his forge or in the streets as he learned them so as not to establish any pattern the guards might notice.

After a few weeks of the new patrol rotations, Mateus was waiting for the forge to clear of the two last customers for the day. Seeing Mateus outside as he escorted his customers to the door, Simão pulled the shutters to declare the forge closed for the remainder of the day. Once the alley was clear of all customers, Mateus slipped quickly into the forge, locking the door behind him.

"Simão, he's back."

"Who, The Inquisitor? Are you sure?"

"We've been getting reports from both sides the past couple of days that he is sweeping the countryside, trying to stay hidden and avoiding contact with any creatures. His eyes are solidly black now, and the Tenenbrani report seeing some of the same creatures again that they saw when he came here last time. They are as confused as we are about why he isn't a Tenenbrani himself yet."

"I'll add them to the list of us confused by it. That is curious. Anything else?" Simão pretended to rummage through some nails to give to Mateus as a pretense for their meeting in case anyone happened to look through the window.

"A patrolman, Bartimeu, went down last night. We found his body this morning."

It had been so long since they had had a patrolman die while on duty that it took Simão a moment to process and shift from his earlier exuberance to inquisitive grief. Bartimeu was a Newer recruit with a lot of promise. Young, energetic, and friendly, the short, muscular ginger always had a kind word for everyone he met.

"Was it an attack?" was all he could think to ask at the moment.

"He was meeting with a Tenenbrani, Maefe, and never came back. The meeting never happened, apparently, and Maefe was seen at the next patrol switch to find out what had happened. After his report, he went out again in search of clues and found a mangled body deep in the glade to the west of Tomar." He chose a couple of nails about the same size and started fishing for a coin in his bag.

As he handed Simão the coins, their eyes met. "Bartimeu, we salute you for your sacrifice," They whispered together. They paused, making a slight bow and hand gesture on their chest in respect for the dead.

"Did they collect him for the Pit?"

Mateus nodded.

Simão accepted the coin, gave Mateus the nails, and walked him to the door.

"As long as the Inquisitor is still outside of Tomar, maybe we can get lucky again, and the Pit will give up some of its dead for us. Let's meet at the Pit tonight and see if we learn anything. If he was alone, that may be our only source for information about what really happened."

Mateus agreed, said his farewell, then left the forge closing the door behind him. He returned to his place to rest until it was time to get ready for their rendez-vous well after dark.

At midnight, Simão stuck to the shadows until he reached the eastern section of the northern wall nearest the Pit and waited. When the moonlight struck the symbol on the keystone of the tower arch, he checked the guards to ensure they were turned away, stood in view of the keystone, and made the requisite hand gesture over his chest. He made his way across the alley to a secret door in the wall by the marked tower, and as he approached, a section shimmered and disappeared, creating a doorway. Simão crossed through, and the doorway sealed itself back into oblivion.

Mateus was already at the Pit. As one of the key guards in the patrols, he had requested permission to check the Pit in case any creatures came for fresh food. He was thus prepared with staff and sword and not worried about any guards seeing him. Not to alert anyone else to Simão's presence, Mateus simply gave one short nod in the general direction of his friend and mentor. Nothing had happened yet, though the time was approaching. He was glad of it; he didn't want to be alone when Bartimeu arose from the Pit.

Hiding in his spot behind the large sage bush, away from any townspeople's prying eyes, Simão waited. The Pit hadn't given up any of its dead since the Inquisitor had arrived, and he hoped their vigil wouldn't still be in vain. As the moonlight fully illuminated the shrouded bodies in the Pit, the freshest bundle in the Pit began to shift. Soon after that, the spectral of a brownie emerged, becoming corporeal as they watched. Simão reached the edge of the Pit and offered a hand to help the brownie out. Not needing one, the brownie alighted next to him, and Simão restrained him gently.

Speaking quietly, Simão intoned as he reached out with his mind towards Bartimeu, "Remember who you are, Bartimeu. You are now a brownie with Bartimeu's soul and are a friend to us as we are to you. Remember who you were..."

Mateus came and sat on the other side of Bartimeu, offering an open palm in a sign of non-aggression and invitation. Bartimeu closed his eyes, trying to recall what he could of his life and allowing time to acknowledge this new manifestation.

Simão? Mateus? Bartimeu touched his paw to Mateus's palm, then sat erect, gazing at the two of them.

They heard the voice in their heads, as they always did when communicating with the Clairdani.

Relieved that the Pit was again relinquishing its hold on death, Simão had questions and a task for Bartimeu. *Do you remember what happened while you were on patrol last night? You disappeared, and Maefe never met with you. He found you later, so we were able to bring you here.*

Bartimeu gazed into the distance as if trying to see where he had been. *I remember going out to meet Maefe. He was a little late, and I was distracted by what I thought was a Clairdani trying to get my attention. I followed it, thinking it might lead me to Maefe, which would explain why he was late. I had just rounded a large tree when suddenly I was attacked from above by a Tenenbrani with wings and fangs, and I fought to protect my head and neck. I heard its voice in my head, asking me if I could hear him and what I was doing out in the forest alone near the creatures. I didn't know what to answer, which didn't please him. He was able to pick me up easily and fly me above the trees, and I think I saw one of our griffins flying towards us. I'm unsure what happened after that, because then he dropped me back into the forest. I remember falling, then nothing.*

Simão muttered to himself, "Wings and fangs… sounds like what the Coachman ran into, too." *Mateus* nodded his head in agreement. *I imagine the griffon was able to fight him away from Tomar, although not in time to save you. We are sorry, my friend.*

Bartimeu, Simão continued, *I am going to need you to figure out what attacked you and find out if there's a connection to the Inquisitor. When you know, send a message via our owl or lark network. I've heard he's about, and he might be nearer than we thought. Lastly, see what you can do to help keep the patrols safe and warn them to go in pairs if possible or stay closer to Tomar if not. This new Tenenbrani doesn't seem to be connected to Tomar or within reach of our own network. Stay safe and be careful!*

Bartimeu lifted a paw in salute and darted away towards the southern forest and the lairs of the Tenenbrani.

"We'll need to keep our ears open for any news concerning the Inquisitor and this new Tenenbrani," Simão cautioned Mateus. "Have you heard anything about what the Magistrate will do about this attack?"

"I think he won't round up the town for protection since we went deeper into the forest rather than the forest creatures coming to attack us. He will probably announce that it was a Traitor who got his justice and leave it for now."

Simão agreed and glanced up at the guards. They had their backs to them again for the next walk along the wall. With the moonlight once again illuminating the marked keystone, Simão repeated his gesture, walked towards the wall, and crossed back into Tomar. Hopefully, Bartimeu would have some information soon. In the meantime, he would need to give orders of renewed caution to the patrols and pray the more blood-thirsty Tenenbrani weren't returning for more.

Chapter 33: An Unwelcome Visitor in Tomar

The day after their informative visit to the Pit, the Inquisitor was frustrated that the patrol Traitor hadn't given him any information before he had been chased away by a griffon. *Where were Griffons hiding around here?? Were they Clairdani, or a separate element altogether?* He had never even heard of griffons beyond folklore, and he had been more surprised than afraid of what the griffon could do when he dropped the Traitor the night before. *I would have liked to see what he could do with the likes of me!*

These thoughts plagued his mind as he searched the spot in the forest where he thought the patrol Traitor had lain before being interred in the Pit. Any clues, paper, marks, would be helpful in discovering which other Tomarans were traitors, where they met, or how they contacted and worked with the Tenenbrani. The Codex had been beneficial but was limited in that neither the Advocate nor the gaoler knew the specifics of how the Traitors communicated and met within Tomar, necessitating his physical return to the accursed town. The Clairdani he had left back at his palace had been less than helpful with what really mattered – unravelling the Traitor's web of deceits. Once he had conquered the Traitors of Tomar, the only ones who dared to defy him and remain unfearful of him, he could truly rule over the rest of the lands of Lusitania!

His keen eyesight scoured the area carefully. He knelt down where he believed the body had dropped and felt around the leaves and scant grass in case anything felt unnatural. A little to the right of where his head may have hit, he felt something spongey and smooth. It was tinted brown, but he couldn't tell more than that. It blended in with the dirt and everything else in the forest. On his way back to his mount, he continued to try and clean it and stopped at a stream to clear the remaining debris and dirt from it. It was folded a bit, and unfolding it, he saw that he was mostly transparent, curved in a circular conical shape, and the size of a berry. At last! Something he could use to round up Traitors!

The next day, the Inquisitor came riding back into Tomar. The townspeople saw him coming and most quickly dispersed and had closed up their houses by the time he got to The Magistrate's house. Ma'elrich wasn't fazed by this unwelcome from the town. He only had need of Rowan at the moment.

"Rowan! How are you!" he boomed as he approached the Magistrate's enormous home on the market square.

Startled by the sudden appearance of someone presumed to be dead, Rowan put down his ink quill and called to his aide. "Oliveiro, come with me. He's back, apparently from the dead."

The two men emerged from the house, Rowan in his politician's role once again. "Good to see you, Ma'elrich, dear friend! I heard you were dead or something and missed the coach back to your palace. Rumors, of course!"

Ma'elrich chuckled, "That was an unfortunate day, for sure. I was knocked out, and when I came to, the coach was long gone, and only a dead horse remained to give any evidence of what happened. I'll have to get the coachman's story someday!"

"I can arrange that while you're here."

When Ma'elrich wasn't immediately forthcoming, Rowan continued, trying to prompt a response. Conversation with Ma'elrich never seemed to go well.

"So you've returned! Have you discovered something in your travels or forgotten something here perhaps?"

"I've discovered something, Rowan. Let's go indoors and away from the prying ears out here in the open."

Rowan gestured toward the house, sending Oliveiro ahead to prepare refreshments in his home office.

After sitting and allowing Oliveiro to pour them tea, Oliveiro bowed out of the room. Ma'elrich took that as his cue to begin. Pulling out the green translucent conical piece he'd found in the forest, he held it out to Rowan.

"Have you ever seen anything like this before?"

Rowan reached out to receive it in his hand so that he could inspect it more closely.

"I've never seen anything like it! What do you think it is? A covering of sorts for something?"

"I'm not sure either." The two men sat thoughtfully. After a few moments, Ma'elrich continued. "Do you know anyone with green eyes?"

"Green eyes?" Rowan sat back, surprised. "All humans have brown eyes. Only cats and such have green eyes... Have you ever seen green eyes?"

"I have... once. When I was questioning the gaoler, towards the end, his eyes turned green. I thought it was maybe something I'd done, but now I wonder." He gave Rowan some time to process this before adding, "And this piece is the exact shade of brown of most everyone in the town."

Rowan was beginning to understand now. "So do you think there might be more people in Tomar with green eyes, but we don't see them because they are somehow covering them with these?"

"Exactly."

"Where did you get this, if I may ask?"

"As I was returning, I heard about the man attacked in the forest somewhat beyond your town borders and thought I'd look. I figured a traitor might easily go out to meet with creatures to help plan attacks, and wondered if there might be some clues. This was the only thing I found. If he had it in his eye, it may have popped out during whatever skirmish he had with the creature he was meeting with. You'd think they'd know better. I guess he got the gift he thought he was giving!"

A missing piece snapped into place for Rowan. "So, we no longer need to use the patrols to stop the creature attacks! We can find the Traitors in the town itself and stop them from letting them into the town!"

"Yes, exactly! That's what I've come to do. Together, we can rid ourselves of these Traitors and end the attacks once and for all."

Chapter 34: The Traitor's Downfall

United, at last, Rowan and Ma'elrich decided to plot the traitor's downfall carefully.

"I thought you were going to stop the patrols immediately, Rowan, so as not to allow any Traitors to converse with their monster friends! Why are they still able to go beyond the walls?"

"We are carrying on as if nothing has changed until everything is ready, Ma'elrich. The less warning they have, the more Traitors we will ensnare in our nets!"

"Exactly, give them no warning and no chance to escape either! Plenty of townspeople saw me and are probably trying to leave town or hide somewhere while I am here. We have to lock the town gates and tell everyone that for their protection, no one is to leave for a fortnight. We will start our checkpoints within a couple of days at most. What we need to do now is choose which of the guards we trust the most to form our Justice Patrol. Have them create the checkpoints for us and tell them what to look for in the eyes."

"And those we catch... Will they be bait for the Tenenbrani or for other Traitors? We know the Traitors bring the Tenenbrani into Tomar. However, if we could rid ourselves of the monsters, there would be no issue with the Traitors. They don't seem to do harm to others themselves."

Rowan's inability to take strong action and see the bigger picture infuriated Ma'elrich. Politicians always wanted to stay the course and only do what they had to without getting their own hands dirty.

"Rid yourselves of the Traitors, and even with monsters in the forest, they won't have a way into the town at all! As terrible as it might be, ridding Tomar of its Traitors will be the end of the attacks. You have to focus on that outcome."

Rowan nodded and pulled out the roster of guards and patrols. For the next couple of hours, they created three groups of Justice Patrols. While most of those selected would be responsible for manning the checkpoints, a select few would be detailed to either Rowan or Ma'elrich for carrying out or relaying their orders.

"Can you verify that all of these are clean and not Traitors, Rowan?"

"I can. They are loyal to Tomar and to me. I would swear my life on it."

"Then ensure the lists are posted in the town square, recall the Patrols, and then lock the town gates. We will spend tomorrow with these new squads, working out how and where to set the checkpoints, set up teams, and ensure the details have enough information to know how to answer all questions. The less time they have to prepare for our checkpoints, the more thorough we will be in catching them."

"Adair!" called Rowan.

Adair, who served as both town hall sentry and the town crier, came quickly, "Yes, milord?"

"Assemble all of Tomar to the town centre. Send out the word that because of the recent attack, attendance will be mandatory. Once you are sure all are present, read this Decree to them. Then read the three lists." Rowan thrust a hastily written scroll into his hands. "Once those are read, announce that anyone on the list must be here tomorrow as the sun rises while everyone else is on lockdown for their protection. Anyone found not following the decree or reporting as required will be taken by the guards and executed at sunset."

Looking like he might have questions, Ma'elrich cut him short. "Let's go, now!"

"As you wish, milords." And Adair hustled out of the building.

The evening of the second day, at sunset, Rowan and Ma'elrich watched as five manacled traitors were marched into the gaol. The more interesting spectacle was one badly-beaten woman who hobbled forward slowly as the guards shoved her up the collection of faggots and branches that had been piled around the base of the town's small, square punishment post. All eyes were upon her as she shrieked her insistence on her innocence and the injustice of her pain. Everyone in the market square seemed to hold their breath, gripped by the raw emotion that echoed through her desperate plea. Her voice, a heavy melody in the tense silence, echoed against the stone walls around them. While the weight of her words hung heavily in the air. Some onlookers exchanged uneasy glances, torn between empathy and skepticism, while others watched with more hardened expressions, unmoved by her impassioned protestations. Parents held their children close to them, shielding them as much as they could without violating the law that all eyes must see all executions. Rowan was sure there were more traitors in their midst, but five would be a good beginning. Their treasonous web should dissolve quickly now.

The manacled prisoners were made to stand at the entrance to the gaol, in plain sight of the execution and observers but not within earshot of anyone, lest they be able to pass along any messages to anyone. The doomed woman's thin arms, deformed from recent beatings, were forced into the manacles near the top of the post, stretching her frail, torn frame so that she could barely stand on tiptoe. Comfort was not a consideration. Unlike the majority of the onlookers, the guards were unmoved by the suffering before them and continued their preparations for the impending execution.

Adair stood near the post, reading out her crime for all to hear. "…for trying to avoid a checkpoint and resisting arrest, she shall be condemned to burning at the stake until dead." He did his best not to show any waver in his voice that would show his abhorrence of such punishments. He did as he was commanded and drank heavily to avoid the nightmares that always followed.

With a gesture from Rowan, the guard executioner touched the torch to the faggots, which smoked profusely. Whoever had piled the wood had mistakenly taken either green wood or gotten the wood wet, for it was more smoke than fire. This was a blessing, for after a few minutes of smoke inhalation, the woman slumped down dead, hanging from her manacles, before the flames charred her remains to ashes. Once the flames took her, Rowan and Ma'elrich stepped from the window, eager to applaud themselves on a well-executed traitor's trap and their hopes for the next couple of days.

"Did I not tell you that a lightning strike yields the best results, Rowan?" Ma'elrich gloated. Smudged soot and dank sweat coated his plain overcoat, tunic, and rough-sewn trousers. He refused to wear better clothes when interrogating prisoners, preferring clothing he could either burn or toss away at the end of the day.

"You did, so were you successful so soon? I thought it might take a few days to break them down for any information," Rowen replied.

"I am the Inquisitor, am I not?" Ma'elrich's chest swelled with an unmistakable pride. "My results are legendary, and as you can see, they speak for themselves. I didn't even need to question all of them. After the first one was dragged back to her cell, she died soon thereafter – weak disposition, of course. When the guards selected the second traitor, they chose the frailest of the lot, who broke down very soon after being placed in the chamber. We released him back to his cell after he gave us the one piece of information since it was enough to help us catch the rest of them."

"One piece of information was enough?" Rowan asked, incredulous. "What was it?"

"Where they have their secret meetings in town. It's in the basement of Simão's forge, where his apprentices live while they are training with him. With the decree, they are likely to have a meeting any night now to plan how to escape, which will be our time to attack!"

Rowan's admiration grew at this new action-minded side to Ma'elrich. What a change from the malevolent fear-monger he had been previously, and perhaps showed he was someone he should be cautious of himself. "Will you be using your detail guard or the checkpoint guards for that task?"

"Both. I don't want any to escape, and with more soldiers, there will be more hands to grab them and more feet to run after any that might escape."

"Well thought, my clever friend." Rowan pictured the capture of many traitorous men and women dragged through the town towards his gaol and smiled.

Half a fortnight later, Ma'elrich stood facing his five flushed detail guards. Despite their torn and battered clothing, they all stood with their arms plastered to their sides, legs as if glued together, very tall and straight, breathing heavily. They had just returned from their raid and subsequent herding of traitors to the gaol. After the days they spent setting up the raid and hours capturing and imprisoning the large group of traitors, Ma'elrich began his pacing around them as he liked to do when interrogating others. It helped him see how much each fidgeted when being questioned, and the mind game made him feel more powerful.

He pointed to the sandy-haired, chiseled man standing at the right end of the group. "I'll start with you. How many traitors have you all chained up in the gaol?"

Sweat beaded on his brow, and he tried to mentally count how many rooms were now full and how many manacles were in each room. "About forty-three, sir."

Forty-three? There were that many townspeople acting against their own people? Including the five they caught in the checkpoints, that made forty-eight...

Tapping the tallest detail guard from behind, Ma'elrich asked, "And how many got away?"

The tallest detail's hairy neck convulsed as he swallowed hard. "No…none, sir, to my knowledge. We had all entrances and exits covered, and we had the element of surprise on our side. Once they realized they were all being bound and carted off to the gaol, they were everywhere: trying to exit through windows, fighting their way through back doors and trap doors… but we were able to channel them through one door so all were bound and accounted for."

Ma'elrich paused in his pacing. His eyebrows rose in adoration of this well-executed plan.

"Good!" He stopped in front of the shortest guard, who was the only one he could see eye to eye. Glaring into his eyes, he had one last burning question.

"Can you personally guarantee that all of them were in the meeting?"

"Yes, sir. We watched as these traitors arrived at the forge in ones and twos, slinking in from the shadows. The last one looked around, then locked the door behind him. At that, we surrounded the building and waited by windows out of sight to verify that it was a traitors' meeting. As soon as their leader started the meeting, half of us broke down the locked door and tore into their meeting room. We had about twelve of them bound before they figured out that we were the Justice Patrol and there to arrest them. Those of us who stayed outside the forge were able to capture anyone who tried to escape, hold those who were bound, and watch for any newcomers. No one else came within sight of the forge." Stealing himself, he stood up a little straighter. "You have my word."

Ma'elrich considered this final statement. "I will hold you to that. If I find that any traitors were not caught in the raid, you will share their same fate."

Chapter 35: A Message in a Bottle

After a long trip to find answers, Anehta finally returned to the caves and was distressed to find no one there! She had important news and no idea where exactly either of her friends might be! Exhausted, she decided to try to rest a bit and hope that either Metulas returned by that time or she had enough strength to try and find where Luz might be.

What seemed to be only moments later, Anehta was woken by the low humming that was Metulas' attempt at singing. Since there were only a few caves that Metulas could actually fit his bulk into, he had resorted to singing and breathing fire to get their attention when they were asleep.

Alright, I'm awake! Anehta flew to the mouth of the cave and playfully butted heads with Metulas.

Happy to see you too, Anehta, Metulas replied to her enthusiasm. *Were the elves what we expected them to be?*

An interesting group, they are indeed! And Anehta told Metulas everything she could remember. What the elves looked like, how they postured themselves differently than anything she'd seen before, what had happened at the council meeting, how the king had captured her, the clue, and that the elves weren't going to be any more helpful at this time.

Disappointing, but not unexpected, Metulas sighed. "Well, we have persevered without them so far. I suppose we can finish this without them, too. It will take everything we have to give, though, and we will need some more serious plans to make things change."

Where is Luz, Metulas?

She is beginning her search for the writing of the curse itself. From what you said, I'm now convinced the curse was written on a magic stone that the elves can carve into, but no one else can see the carvings. 'their writing and their methods'... I wonder...

What do you think they meant by that? Anehta asked.

I'm fairly certain that they mean they wrote the curse in elfish in that special ink that only shows in the moonlight. That much, I told Luz, although that makes it hard to find unless you know where to look. The humans probably never knew they were cursed, which would be true to form for the elves. Since elves abhor lies, they speak truth, although they have their own ways of not being straightforward. It would be true elfin fashion for them to have cursed the human race while they were sleeping or dying or incapacitated in some other way. By placing the writing of the curse on the battlefield as they all lay dying, the humans were within the presence of the curse, even if they weren't exactly able to see it or understand it. It was still binding since it did fulfill the rule that all parties must be at the place where the curse is placed. The fact that everyone who saw the placement died before relaying the curse to the rest of the people was immaterial to them.

And the dead tell no tales. Did I tell you their king put a truth oath on me? They are definitely a tricky lot. We will have to be on our guard. Is there anything he told us that will help us find this curse stone? And have you learned anything that will help us all break the curse?

There is one thing I just thought about from something you said and something I did learn recently. Since it's written in elfish ink, we should be able to create something that will draw us to that substance. It wouldn't work in the forest since the ink comes from rare herbs that are fermented and added to other ingredients in the forest. However, since none of those elements are between here and Tomar, any pull would indicate that the curse was in that direction.

So Luz could use this object to help guide her to the curse stone? That would save us so much time! For the first time in a while, Anehta finally felt they weren't going to fight a losing battle and might actually be able to make some progress.

I believe so... can you go find something easy and light for Luz to carry as she searches for the stone?

Happily, Anehta flew off, bringing back one object after another until they agreed on a y-shaped small branch that would be small enough to hide in a bag.

Metulas gently placed the small branch on the ground and, with meticulous care, breathed a greenish dragon fire upon it that Anehta had never seen before. To Anehta's amazement, the branch did not succumb to the flames in any way. Instead, it seemed to glow green for a few moments before the glow slowly faded and seemed to disappear into the branch.

Hmmm... It doesn't look that different. Are you sure that works? Anehta asked curiously. She didn't want to offend Metulas.

Come look at it again, closer this time. I promise I won't singe you...

Anehta hopped over to the branch. It didn't seem any different to her from before until Metulas breathed warm air on it without any fire. Slowly, a bluish light emerged on the surface, a fanciful script that seemed to dance with ethereal light. The characters glowed briefly before fading away as swiftly as they had appeared.

Stupendous! Anehta gave a little flip in her excitement, landing awkwardly and rolling a bit before being able to get back on her feet.

Let's take this to Luz together. It'll be good to ensure she knows how to use it.

A couple hours later, the flying pair of friends finally spotted Luz near a cool spring in Batalha, the last one before entering the sandy, lifeless desert that separated the region surrounding Tomar from Batalha. Seeing a large, familiar shadow on the ground, Luz looked up and hailed her friends as they alighted near her.

"Anehta! You're back already!" she exclaimed, giving her dear friend a squeeze. Anehta squeaked in response.

Yep, and we think we have something that will help you find the curse stone!

With that introduction, Metulas brandished the small branch with a flourish and handed it to Luz.

Luz eyed the small branch carefully. Not knowing exactly what to say, Luz said, "Thank you?" After another moment of thinking of what to say without offending them, she added, "So, is this a special stick, or should I have remembered to put one in my pack before I left to help me roast the potatoes at night?"

Anehta and Metulas shared a knowing smile.

Let me show you, said Metulas as he breathed on the stick. The elfish writing glowed briefly, then faded away.

It's a magic stick! Wonderful! Um... what does it do, other than glow then? inquired Luz curiously.

This stick has been enchanted to lead you to the curse stone. Like pulls to like, so this stick has the elfish writing on it and will draw you towards other elfish writings. Since there will be many such writings north of us where the elfish kingdom is, only let it draw you either south or west. One thing I have learned since you departed was that the last battlefield was so fierce that the land itself wanted to forget about the blood. With the curse, everything that was on that battlefield would die, including the vegetation and any other lifeforms that were on the battlefield when it ended. Thankfully, most of the larger creatures were able to get away from the noise and bloodshed and flee into the forest. The plants and insects weren't so lucky, which is why it is a dry, dead desert here even today.

"Do you mean to say this desert right here is where the last battlefield was? Do you think this is where the curse was then, or did the elves tell you where they laid it?" Luz started to scan the horizon, looking for any rock that might happen to have the curse written on it.

Anehta piped in, *They claimed to have placed it in plain sight of the humans who were still on the battlefield as it ended. So the stone is either still on the battlefield, or someone moved it. Hopefully, the stick will help you find where it is now.*

"This could be very useful, indeed!" Luz turned over the stick a few times, looking it over as if for instructions. "How do I use it though? I don't see it pointing me towards any direction right now."

Hold the stick with both hands where the two parts form a "V." Yes, like that. Now, focus on the curse stone. Try to imagine a stone with elfish writing in glowing blue letters... instructed Metulas.

The stick twitched suddenly, and Luz dropped it in surprise.

"It moved!"

Exactly as it should! This time, rather than drop it, hold it and let it pull you towards the stone. It will stop moving as soon as it loses its physical connection to you, so it shouldn't get away from you. When you get near other people though, try not to use it where they can see you. They might get some ideas and take it from you.

Luz nodded and smiled up at Metulas, hope and gratitude shining in her face.

I'm coming with you, Luz, for today at least, to help keep you safe. Metulas has much to do and figure out at the Cidade, and I'll check in with him every couple of days to keep you both up to date with the news. I also need to do my rounds with our people to see what they know about the Inquisitor. The elves heard he was roaming the countryside and had captured some of the Clairdani. He may already be in the area near Tomar or even here looking for you.

With that, the three said their farewells, and Metulas flew back to his work with the old dragon heart in Batalha. After watching Metulas' departure into the distance, Luz put her pack on her back and picked up the branch with both hands. There was a definite pull towards the west, thankfully just strong enough to keep them moving at a solid pace and not a trot. Looking at Anehta who was still standing still, Luz called over her shoulder, "You coming?"

Anehta gave a hoot of affirmation, and the two started their journey tracking the curse stone.

Much to their surprise, the stick did not lead them on a direct path in any way! By the end of the third day, it seemed to have led them through grasslands, then lowlands towards where Metulas had indicated the Cidade dos Corações lay. There was a haze over the area as if there were magic that protected that area from humans seeing it. The twig enabled her to enter the area, but before she reached any of the interesting caves beyond the mounds of dragon bones, it pulled her away from the area in another direction. Soon, it was clear that the stone was not still in the Cidade as they were led back to what seemed to be the entrance.

After some frustration and confusion, Luz finally took one hand off the branch. "I feel it pulling us away from here, back towards the battlefield."

Maybe this is where a lot of elfish writing or magic is, so it was drawn here first? If humans are magically repelled from here, then it won't be here now if the curse rock is with people, right? Offered Anehta insightfully.

"Very true. OK, then let's see where else this will lead us. Ready?" Luz put both hands back on the branch, and they turned around, pointing the stick towards Tomar again. Although the stick seemed to lead them meandering hither and yon, at least they were moving in the general direction of the town of Tomar itself. Largely, the journey was thankfully uneventful other than stiff joints from holding the branch continually, and they slept very well each night, Luz tumbling into her sac each night from sheer exhaustion.

The Clairdani, hearing from Anehta that Luz was fully recovered and on a new quest, took turns to keep her company. Happy to see her alive and well, they also kept guard overnight and brought them news of the countryside, the Inquisitor, and Tomar. Most importantly, with the Clairdani around, Anehta was able to travel more freely between Luz and Metulas, so that soon everyone was up to date with the happenings in Tomar and around.

The Clairdani were also able to fill in additional news that they hadn't gotten from The Enlightened. After her escape from Tomar, there had been a very strict lockdown, and fewer people had been buried at the Pit. Without Simão and the others meeting there, any newly created Clairdani didn't realize they still had a human mind, heart, and joint purpose with the Enlightened. Consequently, the Clairdani were not sure if these newer Clairdani would be part of their cause or not or even reachable through their link. Sometimes, they reverted to their animal instincts, finding a simple solace in being free in the forest and not still tied to the pains that surrounded the town of Tomar and their past.

"I'm sure they will be on our side, don't worry. They won't join the Tenenbrani, and now that I'm back, I can help them reconnect so we can communicate with them," Luz assured them.

The Clairdani seemed to be assuaged by her confidence and didn't argue the point, happy to take turns in her company. Despite her carrying a small branch all the time, the Clairdani never mentioned it, and Luz felt it would be best not to explain to the Clairdani about the curse stone. This was their own personal quest, with all of its dangers and mystery, and the fewer beings who knew about it, the more successful their mission would be. After a week of meandering in the desert as if they were led by a wayward child, the stick gave an abrupt halt in the middle of the desert between Batalha and Tomar. Looking around the spot, there was nothing there except sand. Luz put the stick down in case it needed to recharge and put both hands on it again. It shook but made no pull in any direction.

Maybe the branch is tired? Do inanimate, enchanted objects need rest?? Decisively, Luz announced to the Clairdani, keeping her company, "Let's rest. We've been travelling for quite a while, and it seems we are getting closer to Tomar. Let's take some time to check our supplies." She looked meaningfully at Anehta, trying to tell her with her eyes that she needed her help.

Is this the place? Whispered Anehta when she had flown down to Luz's shoulder.

"It must be. The stick stopped here and isn't wanting to go anywhere. Help me look around, and tonight, when the moon is out, we will check to see if any of the rocks we find are marked."

After an hour of searching and pretending to search for wood for a fire, they found a couple of stones that were large and flat enough to be candidates for writing. They decided to make camp close to them and practice sparring til dusk. In the depth of the night, the moon rose, and assured that the Clairdani were resting, they checked the stones excitedly for any writing. They were blank. They spent a couple more hours looking in wider circles to see if there were any other stones they had missed, but only the two they already saw were in that area. Sad but not discouraged, they returned to camp and slept until the sun awoke them the next day.

After first light, Luz took hold of the stick once more and thinking about the curse itself, the stick gave another pull towards Tomar. Relieved, Luz trailed the slow progress through the desert, finally reaching the outskirts of Tomar. It became evident that the elusive stone lay somewhere within the town itself. With the Inquisitor entrenched within Tomar and the Traitors securely in chains, she knew she needed a plan.

Chapter 36: Home Squatters

On his way to Cenellot and Noyette's cave from his newly made tree-dwelling in Sintrentejo, Florenço noted how many elves, flora, and fauna he saw. Not too many elves choose to live this far from the elfin center; indeed, he saw very few. Inwardly, he sighed a breath of relief. There would be fewer eyes spying on them and reporting to King Abrimel.

Just at the border, he saw Markus as if he were waiting for him. They exchanged their respectful bows, and Florenço patted the side of Markus' head.

What is it, my friend? You seem worried!

The Enlightened of Tomar have almost all been captured two nights past. The Inquisitor has made an eventful return, and he has somehow uncovered the secret of the eye covers that concealed their distinctive green eyes. He was able to use that information in street checkpoints, and one of those caught told them about Simão's meeting place. Almost all of them are now in chains. Mateus is part of the detail and was able to get Simão and a couple of others out, and these fugitives are now also in hiding in the forest. I didn't bring them here, of course. They wanted to stay near Tomar to see what they could do to help free the others.

This was too much to pass along to Cenellot and Noyette all at once, and it strengthened his resolve to move them into Sintra.

Come with me, Markus. I will be moving Cenellot and Noyette to Sintra this evening, and we could use your help, company, and protection.

I will, only because I promised Simão to see them safe, and this will be in keeping with that promise. Without their patrols, we have no way of working with our spies within the Tenenbrani. I forgot to tell you – somehow, the Inquisitor managed to trick some Clairdani into his palace, Almourael, and is holding them captive as well. We do not know what the purpose of their capture is, although others have reported that he was demanding answers from them. He knows no limits to the amount of evil he pursues, and we do not know anything more about their well-being other than fearing the worst.

Florenço shook his head at the sad news and wondered how such an evil as the Inquisitor had been hidden for so long. For now, Tomar was not anywhere close to Sintra, but this news clearly meant there would be no returning to Tomar for Cenellot and Noyette.

Even more resolved to ensure that Cenellot and Noyette would remain safe, Florenço and Markus trotted to the cave, wondering between them what the future of Tomar might be. Very soon, they saw Cenellot and Noyette at the entrance as if expecting them.

Seeing Florenço, Cenellot ran to him and hugged him. "Florenço, Markus! We are happy to see you!"

I am happy to see you as well! Show me the greeting I taught you, Cenellot. Remember, we don't show such outbursts of emotion in the elfin kingdom.

Laughing at himself, Cenellot retreated a few steps, then displayed the hand gesture over his heart and to his face, saying in Elfish, *My heart is gladdened by seeing you.*

Markus bowed in greeting. *You've done well in such a short time, Cenellot!*

Florenço and Cenellot both beamed at the compliment.

Cenellot, I need to speak to you and your mother. Is she nearby?

Cenellot nodded and walked quickly into the cave, returning with his mother right behind him. Her smile warmed Florenço's heart, and he gave her the same hand gestures that Cenellot had just offered to him. She returned the gesture as well, smiling as she did so.

They had made great progress in the few short weeks they had been working on learning the elfin customs and mannerisms, although the language was still difficult for them.

Impressed, Markus noted, *you may yet do well with the elves!*

Cenellot, I have important things to discuss with you two, and I need you to relay the news to your mother. Agreed?

"Mother, Florenço has some important news. He will put it in my mind, and I will relay the message to you. Will that be alright with you?"

"News? From Tomar or from the elves?" she replied.

"Both," answered Florenço.

Florenço and Cenellot stared at each other for a few minutes. Every once in a while, Markus seemed to nicker and add something to the conversation. Once all three had stopped looking between the three of them, Cenellot turned to his mother.

"They say that the Inquisitor left Tomar but has returned worse than before. He has captured Clairdani and has now imprisoned most of the Traitors in a raid with plans to execute them soon. We will never be able to return to Tomar safely. Also, Florenço petitioned the elfin king, King Abrimel, for our refuge with them, and he refused. Despite this, Florenço has built us a house in the tree tops near the border of the elfin lands where we should be safe. The elfin lands are protected by magic so that humans cannot see or find them, so if anyone tries to find us, they won't be able to see us inside their lands."

Florenço and Markus nodded their heads in agreement.

Noyette took a few minutes to process all this information, then asked, "So are you asking us what we want to do? As I see it, we have two options: one, stay here and train so that if we are attacked someday, we can defend ourselves and never have more interaction with people other than you two; or two, hide in this house of yours in the elfin lands where we won't need to defend ourselves but will train and learn customs just as we are here. So either we have freedom but fear of attack, or we have few freedoms with no fear of attack."

Florenço knew the difficulty of the decision and could only gesture with his hands that he was sorry for the pitiful options available.

With all the traitors in prison, there won't be anyone to check on you. The Clairdani know that we are watching over you now, but they aren't allowed to tell humans about us, so those in Tomar don't know that you are being taken care of. Without their help, they won't be surprised if you don't stay at the cave."

In a few phrases, Cenellot translated all for his mother.

"What do you think, Cenellot?" she asked. "Should we stay here as we have and hope the Inquisitor and Tenenbrani

247

won't find us, or should we move to this Elfin house of Florenço's and test our learning of the Elfin ways, customs, and language?"

I know you will never look like elves. However, if you can learn the language, customs, and swordsmanship, you can blend in from a distance. We can hope that with enough time and training, you will go undetected until a time when the king might change his mind.

Cenellot relayed the message. "Mother, I think we will be safer with Florenço in Sintra, even if we have to stay hidden. Hopefully, we won't have to hide forever, and we can try to make ourselves seem useful to them when the time comes."

Noyette cast a nostalgic gaze over the area, her eyes lingering on the familiar sights that held memories close to her heart. All that they had learned and experienced over the past months came back to her. While they were mostly pleasant memories, she was ready to move on from a damp cave, especially if they might be spending more time inside their new place.

"Give us time to pack what is here, and we'll follow you."

Towards dusk, the four of them furtively hiked to the borderland of Sintrentejo, each of them laden with what goods they could carry. Markus carried as much as he could to make their journey quieter and lighter. Florenço had assured them that they would have everything they needed in Sintra, although it would be better if he weren't suddenly looking for items such as women's clothing if they were trying to avoid detection.

Just as the moon rose, they managed to reach the tree house Florenço had built for them. Cenellot stood in awe, his eyes widened with the anticipation of this new adventure. Every emotion he felt, unspoken, resonated in his eyes as he took in everything around him. The hazel tree Florenço chose was the largest tree he had ever seen! It was at least as wide as he was tall, with a small, spiral staircase hewn into the bark reaching into the canopy. Markus whinnied his approval quietly.

Noyette's eyes were also wide from apprehension and admiration. The elfin workmanship was beyond anything she had ever seen before! She had never lived anywhere other than Tomar, and then she lived in a cave and now a tree! If her family saw her now, they wouldn't know her. Despite its beauty, the house didn't look very big. *How do we live in a tree without falling out of it?*

Unpacking the bags from Markus, they said their farewells, and Markus departed silently to return to Tomar and help where he could. Florenço gestured them up the staircase, checking the surrounding area as he followed behind them. As they passed into the canopy of their tree dwelling, they stepped onto a large, flat, polished wooden decking that flowed into all the main branches of the hazel tree. These formed the bones of their new house, and there were multiple smaller decks all connected to the main flooring by ornately hewn staircases. Both living branches and flowery vines had been woven together to give a sense of privacy walls. High window-like openings gave them a bird's eye view of the surrounding forest while protecting them from being seen from below. Exhausted by their travel, Noyette sat on a large, carved branch that rose out of the flooring, inviting anyone to sit on its seat.

"You'll find beds for each of you in the adjoining spaces. I'll remain here tonight to help with any questions and ensure all is safe for you."

The two weary travelers each claimed a bedroom space, finding a hollowed wooden basin with a jar of water waiting for them. Within moments, they were each asleep under soft grass woven bedding, their heads resting on pillows of downy reeds. For the first time in many months, they felt they were allowed to relax, unburdening themselves of the anxiety and worry that had plagued them since they left Tomar.

Early the next morning, Cenellot and Noyette awoke to see that Florenço had set up breakfast for them in the main room. Seeing them, Florenço gave them another traditional elfin greeting. *My heart is honored to see you again,* which they returned. All enjoyed the variety of fruits, vegetables, and bread that was on the table and fell silent as the meal ended. This would be the start of a new life for them, and the enormity of that moment weighed on them.

"This is amazing, Florenço! We can hardly thank you enough for having created this for us!" gushed Noyette, enthralled at all this forest elf had done for them and asking for nothing in return.

Cenellot nodded vigorously in agreement and translated the human speech for Florenço. Using the elfish, he continued, *Will I get to train with other elves now? I've been getting much better with my swordsmanship...*

Florenço smiled to stifle a laugh. *I'm sure you are! You've been working hard for a while now! It will take time though, for many reasons. I have a plan that I hope will help convince the king that you are a help to us, not just refugees asking for handouts.*

For both of you, we must continue using the elfish as much as possible. Learn new words every day, and practice even between yourselves so that you will not need any translation. Continue using the customs, and I have brought you both clothing that will help you blend in with the elves and the forest.

Cenellot, we must continue you in your training – swordsmanship, horsemanship, archery, hand-to-hand combat – but also geography, history, rituals, and grace. Know that there are not many children here for you to train with since we elves live for a long time and have different customs from you regarding children. Children begin training at an early age, and both boys and girls train their entire lives, so that anyone can defend the forest and our people. Combined with our natural strength and speed, even those a little younger than you would be able to defeat you easily.

Resignedly, Cenellot acquiesced. "Could I eventually become as good a warrior as my father was at least?"

We will see what we can do, I promise. Please relay this next bit to your mother: She will need to train as a healer since that would be the most likely way she can stay here and not be a trained warrior like the other female elves. It would not be too unusual. There are quite a few elves who refrain from any violence and prefer to work with the healing arts instead. I will work with her to teach her what I know, and she will need to learn to read elfish so she can read the books that are here, written about healing. Can she do that – learn to read Elfish and train to be a healer?

Cenellot relayed the message to Noyette, who grew flustered at the thought of the tasks. "That's a lot to learn in a short space of time!"

"You have all the time you need, mother. Remember, we are safe, and nothing will harm us here."

Noyette sighed. "I will do my best to train and learn as much as I can in hopes that the elves will eventually accept me as well as you have, Florenço."

Florenço nodded his acceptance of their agreement. They had a plan for how they might stay. How long they could last before King Abrimel found them, he did not know.

Lastly, I need to ensure that anyone we interact with will not tell the king that I am harboring fugitives here, or we will all be imprisoned. This far away from the center of Sintra, we will mostly encounter other elves who are also not fond of King Abrimel. However, any one of them might use the information as a bargaining chip with him to restore lost favors. If you do get to speak to any elf, be very careful of anything you say to anyone. We weigh our spoken words very carefully, which is why we tend to speak into each other's minds in our everyday speech. Spoken and written words are both considered binding promises, so you must speak carefully and respectfully at all times. This may be the biggest challenge for you, although I know you are well-intentioned.

That is enough for now. I need to return to my other dwelling, give my report of how you two are faring in the cave, and get more supplies. Please rest here, put away your belongings, and we will continue your training when I return.

Chapter 37: A Dragon's Heavy Heart

While Anehta and Luz continued with their slow search for the curse stone, Anehta had been reporting back and forth between Luz and Metulas so they could still work together and share ideas as best they could. While retracing the stone's pathway, Metulas had been using the time to draw out the old dragon from his reverie. Without the distraction of humans and Clairdani, perhaps the ancient dragon would offer some dragon-to-dragon advice or aide, or so he hoped.

After a full fortnight of travelling, Anehta had come with the news he had thought was a strong possibility: the curse stone was within the town of Tomar. Most likely, he thought, the cursed object would be this same object in the Magistrate's office, given the power it seemed to have and the fact that the elves were only laying claim to one. Although Metulas had made some progress with the old dragon, it was clear he was still holding the most critical information to himself.

In desperation, Metulas flew with the old dragon's heart to the Cidade, telling Anehta to stay with Luz outside Tomar til the new moon, and then he would send word. For this excursion into the Cidade, he needed to be in the mindset of a dragon in the company of other dragons. What he had not told either Anehta or Luz was that, like all dragon lair sites, there were caves that only dragons were able to enter or find in the Cidade, called the Grottos dos Ossos. These Grottos were his quest, the secretive caves that the dragon heart had finally told him about after weeks of silence. Despite the vitriol the old dragon's heart spewed, Metulas felt more connected to his own magic when he felt the old dragon's heart's presence. He had been alone for so many centuries that it was comforting to hear the deep, growling voice and feel young again. As they approached the caves in the Cidade, the old heart's punctuated grumbling awoke Metulas from his reverie.

Those thieving elves! We had stores of treasure here, even towards the end of our war with the humans! Metulas could only imagine it, having never seen the fabled treasures that the humans and dragons shared in bygone eras. It was true. The elves had certainly been here, although not any time recently. Their magic felt earthy, unlike the dragon magic, which felt more like air and fire. They may have taken the treasure from the Cidade, but they wouldn't be able to enter the caves. With the heart in hand, Metulas followed the feel of dragon magic towards the hills in the center of the Cidade and hoped the heart could lead him to any other clues about curses and how to break it.

He searches far and wide, for many nights on end, to see if the differences in moonlight or sunlight show any indicated writings and clues around the caves. Finally, Metulas felt a change in the dragon's heart, and, looking down, he saw a cave opening! He descended slowly to avoid disturbing any dust or objects below and alighted at the enormous cave mouth. Metulas gaped at its expanse, seeing multiple cavernous tunnels branching from the one huge opening space. Unlike other cavern systems, every cavernous tunnel was large enough to accommodate the bulk and height of large dragons, the luminescent walls emitting a dull light.

Adjusting to the dimly lit glittering gloom of the large space, Metulas began to discern large wooden chests, golden objects too big for the chests strewn about the floor, and a heavy layer of dust covering everything. An earthy and fiery magic penetrated the air and seemed to buoy them with an energy he hadn't felt since before the wars began.

As he explained what he saw to his compatriot, the old dragon heart sighed. *I wondered if we had hidden this away before the elves joined us in the war. With no one left to claim it, they would have taken it to their realm as their own as a tribute for their assistance. I remember when all of this was ours, and there was peace. Thankfully this at least seems to still be ours.*

Metulas shared a great sense of longing with him, remarking, *peace would be welcome again!*

It would, came the gravelly reply.

Purposefully avoiding any mention of humans, Metulas directed his attention toward a discussion focused on a peaceful outcome instead. *Do you think breaking the curse that caused the end of our race would help restore peace? Or how else can we halt the influence of the elves' magic over the land here?*

Humans are not a peaceful race, so ending a curse that causes them torment will not necessarily create peace. Although, humans warring with each other does allow the elves a sense of peace outside the human realms. In the end, the scheming elves achieved almost all of what they had hoped for: peace, riches, and sole control over the land. They may not have all the riches, given the treasure we see here, but they most definitely raided the Cidade and took anything they found of value with them to their realm.

Metulas pondered this insight into the elfin mind and world. In this space, maybe the old heart would be more willing to answer helpful questions?

What can you remember about how they cast their curses and spells? When they are written down, are there protections in place?

Specifically, why weren't her powers able to overcome the magistrate?

The heart grew quiet and seemed to recede into itself. Metulas worried that he had overstepped his confidence and laid the heart on one of the open chests. After a long while, the heart finally replied, *the elves didn't need to protect the written magic. Once it was written, the words were binding to all parties involved and in sight of the words as they were written. Many times, they might place anti-magic spells on the object that was infused with the spell or curse to protect it. From what I recollect, usually, the spell keeps others from recognizing it, being able to see it, or makes the object seem like it is something other than what it is, keeping all but the original spell weavers away.*

How does a curse written down get broken, then? Can anyone but the original spell weavers change the curse itself? Metulas was beginning to realize there would be no end to the Tenenbrani until they threatened the elves enough to force them out of hiding.

If the curse has been infused into an object, then destroying the object would break the curse. However, the protections make the object nearly impossible to destroy. The old dragon finally told Metulas what he wanted to know about how to break the curse. It was a torrent of information, as if the dam of hostility had finally been broken and the information that had been closely guarded was finally finding space to invade. Successful at last, Metulas gathered the old heart in his arms and flew quietly back to Batalha.

His mind was full of what he had learned, and his heart was heavy with his thoughts.

Right before the new moon, Metulas was mindlessly playing with his dinner, an old doe that had gotten lost at the edge of the desert by Batalha. His mind was partially on the need to eat before being around the Clairdani, which he was restricted from eating, and mostly on how to help Luz retrieve the stone or, at a minimum, read the inscription if there was one. A golden eagle descended and settled near the neck, turning its head to gaze up at the daydreaming dragon.

Brave of you, settling where I could toast you, Timaeus! Metulas didn't want anyone or anything, especially this particularly gossipy eagle Clairdani, to think he'd been startled.

Nice to see you, too, Metulas! Where are the others?

They are outside Tomar. What news? I haven't seen you in an age..and you always have the best sources for what's going on beyond Batalha.

At the compliment, Timaeus fluffed his feathers as he puffed up his chest. *I'm sure you've heard about the Inquisitor's raids, both in and outside Tomar? Never before have humans targeted us, and we are hoping to work even closer together with the Enlightened in case he decides to eradicate the Clairdani as well as the Enlightened. Without either of those groups, the Tenenbrani will overrun Tomar and the surrounding area, and all will parish!* Timaeus grew more agitated as he spoke, threatening to spoil the dinner Metulas hadn't gotten around to eating yet.

We know, we know... Metulas tried to re-steady his friend. In a few sentences, Metulas told Timaeus the basics of a plan he was devising.

The elves... that would be interesting if they agree to help. This whole mess is partially their fault in the first place, so I would think they should help sort it. When we forget the original cause of an error, we should be forgiven of any remaining debt paid afterwards. Timaeus nodded his head towards the deer's innards, which had been causally tossed to the side, and Metulas gestured that he could have that part of the meal.

Perhaps if all humans understood about the curse, it would make them reconsider their own actions? The Enlightened were able to figure it out, although most others seem too afraid to even listen or pay attention to anything, human or otherwise. That might be a piece of the plan we need to put in motion, especially if we can't break the curse itself.

What can we Clairdani do to help? We will have to work together if we're going to bring this Inquisitor to justice!

Metulas pondered the options of what needed to be done and who could do each piece best. *With the Inquisitor not in his palace, could you organize a rescue of those Clairdani imprisoned? We will be working on freeing Tomar from the powers of the Magistrate and the Inquisitor, and anything you and the forest Clairdani nearest Clod Pollux could do would be most welcome. Before you go to his palace though, I have something for you to do...*

For the next while, Metulas outlined his plan then dispatched Timaeus toward Tomar with the mission of locating Simão and reuniting him with Luz until Metulas could join them later.

Chapter 38: A Kidnapping Plan

At the Pit after dusk, a shrouded corpse slowly rolled towards the edge of the Pit. It moved so slowly that none of the gate or wall guards noticed its movement as it slowly stood upright under one of the overhanging tree branches. All at once, the figure climbed into the tree branch and disappeared. Laying on her front under a dense copse of bushes a little ways away lay Luz, her eyes watching the Pit cautiously. She had never seen anything but Clairdani climb out of the Pit, and this shrouded figure was no Clairdani! "Anehta, did you see that?" she whispered.

Anehta was staring where the figure had disappeared, her eyes large onyx beads in disbelief.

"Fly over there and find out who or what that is, would you?" Luz half-gestured, half stage whispered in her excitement.

Anehta turned her large eyes on her in continued disbelief of the request. These were the times when she hated being small. She was not the brave one of the three of them, and yet once again, they would have her do the dangerous sleuthing.

Luz, in an attempt to avoid raising her voice but still delivering a firm whisper, scolded Anehta while simultaneously trying to encourage her, "You are brave, you can do this, Anehta! The guards won't notice you, and you can fly up that tree much quicker than I could climb it…"

Anehta, initially hesitant, met Luz's gaze with a mix of uncertainty and determination. After a moment, she took a deep breath and replied, "I know, I know… OK, I'll be right back."

A few minutes later, she returned in good spirits. "Guess who it is? It's Simão! He's been hiding in the Pit, so you can't believe how much he stinks…"

"Simão? Really?" Luz cut her off.

"Can you find a place for us to meet beyond the lights of Tomar so the guards can't see us?"

After more flying between the two conspirators, Luz and Simão met behind a bush beyond the reach of Tomar. She gave him a fierce hug after they both acknowledged each other with their identifying hand gesture. Anehta was right. He did smell of rotting meat and decay. She held her breath when he got too close.

"It's so good to see you alive and well, Luz! Timaeus was here last night and said he was told to have us meet until Metulas could be here himself." Simão whispered.

"It's good to see you, too! How'd you escape?"

"Mateus is part of the detail, so he was able to let me out of a window he was guarding and send me to a neighboring street to hide until the raid was over. They had to act as if they got everyone, or the hunt would still be on. We're hoping to free everyone before the Inquisitor or the Magistrate get any ideas about public executions…" Simão's voice trailed off, not wanting to dampen their high spirits.

"Good planning. I hope they don't discover Mateus's secret! We are working on a plan to free all of Tomar within the next few days. I hope that's soon enough. Do you have contact with Mateus?"

"I do. He is able to visit the Pit almost every evening."

"Good. Once Metulas gets here, we can tell everyone the plan and get help. Is there anyone else left in Tomar that I could stay with for a couple of days?"

"You could stay above the Forge! The whole place is boarded up, so no one will look inside but you'll have to be very careful not to have any lights visible. There may even be some food still there that's edible. What do you say?"

"So home, sweet home!" responded Luz exuberantly.

Luz was able to find some clothes at the Pit that would serve as her disguise, and she used the secret entrance to enter the town in the middle of the night once she knew the guard wasn't watching that section of the wall. Once through the wall, she and Anehta snuck carefully into Tomar through the empty streets to Simão's house as quietly as they could.

After rising early and an uneventful day of watching the townsfolk of Tomar, Luz was eager to test her "divining rod" in town to see where exactly the curse object might be. She had been testing it quietly, and each time she thought about the cursed object, it pointed her towards the Magistrate's office. It must be the same object that was preventing her from connecting with the Magistrate!

"Patience," chided Anehta. "Metulas will be here tonight with the new moon, and we can go then. That stick doesn't need sunlight to work. Besides, the reports we've heard say that everyone is on the lookout for green eyes and knows to check for eye covers, so it's better to wait until dark when it's easier to avoid the checkpoints."

Chided, Luz diverted her frustrations and energies to the forge itself. By that evening, Luz had reorganized and cleaned everything in Simão's forge despite Anehta's protests. "If anyone sees this, they will think Simão is still here and not locked up with the others!" She admonished quietly.

"No one ever checked here before, so how would they know that Simão doesn't always keep this place this neat?" Luz retorted, a bit too much above a whisper.

Anehta signed and hoped that no one would need to examine Simão's forge and lodging before they were able to execute their plan. She helped Luz where she could, keeping their voices down while they could hear townsfolk in the streets and alleys below. Once it grew very dark after the sun set, Luz found a spy hole in the north-facing wall and watched both the guarded gate and the secret exit leading to the Pit. As soon as she saw Mateus creep through the wall, she slipped out with Anehta and followed him out beyond the Pit to meet with Simão.

At Luz's approach, the two men stood, and the three signaled with their hand gestures they were indeed part of The Enlightened. Mateus had news to share, and Luz had a plan to explain.

Mateus began, "The Inquisitor has been torturing our friends for information about the Tenenbrani and Clairdani, trying to find out which ones they are working with. So far, no one has said anything, and although terribly broken and mangled, they are still alive for now."

"Good. Let's hope things can stay that way for now. Were you able to meet with Markus, Simão? We might need his counsel as well once Metulas gets here," Luz began.

As if announced, they heard a flap of wings and felt the strong depression of wind pushing them as Metulas landed further into the shadows and then took the two large steps to reach them. At the same moment, Markus trotted towards them, nodding his head in greeting.

Yes, we will need the Clairdani for our plan. We must make haste to set the plan in motion if we are to save our imprisoned friends.

"What's the plan, then? You both sound like you have one ready?" asked Simão eagerly.

In the dark of the new moon beyond the eyes and ears of Tomar, Metulas and Luz explained the details of their plan, each adding details and answering questions until everyone knew what they needed to do the day after next.

Two days later, on Quinta, Anehta stood as still as possible on the founder's statue in the main market square. It was mounted on a large base, making the statue high enough that most people's eyes never looked beyond the base and its inscription. From there, she could see most of the main buildings of Tomar, and today, she watched the gaol's guards' entrance carefully. She had watched as the Inquisitor sauntered into the gaol as soon as the sun arose, and the new shift of guards along with his detail marched in soon thereafter. She imagined what Mateus was doing in the gaol now. Hopefully, all was going according to the plan. He should be checking in on the Inquisitor to see if there was anything special he needed to do to help with the interrogations today. Hopefully that sped up his preparations and set him to work a little sooner. As soon as the Inquisitor and other guards were distracted by the other prisoners, he would tell the guards near him that the Inquisitor had asked him to run an errand to the Magistrate, and he would leave the gaol. That should take... *there he is! He's signaled that all is good. That's me off then while he goes to the Magistrate.*

Anehta flew slowly toward her goal of the western wall outside Tomar, stopping occasionally as if she were snacking on insects. If she flew too quickly, it might seem she was on a task, and she needed to appear to be just another bird-like animal flying in search of food. Finally, she crossed over the western walls and into the deeper forest, where the others were waiting for her.

All is going according to plan so far. Anehta reported.

"Well done, Anehta! Markus, is your team ready? Remember to go towards the northern gates. We need a witness to the Magistrate's kidnapping to lure the Inquisitor to follow," reminded Luz.

We are. I'm on my way to meet them now.

With Markus' departure, Luz spoke to Simão. "With the Magistrate gone, we will hope to get the Inquisitor to follow soon. Remember, you and I will sneak into town once everyone is distracted by the Clairdani approaching the gates. You will need to hide in Tomar, start prodding people about how poorly run the town is under his control, and encourage them to resist his rule as much as possible. The gaol is already full, so he may think twice about putting more people in it and just impose an even tighter martial law. Tell them to stay strong. This plan should only take a few days if they can hang on that long. We have to believe we can beat the Inquisitor and have him leave Tomar forever."

Before long, a cacophony of animal vocalizations emerged from the west, gradually advancing toward the northern gate. The distinct sounds hinted at an approaching commotion, adding an element of trepidation to the already charged atmosphere. Mateus reached the Magistrate's office at that moment. As he knocked on the door, the Magistrate called for him to enter. He was standing by the northern window, trying to make sense of what he saw out the window.

"Sir, you're needed at the Northern gate..." Mateus began as he entered the room.

"What? What's happening at the gate? Is that what the commotion is about?"

"We aren't sure, sir. However, it seems that they are coming to Tomar peacefully although noisily."

Rowan gave a curt nod as if to convince himself that he could take charge of the current situation. As he passed by Mateus, he gave him a nod in acknowledgement of Mateus's bow towards him. Mateus guided him down the stairs, through the town streets, to the northern gate, carefully parting the crowds so the Magistrate could get to the gate as quickly as possible.

That's my cue, said Metulas. *Remember that once you find the cursed object, Luz, you need to leave before The Inquisitor takes over the office. He shouldn't be there during the night hours, and there won't be any moonlight for a few more days yet. As soon as you can see the writing, copy it down and bring it back to Batalha. I will expect you in half a fortnight back at home, ready to help entertain our, um,... visitor.*

With two tremendous flaps, Metulas was airborne and out of sight. Luz waited with Simão while Anehta flew to the top of the western wall as a lookout. Once it seemed that everyone had gone to the northern gate to watch the Magistrate deal with the Clairdani, Anehta flew at the larger of the two guards still guarding the western gate. She bumped into him as hard as she could, then landed, as if stunned, on the ground a little way along the wall to distract them. She had grabbed one of his shiny medals, which she still had in her talon while she lay there upside down. As soon as the guards noticed the missing medal and where it was, the chase was on, for suddenly Anehta wasn't stunned anymore and was stealing the medal! Once both guards were distracted, Simão and Luz slunk around the gate doors, entering unobserved and immediately going their separate ways.

After helping the Magistrate arrive at the Northern gates, Mateus returned to the gaol to pretend nothing had happened and help convince the Inquisitor and the guards that nothing was happening outside if they got suspicious. Ignoring the sounds of interested villagers running to the northern gates was difficult, so he decided to ask the inmates for a distraction. He quietly spoke to one of the enlightened prisoners, telling him to start singing and continue no matter what else was said or happening and see how many he could get to sing loud enough to cover any noises in the streets. He knew this would also infuriate the Inquisitor, and he hoped no one had seen him talking to The Enlightened prisoner or he would be joining them. There was no saying how The Inquisitor might react to the noise, but as long as he stayed within the gaol system, all would be well in the end.

Beyond the walls, The Magistrate stood astounded as a multitude of creatures came into view, an unexpected gathering that surpassed anything he had witnessed before. The sheer number and diversity of the beings left him in awe, prompting an ipromptu reevaluation of the situation unfolding outside the city walls. He had only ever seen them one at a time, and usually in the midst of townspeople running chaotically from their voracious appetite. Behind him, he ordered the gates barred shut to prevent any destruction of the town or its people and all guards to remain on the walls with orders to shoot arrows through the creatures if they attack.

Rowan stood outside the gates facing the hoard of creatures coming from the west in as calm a decorum as he could muster. As long as they didn't seem hostile, he was not going to run. *They seem determined and excitable about something I don't understand, but otherwise, not threatening.*

At fifty paces from the Magistrate, Markus halted the group. Simultaneously, they ceased their cawing, whinnying, and growling and the effect was deafening. Looking over his shoulder, Markus signaled to the Clairdani to greet the Magistrate. As one, they bowed in his direction. Their job was to hold his interest and help him begin to see that they were not all bloodthirsty creatures, and so far, Markus was proud of them.

Rowan stood frozen in disbelief! These creatures seemed more human-like than any other creatures he had ever encountered, and they seemed very tame and approachable! All along the wall, the guards held their collective breath as they watched their Magistrate take a tentative step towards a hoard of wild creatures...

An ominous thud sounded to the east of the magistrate as they were all buffeted by a warm gust of wind. Something invisible pulled the magistrate into the air, quickly taking him out of sight of the town and range of the arrows! At the same moment, the Clairdani raced away, lest any guards get the idea that they were behind the Magistrate's disappearance. Arrows flew in the air, although many guards held off, not wanting to hit their Magistrate.

Within moments, there was no evidence that anything had ever happened other than the loss of their Magistrate. No creatures were in sight, and there was nothing left behind outside the walls of Tomar. He had simply… vanished! "Hold your arrows! He's gone. You two – go collect the arrows for us," commanded the guard captain.

So ordered, the two guards that had been standing next to him stomped down the stone stairs into the area that had just witnessed an unimaginable site. Guards shouted at them over the wall, pointing to arrows they could see to help the two on the ground collect all the arrows. They also went to the spot where the Magistrate had disappeared to see if there was any evidence of what had taken him.

Hastily returning to their fellow guards and captain, the two guards interjected information faster than they shot arrows.

"… large footprints, a half finger deep in the ground…"

".. and it must have had a tail, there were flattened grasses a length away from the footprints…"

"… we've never had anything invisible before!"

"… the air was warmer where it must have stood. What could that be?"

Bewildered, the captain dismissed the guards until he had clear further directions, although the first item would be to determine who would be the temporary leader for Tomar…

Meanwhile, Luz and Anehta were able to find their way quietly into the Magistrate's office without being seen. Using the divining stick, Luz allowed it to pull her around the room until it finally stopped, vibrating behind his large desk against a stone wall.

"Do you think it's one of these stones?" Luz whispered to Anehta.

Anehta just pointed her beak at the enchanted stick, hoping the stick could be more precise. Looking all around and poking at various stones with their enchanted branch, they couldn't be sure whether the object was a large stone or something else hidden behind the wall.

After a few more minutes of checking for loose stones or any markings on them, Luz grew worried about being found. "We've been here too long already; let's come back once the moon is up and see if we can find it then."

Agreeing with her, the two left just as quietly down the stairs. The town was abuzz with the news of the Magistrate's bizarre kidnapping, and in all the mayhem, they found it easy to navigate through the town to Simão's forge to rest until the town fell asleep.

Chapter 39: Cave Life

Once far enough away from Tomar that no one could see them, Metulas halted his invisibility and allowed Rowan to see him. Not that it mattered. Rowan had fainted from fear as soon as he had gone above the tree tops! Carrying an unconscious body was no different than carrying other animals he had brought back for meals, although he had hoped for more of a conversation or sport with this one.

As they neared the caves at Batalha, Rowan began to gain consciousness and started to struggle to see where he was. Metulas flew to the smaller caves near the top of the mountain, hoping the height and isolation would help him calm down. He knew that would not be the case as soon as he placed the Magistrate in the cave, somewhat gently. As soon as he flew away, the Magistrate had stared first at him, having never seen a dragon. Then, seeing the height of where he was, he scurried as far back into the cave as he could, screaming as much as the small deer and rabbits did when they sensed death coming. Metulas shook his head, unable to help this human gain his sanity. Hopefully, Anehta would be coming soon and would help coordinate what help they could offer him.

For now, Metulas was the only connection he had, and he would need to do his best. There was a small pot Luz kept in her cave for water and perhaps something to lay down on. Thinking of these, he reached far into her cave and retrieved both the pot and some bedding with his outstretched foreleg. Filling the pot from a stream nearby, he then flew back to Rowan. The man was lying flat on the cave floor at the entrance, peering over the edge, his round, brown eyes terrorized and mesmerized as he watched Metulas warily . As carefully as he could, Metulas placed the water pot and the bedding in the cave, far enough away that if the man startled, he wouldn't knock the pot over right away. *So far, all is good.* He remembered Luz's warning not to smile or do anything else he thought might be friendly and laughed remembering her re-enactment of someone being scared to death seeing so many large, sharp teeth all at once. *Metulas* glanced at Rowan, then gestured to the pot and bedding in what he hoped would be construed as friendly. *He seems frozen, although I can hear a heartbeat and his eyes are watching me. Maybe Anehta will have better luck!* With that thought, Metulas took to the air and returned to his cave well below where the Magistrate lay.

As the day wore on, Metulas kept looking towards Tomar, hoping to see Anehta returning soon. He knew they would be resting until they could see the moonlight this evening, which meant time for the Magistrate to reflect and, for him, time to plan. He retreated into his cave to rest until the Magistrate settled down. He wanted to go hunting... food always soothed the savage beast.

Rowan's eyes watched the dragon as it flew away and back to its own cave lair. He was genuinely surprised to still find himself alive – weren't people the favorite food of dragons? The fact that it hadn't managed to eat him yet was beyond him. Maybe it liked to play with its food first? Looking around, he didn't see any other bones in the cave with him, although there were quite a few bones scattered around the ground far below the caves. Perhaps this dragon kept people alive until it was hungry, like people do with farm animals? That must be it. It was waiting for the right moment, then it would play cat and mouse with him when he got hungry.

As time snailed past, his fear slowly transcended to anger. *How dare this dragon take me away from Tomar? What had I done to deserve this? I had only been trying to reach out to some of the creatures and possibly make a turn for the better for Tomar, and now, this! And for what? Was he here to starve or a meal for later?* In frustration, he screamed at the heavens, venting about his misfortune. As his mood slightly improved, he resolved to inspect the interior of his cave, curious about what other surprises might be lurking within.

As the day progressed into deepest night, Metulas caught sight of Anehta making her way back from Tomar in the enveloping darkness. As expected, she was alone. On the night after a new moon, there wouldn't be any moonlight yet. Finding the curse stone might take a while, and Luz should stay in Tomar until she could get the curse written down. They could manage with the Magistrate until then, perhaps. Anehta drew close, then landed softly on Metulas' right elbow.

Hello, little one. How is Tomar?

All went as planned. You were stupendous! I still can't believe you managed to make yourself invisible – that was fantastic! The whole town is talking about it, and the Inquisitor has assumed control of Tomar. Everyone hates him already, so we will see how long he stays in charge before there's an uprising. They are despondent at his return and rise to power!

Eager to hear more about the curse stone and help Anehta refocus, Metulas asked, *And how did your search of the office go? Were you able to get there undetected? Did you find the curse object? Is Luz safe?*

Yes, yes, everything went fine. The Inquisitor is locked away in his office, trying to put order to the chaos in town by having the guards enforce a lock down. There can't be any complaints with no one in the streets, right? He says it's for everyone's safety as if you would go after anyone else in Tomar...

Metulas gave her a look that told her she was rambling a bit.

OK, ok, yes, Luz is fine. We got to the office, and her enchanted stick pointed her to the wall of stones behind his desk. We didn't know if it was one of those or if the actual curse object was behind the wall itself. We were going to wait until the moonlight to see if there was writing on any of them, but with the new moon, that would be a while. She is staying in Simão's place until there's enough moonlight to capture the writing. Then, she will come back. And if you could help with a ride, that would be even sooner...?

Metulas harumphed. *A ride would make her get here that much faster, true. I'll go to Tomar as soon as I see enough moonlight. In the meantime, I need your help here.*

Oh? I forgot to ask! How is our Magistrate doing?

He's not happy about all this, of course. He probably needs something he can eat, so I've been waiting for you to return. I managed to give him Luz's pot of water and bedding, at least. You're the first Clairdani I've seen and been able to ask since this morning, reported Metulas.

I'm sure Luz left something here that humans might eat. I'll go bring him something. I can go out in the morning and find other friends to help out. I saw Timaeus at Tomar. Is he here somewhere?

No, Timaeus is working on freeing the Clairdani, who are trapped in the Inquisitor's palace. You have the right idea though. I put him in one of the caves at the top so only those who can fly or crawl over the rocks easily will be able to help.

You did? Why that one? It's a bit cold up there, and now it'll be harder for our forest Clairdani to help out.

Let's just say I haven't forgiven him completely for what he did to Luz yet. She suffered a lot worse under his care. Maybe it'll make him think about how he treats others.

Anehta shrugged her shoulders in understanding. *I'll bring him something to eat and see if I can talk to him or at least begin to understand that not all of us creatures eat humans.*

Anehta managed to find some nuts in Luz's cave, and putting them in a pouch, carried the pouch to the Magistrate's cave. Landing at the edge of the cave opening, she saw him sitting on the bedding a little way in from the mouth of the cave, gazing at the night sky. She hopped towards him with the pouch, put it in front of him, then hopped away so as not to frighten him. He looked tired and haggard, with the little hair that he had still wind-blown from the flight, his clothes askew from the flight and perhaps some sleep and frustration. His brown eyes looked at Anehta, and she sensed resignation in him. She nodded towards the bag, and he slowly opened it. Taking out a nut he seemed to recognize, he ate it, then tentatively, he tried another one. Hunger took over, and before long, the pouch was empty. He gave the pouch back and just stared at her.

"If you can understand me and know who I am, then I demand that you tell me why I'm here!"

274

Anehta was able to understand the human speech, even if she wasn't able to speak it back. She was only able to shake her head in response to his demand.

"So you can answer questions but can't tell me anything?" Rowan asked.

Anehta nodded her head.

"Now we're getting somewhere! So am I a prisoner?"

Nod.

"Am I going to be tortured?"

Vigorous shaking this time.

"Oh? That's good, that's good... Am I going to be eaten by that dragon?"

Again, vigorous shaking.

"OK, so I'm here as a prisoner but not to be tortured or eaten? Sort of a guest of the dragon, I guess?"

Anehta shrugged. He was actually more Luz's guest, but he would find that out soon.

He grew quiet and thoughtful, so Anehta took the pouch and flew back to Metulas, who had company.

A brownie Anehta had never met before was catching up with Metulas.

Anehta, meet Bartimeu, Bartimeu, meet Anehta.

Bartimeu? The one that fell from the sky?

Yes, the same one. It's my fault that so many of the Enlightened are now imprisoned. I should have been more careful, and when my Tenenbrani contact didn't show up, I should have returned to Tomar and not ventured further out.

So, I'm here to help. Simão asked me to look into the connections between the Inquisitor and the Tenenbrani that attacked me, and so far, I haven't found any. He also asked me to warn the patrols to venture out in pairs, although that's moot right now with everyone on lockdown and most of the Enlightened in the gaol. I want to help. What can I do?

In response, Anehta and Metulas eagerly filled him in with his helpful duties, and before long, the three of them had a plan to help the Magistrate.

The next morning, Bartimeu scrambled to the top of the mountain. He looked in to see how the magistrate was doing after a night without a comfortable bed. Between the wheezy sounds of snoring and the absence of any leaves inside the cave, the Magistrate had evidently been able to use the leaves in the cave to help soften his bedding. All curled up on top of the bedding in his dark grey tunic and wrinkled black cloak, he resembled a large, shivering granite rock. *He must be a bit chilled; I'll have to remind Metulas to set a fire for him for tonight.* As Rowan began to stir, Bartimeu laid down a pouch containing a few quail eggs and scraps of roasted meat on the foot of the bedding, still warm from Metulas ' quick fire-breath. Rowen's eyes sprang open, and seeing the brownie next to him, the Magistrate startled, almost knocking the eggs and meat off the bedding. Fearing an outlash, Bartimeu quickly retreated out of range.

Rowan groaned. "I was really hoping it was all a bad dream, but I'm still here," he said to the brownie, not expecting any response. With his dirty and unshaven face, frayed edges on his clothes, rumpled hair, and his ranting, he looked a bit like a madman. Surprisingly, the brownie shrugged in response and gestured to the food.

Rowan stared at the brownie for a minute as the fact that this creature seemed to understand him. Hesitantly, he asked, "Can you all understand us? I mean, all of you that don't seem to want to eat us?"

Bartimeu wasn't exactly sure how to answer the question, so he half-shrugged and half-nodded.

"I demand that you and your friends take me back to Tomar!" the Magistrate roared. If these creatures could Understand him, that meant they could be bullied. "You have brought me here without invitation, starved me, frozen me, and now I have no purpose in being here? Bring me someone who CAN answer my questions, or the next creature who comes here will be my permanent company!"

Bartimeu darted out of the cave and down the mountain side, disappearing again at Metulas' cave.

"I want real food, not this wild man stuff!" *What I wouldn't give for just a plain bowl of porridge! Something civilized to eat, at least!* Still grumbling, his hunger finally ended his protesting fast, and he ate the proffered foods heartily. *And someone other than just myself to talk to would be nice...*

With only his mind for company, Rowan was struggling. He had had such a wonderful life in Tomar – everything he asked for: food, power, friends, love – and now everything was gone. What was his future now? Could he somehow escape and get back to Tomar? *Not with the dragon as a babysitter. I'll never get out of here!* He spent the remainder of the day alone, and no one disturbed him again. While he slept, fresh water and food were brought for him, and each night from then on, there was a fire set up that kept him warm till the morning but no company of any kind.

A few evenings later, Metulas noticed the quarter moon and called for Anehta and Bartimeu.

There's enough moonlight now to read any writing on the curse object, so I will go find Luz and help her translate the curse if possible.

And we will stay here and watch over the Magistrate? Anehta asked.

Actually, Anehta, I think you should come with me. For now, Bartimeu will have to watch over him alone. When I bring Luz back with me, we will see if she can influence him to our cause. While she is working with the Magistrate, you will be in Tomar. See if you and Simão can convince the Inquisitor that he needs to find us. You might need to start the town in an uprising to drive him out if he doesn't come here on his own.

Or maybe haunt him when he sleeps so that he thinks he's going mad again? Interrupted Bartimeu.

That would do nicely, Bartimeu! Anehta, would you be able to work out that type of plan with Simão? The Inquisitor needs to leave Tomar before he starts executing our Enlightened people. Secondly, out around the countryside, he seems to be imprisoning the Clairdani, so we need somewhere to neutralize him. Third, he may already know we are here, but if he doesn't, we are more likely to be able to handle him alone than when he's with others. I think here in Batalha we can neutralize him and hopefully, I'm big enough to keep him under control...

Anehta and Bartimeu laughed. *There's nothing bigger than you, Metulas! Even the griffons at the borders are only half your size!* Bartimeu agreed.

Simão and I can come up with a plan to get the Inquisitor out of Tomar, and I'll lead him here. So, by the full moon, we should be back. Just let me know which cave you want me to bring him to when I get back.

Agreed, answered Metulas. *Bartimeu, I will leave you some cooked meat for our Magistrate, and we will return within two days. Will you be able to handle the Magistrate for that long? Remember not to let him see you. We have shown him kindness, and he sees it as punishment. He needs enough time with his own thoughts to reassess his life and future, and possibly, when he feels completely alone, he will be willing to listen...*

That, I can do.

Chapter 40: A Break of Trust

Cautiously, Cenellot peered over the windowsill of his room to see if the area was clear, as he had every day for the past fortnight. Although Florenço told him that he had been making progress with his circle of fellow elfin watchers, not all agreed that he and his mother should be granted space within Sintrentejo. Even as a borderland region of the elfin lands of Sintra, no one dared to defy the king if the king had already denied the request. Florenço had conveniently forgotten to tell many of them of the request to the king, hoping they might not make it an issue, but the news was ubiquitous. However, he made sure they all understood that he was going to make another formal request to the king and they shouldn't alert the king to their presence until he had done so. Until Florenço had the king's permission, Cenellot and his mother had to be invisible.

Cenellot caught a glimpse of an elf in the clearing and immediately ducked behind the window ledge, almost falling backwards in his haste. It was a young elf, he thought, only about half as tall as Florenço, and had a tall bow in his hand and a quiver of arrows on his back. He was thin, like all elves he had seen, with a sense of toughness in his thinness. He and his mother had been learning the elfin rituals for washing to help them blend into both the forest and the elfin community, and he hoped that this young elf couldn't smell them here. He held his breath and looked out of his room to the main chamber to see if his mother had also sensed the danger.

She was seated as still as she could on the floor of the main chamber, cross-legged as most of the elves sat. Adorned in the forest-green and tan-colored elfin garb bestowed upon them by Florenço, she almost appeared like a miniature tree, her tall and slender figure enhancing the illusion. Despite her initial awkwardness moving in the unfamiliar attire, she was determined to show respect for elfin traditions and she slowly adjusted well to the much fewer layers of clothing. The seemingly delicate fabric clung to her frame, emphasizing her graceful form. These past few weeks, she had also really taken to the new customs and was making good progress with the spoken language as well. He wished he could speak mind to mind with her, especially now when anything said would be overheard below, no matter how quietly they spoke.

There was pressure on the staircase to their dwelling, and Cenellot peeked out the window to see if the young elf had decided to visit uninvited. *He's still out there, so who's coming up the stairs?*

Florenço! Cenellot thought loudly, not wanting to move too soon and alert the young elf to others in the dwelling. Quietly, Cenellot descended the stairs to the main chamber to meet their friend and hear what news Florenço brought.

As their eyes met, Florenço, Cenellot, and Noyette shared the traditional greeting with their gestures, and Florenço smiled brightly, an emoticon of calm excitement. "I've brought a trainer, Cenellot. Come meet Paenel."

With that introduction, Florenço led Cenellot and Noyette down the steps to the cushiony forest glade below. Seeing them emerge, Paenel strode calmly and somewhat stiffly towards them as if his muscles were extremely tight. Cenellot knew not to judge the age of an elf by their appearance. However, Paenel's business-like manner, coupled with his ebony black clothing, hair, and eyes, made Cenellot wonder if they were close to the same age. Paenel gestured in respect to the three of them, which was returned, then watched Florenço as if trying not to stare at these humans pretending to look like elves and failing.

You have been making tremendous progress, Cenellot, so Paenel has agreed to come every morning and train you in how to use the bow and arrow. Since each of us can only spend a little time here each day, this will allow you the maximum amount of training and hopefully draw less attention to your presence here. So far, this has been a safe distance away from anyone, and Paenel lives close by, meaning he won't be seen by anyone when he comes. He has agreed to keep this training to himself, with the understanding that your training may be what allows you to stay in Sintrentejo, explained Florenço in slow elfish so that they might understand.

Standing next to his mother in case she needed a translation, Cenellot glanced her way and saw that she understood as well as he had. *How do I get a bow? Do I need to use yours for a while, Florenço?*

Both of the elves laughed, making Cenellot feel foolish for his questions.

It will be a while before you are ready for a bow, human. For now, we will train your muscles, and when you are ready, you will make your own bow, declared Paenel in his first demonstration of being a trainer.

Cenellot looked to Florenço for confirmation, which was answered with a head nod. *If you are ready, Cenellot, you may start now. I will work with your mother with herbs while you train.*

Paenel took Cenellot to the stream close to the border of Sintrentejo in the direction of their cave-dwelling, and taking off his dark green elfin jerkin, he jumped casually into the water. The droplets that landed on Cenellot made him shiver with the sudden cold, although Paenel didn't seem to be bothered by the temperature.

Take your tunic off and jump in. The first lesson then is this: the water can only have as much power over you as you let it have. Embrace the cold, let it become part of you, and it cannot control you.

Easier said than done, thought Cenellot as he divested himself of his warmer clothing. Thin as it was, it provided a surprising amount of warmth when put on, and removing that warmth immediately brought goose pimples to his skin. He didn't look forward to getting even colder.

Seeing his hesitation, Paenel splashed a huge wave of water towards him. Dripping wet, Cenellot jumped into the water in resignation as well as in an effort to splash Paenel back.

The water provides us resistance and trains our minds as well. For today, follow what I do and continue to do the same motion until I say we are finished.

Paenel used both arms to push through the water, first forwards, then backwards, halting after each stroke. Cenellot tried to emulate the motions and splashed himself until he sputtered.

Try to keep your shoulders under the water, and don't break the surface while you move.

Determinedly, Cenellot continued to push the water back and forth under Paenel's watchful eye. The repetitive motion, coupled with Paenel's constant corrections, began to take a toll on Cenellot. His arms and shoulders ached with the effort, and the once-refreshing water now felt like an insurmountable force. Paenel's guidance was invaluable, but the strength required for the skill proved to be a formidable challenge for Cenellot's young body. As the training session progressed, extreme fatigue set in, making each stroke more difficult than the last.

Struggling to even stand up in the stream after a couple of hours, Cenellot felt the weight of frustration settling in. The water now seemed to mock his attempts at mastery. Paenel, sensing his struggle, decided this much was enough for today. *Rest, and I will see you tomorrow,* Paenel said as a farewell, and he raced out of the clearing.

This training pattern continued for a fortnight, and despite his initial misgivings and constant soreness, Cenellot was making some progress. However, just as he had the first time he laid on the bank of the river, Cenellot felt he might never be able to move again. He had never felt so tired! By the time Cenellot finally dragged himself out of the water, his limbs were heavy, and his breath labored. He lay there in the grass gazing at the sky, listening to the sounds of the forest all around him. A new sound, like that of leaves rustling, alerted him, and he rolled over to see what it was. He rolled into a long, thin foot, and a moment later, he was yanked up to his feet.

This must be one of them, Mishmarel, said the voice attached to the foot.

Bind him and bring him to me. We need to find Florenço and the other human as well. Check around the area. They were not in the tree dwelling when we just checked.

Cenellot felt himself bound hand and foot by vines, then carried to the elf he assumed was Mishmarel. Cenellot began the traditional elfin greeting. *My heart is gladdened to see you...*

Don't think you're going to win me over with your elfin speech, boy. You have trespassed on our lands and must be judged by King Abrimel, interrupted Mishmarel, pushing him roughly to the ground. Other than Mishmarel, Cenellot counted three other elves searching for his mother and Florenço. They were so quick, hopping from behind one tree to the next, it was nearly impossible to see them move! *No wonder I didn't see or hear them coming. As quiet as the wind, their steps are barely audible!* Thought Cenellot.

Not long thereafter, Florenço and his mother were vine-bound and being shoved into the clearing next to him.

That's all of them, Mishmarel, one silvery-haired elf, reported.

Let's take them to see the king then, replied Mishmarel, and he used a long, thick vine to connect the three prisoners in a line. He held one end to lead the way while the other three stood next to each of the three prisoners as if they were dangerous criminals.

Although bound, Cenellot and Noyette were allowed to see more of Sintrentejo than they ever thought they would. As they continued along, they saw more tree dwellings, each one ornately carved and shaped, and more elfin faces watching them as they were marched past. In so many ways, these were different than the people he knew – the elves had colorful hair instead of the plain browns or yellows, pointed ears and sharp features, and a glow to them rather than the general feel of dirt and grime in Tomar. Yet their curiosity, sense of law and order, and dedication to work were familiar. *Hopefully, reason will be something familiar too...*

That hope was dashed as quickly as they entered the council chambers. Mishmarel led the small line of prisoners straight through the entrance into the council room, where the king stood in front of his throne. Alameas stood slightly behind him, standing as straight as his long, gingery hair. Seeing the humans and Florenço enter, King Abrimel signaled for the guards to bring them in front of him, then had the guards form a semi-circle around them in case they decided to try and run.

Florenço, I remember that you came to see me not too long ago to request asylum for two humans. Are these the two you were referring to?

Florenço nodded his head in affirmation.

After our discussion, did I not say you would be allowed to assist them while they remained outside of Sintrentejo in their own dwelling?

You did, Your Highness. With the Inquisitor's increased...

No excuses or discussion! Shouted the king. *We are aware of this inquisitor's movements and have not deemed them sufficient enough for our attention of any kind. By bringing these humans into Sintra, did you think that perhaps other humans might come looking for them and enter Sintra uninvited, bringing their malice and greed with them?*

Florenço began to defend himself and the humans. *Your Highness, the Inquisitor is somehow aligned with Tenenbrani...*

With growing anger, King Abrimel replied, *The humans in their variety of forms tend toward self-destruction. Whether that comes sooner or later is no concern to us. You put us all in danger by allowing them to cross into our lands! For the endangerment of your people, you will be grounded.*

Murmurs filled the hall in astonishment at the verdict. No elf had been grounded since the Dragon Wars, and its use was reserved for only the worst of crimes. The thought of any of them having to suffer in a dark room with no sunlight, pressed between two stones so no living earth touched him, was enough to send ripples of goose pimples around the room. As forest creatures, they depended both on sunlight and vegetation for their sanity and health. Grounding was as close to a death sentence as they dared. The death sentence itself was only meted out to non-elves.

Florenço's head drooped in shame. At the king's beckoning, two identical elfin guards untethered Florenço, taking him behind the throne dias, where their quiet footsteps faded into silence as they descended a dark, circular stairwell.

Addressing the remaining guards, King Abrimel also ruled against Noyette and Cenellot. *As for these two humans, they will remain in our custody indefinitely until we determine how best to use them. Other than their basic necessities, no one will interact with them or acknowledge that they exist in Sintra.* Glaring at those few elves in the hall, he added, *Are we understood?*

As one, the elves saluted the king with their fists crossed over their hearts, giving a short vocalization of agreement. The two elves accompanying them to this council grasped the vine rope and pulled Noyette and Cenellot roughly towards the same descending staircase. Unaccustomed to the rough handling, Noyette began to voice her disapproval and protest, "Why can't we become part of your community? We aren't like the others! We are learning your ways and language and can be helpful..." Although her voice was unintelligible to almost everyone and was ignored by all before it was cut off by distance.

As they too were dragged down the darkening staircase, Cenellot was entranced by the contrast to the gaol cells he was expecting. Ensconced small torches along the walls gave a low glow to the space, and rather than small, narrow, dank passages into gloom, this space was an expansive cavern with cells along the walls for all to see. As their eyes adjusted to the dimmer light, Cenellot tried to see what the other prisoners looked like. He didn't see any skeletons, thankfully, although many of the prisoners were not elves either. Many were Tenenbrani, occupying a variety of cells according to their size, and the few elves that he did glimpse seemed an angry lot. These elves had lost the glow to their skin that the free elves seemed to have, and their hair was of darker hues – blue or purple. One even had forest-green hair... *was that a troll?*

Seated in the heart of the cavern was their keeper, an aged elf, slender and clad entirely in white, a reflection of his matching hair and skin. As they drew near, his mesmerizing blue eyes felt like they were piercing into the depths of their souls as though passing final judgment. The weight of his gaze left them with a disconcerting feeling, a mix of anticipation and apprehension. After a minute or two of scrutiny, he indicated to the guards, telling them to *Put Florenço in cell 70R7UR4, and the humans can be put together in cell G374 since they are a youth and its mother.*

Cenellot and Noyette were led up a small set of stairs past quite a few Tenenbrani whose stench and breath made Noyette almost collapse from fear. After passing a few empty cells, one of the guards pressed his hand against the vine bars of one larger empty cell, and the vines parted. Once they both entered, the cell doors reknit themselves shut, and their guards left without a word. Noyette felt destitute. Their world was getting ever smaller this past while just as the world should be opening up for Cenellot, and now their only chance at a future was shut to them! She threw herself on a mattress, attempting to hide her tears. There were two mattresses with bedding, much like those Florenço had brought for them, a jar and bowl for water, and a rather large hole in the floor near the edge that seemed to exit the room, leading somewhere. While Noyette laid on her woven mattress, Cenellot stood at the vine bars. He didn't see where they had taken Florenço and hoped he wasn't too far away. *Florenço? Can you hear me?* Cenellot thought, hoping it would travel further than sound.

I can, Cenellot. Don't give up hope, either of you! He did not have you executed or mention physical punishment for you. Practice what you've learned as much as you can daily, and we will have to wait and see what the King decides. Florenço's voice sounded strained and tired, and Cenellot tried not to give up hope. They had to believe they would survive this latest adventure, or they would be lost.

Chapter 41: What Was Lost, Is Found

As much as Ma'elrich enjoyed being allowed to rule Tomar without Rowan always questioning his orders and motives, the barrage of questions about when he would go find what had happened to their Magistrate made him weary. Imposing a curfew at dark and limiting how often people were allowed to leave their homes had only intensified the number of questions barraging him when they were allowed to see him. Frustrated with the interruptions, he retreated back to the Magistrate's office with orders for him not to be disturbed so he could formulate a plan that would help him feel more empowered in this town.

The guards collectively shook their heads. Whereas the Magistrate had tried to impose harsher rules to help catch the Traitors, the Inquisitor had already achieved the goal and seemed to be punishing the town anyway! With the Traitors all in captivity, there was no reason for the continued curfews and lockdowns. The few interactions they had had in town, on orders to arrest anyone out after curfew or asking too many questions, had only led to more distrust and unrest within Tomar. The Inquisitor was clearly not interested in Tomar's citizens and their well-being; rather, he had a singular goal in mind and was unable to change his focus when Tomar needed him to.

Mateus listened to their grumblings with growing interest. As part of the Inquisitor's detail, he had to be very careful not to show any disloyalties, although he had to balance that with the needs of Tomar and The Enlightened.

Entering the Magistrate's office for the post-curfew daily report, Mateus approached the large wooden desk. While he waited to be acknowledged, he noticed that the air here always seemed different than in the rest of Tomar for some reason – colder, less friendly somehow. The Inquisitor finished writing his latest restrictions on Tomar, and said shortly, "Report."

"All of Tomar are in their homes, secured for the evening, sir. There was only one warning given today during the market and no arrests."

"How goes it with the Traitors in the gaol? Are any of them talking yet about how they contact the creatures to attack us?"

"Not so far, sir. Diago and Tiago are still working on them."

"I can help with the interrogations if you need me. I'm busy trying to keep order in this blasted town right now. All these petitions for market spaces, correspondence, pleas for clemency... I don't understand why anyone would want to be in charge of a town. It's all paperwork!"

Mateus let the frustration dissipate for a few breaths before responding. "Perhaps..." Mateus started cautiously, waiting to see if he would be encouraged to offer a suggestion. When The Inquisitor looked up, interested, he continued. "Some of us might be able to handle some of these other mundane tasks for you, sir? Then, you could focus on what you would like to focus on?"

The Inquisitor glanced quickly at the top right-hand drawer of the desk, giving a grunt. "I might consider that. Let me think on it... In the meantime, tell me. What are the people grumbling about most now?"

Mateus hesitated. Knowing that whatever he told him would be the subject of new controls, he looked for something nonthreatening. "They worry about what happened to the Magistrate mostly… May I speak plainly, sir?"

"Of course, Mateus. I've come to trust you completely."

"We know that all of the Traitors are in the gaol, and yet everyone is still in lockdown as if the Traitors were around the town enabling monsters to enter Tomar. Without the Traitors out and about, couldn't we allow the citizens more freedom to move around Tomar itself at least? Maybe we can reinstate the patrols inside Tomar for any protection they would need?" Mateus suggested.

Ma'elrich growled threateningly and looked Mateus in the eye. It was terrorizing, and Mateus understood then why he was such a successful inquisitor. "They all think that everything should be just as it was when it was just Rowan here – all the gates open to anyone from anywhere, people milling about as if there aren't still monsters out there that could take someone at any time? There must still be people plotting if someone coordinated with the monsters to take Rowan! Even with the Traitors in prison, there must be others still sympathetic to their cause and these we have to rout out!" The Inquisitor's face had slowly turned from his normal ashen grey to molten, and his eyes began flashing black, spittle dangling from the tips of his mustache.

Mateus was alarmed, although his training helped keep his mind calm so he could think. *So, indeed, he is about ready for his transformation! We will need to start planning for his evacuation when that happens and for Rowan's return.*

"Perhaps a smaller detail could go door to door and demand a pledge of loyalty to Tomar? They would be given a badge which would allow them the freedom to walk about the town?"

The Inquisitor thought long and hard about this suggestion. "Have we been able to replace all the key positions that were previously held by Traitors? I believe we still needed a tax assessor and market ombudsman, at the very least."

"I can have those positions filled by tomorrow morning, sir, and I can have the detail guards obtain loyalty pledges then as well. I will ensure that our guards are posted more visibly around Tomar, both day and night, to keep the order so you can do your own work without disturbances."

"Those loyalty pledge badges will cost money… "

"Of course, sir. I will ensure that money is documented and brought to you each evening, as well as the list of anyone who might refuse to sign the pledge."

"That will do, thank you, Mateus. I will look for those tomorrow evening and perhaps walk about Tomar myself to see how everything is going."

With a snap, Mateus drew himself up straight, turned, and left the office. There was much to do before dawn and lots to discuss with Simão and the other detailers.

Anehta was waiting for Mateus in a shadowy corner of his front doorway, and lost in his thoughts, Mateus almost stepped on her. The sudden flurry of wings startled him, and he drew his short dagger automatically, ready for an attack.

Mateus, it's just me, Anehta!

Mateus still looked around the area, making sure his dagger might not be needed anywhere else before sheathing the blade. *You can't be too careful here, especially since there's still a curfew in place, and no one should be out and about.*

Well, technically, the curfew only applies to you humans, right? So I'm safe enough, countered Anehta.

Yes, although being a creature that isn't a normal pet makes you a target no matter what time of day it is... Mateus changed the subject, focused on what needed to be done and soon. *So, is anyone else here, inside?*

Yes, both Simão and Luz are here. Metulas is outside Tomar, waiting for Luz.

Mateus quietly opened the door, and after closing the door, found the torch nearby and lit it, highlighting the warm faces of Simão and Luz sitting quietly at the small, wooden table against the wall of the one-room hut. After the death of his family, Mateus had not been able to live in his parent's place and sold it soon thereafter. This much smaller hut was enough for his basic needs as a guard, and its small size meant it wasn't ever under scrutiny of suspicious meetings. As Mateus took the two strides to arrive at the table, Simão and Luz stood, and the three grasped each other's forearms in a warm triangle of greeting.

"I have news..." started both Luz and Mateus at once, then smiled at laughed quietly.

Simão exerted his leadership. "We all have news to share. Luz, since I know you need to leave soon, tell us your news first. Then, Mateus can give us news you need to hear first, then you can go work with Metulas."

"We have the Magistrate in Batalha. He's unhappy of course, but otherwise fine. I need to go to him and see if I can succeed in the caves where I failed last time in his office. We think the key to the Tenenbrani transformations has to be in the Magistrate's office, so we need to be able to get in there when the Inquisitor's out," explained Luz quietly.

"I just left him in that office. He'll be there for a little bit, I think." Mateus answered the unasked question of when the Inquisitor would be out. "I have been trying to convince him to allow Tomar more freedoms, and we arrived at a pledge of loyalty that people could purchase to allow them to move around Tomar as they would like."

Luz and Simão both grumbled at that. To have to pay for a freedom that was supposed to be free was certainly tyranny and favored those who weren't already struggling with the newly reimposed limits on trade.

Sensing their malcontent, Mateus added, "It was the only thing I could think of at the moment that he would let us guards handle while he stays in his office doing whatever he wants to be doing. It bought us a little time, although it might keep him in the office for a bit. He kept looking at the upper right-hand drawer of the desk, so maybe there are plans or items there that we could look at to know what his plan is? He was excited to get all the Traitors imprisoned but still is acting as if he hasn't won, so I think he's still after you, Luz, and won't quit until he has you as well."

"So, we need a plan to get him out of the office during the night so we can get into the office and another plan to get him out of Tomar," summarized Simão.

"Simão, his eyes were flashing black and red again, so he's definitely on the verge of transforming into a Tenenbrani," Mateus warned.

"We've been suspicious of that for a while now, but so far, he's not succumbed. I'll see what I can do to get a safe passage for him out of Tomar before anyone gets hurt when he does."

"Good. You should be safe for now if you're in disguise. Just remember to stick to the shadows. I've been able to convince him that all the Traitors are imprisoned and that you died in the raid. Since the meeting was at your forge, it would be hard to believe that you weren't involved somehow, so make sure you aren't recognized."

Simão turned to Luz and Anehta. "You two have your responsibilities at the Magistrate's office. STAY SAFE! We can't afford to lose you again, Luz! Once you've done what you need to do, you need to return to Batalha and work with Rowan. Mateus, I assume you will be up all night working with whatever guards don't have families to put together a system for tomorrow?"

"Unfortunately, yes, and we might even discuss what we can to convince the Inquisitor that he needs to go looking for our Magistrate... "

"That will have to wait til after tonight's events. Best of luck to you, all of you. While I'm thinking of a plan for his Tenenbrani outburst, I'll be in or near the tavern near market square looking for people we can trust. Come get me if you need me, any of you."

"Agreed," they all whispered.

Near the town hall, Luz practiced her disillusionment. She hadn't had the strength since before her imprisonment and hadn't tried it again. Now, she desperately needed use of her ability if she could manage to muster the energy.

"How's this, Anehta?"

Pretty good, actually, just remember not to be in the light where your shadow will give you away, Anehta pointed out.

"Right," responded Luz, and she moved under the eaves of the building so her shadow blended in with the surroundings.

Perfect, whispered Anehta.

Under the light of the half-moon, the two waited across the town square from town hall, in perfect view of the Magistrate's main window, still alight even as the night watch called ten bells. A couple times, Anehta flew up across the window to check in to see if perhaps he was asleep and found him working on something in the moonlight. Once the moon set at twelve bells, they saw the light go out, and a few minutes later, the Inquisitor emerged, heading towards The Magistrate's house.

"He's wasted all our moonlight!" hoarse, whispered Luz, frustrated. They need the moonlight for their own purposes, and now they'd have to wait another day.

If he's also working on something using moonlight, then we won't be able to do anything in the office at all! Let's tell Metulas, and maybe we will have to come back after the Inquisitor is out too, and Anehta flew north of the Pit to bring Metulas in on the plot.

Following Metulas' instincts, the trio was at least going to evaluate the situation in the office once more before they returned to Batalha. Within the hour, Luz was inside the office, Anehta having been able to access the room using the partially opened window and opening the door for Luz. Metulas, as invisible as he could be, was still as solid as ever. He landed as gently as he could in the large town square and twisted himself so that he could get his eyes near enough to the window to see.

We think it has to be here, behind the desk, although whether it's one of the stones or something behind the stones, we don't know, said Luz in her mind to Metulas and Anehta. *But without the moonlight, we can't know where it is exactly.*

Metulas thought for a moment. *If it were out in the open like that, the moonlight during any evening meeting may have divulged the curse to anyone in the room. Let me try something – move to the other side of the room, you two.*

Luz and Anehta did as instructed and watched in amazement as Metulas blew fire-hot smoke from his nose into the room towards the stones behind the desk. They held their breaths and closed their eyes, then opened them when they felt the coolness of the air return. There was a glow to the stones behind the Magistrate's desk, but also underneath the desk, and underneath the desk where moonlight would never shine, there was definite writing!

Luz and Anehta rushed over, only to see the writing fade. Excited to finally find the curse words, they moved the desk to make the flooring more accessible. Luz searched hurriedly through the desk to find something to trace the writing on the floor. When she was ready with a piece of slate from the back of a drawer, she called to Metulas to direct his warm breath on the stones again.

This time, Luz used the slate piece to trace the letters she saw on the floor. She grew faint, being that close to the curse itself, and Anehta grew alarmed at her pallor.

Are you hale? You look dreadful! Asked Anehta, fanning her with her wings to bring her fresh air.

I'll be all right. Let's just make this as quick as we can. The longer I stay next to this stone, the weaker I feel.

Anehta sat where Luz could lean against her, willing her strength into her. They had to repeat the process a few times, since she could only copy a little before the writing faded, and each time, Luz would step away and get some distance from the stone before returning. At the end, Metulas was able to see it through the window and translate it to them:

As long as mistrust endures,

And hearts of flesh act as stone,

Hate will become its true form,

Their stone hearts manifesting as flesh.

What was lost must be found,

What was hidden, returned,

What caused hate, reversed

By a willing sacrifice that reunites

What was mistakenly separated

And restores stone hearts to flesh.

The three stood in thoughtful silence as they reflected on what they had heard until Metulas shifted outside the window.

Memorize it, Luz, so we can write it in Batalha and think about it later. For now, erase the markings Anehta, and let's get back home. Anehta will stay here to help draw the Inquisitor out to us.

Chapter 42: An Unlikely Change of Heart

With Mateus departing the office, Ma'elrich's mind plunged into a freefall of thoughts, consumed by the urgency of translating the Codex without any interruptions. *If Mateus and the guards can handle the townspeople, line my coffers, and all while I have peace to hunt down this Advocate, that will do well for me!* Looking out the window at the moonlight, he pulled out the codex from the top right-hand drawer of the desk. He had translated much of it, and while it said nothing of the eye covers and such, it did speak of the Clairdani and Tenenbrani. The creatures appeared disinterested in Tomar itself, especially in the absence of the Traitors. The passages concerning the city might have been merely wild rantings of a damaged girl's desperate grasp on hopeful ideals rather than an accurate representation of their intentions.

What he hoped for now was more about where exactly to find the Advocate beyond the desert. That last bit would allow him to root out the last bit of those traitors who had taken his father from him and made him what he was. Revenge would be so sweet! This was one of the last few elfin-inked pages of the Codex, and he hoped the moonlight was the right lighting for this last mystery! He squared his shoulders, rolled his head, and set to work.

The moonlight allowed him to translate the next two pages, and his excitement grew as he traced the words into the Codex:

Anehta and I do everything together while Metulas watches mostly. He's too big to play the games with us usually. Mostly, he sits in his cave until he gets hungry, and then he gets something big enough for dinner for all of us...

300

Turning the page, the next page was blank! The moonlight was gone for the night. *Tomorrow...*

With the end of his transcribing for the evening, Ma'elrich re-read what he had just transcribed. *So there are two others with her, and they all live in the caves. They must be rather large for all of them to live there. Maybe it's part of a mountain range? That should be easy to find if I go across the desert far enough...*

With that happy thought, Ma'elrich closed the Codex, blew out the candles, and carried the Codex out of Rowan's office with him to his room on Rowan's estate. Thinking of the following day, he packed a small bag and organized his thoughts. *After a quick check-in on Tomar to ensure the guards had control over the town, I could slip out across the desert to the north and look for these caves. No one would need to know that I left except possibly Mateus... Yes, I'll tell Mateus that the guards must control the town for a few days although he need not know why. Ensuring the loyalty pledges are paid and awarded will take a fortnight. That should be enough time...* Drained and weary, he crawled into bed, falling into sleep with contented thoughts and hopeful plans for tomorrow.

The Inquisitor dreamed and thought much about the Codex and the Advocate, and when he was finally fully awake, he felt strong enough to at least try to find this Advocate. After a hurried check-in with Mateus to emphasize the importance of the town under the careful scrutiny of the guards, the two of them walked through the main avenue discussing the plans Mateus had created for the loyalty pledges. Distracted, the Inquisitor nodded his head in agreement with everything and, at the end of the street, hastily made his excuses and returned to the office for his bag.

Hiding in a shadowy corner across from the town hall, Anehta watched the Inquisitor as he departed the town hall. *Interesting... now where might he be going?* Looking furtively around the square to determine which guards were ensuring the market square was empty, he then walked along the building to a nearby alley. Anehta flew the short distance to track where he might be going, all the while ensuring she wasn't seen. At the north gate, he halted and looked for the guard on duty. As requested, the gate had been bolted shut until the loyalty badges were distributed and would allow for exit and entry.

"Open the gate, guards. I have business to attend to outside the walls."

The guards shot a questioning look at each other but otherwise gave no sign of wavering from the command. One of the guards quickly descended the stairs to open the smaller door embedded within the wooden gate and followed the Inquisitor to the outer iron gate, opening the iron sally gate for him to pass through. Without a word, the guard relocked both gates and returned to his guard duty, watching the Inquisitor's direction.

As the Inquisitor made his way through the gates, Anehta simply flew over the gates to a nearby tree. As he neared the desert, she saw him check his bag, then move deliberately into the desert and continue north. *I wonder if he figured out where our caves are, or is he just checking the countryside? I had better put a warning out to the Clairdani to let Luz know he is on his way. He might need some company too...*

Knowing it wouldn't be difficult to track the Inquisitor as he crossed the desert over the next couple of days, Anehta flew back west towards the forest to alert anyone she could find to send out word that the Inquisitor was no longer in Tomar and was possibly looking for Luz. I alert in place, she gathered her courage and flew back to follow the Inquisitor. She did her best to stay far enough behind that he didn't see her hopping among the sparse vegetation. Even from her distance, she could hear his stomach protest his departure without food. Occasionally, he seemed to look around, possibly for something to eat, and she hoped that her natural desert camouflage worked well enough. *What I wouldn't give to have Luz's ability to be invisible!* There wasn't much to eat in the desert for those who weren't accustomed to its natural menu, and most of the menu only appeared at night. What small creatures existed in the daytime desert were alternately ignored or eaten, raw apparently, and Anehta shuddered inwardly at his habits. *In many ways, he seems more beastly than human! Perhaps... I'll go on ahead and help get things ready for his arrival in Batalha.* Just as she flew ahead of him, though, a sudden cold draft of wind knocked her over, and she was blown to the ground. The next moment, she felt a cold, callous hand around her throat.

In her mind, she heard his cold voice. *I am only looking for the Advocate so I can talk to her, nothing else.* The Inquisitor lied easily.

Release me, and I can fly to her. Then she can meet you here. Anehta tried to bargain.

The Inquisitor slowly released her and broke into tears, hiding his face in his hands as he continued. *I'm so sorry. I can't seem to help it! I've been cruel for so long, and I want to be better! I hope the Advocate can help me!* He lowered his hands and glanced up at Anehta, who had flown to the ground in front of him to see what was happening.

He has green eyes? And he's speaking to me in OUR language? He must have become one of the Enlightened, instead of a Tenenbrani! Happily, Anehta hopped around, eager to bring him to Batalha to learn from the Advocate herself. The Inquisitor smiled in return and held out his open palm. Seeing the gesture, Anehta perched on it, giving him directions and mindless chatter as they continued their journey through the desert.

As soon as they made camp for the evening, Anehta said she would check the surrounding area to make sure all was safe, leaving the Inquisitor to his own dinner preparations. The desert came alive at night, and quite a few Clairdani and desert animals were moving around. Seeing a tall arm of a prickly pear cactus, Anehta decided to rest for a moment and had almost reached the cactus when she suddenly found herself underneath something with a lot of fur. Stunned at first in fear, lest it be the Inquisitor or a Tenenbrani she hadn't seen, she winced and made herself as small as possible so as not to seem worth the trouble to eat her. She was released, and standing up, she saw a familiar-seeming brownie laughing at her. Sputtering, she began to right herself, only to be scooped up, tossed into the air, and cuddled.

Happy to see me, are you? Anehta asked.

The brownie held her at arm's length to see her more clearly, and her eyes traveled past Anehta to the Inquisitor. Dropping Anehta quickly, the brownie scuttled behind the cactus with lightning speed, ensuring the Inquisitor hadn't seen her. Anehta looked behind her to see what had spooked her friend, then flew behind the prickly pear to talk to her.

He's scary, isn't he! Anehta whispered, having a bit of fun with her friend in retaliation. *I didn't see him. Thanks for the warning! I wonder what he's doing out here?*

You smell a little of him. You've been near him all day today! Said the brownie, suddenly wary. *You're one of them now, are you?*

No! It's not like that at all! I still think he's scary, and I don't trust him either. He is able to talk with us, though, and he has green eyes now, and he asked if I would lead him to see Luz, who's already waiting for him, so that's what we're doing now. Anehta realized she was rambling a bit as she tended to do when she was nervous.

Interesting... do you want me to tell the others that he's on our side now?

I wouldn't, not just yet anyway. Anehta cautioned. *As I said, I still don't trust him, whatever his story and eye color. Let's wait until after Luz and Metulas meet with him to see what happens. You could tell the others to keep a lookout for anything odd and give me any reports after he's gone to bed. That way, if I don't check in to get your reports, you can send a lark message to Metulas that something happened to me, and they can come rescue me.*

With an agreement reached, they parted ways. Anehta made her way back to camp, a newfound calmness enveloping her regarding the plan to bring the Inquisitor to the caves. Glancing over at where Ma'elrich slept, she nestled into a small hollow within a dead cactus arm. From there, she had a clear view of their surroundings, and after ensuring all was calm, she was soon fast asleep. For the next two days, they developed a routine of departing just as dawn began and collecting what water they could from the food bowls they had left out. Anehta would then fly a bit ahead for Ma'elrich to follow, stopping for food before 'he sun's heat zapped their strength. They would set up on the shady side of either rock formations or a flock of cacti and rest, then walk again until the edge of dusk before setting up camp officially. After Ma'elrich fell asleep, Anehta would move away from camp and wait for any Clairdani in the area to catch up on the news of the area and relay any insights she had in return.

The report from Batlha was that Luz and Metulas were ready for them in Batalha, and Rowan was growing indignant with his imprisonment. On the other side of the desert, all seemed to be going well in Tomar with Mateus and the guards in command. Mateus had even been able to hold off further interrogations of the Enlightened, although there were some musings within the town that perhaps Mateus was too sympathetic towards them. *I hope Mateus doesn't stretch himself too far and get imprisoned himself! After Hawthorne's fate, I wouldn't want the same to befall Mateus!* With cautious hope, Anehta focused on the task at hand, knowing that if they succeeded with these two men, Tomar would know the truth and that knowledge would begin unravelling the curse upon them.

Towards the middle of their third day, Anehta pointed ahead to some dark, bulbous storm clouds on the distant horizon.

"Should we set up camp now for when that storm hits us?" Ma'elrich asked.

Those aren't storm clouds. Those are the caves up ahead! We should be there by dusk today. She tried not to sound too eager to be finished with this journey. Usually, she flew, and it only took a few hours. Walking, or only flying a little bit at a time, made the trip interminable, especially with the current company. Additionally, although he had tried to be pleasant and even asked her to call him "Ma'elrich," there was a noticeable absence of kindness or warmth in his questions, reminding Anehta that he was truly a torturing inquisitor and not a conversationalist. . Rather, he remained stiff and reserved, maintaining a clear boundary that seemed to declare further friendly conversation impossible. This coldness made the trip feel longer than its actual duration, and already, it seemed that their discovery of the curse writing itself was many moons ago.

Ma'elrich was also eager to finish this dry journey across the desert and finally capture this Advocate! Anehta hadn't been very disclosing about any information regarding what he would find at the caves, despite his attempts at casually asking what the Advocate was like, who Metulas was, or how they lived so far away from any towns nearby. In fact, she had been very cagey and stilted in her responses, and from his experience with interrogation, he knew she still didn't trust him. *Trust takes time,* he reminded himself.

Their thoughts filled the last few hours' journey to Batalha, the caves growing with each step. At a spear's throw away, the mountainside seemed to reach nearly to the heavens, casting deep shadows to the east from the setting sun. With very little vegetation on its surface, the cavernous mountain seemed like an overgrown pumice stone with all the cave mouths facing them. At the distance of a stone's throw, two figures erupted from the largest of the openings, almost halfway up the mountainside and impossible to reach without wings of some sort. One of the figures seemed human. *That one must be the Advocate.*

"Is that a dragon??" Ma'elrich asked Anehta in astonishment as the second figure's wings spread wide and revealed the largest creature he had ever seen. With its red-golden hue, the dragon looked as if part of the sun had melted and now flew towards him, with the Advocate riding on its back.

Yes! Anehta answered, almost breathless in her clear admiration for her friends.

With a thunderous thud, Metulas landed almost on top of Ma'elrich, gold eyes glaring into the green. Luz stood, spear in hand, and jumped off his back, tumbling gracefully to the ground. Walking towards the two male figures, she put her hand on Metulas, calming him enough that he stopped glaring at Ma'elrich with as much hatred.

Excitedly, Anehta made introductions. *Metulas, Luz, this is Ma'elrich, otherwise known as the Inquisitor.*

"I hope you don't mind me intruding like this. Anehta has been kind enough to guide me to see you. After all I've read about you, I feel I have come to understand you and your cause, and I wanted to get to know you more... personally."

Anehta flew up to Luz's shoulder, leaning her head against Luz's. Speaking only to Luz, Anehta whispered *I don't trust him, but maybe you will be able to convince him we can work together against the Tenenbrani and end all of the misunderstandings once and for all? If we are united, then maybe we will be one bit closer to eliminating this curse forever?*

Luz nodded and stood as tall as she could to face Ma'elrich. "Welcome, Ma'elrich. We welcome the opportunity to get to know each other and come to a mutual understanding about what has happened to Tomar. For now, we have a place prepared for you so you may rest. We will ensure your needs are met, although we ask that you not leave your safe space while you remain with us. If you can agree to these conditions, we will show you to your lodging."

With a curt nod, Ma'elrich agreed. Luz came forward with a long white strip of cloth.

"It's already dusk, and difficult to see anything already. Is a blindfold truly necessary?"

"The blindfold is a necessary precaution, and we promise that you will remain safe. We can remove the blindfold once you are safely in your lodging."

Apprehensively, Ma'elrich agreed, and Luz tied the blindfold over his eyes as the night fully blotted out all light. Only the faint glow of a fire in the cave Metulas and Luz lived in gave any light to the mountainside. Once blindfolded, Metulas gently closed a claw around him and carried him to a cave within hearing distance of Rowan. Seeing some large, flying creature glinting in the starlight, Rowan hailed them, throwing caution to the wind as he remembered he was a commanding magistrate who was above fear and cowardice. "You, whatever you are! Come rescue me!"

In flight, Ma'elrich thought he heard a familiar voice, although the wind kept much of the sound from reaching him. "Who's already here? Are you collecting people here as if it were a prison??" asked Rowan, shouting to be heard over the wind in his ears.

"Rowan?" asked Ma'elrich, who then began to squirm and fight to be freed. Metulas' growl resounded across the mountainside, stilling him temporarily. *Be still, human. This is not a prison for you. You are safe and will have your questions answered as long as you abide by the established agreement.*

With that, Metulas placed Ma'elrich on his feet at the mouth of a small cave, which had already been set with bedding, a firepit, water, and some food. Turning Ma'elrich around, Metulas used a small finger claw to release the blindfold. With a quick breath, he also lit the bramble in the firepit for Ma'elrich to stay warm. The fire gave the only welcoming warmth in the area, giving the cave itself a haunted air from the shadows the flames cast along the walls. Ma'elrich turned away from the cave to look over the valley and stood dangerously close to the edge. From the cave mouth, the view was tremendous until he looked down. The height was dizzying, and Metulas pulled him back away from the edge of the cave. *Rest, and stay away from the edge until you are used to the height. I promise you that you are safe. You are close enough to Rowan to speak to him but not see him or know where he is. You may speak, but you may not visit him yet.*

At that moment, Anehta arrived to check on Ma'elrich and inspected the cave itself. *I can spend the night up here with you for company and make sure all is safe for the night.*

"I'll be fine, thank you, Anehta. Metulas set up the fire, and there's enough material here to set up a comfortable place to sleep."

No trouble, I found a small hollow in the back that would be perfect for me!

Assured that all was well, Metulas flew back to his own cave, leaving Ma'elrich under Anehta's watchful gaze once again. Ma'elrich sat at the fire and ate the provided food,

310

seemingly oblivious to the heights at the moment. Anehta gathered a few twigs and moss from the stones nearby, helping herself to a few juicy insects she encountered along the way. Finally, full and happy, she sang to herself as she made her spot cozy enough for her to sleep. Exhausted from their journey, the two of them lay on their respective bedding and watched the pinpricks of light shine through the clear dark sky in silence until they both fell asleep.

Chapter 43: The Meeting of the Minds

After Luz and Metulas arrived back in Batalha, the two of them agreed on a new plan for converting the Magistrate to their cause since being with the curse stone for so long may have fortified his inability to see beauty, truth, and humanity. For the first couple of days after their return, Luz solicited the Clairdani to encourage more animals to come to the area, especially near the mountainside where the Magistrate could hear them.

"What do you think about us training with the Clairdani? We never have, and we should start learning how to work together with them. We will, of course, take the lead, but having their strengths with ours could offer more possibilities. It might also help our Magistrate begin to see the differences between the Tenenbrani and the Clairdani?" asked Luz.

Metulas reluctantly agreed and in the agreement made with the Clairdani, he had to compromise not to eat any animals in the immediate area while they were helping with the cause. This meant he would need to travel much further for his meals, and they agreed to come at whatever time needed to work with a satiated dragon rather than a hungry one.

The next day, the Clairdani, led by Bartimeu, Luz, and Metulas staged multiple animal encounters in the area and trained as hard as they could. They hoped to make as much noise as possible to draw the Magistrate's attention and begin to see that the violence wasn't directed at Tomar. As they flew fantastical aerial maneuvers, practiced their sword-horn play, and worked on their strength against the rocks near the mountain, the clashes sounded convincingly real, startling the unaware animals into stampedes or squawking flights amid the deafening clamor of battle. At the first sounds of combat, Rowan's curiosity drew him to the edge of the cave. Seeing the battling creatures made his heart race faster, and when the animals began fleeing the scene that moved all around them, he shrank into the recesses of the cave for safety.

In the evenings, partially to entertain the number of friends staying overnight and partially to touch the Magistrate's heart, Luz sang the songs she remembered from Tomar. Many of the Clairdani made requests, unable to sing themselves as they used to as humans, and they enjoyed the youth in her voice as she sang. Among the melodies, there were older songs sung in the language of animals that Metulas had patiently taught her. These songs told tales of bygone days when animals and people worked harmoniously. As the tunes unfolded, a yearning for those days swept through them, causing them all to sway together, bound by a shared longing for the times past. On the first evening of song, the Magistrate cowered even more in the back of his cave, covering his ears and hiding completely under the woven blanket they'd given him. *I will not let them curse me; I will not let them curse me...* he chanted to himself. His chanting blocked the music, and every once in a while, he would stop to check if the music had ended. In between musical numbers, he heard laughter and chatter and the beginnings of a new tune. When the animal language songs began, he forgot to cover his ears, entranced by the simple beauty of the syllables and notes. Unconsciously, Rowan stood up and walked to the edge of the cave, looking down at the happy circle of friends around the fire.

Seeing Rowan at the edge of the cave, Bartimeu signaled with his eyes to Luz, who noticed that Rowan was showing

313

interest. After the next song, she whispered a plan to Bartimeu, who agreed to take care of the plan details. As Luz sang the last few songs, Bartimeu quietly moved around the group, talking to each of the Clairdani and getting many of them to agree to the plan. It would be enough, they hoped.

Beginning that next morning, a different Clairdani brought each meal to the Magistrate, and now they were intently visible. After delivering the meal, each would wander around the cave a bit while he ate, offering the Magistrate an opportunity to try to communicate with them or at least look into their eyes. As these selected Clairdani had all been victims of his own wonton sense of justice, they hoped to be able to convey to him their connection to Tomar however they could. He adamantly refused to glance in their direction or express gratitude for the meals. Instead, he opted to turn his back to them, fixing his gaze over the valley as he ate. When he finished, he would place the bowl or wooden plank behind him and wait for each Clairdani to leave.

After so many innumerable days of being captive, these last ones with these strange animals delivering meals, battle all around them, and strange music in the evenings had brought a sense of calm to Rowan's life. Although he didn't care for any of these creatures, his loneliness had abated somewhat, and he continued to think of the people of Tomar and wonder whether they missed him. *Why hasn't anyone come to find me? They could have tracked my captors and been here by now, for sure! I wish I could remember exactly what happened after I reached out to touch one of the creatures near Tomar and when I got here!*

Rowan still had not seen Metulas, who had been careful to stay either in the shadows or out of sight of the caves when he was out and about. *In fact, when Ma'elrich arrived in*

Batalha, and Metulas flew down to greet them, Rowan was sure what he saw was only a reflection of the sunset on the reflective mountainside. Hearing the faint but familiar, gruff voice of his friend Ma'elrich made Rowan wonder if he was losing his mind and imagining his friend flying nearby! *Has Ma'elrich come to rescue me? Where are the guards to help fight my captors? Did he come alone??* Rowan shook his head, bewildered at his friend's stupidity. Now, they were both prisoners, and no one would be coming to find them!

The evening of Ma'elrich and Anehta's arrival, after Ma'elrich was sleeping soundly, the four of them talked long into the night of all that had happened and what they should do with the Inquisitor and the Magistrate. After a long evening of discussion with Metulas and Bartimeu, Luz agreed she should at least talk with Ma'elrich and allow him to explain himself. The Magistrate was softening but not ready to understand the truth of the curse yet. *We will be there with you, Luz, just in case. He may have changed, or he may be pretending, which is the only thing we need to know at the moment.* Anehta pledged her support, and Bartimeu nodded his agreement.

The next morning, Luz wandered up to Ma'elrich's cave, choosing to hide her flying abilities until she knew more about him. Bartimeu and Anehta bounded up from a different direction so as not to alarm Ma'elrich and be able to intervene quickly if needed. When they were both in place, Luz climbed up the last bit, pulling herself up over the cave mouth opening.

"Good morning, Ma'elrich, is it?" Luz began, trying to keep things light and friendly. The figure in front of her still resembled a troll in both bearing and demeanor. Thankfully, he didn't smell like one, at least! At the same time, she noticed that, indeed, his eyes were green, as Anehta had said. In the dark, it had been hard to tell what the morning light now showed plainly.

"Yes, and you are … Luz?" he asked in a polite response.

Luz gave a short nod in affirmation. "Were you able to sleep well enough? The sounds of the open air and the light of a starry night sky can be difficult for some to find sleep," Luz commented in an attempt to keep things as polite as possible and allow him to state his purpose when he was ready.

"I did, thank you. Anehta kept me company for part of the night, and the cave helped make me feel less exposed to the elements."

They both kept silent for a while, not wanting to break the comfort it offered them. Finally, Luz prompted him. "So, you were saying when you arrived that you had read something about me? I didn't realize there was much in print or anything about me, certainly!"

"Ah yes, well… it wasn't exactly a book I found in a library. It was a codex, a book carefully written in special ink, with a special lock and key, that the guards found and gave to me. It was Hawthorne's notes that he wrote about you while you were in the gaol in Tomar."

At her reaction to both the name Hawthorne and her imprisonment, it was clear that she had no idea Hawthorne had written anything about her. *All the better that she didn't know… she probably wouldn't have given him as much information as she did if she had known it was being written down!*

Remembering to stay calm and not reveal emotions, Luz remarked, "I wasn't aware that any such book existed. What exactly was in it?"

Careful, don't tell her too much! He had to remind himself. "It was mostly about your childhood, the Clairdani and Tenenbrani, and how you found Metulas and this place."

"Where does Hawthorne fit into this?" she asked.

"Hawthorne clearly came to trust you and, through you, began to believe everything you told him about the transformations and the ongoing battles between the Tenenbrani and Clairdani. Through his eyes, I began to see what a wonderful being you are and that it's the people that are cruel and evil, not the creatures themselves!" He shed a couple of tears and took a moment to wipe his eyes.

"So, if you've known about how things really work in Tomar for a while, why are you coming here now after you've still continued to persecute our people??" Luz's voice grew louder as she grew angrier at the continued persecutions when he knew it wasn't their people who were the source of the evil in Tomar.

"I know, I know… after the last page that I translated in Tomar, I wanted to come out here and apologize for everything I've put you and your people through and see what we could do together to make things right again in Tomar."

He bowed his head, seemingly remorseful for all the shameful things he had done to her people. After a minute to allow his story to absorb, he added, "I've come here to ask for your forgiveness, and I hope that you will let me replace Hawthorne as one of your protectors for life."

Luz looked at Ma'elrich searchingly and waited for him to return her gaze. She held his gaze, searching not only with her eyes but with her soul deep into his heart to see how true this conversion was. In his heart was division, although it wasn't clear what type of division or what the two parts represented. She would accept his request but keep her wariness and guard up around him until the division in his soul was absolved. She hoped it was because it was a very new transformation, and as it grew stronger, perhaps it would completely control his soul.

"I will accept your apology and role as one of my protectors for life," she decided and gave him a hug of acceptance into her group. "Thank you for sharing your story, and please make yourself at home here in your cave. The Clairdani will be here with food for you, and we will talk again tomorrow. There is much to discuss!"

And bidding him farewell, Luz jumped off the edge of the cave mouth and ran lightly down the mountainside out of sight.

Metulas was waiting for her, eager to hear her assessment of Ma'elrich's character. As she entered, he noticed her flushed face and light demeanor. *Good news, then?*

"Well, his eyes are indeed green, so perhaps his conversion is still very new and needs time to manifest itself. He seems divided, although I'm not sure if the division was this new conversion slowly taking over his previous self or something else. He offered to be one of my protectors for life out of remorse for what he's done to Tomar."

Did you accept his offer?

"I did, although I agree with Anehta that we need to watch him carefully. If this is a true conversion, do you think this might be the change that was mentioned in the writing of the curse? If so, that may be the additional strength we need on our side to help rid ourselves of the evils of the Tenenbrani forever!"

Curses and prophecies are odd things. Often, it is after events occur that we finally understand their true meaning. We should not do anything different to try and make the curse end, for doing so might make everything worse! We know the events that could end the curse, and by doing so, we have potentially already changed Tomar's future. I'm confident that the choices we are presented with will happen regardless of what we know. If the time for the curse to end is at hand, then the choices we make will bring about the end of the curse.

"Why did we risk our lives getting into the Magistrate's office and learning the words of the curse then if the words don't matter?"

Think about everything that's been set in motion because we discovered the curse was inside that office. We realized we had to get the Magistrate out of his office and away from the powers in that stone...

"If the curse had been somewhere else, perhaps Tomar's magistrate wouldn't have been as cruel, encouraging cruelty around him and causing so many transformations. So, by removing him from the strength of the curse, maybe that alone might help save Tomar?"

Only time can tell. Moving the Magistrate away from the curse doesn't end the curse. There are other people still physically close enough to it for its power to influence them.

We must believe that this is a first step, and if we do what we feel is best for everyone, we will be helping manifest the curse to its end.

"I think I understand you. So, the Magistrate should be growing kinder as he stays away from the powers of the curse? He hasn't changed that much since he's been here…"

Everything takes time. He's been close to that curse stone for many years, and he's only been here for a fortnight. He is beginning to show a willingness to accept another truth from what he's always known.

Luz began to show her impatience, shifting her weight from one foot to the other. Even though the curse had been in place for as long as anyone remembered, being so close to abolishing it and having to wait was going to be excruciating! A sense of eager anticipation and restlessness swelled within her heart.

The people of Tomar are safe for now from either of these two tyrants. Think of that!

"But not from the Tenenbrani, and Simão is essentially working with all of our contacts alone! It's only a matter of time before he gets attacked by one of these other Tenenbrani while he's meeting one of them."

We have to hope he will stay within Tomar until he has someone to help him. Simão and Mateus are intelligent and careful. They will be safe enough.

"I suppose that is all we can do for now."

Metulas nodded his head, sensing she had more to discuss.

"As for Ma'elrich and his conversion, do you think he might be able to explain the truth to Rowan? They've worked together for a while now, and maybe Ma'elrich knows how to approach Rowan so that he'll listen?"

Yes, I think you have a clever idea there. Go speak with Ma'elrich and see if he would be willing to convince Rowan of the truth, given all that he knows of us. Once Rowan converts, we can take them back to Tomar, remove the stone from the office, and release the Enlightened from their imprisonment...

"Tomar would be a completely different town if they were all united and understood that they were under a curse!" Luz's eyes were aglow with thoughts of a free Tomar, where the Enlightened's work with the Tenenbrani wouldn't been suspicious.

Focus on what is at hand, my dear Luz. It might take a long time to undo the power the curse has on the Magistrate, and hopefully, he isn't too foregone to be able to return. His eyes were flashing the first day he was here, and we don't know if the curse is reversible. He hasn't transformed since he's been here, at least.

Luz took a few moments to help calm her mind and focus on the present moment, not on what could have been or could be in the distant future. The far-off look in her eyes faded, and her resolve returned. "I'll bring Ma'elrich his noonday meal and have a chat with him about Rowan. I'll let you know what we decide."

At noon, Luz managed to bring a bowl of various edible nuts, roots, berries, and even a small roasted mouse for Ma'elrich. Graciously, Ma'elrich accepted the meal and sat down to eat.

"How do you find your lodging? It's very different from your place in Tomar, I'm sure!" began Luz, making idle conversation while he ate.

Ma'elrich vocalized something that sounded positive enough while still eating. Luz decided to give him time to eat alone and sat down at the cave mouth edge with her legs dangling off the mountainside. After a few minutes, Ma'elrich came and stood nearby, handing her the empty bowl back.

"Thank you, Luz, for the meal. I imagine having a dragon to cook your food saves time and space?"

"It might save some time, although I think Metulas takes up more space than any small fire would!"

They both laughed at the thought of a dragon the size of a small fire.

"Stone-walled caves are a good place for a dragon to live; fewer chances of anything catching fire," offered Ma'elrich as they collected themselves.

"It's been very safe, yes. Most creatures fear the dragon's claws more than his fire, although they both offer protection."

They sat in silence for a minute while Luz thought about how best to start her request.

"Ma'elrich, how well do you know Rowan?"

Surprised at the question, Ma'elrich stared for a moment before answering. "We were close friends once, many years ago. I am from Tomar, actually. He and I were neighbors, and our parents did everything together, so we naturally got to know each other very well. Anytime either of our parents punished us too harshly or showed their tendency to bloodthirsty anger, we would run to the other's place for safety to wait for the storm to blow over. When I was about 10, the Traitors led a Tenenbrani into Tomar, and that Tenenbrani killed both my father and mother. My father's body was never found, and my mother's broken remaining parts were beyond recognition.'

"I am so sorry for your ordeal; that must have impacted you immensely!" Luz tried to comfort him.

"It did. Rowan's parents were willing to take me in, but I needed to get away from Tomar. I couldn't stay somewhere where nightmares of those creatures would haunt me every night for life, and my father's brother in Cold Pollux took me in for his own. He had no family, so we became a new family of our own. When he died many years ago, he left me everything."

Luz looked into his eyes, searching for any sense of loss that might still be there. Strangely, she didn't see loss in his eyes. Only cold.

"Do you understand now that it might have been your father who transformed and caused your mother's death?"

"I suppose that is what happened. My memories from that night are very vivid, and I was at Rowan's place when they died. He saved my life, after a fashion. Since then, though, we didn't see each other again and we had different lives. He became the Magistrate like his father was before him, and I became the Inquisitor." We only knew about the other from what news travelled around the area, and I guess we are both competitive and always want to outdo the other, whether it be in influence, wealth, prestige... Since I've been back in Tomar, things have grown more strained between us.

We don't appreciate each other's methods of finding truth or controlling a town."

"I see… We are hoping that you might be able to put the competition aside and remember your friendship from long ago. Perhaps then, you can use your connection and influence on Rowan to help convince him of the goodness and rightness of the Enlightened and Clairdani? We've only had limited success, and perhaps if you shared your story with him, he might be more open to the idea?"

Before she even finished, Ma'elrich shook his head. "He's too full of his own malice. He would never understand your side. It's a matter of pride for him that he won't ever admit he may have been wrong."

Luz sighed and stood, ready to go.

"I could try though, I guess," offered Ma'elrich, watching Luz's dejected form stand up straighter with the hope he had just given her.

"Oh, thank you!" sang Luz sweetly, and she gave him a hug of thanksgiving. "We can work together at first, and if a united front doesn't work, we can leave the two of you alone and see if you have better luck alone."

"I will do my best, although I don't know that he has any more regard for me than for you, given recent events," replied Ma'elrich.

"We will see," Luz decided, then departed.

A little while later, a humongous golden eagle appeared, whose golden eyes were each the size of a man's fist. As she landed, she bent her head to gaze into Ma'elrich's eyes. *I will carry you to see Rowan. Luz will meet us there. Step onto my talon and hold on to my leg so you won't fall as we fly. It isn't far.*

Ma'elrich did as he was asked, and the two flew away from the mountainside into the air. The eagle went around the backside of the caves, continuing to the other side of the cavernous mountainside. She set him down at the mouth of another cave, slightly larger than the one he had just been in, about halfway up the mountain this time. Gently, the eagle alighted on the edge of the mouth edge and allowed Ma'elrich to disembark onto solid ground. As soon as he stood in the cave, she took off again.

A few minutes later, Luz appeared, climbing up onto the cave ledge. She never seemed to be out of breath! He watched her admiringly, and she stood and smiled.

"I thought neutral ground might be a good place to start our meeting. It'll be yourself, me, and Rowan. Metulas will come later if we feel we need him."

"Is Rowan coming here then?"

As in answer, the same golden eagle appeared, holding a squirming Rowan in its talons. He was beating on the talons with his fists, causing the eagle to flinch and suddenly drop in height at the stronger blows. Together, they appeared like bobbing toys in the water. Finally, the eagle approached their cave, and she set Rowan firmly on the cave ledge before folding in her wings. Rowan steadied himself, then ran to the edge and was sick. *He's worse than my fledglings ever were when we'd have to move them! Will he be alright?*

"He'll be fine," laughed Ma'elrich, despite his friend's discomfort.

With the assurance, the eagle departed, Luz's thanks sounding on the wind.

After a few minutes of breathing deeply on the edge, bent over with his hands on his thighs, Rowan was finally able to stand up and face Luz and Ma'elrich. A fortnight of being away from his pampered life showed. His once-impeccable outer black robe was frayed and worn, and a few small holes had started around his elbows and the lower edge as well. Stains dotted his tunic and trousers, and his hair, once a helmet of gleaming black, was escaping from his head using all possible routes at once. Luz and Ma'elrich schooled their faces so as not to alarm the already unsettled man.

"Good to see you, Rowan!" Ma'elrich stepped forward to grasp forearms with his friend and pull him a bit further away from the edge of the cave ledge.

Registering that his friend was in front of him, Rowan asked, "Were you the one I thought I saw the other night coming to the caves here?"

"It was, although I came by choice, not by force. It is good to see you, Rowan. You seem to have been treated well enough?"

In response, Rowan only harrumphed. "I've been kidnapped, starved, scared out of my wits, ignored, and deprived of my livelihood. How do you think I'm doing?"

"Well, put that way, I can see your point."

Luz moved slightly, and it caught the men's attention. Rowan stared at her as if he had never seen her before. *Is this the girl behind all of this?*

To cover the awkward moment, Ma'elrich made introductions. "Luz, may I present Rowan, Magistrate of Tomar. Rowan, may I present Luz, also known as the Advocate, who lives here and would like you to join her cause."

Luz laughed inwardly at his forthrightness. Rowan gave a short burst of incredulous laughter. "After all they've put me through, they want me to help them?"

Luz felt they weren't getting off to a good start. "Please, Rowan, I think there are too many misunderstandings, and it would help if we sat down and explained our side so you could understand what our cause is. We will understand if afterwards you still don't want to help us."

With a guttural harrumph, Rowan agreed, and the three sat on the largest rocks they could find for seats. For the next hour, Luz told Rowan everything about the transformations of the Tenenbrani and how Clairdani and the Enlightened are working together to save Tomar from further Tenenbrani attacks. Throughout her explanation, Ma'elrich would interject with an occasional "and that's why we thought…" or other interested grunts.

When Luz finally finished, Rowan turned to Ma'elrich. "And you believe all this nonsense?"

"I believe their version is the truth, Rowan, not nonsense." As the two men stared at each other in a game of staring chicken, Rowan finally noticed Ma'elrich's eyes.

"You traitor, you have the green eyes now too! How could you turn on me? We were like brothers!" Rowan genuinely felt betrayed, the only sane person in this chaotic world of talking, murderous creatures.

Ma'elrich turned to Luz, his look clearly reiterating his inability to influence his prior friend.

"Can you believe that we are not trying to hurt any of the townspeople? Even if you don't believe in our cause, can we, at a minimum, call a halt on hunting the creatures outside the walls of Tomar and executions of any of our Enlightened?"

Luz attempted to put a bit of her own power of persuasion into her words, hoping that without the curse stone's powers in the area, hers might begin to have some effect. She didn't sense any shift in him, although no shift was better than the negative shifts before her captivity.

"That will only encourage even more attacks in Tomar without the deterrent of punishment for their crimes! I cannot agree to those terms." Rowan declared.

"We are working in our own way to stop the Tenenbrani attacks on Tomar. Our ways aren't the same as your ways, we know, although they are not wrong just for being different. We must build trust within Tomar and understand that we all want these attacks to end."

Rowan, having nothing more to contribute, exchanged defiant glares with Luz instead. Neither was willing to yield ground. Staring into his black eyes, she noticed flashes of red, indicating a potential transformation was imminent. Realizing the urgency, she knew she had to leave immediately and devise a plan in case the transformation occurred in the next couple of days. "We will leave you two here so you are no longer isolated from others. I will visit each day to see if you are willing to consider a truce. Until then, peace."

Without waiting for their approval, Luz somersaulted over the side of the cave ledge to burn off some of her frustration and ran down the mountainside to Metulas' cave.

Ma'elrich began, trying to reconcile with his friend. "I'm sorry for any steps I took in Tomar that may have gone too far to help control the chaos within Tomar. Believe me, it was all in the name of protecting them from further attacks."

Rowan seemed to soften a bit and turned towards his old friend. "Well, Ma'elrich, the past is the past. All is forgiven, as we are stuck together for now." The two men stared at each other, brown eyes looking into black, now flecked with red.

Rowan flinched. Ma'elrich's eyes were now brown, not green!

"What's going on here, Ma'elrich? How are your eyes now brown? I know they were green before!"

"They use eye covers, so why can't I? I needed to get them to trust me so I could come find you and possibly rescue you. If possible, we might even be able to destroy these Traitors at their source!"

Rowan had to laugh at his machinations and release the stress he had felt being the only sane one left in this strange world. "So, you don't believe any of what they're telling you?"

"Oh, I believe that there are possibly some creatures out there that are less bloodthirsty than others, just as there are both kind and cruel people. But are people turning into these creatures? That sounds like a lot of fairy tales we tell our children to make them behave!"

"So, the codex you were working on was just that, a lot of those fairy tales about these creatures?" Rowan tried to summarize.

"Well, no, I'm sorry for misleading you there. I actually was able to read the codex in its entirety, and it's everything Luz ever told Hawthorne. It has her life story, much about the different types of creatures they work with through short stories that happened in and around Tomar. It also mentions much about this place, although there was only a vague suggestion of where it was. That was what I finally figured out – that this place had to be across the desert that we always thought was the end of our world."

"You kept all of that from me? Why?"

"I was waiting to have the codex finished in its entirety, and I was collecting the names and places mentioned so I could follow up with you," Ma'elrich lied to cover his selfish designs.

Standing up, Ma'elrich walked around the edge of the cave ledge, searching for anyone or anything that might be listening to them. Rowan watched him warily. Seeing nothing around, Ma'elrich continued. "Rowan, if we could simply execute Luz here, all of our problems would be solved! Everyone dotes and depends on her; without her, the Traitors would fall apart!"

"So, we just wait for her to show up and kill her?" Rowan did a poor job of disguising the glee in his voice. After months of torturing Luz, he would enjoy just snuffing her out of existence since now they had all the information they needed to rout the Traitors.

"Of course not. I've won their trust though. With the green contacts, they all believe I'm now one of them and think I'm trying to convince you to agree with them. We just have to play along for a little while, then when she's vulnerable, we strike. We just need to figure out exactly how…"

With enthusiasm, the two men huddled in the cave, like trolls around a bonfire. They engaged in lively banter for hours, discussing the various means and weapons they could create to ensure the success of their plan. As a Clairdani stag came to bring them their evening meals, Rowan was again terrified, and Ma'elrich took the opportunity to help him understand these creatures.

"Don't be afraid of them, Rowan. Remember, they only bring us food to help us, not hurt us. Try this."

Ma'elrich approached the stag, staring into its eyes. After a couple minutes, the stag turned away and put food down for Ma'elrich.

"See, gaze into the animal's eyes, and imagine yourself saying 'thank you' to it. Stay calm. It will then put the food in front of you. He's waiting for you to accept him and acknowledge that he's not an enemy."

Hesitantly, Rowan mimicked his friend, imagining himself saying "thank you" while gazing into the stag's eyes. Having not said "thank you" very often in his life, it was a very odd feeling saying such to a creature. He also had the odd sensation that this was someone he had seen before somehow. He shook himself of the possibility. A creature he had met before? Impossible!

"So, is there something to their declaration that when innocents are murdered or executed in Tomar, they also turn into these creatures?"

"Who knows, and does it really matter?" replied Ma'elrich flippantly. "I just pretend to be kind to them, and I get what they want to give me. I notice that we haven't been given our bedding or fire yet, so perhaps this is part of a test of trust?"

Rowan shrugged, "We shall see. It will be a cold night without those things, and I don't know that we can call for anything. We seem to be at their mercy here."

As hoped, other Clairdani came shortly after their meal to bring firewood and fire and again after sunset to bring bedding. As practiced, the two friends went through the ritual of staring into the eyes of the Clairdani before being given the desired items. Each time, while Ma'elrich seemed unperturbed by the encounters, Rowan sensed a connection with each of these creatures.

Unnerved, Rowan busied himself with preparing his bedding near the fire for warmth. Still unsure of himself, he mumbled an evening farewell to Ma'elrich and settled on his bedding for the evening. That night, dreams of all the people he had had executed visited him, staring into his soul. The next morning, he woke in a cold sweat and did his best to hide it from his friend.

Chapter 44: The Battle of Batalha

The next morning, Metulas wasn't as convinced that Ma'elrich would succeed where they had failed. *It may have been too early, and Rowan convinced Ma'elrich that the Clairdani and Enlightened are fantastical stories your mind made up while you were recovering from your brutal interrogations.*

As Luz thought about how she might be able to keep the two men's progress moving forward, the dog-sized fire salamander that had taken lunch to their guests returned. She dropped the bowls near Luz and looked between the two of them to report.

How are they? Did you see any progress with Rowan? asked Metulas anxiously.

The Inquisitor is teaching the Magistrate how to work with us, actually! In detail, the fire salamander reported all that had occurred as preamble to giving them their meals, and any discussion during the meal.

The strange thing was that when I looked into the Inquisitor's eyes, I didn't see anything. But when I looked into Rowan's eyes, I felt a connection like he possibly recognized me! It was very brief, but there was a definite shift somewhere. He didn't admit any connection to the Inquisitor, at any rate. He did ask if the stories might be true, and interestingly enough, the Inquisitor laughed and said it was fairy tales rather than admitting its truth.

This mercurial aspect of their newest guest was enlightening. "Why would he lie to Rowan and pretend it's all fantasy?" Luz was annoyed with herself for having trusted him at all when she sensed some duplicity in his soul. *I was hoping the duality I saw In him was the truth slowly transforming his heart, although perhaps this is something else entirely?*

Metulas only blew a bit of smoke from his nostrils, showing his share of annoyance with their guest. *I will have to investigate this myself as well and see if the heart has any answers.* His eyes seemed to drift away from them to times long ago, then slowly return to where they were.

Luz, how did you feel near Rowan? Any drops in your power in his presence? Metulas inquired.

"None, thankfully. The power only seems to radiate from the curse stone itself. Without the curse's influence, his attitudes seem more malleable. If he is very susceptible, it may be a battle for his soul between us and the Inquisitor." Luz said insightfully.

You may very well be right, Luz. In which case, you will need to use your influence to win over Rowan yourself. Tell him the stories of the Clairdani he might remember, the Tenenbrani that have converted, and any stories you know about Tomarans connecting with Clairdani they had known when they were still human. It may be that he was reaching the time for his own transformation, and your influence will be even more critical for that very reason.

Luz nodded and stood up. "And anytime I'm there with them, they can't conspire against us. Do you think we should just split them up again?"

Metulas thought about this strategy and voted against it. *Let's see how well you are able to influence him first. If, by the third day, we see no difference in him, we will separate them again. Together, you might be able to influence Ma'elrich as well or see any patterns in his alternating dispositions.*

334

Resolute, Luz nodded and began her ascent to their cave. She would need to begin as soon as possible to ensure that the two men's doubts didn't completely undo any newly planted ideas. After a quick glance at Metulas for assurance, Anehta followed.

The first visit did not go as planned. Luz popped over the cave edge a little after breakfast, and the two men were still discombobulated in their dress. Just as Luz turned her face away, Anehta had overflown the cave the first time, and trying to make up for being late, she flew too fast and suddenly, seeing Luz turn toward her, had knocked herself out by misjudging the height of the cave opening after flying around her. The three of them then spent the time trying to revive her, checking her for injuries, and sharing stories of their own follies through the years. Bartimeu arrived with their noonday meal, signaling time for them to take a break for themselves as well. With fond farewells, Luz and Anehta departed, promising to return soon after they ate as well.

For the next three days, Luz and Anehta returned between meals to talk with Rowan and Ma'elrich, entertaining them with stories of the various Clairdani and Tenenbrani's transformations and explaining to them how things really are in the magical world. Luz made sure to use names he might recognize when talking about various Clairdani – who they had been in Tomar and who they were now. All around them, they still heard the eclectic battle sounds of the animals around them, and being very familiar with their sounds, Luz introduced each of the various creatures to them by their sounds. Giving the men the creatures' names, if she happened to know them, and their stories, Luz was making a tangible connection between them and these creatures. After the second day, Luz noticed that Rowan's eyes no longer flashed red and had softened from their harsh black back to their brown color. Encouraged, Luz put as much of herself into her words as she could, looking for any further changes and noting any changes to Metulas in their evening discussions.

Ma'elrich observed Rowan's eye changes as well, though without sharing the same level of enthusiasm. While they ate each meal, Ma'elrich would try to find bits of bone he might be able to use; and in the evenings, he would look for sharp stones or grasses he could work with to create a lethal weapon. He reminded Rowan what their plan was and ensured Rowan was back on track once Luz left. *Yes, she does have some kind of mental abilities that help her convince others to believe her. Thankfully, I seem to be immune to it. Physically though...* Luz didn't seem very strong physically, and two strong men against one frail girl were good odds in his book. The most the little owl could do was peck at them, and that was easy enough to shrug off.

It was true. Despite himself, Rowan found himself looking forward to her visits. Not only was she as different from Ma'elrich as light is to dark, but her explanations of the creatures around them and their origins were beginning to make more sense to him than the explanations he had gotten from Ma'elrich. Ironically, learning to really look into the eyes of the Clairdani had started a slow burn of understanding that grew with each visit. At the end of the third day, as the fire salamander delivered their evening meals, Rowan finally recognized the fire salamander as the woman he had burned at the stake for being a suspected traitor! "Veronica?"

The fire salamander seemed as surprised as he was that he remembered who she was! Slowly, she nodded her head, and their eyes met. As the realization of who she was dawned on him, remorse overwhelmed him and held him frozen as the full extent of what he had done, not just to Veronica but to all the people he had ordered executed through the years. Seeing his friend frozen, Ma'elrich helped him return to his bedding and lie down.

"What happened, Rowan? Are you feeling ill?"

Rowan could only shake his head.

"Is there anything I can ask them to get for you? Water? Your food is here...," offered Ma'elrich, collecting the items he named and placing them near Rowan's bed.

"I just need to rest. Yes, just let me rest." Rowan insisted.

Ma'elrich looked at the fire salamander and gave her his bowl. "Tell Luz that she shouldn't come this afternoon because Rowan needs to rest. We will see her tomorrow." Hesitatingly, the fire salamander looked first to Rowan, then to Ma'elrich, then slowly slithered down the mountainside.

Not approving of weakness of any kind, Ma'elrich worried that his comrade was starting to believe all the tales Luz was telling them. He would have to dispatch her alone tomorrow before Rowan converted to her cause. If that ever happened, all would be lost. He needed his friend to stay strong with him and help revenge his father's death! While Rowan rested, Ma'elrich worked on his weapon, honing its sharp edges and putting hot tallow on the grasses to strengthen them. At last, it was finished. He practiced retrieving it from his pouch, ensuring he could do so swiftly to catch her off guard in the morning. Content, at last, he lay down to sleep near his friend.

Veronica slithered quickly into Metulas' cave. *Rowan's converting, I can tell! He remembered me!*

Luz looked up from her food. "Are you sure?"

Yes! He said my name and froze as if finally understanding everything we've been telling him! He had to go lie down to have some time thinking through it all, and Ma'elrich said to come tomorrow to give Rowan some time.

Happy, Luz and Anehta danced a small dance in the cave, nearly knocking Luz's food over.

Carefully, little ones! Cautioned Metulas. *If he truly does convert and become an Enlightened, then we should be able to tell all of Tomar the truth and have them work with us, not against us. Tomorrow, I should go with you, Luz. Perhaps he is ready to meet a dragon!* Secretly, Metulas ensured the old dragon heart was with him. He might need some counsel tomorrow and wanted to make sure the old dragon heard everything he did in the morning.

The next morning, the stag, Martim, brought the men their breakfast. Both men were up and ready to eat, although when Rowan saw him approach, he began weeping! Carefully, Martim gazed into Rowan's eyes, and very faintly, he heard Rowan whisper, "I am so sorry for having misunderstood you and having you wrongfully executed. Please forgive me!"

Surprised, Martim nodded his head and turned to let Rowan get their food from his backpacks. As he did, he decided to introduce Martim to Ma'elrich. As the details were still vague, Rowan guessed many of them, gesturing to Martim to either confirm or negate his assertions about his life and execution. As Martim left, Rowan turned to his friend. "And it must be true, Ma'elrich! All of these Clairdani serving us were wrongfully executed, and since they were innocents, they were transformed into these magnificent creatures who can work with us in peaceful ways! There's nothing to fear here, they are the same kind, loving souls from before!"

Ma'elrich had had enough. "Now, listen up. All of these creatures have one thing in common – they all have grudges against you and Tomar. As soon as they are organized, they will rise up against Tomar and destroy everyone in it! These might be the smaller ones, so they seem harmless but trust me, they all have means of vanquishing an assumed foe!"

Just then, Metulas arrived with Luz on his back. The two men turned as one and stared. Flapping his wings to stay still, Metulas was a magnificent and powerful creature! Luz slid off of his neck, landing at the edge, and Metulas hooked his claws in the mountain so that his face was next to the cave. Rowan's eyes doubled in size as he took in the enormity of the creature staring into the cave at him. Luz made introductions to help ease the tension. "Rowan, this is Metulas, the last remaining dragon in our world. Metulas, this is Rowan, the Magistrate of Tomar."

Rowan and Metulas' eyes met, and something finally fell into place for him. They were each a leader in their own right, and each needed to know the truth of the other. For the next few minutes, Metulas and Rowan were transfixed while the others watch in amazement. Using his dragon ability to send mental pictures, Metulas shared all he could. Rowan saw, heard, and felt Metulas' story in an instant– his early life during the dragon wars, his seeming abandonment during the last battle, his enduring loneliness over the centuries, his spite of humanity, and then his accidental encounter with Luz and their friendship that spawned a new leadership helping to fight and transform Tenenbrani. In turn, Metulas sensed Rowan's early friendship with

Ma'elrich, his abuse, the loss of his friend, and his decision to focus his hate on the Traitors, which grew as he spent more time in the office. There was a sense of shared understanding and unity between them then, and Rowan was at ease with Metulas' large head at the entrance to the cave.

Luz waited until the end of their exchange to add to their story. "We know that it is a curse that causes the people of Tomar to transform into these creatures, and we hope that together, we might be able to break this curse. With no curse, there would be no attacks, and many innocent lives could be spared!"

"How would we fit into the plan for breaking the curse? We have no powers of our own…"

"Are you agreeing to be part of whatever plan we can create that will help stop the curse from transforming the people of Tomar?" Luz asked excitedly.

"Let us think about it," interrupted Ma'elrich harshly, pulling Rowan away from Luz and forcing him to look away from the dragon. "We can let you know later."

Abashed, Luz wandered toward Metulas, giving quizzical glances at both men. "As you wish. I will return after midday."

After midday, Luz finished her training with Anehta and continued up the mountainside to Rowan and Ma'elrich's cave. As she approached, she heard the two arguing loudly. *What is going on? Aren't the two of them on the same side?* Since neither seemed to have seen her yet, she decided to listen out of sight for a while.

"This is it, Rowan. We have to act now!"

"What if I don't want to follow through anymore?"

"But Rowan, you know all of this is false! Who do you trust more, your best friend from childhood or these crazy talking animals led by this little girl with fantasies? They need you because you run Tomar, and they are tired of being hunted and imprisoned. They kidnapped you, remember? They have no love for you!"

Rowan didn't respond, and Luz heard Ma'elrich clear his throat and continue more quietly.

"We need to end this. If we can kill Luz, then whatever creatures we find here, we will begin the end of the wonton attacks in Tomar immediately. Remember? That's what our plan was?"

"That was before I understood the truth. These creatures truly are reincarnations of their former human selves and have their memories and kindness to prove that fact! That dragon is a sign that the legends we grew up with about dragons and humans working together might be real, too!"

Hearing the argument escalate, Luz climbed up over the cave ledge. "Anything I can help with here?" Distracted by her sudden appearance, Rowan moved towards Luz while Ma'elrich reached into his pouch.

"We're just having a disagreement, Luz. Ma'elrich is being stubborn and not willing to concede the truth behind the Clairdani and Tenenbrani," clarified Rowan.

While Rowan was speaking with Luz, Ma'elrich had moved closer to them. "Grab her!" shouted Ma'elrich.

Rather than grab Luz and hold her still, Rowan stepped in front of her to stop Ma'elrich from inflicting any harm. Twelve miniature daggers connected by string pierced his neck, forming a red ring that dripped Rowan's blood on the cave's floor as he sank to the ground, unable to form a coherent word with the blood bubbling up into his mouth. Luz knelt down next to Rowan, trying to staunch the bleeding to no avail. She glared at Ma'elrich, who collected the weapon and began to eye her neck as well.

Smelling blood, Metulas arrived a few seconds later. *What... happened!"* he demanded. Ma'elrich stepped back at the sight of the dragon's face and feel of fire. Luz tried to explain the argument between the two men and pointed at Ma'elrich as the murderer. Looking at Ma'elrich, they both noticed his eyes had returned to brown!

"What's going on, Ma'elrich! We saw your green eyes and were giving you time to adjust to your new understanding of this world. In return, you decided to kill us instead?" Luz was so irate and frustrated she fought to keep her tears in check.

"You are both simpletons to think that only one side can use these eye covers. They work in reverse as well, of course, although I don't need them." For emphasis, he quickly changed his eye color to green, then black with flecks of red in them, and back to brown. Luz stepped away from Ma'elrich, towards the safety of Metulas' side.

"You are so eager to have people believe your truth that you accept anyone claiming to understand your world just like you did me. It has become your undoing, and I can now destroy you all with what I know about all of you! I have never been caught in my schemes, despite all your protections in place at Tomar, because..." Ma'elrich's words broke off as he decided to let actions speak for him.

Within seconds, instead of the Inquisitor, a large chimera with three different heads grew. One head was that of a large raptor, another was that of a lion, and the last was a venomous snake. His body was a mixture of the three – black leather wings erupted from the middle of his back, and black feathers that seemed more like metallic scales covered the long, sinuous main body that ended in a tail with two large barbs on either side. His much shorter arms and stocky, powerful legs had become those of a lion that ended in a raptor's talons. Metulas gathered Luz gently into his talons, placed her in a neighboring cave for safety, and then flew a little way off the mountainside to ensure he wasn't trapped on the mountain by this chimera and what it might do next. As they watched, Ma'elrich's elongated body seemed to ooze out of the cave as it grew longer. Once most of his body was outside the cave, Ma'elrich withdrew his heads from the cave and dug his nails into the mountainside. Six eyes now fixated on Metulas.

Metulas immediately launched himself on Ma'elrich. All the power he had kept in check found sudden release, and the two beasts seemed to somersault as they flew in the air, each trying to inflict more harm on the other with their talons, fangs, and fire. Although Ma'elrich had the element of surprise on his side, it was clear that Metulas fought aerial combat well. Their various screeches echoed throughout the valley as they seemed to take turns having the upper hand slashing at the other, gouging large bits of flesh that dripped platter-sized drops of blood on the ground below. Soon, Metulas held the chimera's body immobile in his talons, the three heads in one talon and the wings in the other. The serpent-like tail flashed in the sunlight as it continued to thrash, occasionally landing blows on Metulas' head or tail. Metulas breathed fire on the inflicting tail-mace and tried to grasp it with his fangs to no avail. As they sped to the ground, one last thrash of the mace-like tail caught on Metulas' tail and the base, tearing deep to the bone. Screaming in pain,

Metulas landed on the chimera with his full weight, crushing many of Ma'elrich's bones and tearing one of his wings such that only a few ligaments still held the wing onto his back. Ma'elrich had been able to wound Metulas as well, and the dragon's tail would need careful tending if he were to keep it. Thinking Ma'elrich would be near death with his wounds, Metulas released him to speak to him.

You deserve death for your crimes. Not just for Rowan, but for all the innocents you've destroyed. Your destruction of those against the Tenenbrani proves that you are one yourself, and we will ensure everyone knows of your treachery! Do you have anything worth conveying to anyone who might care to hear from you?

Luz, gripped by horrified fascination, had been watching the aerial combat. Now, she sprinted down the mountainside as fast as she could, eager to offer any healing assistance to Metulas. Fears of both being at death's door consumed her thoughts, and she listened intently for any response or sign of life as she approached. Seeing motion, she hurried down the last hundred feet of the mountain towards the two combatants. Hearing the last of Metulas' words, she put her hand lightly on his front leg and interjected, "He does deserve death, but without Rowan to validate who we are, he's the only one that might be able to tell the truth to Tomar."

In his ire, Metulas only saw red and knew that Ma'elrich would never tell the truth, no matter the cost. However, the small distraction Luz created was enough. Ma'elrich transformed himself into a gigantic eagle and feebly shot into the air, splattering blood droplets in his wake. Within seconds, he was nearly invisible. Luz's hand prevented Metulas from chasing him.

Anehta flew down to help her friend. "I'm sorry he got away," she comforted as she and Anehta put what poultices they could on the wounds. Dragons could be miraculous self-healers, although sometimes the additional help eased and sped up the healing process.

"The Magistrate had converted at the end, too! We were counting on him to help us convince the people of Tomar that we could work with the Clairdani…" Luz continued to lament.

Metulas had been very silent, as if deep in thought, which he sometimes did when he needed to focus on healing or stilling his anger. Luz and Anehta shared his silence as they continued to work on the bandages. As they put on the last poultice, Metulas' eyes popped open as if surprised by a sudden thought. *Thank you, little ones!*

He then launched himself into the air, flying back to where Rowan lay, dead. Gently, he brought Rowan's body to the cave's mouth, then carried it to his own cave where all could assemble. Once Anehta and Luz arrived, he drew out the old dragon heart. As the two smaller companions watched, Metulas began humming something in a different language. they saw flashes of dragons, humans, and battles in their minds, and a light of hope glimmering like a new sunrise. As he hummed, the sapphire heart in his foreclaw began to glow as he held it over Rowan's body. The heart then radiated with a brilliant intensity of light before it disappeared, and Rowan began glowing with the same heart glow. They all seemed to hold their breath in anticipation and watched Rowan as the glow diminished and subsided. Nothing else happened.

What were you hoping would happen? Asked Anehta, tentatively. Death still seemed to linger in the air, as the two friends moved towards Rowan's body.

I had hoped to revive him, at least. I had taken the heart with me as a precaution. I honestly thought that it would be me who needed the heart, and I was willing to sacrifice my own life if it meant the end of the bit of evil called Ma'elrich. With you two, I will survive my wounds and have no need of it. However, this man here could help us. That one line in the curse talked about uniting that which was separated, and I thought that putting a dragon heart together with a human might be some way of filling that. The old dragon gave me the words to use for restoring a heart, and I hoped it might be the correct way to restore him. A dragon heart has never been used for another race of being before. I thought we had nothing to lose by trying.

The three of them sat around Rowan's body, trying to think of another way to help Rowan. The Pit would allow for his transformation into a Clairdani, although that would not help Tomarans understand the goodness of the Clairdani. They needed him to be an influential human so he could help begin the dismantling of the curse. A pulse twitched in his neck, and the wounds slowly seemed to dissolve as they watched Rowan's body. Rather than the grey-white of decaying flesh, Rowan's body was gaining pinkish color.

"His eyes are opening!" Luz announced as she opened her eyes and glanced at Rowan. "He's alive!"

The heart must have worked! Give him some room…

Instead, Luz and Anehta raced over behind Rowan, helping him sit up and making him more comfortable.

Miraculously, his wounded neck had healed completely! Luz gave him a hug. "Welcome back, Rowan!"

"Why do I feel so different, and why do I have memories of times before I was even born? It's so strange..." Rowan wondered aloud.

I had to give you a new heart – one from an old dragon that fought in the dragon wars many centuries ago. Our hope is that you will now have both your own and his memories and will be able to help unite the humans with the Clairdani and dragons with a common purpose to end this curse.

"Curse? What curse?" asked Rowan, and then he suddenly realized that Metulas had answered the question and he had understood him. "Is that why I can now understand you?"

Patiently, Luz explained all that she understood about the curse and how it affected Tomar, even explaining about the curse stone and its power over those in Tomar. After interrupting many times to ask questions, Rowan finally seemed to understand how the curse created the Tenenbrani and Clairdani.

Anehta flew so she could stand in front of Rowan and peered into his face. After a few moments, Rowan began to understand she was talking to him as he heard a high-pitched voice in his head. It was something about being relieved that he was doing well. This mental talking would take some getting used to!

"So, as Metulas was saying, we need your help if we want to halt our people becoming blood-thirsty monsters. If you can halt the persecution of the Enlightened, what you used to call Traitors, that would allow them to continue their work connecting Tenenbrani with their humanity. That will help cut down on the attacks, and we will continue to work together to determine next steps. We hope you can join us as the Magistrate in Tomar?"

Rowan was now up on his feet, able to pace a bit while lost in thought. Finally, he gave his answer.

"I will work with you. It occurs to be that one key obstacle will be Ma'elrich. Who knows where he is and what his connection to the Tenenbrani is? I think joining forces may be our only path to defeat Ma'elrich and these Tenenbrani. I never realized how evil he had become! I know you mentioned you've had success with getting other Tenenbrani to feel remorse and lose their bloodlust, Luz. Do you think that might work for Ma'elrich too? I mean, the Tenenbrani are evil enough without someone who can transform into one at will and deceive others into thinking he's human otherwise!"

We may never know how far the blood-lust has taken Ma'elrich's soul, although we can try to bring back his humanity when the time is right. For now, we need to focus on the people of Tomar, and we will use the Clairdani network to help us determine where Ma'elrich is.

"We will fly you back to Tomar and help you re-settle in as the Magistrate. Mateus is your true friend and will guide you well as well as be a liaison between us. When Ma'elrich returns, I promise to do my best to bring back his humanity."

"We have an agreement then," declared Rowan, and Luz sealed the deal with long hugs for everyone.

After a celebratory meal on the ground in front of the cavernous mountain with all the Clairdani in the area present, Rowan finally seemed at home and truly content. He stood, impatient to get back to Tomar and see everything from this new perspective. With one last round of goodbyes and hugs for Luz, Metulas carefully collected Rowan in his talons and flew him back to the Pit near Tomar.

Remember to avoid your office as long as that curse stone is there! I'll explain everything to Mateus, and he will be your guide. We will be in touch.

With a wave, Rowan marched towards the gates of Tomar, and Metulas waited for Mateus. *Ma'elrich and the Tenenbrani may be out there plotting against us, but with all of us united, we have hope for a better future, and that's something many will rally behind.*

For the first time in a long while, Metulas' heart sang.